Gregg Olsen is a *New York Times* bestselling author of non-fiction and novels, and has contributed a short story to a collection edited by Lee Child. The award-winning author has been a guest on US and international television shows discussing crime.

Also by Gregg Olsen

THE GIRL
IN THE
WOODS

GREGG
OLSEN

CONSTABLE • LONDON

For Jean M. Olsen,
who likes to make everything go smoothly

CONSTABLE

First published in the USA in 2014 by Pinnacle Books,
a division of Kensington Publishing Corp.,

This edition published in Great Britain in 2015 by Constable

1 3 5 7 9 10 8 6 4 2

A CIP catalogue record for this book
is available from the British Library.

ISBN 978-1-47210-948-4 (paperback)
ISBN: 978-1-47211-358-0 (ebook)

Printed and bound in Great Britain by
CPI Group (UK) Ltd, Croydon CRO 4YY

Constable
is an imprint of
Constable & Robinson Ltd
100 Victoria Embankment
London EC4Y 0DY

An Hachette UK Company
www.hachette.co.uk

www.constablerobinson.com

PROLOGUE

Molly O'Rourke worked as a nurse's aide at a convalescent center in Silverdale, Washington, and loathed the early morning and weekend hours that came with the job. It wasn't what she'd envisioned at all. At twenty-seven, the petite redhead with sharp, angular features had expected that she'd be a bit further along at this stage. It was true she was no longer under her mother's roof—and that was a godsend—but she wasn't exactly moving along in life at a fast clip. She rented a slightly rundown house at 509 Camellia Street in Port Orchard, up on the hill overlooking the naval shipyard and its row of hulking gray ships awaiting repair or dismantling. She put a pencil to her budget and realized that the only way she could afford a better place was if she had a roommate or a boyfriend, but that wasn't going to happen. Not with her terrible hours.

Molly wasn't a quitter, but a realist. She stood in the dim light of the parking strip in front of her 1940s house and ran every possible outcome for her life through her head. The list had very few "pluses" and a plethora of "minuses."

She'd completed her training from a quasi-university in downtown Bremerton and was saddled with what she had determined after graduation was minimal skills and maximum debt. Her mother had needled her for paying so much for an education that basically had her changing diapers on the elderly.

"And you thought you were going to be a nurse," Mrs. O'Rourke said, in a cutting way that she'd perfected. "You should have stayed at the doctor's office where you were a receptionist and you had a decent meal benefit. I'm not being harsh. You know, honey doll, I always believed in you."

Honey doll was like a twisted dagger in the gut.

That entire exchange came into Molly's head at a little after 4 o'clock Saturday morning as she stood with her dog while the pooch found a suitable spot on the fringe of a juniper bush in the parking strip. A late-night rain had left the asphalt black and shiny and the lamp on her driveway cast a glistening puddle of light at her feet.

"Hurry up, Candy, I gotta get to work." Molly tugged on the hot pink leash to redirect the dog to the duty at hand. "Honestly, do you have to smell every little thing? Every single time? Can you just do your job so I can do mine?"

Candy, a miniature schnauzer with a decidedly independent streak, was not about to be rushed. *Not ever.* Her silver-furred face tilted at her owner with a look that was probably a kind of canine F-U, but the dog owner didn't take it that way at all.

"Be a good girl," Molly said, relaxing the length of the leash.

Just as hope had been all but dashed, Candy got her act together and squatted.

"Good girl," Molly said, satisfied that she might get to work on time.

Molly looked up toward the top-to-bottom renovated house next door as lights in the upstairs bedroom sent a beam out into the early morning darkness. It was the home of her neighbors, Ted and Jennifer Roberts.

The nurse's aide glanced at her phone. It was 4:15 a.m. She let out a sigh. Ted Roberts had been ill for months. *Seriously ill.* There was a terrible irony to his downward spiral. He'd been a typical Northwesterner—the kind who fishes, skis, kayaks, and generally just lives his or her life in the elements, out in the abundance of outdoor-related activities that make the region the focus of so much attention by sports and lifestyle magazines.

Molly admired Ted for doing all that he did. She was a TV watcher, not a doer. That, her mother told her, was one reason why she couldn't get a boyfriend.

Or a decent one.

"No one wants to marry a couch potato, honey doll," she had said.

Molly knew that. But then again her shift at work made doing anything but flopping in front of the TV out of the question. She hadn't had sex in more than a year. The encounter with an old boyfriend from high school hadn't been of the caliber to make her want a repeat.

Ted Roberts had invited her to go kayaking one time when he was still single, but Molly didn't want to miss a

Gregg Olsen

reality TV marathon she'd been sucked into, and passed on the opportunity.

She wished now that she'd said yes. She liked Ted.

So robust.

So strong.

So vital.

As she stood there looking up at the lighted window, she caught a memory of how Ted had appeared before getting sick.

He was in his forties, but his body surely didn't look it. That former classmate she'd hooked up with looked like he'd swallowed the Pillsbury Doughboy. Whole.

Molly didn't go kayaking with Ted, but she kind of imagined he had been asking her out on a date. She'd never had said yes to that, anyway. Not cool to date your neighbor. Not at all.

"You only live once," he said when she declined his offer.

If that was her window for the older guy next door, it snapped shut shortly thereafter.

It was around that time that Jennifer and her son, Micah, and daughter, Ruby, showed up on the scene. Molly could see a change coming over her friend and neighbor. Even though he'd always had a smile on his face, a joke, a laugh, something that indicated a love of life, Ted Roberts hadn't really been happy at all. Oh he *looked* like he was happy, but that wasn't genuine.

Ted had even admitted one day the previous summer that he'd been filling up his time biking, running, and kayaking to escape the emptiness of his own life.

"You got a boyfriend yet, Mol?" he asked her while he washed his Jeep on a sunny August afternoon.

Molly looked away, embarrassed. "Not really," she said. "I've had a few maybes, but none that I'd ever go out with. The guys I see at work are super old, you know, in their fifties and forties and stuff."

Ted smiled. "Old like me?" he said. His eyes squinted and his gaze challenged her a little. His brow was a crinkled patch of sunburned skin.

"That came out wrong," Molly said, her face feeling hot.

He grinned and flashed his bright white teeth. "No worries," he said. "I'm going to tell you something very important."

He motioned for her to come closer.

"What?" Molly asked, leaning in, keeping an eye on the hose in case he was going to try to drench her in some Ted-like prank.

"I didn't start living until I found Jennifer," he said. "Don't wait like I did. Sometimes the best thing is standing right in front of you."

Molly was lonely and naive enough to think that he was kind of hitting on her. It was a thought she'd like expunged from her memory because he hadn't been doing anything of the sort. Yet for some reason the encounter came back to her while her dog squatted by the bush and the light came on in the bedroom.

Ted was not like that at all. He was no flirt. He was deliriously happy that he had found Jennifer.

With Candy now doing her little dance, flipping dirt and barkdust back toward the parking strip, Molly's thoughts drifted to the last time she saw Ted. It was about a week ago. She went over after work with the better part of a chocolate sheet cake.

Jennifer answered the door. She was in her forties, too, but looked younger. She had a lovely figure, the kind Molly had always wanted—a little larger on top, but not so much that it distracted from her face. Her wrists and ankles were thin—which were always stops on Molly's survey of another girl. Her mother had piano legs and so did she.

"I thought you, Ted, and the kids might like this," Molly said. "They made me take it home. I guess they think I have no life and it doesn't matter if I get fat. Anyway, you, all of you, are always so perfect."

"Molly, you're so thoughtful," Jennifer said. "I'm sure Ruby and Micah will devour it."

"Ah, maybe Ted too," Molly said, almost as a question.

Jennifer turned toward the living room. "Would you like to see him?"

Molly didn't hesitate to get into the living room. It was the real reason she was there. The cake had been an excuse.

She shut the door and followed Jennifer into a darkened living room, where the sole illumination came from the seventy-inch big screen TV.

"You have a visitor, babe," Jennifer said. She turned to Molly and gave her a little look, a warning, it seemed.

Molly could scarcely believe her eyes. Ted was covered in a Navajo blanket up to his neck. His eyes were slits. His face had shrunken to a kind of Edvard Munch gauntness. Even with the flickering glow—or especially because of it—he was a horrific sight.

Ted couldn't even lift his head from the sofa to say hello.

Jennifer stood next to him and stroked his pasty brow.

"If it gets to the point that you can't stay home anymore, Teddy, I'm going to see that you are sent to Molly's nursing home."

"I hope it doesn't come to that," Molly said, trying to lighten the mood. "Our cafeteria is all carbs and no protein. He'll starve there."

Ted attempted a smile.

Jennifer handed him a water bottle.

"Drink some iced tea," she said. "You're getting dehydrated, babe."

Ted sipped slowly from the flexible straw that stuck out only a quarter of an inch from the top of the bottle.

"You are getting better, aren't you?" Molly asked, her heart quickening a little. She'd seen people at the convalescent center who looked better than Ted, and they died.

"I think so," Ted said, his voice a slight croak. "Every day I do feel a little bit stronger."

He closed his eyes and Jennifer motioned for Molly to come to the kitchen where she set the cake on the counter.

"Jennifer, he's going to be all right, isn't he?"

Jennifer opened the refrigerator and rearranged a dozen bottles of iced tea so she could accommodate the cake.

"I don't know, Molly," she said.

With the space barely big enough to accommodate it, Jennifer shoved the cake onto the top shelf. Molly could see that the back end of the cake had smashed the refrigerator wall.

"What exactly is wrong with him?" she asked.

Jennifer shook her head and shut the refrigerator. She had an irritated look on her face.

By what? The cake or the question?

"We don't know," she said, reaching for a towel to wipe off some chocolate that had smeared her palm. "Cancer maybe."

Molly kept her eyes riveted on Jennifer's. "What do you mean, *maybe*?"

Jennifer started walking toward the front door to lead Molly from the kitchen, but the younger woman tugged at her shoulder.

"What do you mean?" she repeated.

Jennifer spun around. "I mean, he won't go in to see the doctors anymore. Believe me I've tried."

"Why won't he?" Molly asked.

"He's afraid, Molly."

"Ted's not afraid of anything."

The two women stood toe to toe.

"You don't know him like I do."

It was a trump card of sorts, and Jennifer played it for all it was worth.

"Then tell me," Molly said. "What's he afraid of?"

Jennifer narrowed her focus. She didn't like being questioned by some neighbor. "That if he goes to the doctor he'll never come home again," she said.

Molly pounced. "That's stupid."

"To you maybe," Jennifer said. "But my husband is adamant."

Husband. It was odd that she referred to him as "husband." Molly immediately saw it as a territorial move. *He's mine.* Candy had a toy cat that she liked to hump, even though she was a female. It was about being territorial. Staking a claim. Saying something is "mine."

Jennifer was humping her sick husband.

"He might die, Jennifer," Molly said.

Jennifer went to open the front door.

"There are worse things than dying," she said.

The young woman wanted to scream at Jennifer's obvious indifference. She knew better. Jennifer Roberts was not the type that anyone wanted to mess with. She was a woman who always got her way.

Molly O'Rourke was not deeply religious, but she gave prayer a try after that encounter. She prayed over and over that God would heal Ted Roberts. Someone so full of life, so happy, shouldn't have to suffer.

CHAPTER 1

Birdy Waterman went toward the ringing bell and an annoyingly insistent rat-tat-tat knock on the glass storm door of her home in Port Orchard, Washington. Her cell phone was pressed to her ear and her fingertips fumbled in her pocket for her car keys. She retrieved a tube of lip balm—with the lid off and the product making a mess of her pocket.

Great! Where are those keys?

"Hang on," she said into the phone, grabbing a tissue and wiping off her hand. "Everything happens at once. Someone's here. I'll be there in fifteen minutes."

She swung the door open. On her doorstep was a soaking wet teenaged boy.

"Make that twenty," she said, pulling the phone away from her ear.

It was her sister's son, Elan.

"Elan, what are you doing here?"

"Can I come in?" he asked.

"Hang on," she said back into the phone.

"Wait, did I get the date wrong?" she asked him.

The kid shook his head.

Birdy looked past Elan to see if he was alone. He was only sixteen. They had made plans for him to come over during spring break. He hadn't been getting along with his parents and Birdy offered to have him stay with her. She'd circled the date on the calendar on her desk at the Kitsap County coroner's office and on the one that hung in the kitchen next to the refrigerator. It couldn't have slipped her mind. She even made plans for activities that the two of them could do—most of which were in Seattle, a place the boy revered because it was the Northwest's largest city. To a teenager from the Makah Reservation, it held a lot of cachet.

"Where's your mom?" Birdy asked, looking past him, still clinging to her cell phone.

The boy, who looked so much like his mother— Birdy's sister, Summer—shook his head. "She's not here. And I don't care where she is."

"How'd you get here?"

"I caught a ride and I walked from the foot ferry. I hitched, but no one would pick me up."

"You shouldn't do that," Birdy said. "Not safe." She motioned him inside. She didn't tell him to take off his shoes, wet and muddy as they were. He was such a sight she nearly forgot that she had the phone in her hand. Elan, gangly, but now not so much, was almost a man. He had medium length dark hair, straight and coarse enough to mimic the tail of a mare. On his chin were the faintest of whiskers. He was trying to grow up.

She turned away from the teen and spoke back into her phone.

"I have an unexpected visitor," Birdy said. She paused and listened. "Everything is fine. I'll see you at the scene as soon as I can get there."

Elan removed his damp dark gray hoody and stood frozen in the small foyer. They looked at each other the way strangers sometimes do. Indeed they nearly were. Elan's mother had all but cut Birdy out of her life over the past few years. There were old reasons for it, and there seemed to be very little to be done about it. The sisters had been close and they'd grown apart. Birdy figured there would be reconciliation someday. Indeed, she hoped that her entertaining Elan for spring break would be the start of something good between her and Summer. Her heart was always heavy when she and her sister stopped speaking.

As the Kitsap County forensic pathologist, Dr. Birdy Waterman had seen what real family discord could do. She was grateful that hers was more of a war of words than weapons.

"You are going to catch a cold," she said. "And I have to leave right this minute."

Elan's hooded eyes sparkled. "If I caught a cold would you split me open and look at my guts?" he asked.

She half smiled at him and feigned exasperation. "If I had to, yes." She'd only seen him a half dozen times in the past three years at her sister's place on the reservation. He was a smart aleck then. And he still was. She liked him.

"I'll be gone awhile. You are going to get out of all of your wet clothes and put them in the dryer."

He looked at her with a blank stare. "What am I supposed to wear?" he asked. "You don't want a naked man running around, do you?"

She ignored his somewhat petulant sarcasm.

Man? That was a stretch.

She noticed Elan's muddy shoes, and the mess they were making of her buffed hardwood floors, but said nothing about that. Instead, she led him to her bedroom.

"Uninvited guests," she said, then pretended to edit herself. "*Surprise* guests get a surprise." She pulled a lilac terry robe from a wooden peg behind her bedroom door.

"This will have to do," she said, offering the garment.

Elan made an irritated face but accepted the robe. He obviously hated the idea of wearing his aunt's bathrobe—probably *any* woman's bathrobe. At least it didn't have a row of pink roses around the neckline like his mother's. Besides, no one, he was pretty sure, would see him holed up in his aunt's place.

"Aunt Birdy, are you going to a crime scene?" he asked. "I want to go."

"I am," she said, continuing to push the robe at him until he had no choice but to accept it. "But you're not coming. Stay here and chill. I'll be back soon enough. And when I get back you'll tell me why you're here so early. By the way, does your mom know you're here?"

He kept his eyes on the robe. "No. She doesn't. And I don't want her to."

That wasn't going to happen. The last thing she needed was another reason for her sister to be miffed at her.

"Your dad?" she asked.

Elan looked up and caught his aunt's direct gaze. His dark brown eyes flashed. "I hate him even more."

Birdy rolled her eyes upward. "That's perfect," she said. "We can sort out your drama when I get back."

"I'm—"

She put her hand up and cut him off. "Hungry? Frozen pizza is the best I've got. Didn't have time to bake you a cake."

She found her keys from the dish set atop a birdseye maple console by the door and went outside. It had just stopped raining. But in late March in the Pacific Northwest, a cease-fire on precipitation only meant the clouds were taking a coffee break. Jinx, the neighbor's cat, ran over the wet pavement for a scratch under her chin, but Birdy wasn't offering one right then. The cat, a tabby with a stomach that dragged on the lawn, skulked away. Birdy was in a hurry.

She dressed for the weather, which meant layers—dark dyed blue jeans, a sunflower yellow cotton sweater, a North Face black jacket. If it got halfway warm, she'd discard the North Face. That almost always made her too hot. She carried her purse, a raincoat, and a small black bag. Not a doctor's bag, really. But a bag that held a few of the tools of her trade—latex gloves, a flashlight, a voice recorder, evidence tags, a rule, and a camera. She wouldn't necessarily need any of that where she was going, but Dr. Waterman lived by the tried and oh-so-true adage:

Better safe than sorry.

As she unlocked her car, a Seattle-bound ferry plowed the slate waters of Rich Passage on the other side of Beach Drive. A small assemblage of seagulls wrestled over a soggy, and very dead, opossum on the roadside.

Elan had arrived early. Not good.

Birdy pulled out of the driveway and turned on the jazz CD that had been on continuous rotation. The music always calmed her. She was sure that Elan would consider it completely boring and hopelessly uncool, but she probably wouldn't like his music either. She needed a little calming influence just then. Nothing was ever easy in her family. Her nephew had basically run away—at least as far as she could tell. Summer was going to blame her for this, somehow. She always did. As Birdy drove up Mile Hill Road and then the long stretch of Banner Road, she wondered why the best intentions of the past were always a source of hurt in the present.

And yet the worst of it all was not her family, her nephew, or her sister. The worst of it was what the dispatcher from the coroner's office had told her moments just before Elan arrived.

A dismembered human foot had been found in Banner Forest.

CHAPTER 2

Tracy Montgomery had smelled the odor first. The twelve-year-old and the other members of Suzanne Hatfield's sixth grade Olalla Elementary School class had made their way through the twists and turns of a trail understandably called Tunnel Vision toward the sodden intersection of Croaking Frog, when she first got a whiff. It was so rank it made her pinch her nose like she did when jumping in the pool at the Y in nearby Gig Harbor.

"Ewww, stinks here," the girl said in a manner that indicated more of an announcement than a mere observation.

Tracy was a know-it-all who wore purple Ugg boots that were destined to be ruined by the muddy late March nature walk in Banner Forest, a Kitsap County park of 630-plus acres. She'd been warned that the boots were not appropriate for the sure-to-be-soggy trek inside the one-square-mile woods that were dank and drippy even on a sunny spring day. There was no doubt that Tracy's mother was going to survey the damage of those annoyingly bright boots and phone a complaint into the principal's office.

"That's why they call it skunk cabbage," said Ms. Hatfield, a veteran teacher who had seen the interest in anything that had to do with nature decline with increasing velocity in the last decade of her thirty-year teaching career. She could hardly wait until retirement, a mere forty-four school days away. Kids today were all but certain that lettuce grew in a cellophane bag and chickens were hatched shaped like nuggets.

Ms. Hatfield brightened a little as a thought came to mind. Her mental calculations hadn't been updated to take into account *this* day.

Technically, she only had forty-three days left on the job.

A squirrel darted across the shrouded entrance to Croaking Frog, turned left, then right, before zipping up a mostly dead Douglas fir.

"My dad shoots those in our yard," Davy Saunders said. The schoolboy's disclosure didn't surprise anyone. Davy's dad went to jail for confronting an intruder—a driver from the Mattress Ranch store in Gorst—with a loaded weapon. The driver's crime? The young man used the Saunders driveway to make a three-point turn.

"Want to hear something really gross?"

This time the voice belonged to Cameron Lee. He was packed into the middle of the mass of kids and two beleaguered moms clogging the trail. "My cousin sent me a video that showed some old guy cutting up a squirrel and cooking it. You know, like for food."

Ms. Hatfield considered using Cameron's comment

as a learning moment about how some people forage for survival, but honestly, she was simply tired of competing with reality TV, the Internet, and the constant prattling of the digital generation. They knew less and less it seemed because they simply didn't have to really *know* anything.

Everything was always at their fingertips.

Ms. Hatfield knew the Latin name for the skunk cabbage that had so irritated Tracy's olfactory senses—*Lysichiton americanus*—but she didn't bother mentioning it to her students. Instead, she sighed and spouted off a few mundane facts about the enormous-leafed plant with bright yellow spires protruding from the muddy soil like lanterns in a dark night.

"It smells bad for a reason," she said. "Anyone know why?"

She looked around. Apparently, no one *did*. She glanced in the direction of Viola Mertz, but even *she* didn't offer up a reason. The teacher could scarcely recall a moment in the classroom when Viola didn't raise her hand.

If she'd lost Viola, there was no hope.

Ms. Hatfield gamely continued. "It smells bad to attract—"

"Smells like Ryan and he can't attract anyone," Cooper Wilson said, picking on scrawny Ryan Jonas whenever he could.

Ms. Hatfield ignored the remark. Cooper was a thug and she hoped that when puberty tapped Ryan on the shoulders, he'd bulk up and beat the crap out of his tormentor. But that would be later, long after she was gone from the classroom.

". . . to attract pollinators," she went on, wondering

if she should skip counting days left on the job and switch to hours. "Bugs, bees, flies, whatever."

"I'm bored," Carrie Bowden said.

Ms. Hatfield wanted to say that she was bored too, but of course she didn't. She looked over at one of the two moms who'd come along on the nature hike—Carrie's mom, a willowy brunette named Angie, who had corked ear buds into her ears for the bus ride from the school and hadn't taken them out since. Cooper Wilson's mom, Mariah, must be bored too. She flipped through her phone's email, cursing the bad reception she was getting.

"It might smell bad," Ms. Hatfield said, trying to carry on with her last field trip ever. "But believe it or not this plant actually tastes good to bears. They love it like you love a Subway sandwich."

Only Cooper Wilson brightened a little. He loved Subway.

"Indigenous people ate the plant's roots too," the teacher went on. She flashed back to when she first started teaching and how she'd first used the word *Indians*, then *Native Americans*, then, and now, *indigenous people*.

Lots of changes in three decades.

"Skunk cabbage might smell bad," she said, "but it had very important uses for our Chinook people. They used the leaves to wrap around salmon when roasting it on the hot coals of an alder wood fire."

"I went to a luau in Hawaii and they did that with a pig," Carrie piped up, not so much because she wanted to add to the conversation, but because she liked to remind the others in the class that she'd been to Hawaii over Christmas break. She brought it up at least once a week since her sunburned and lei-wearing return in

January. "They wrapped it up in big green leaves before putting it into the ground on some coals," she said. "That's what they did in Hawaii."

"Ms. Hatfield," Tracy said, her voice rising above the din of not-so-nature lovers. "I need to show you something."

Tracy always had something to say. And Ms. Hatfield knew it was always super important. Everything with Tracy was super important.

"Just a minute," the teacher said, a little too sharply. She tried to diffuse her obvious irritation with a quick smile. "Kids, about what Cameron said a moment ago," she continued. "I want you to know that a squirrel is probably a decent source of protein. When game was scarce, many pioneers survived on small rodents and birds."

"Ms. Hatfield! I'm seriously going to puke," Tracy called out. Her voice now had enough urgency to cut through the buzzing and complaining of the two dozen other kids on the field trip.

Tracy knew how to command attention. Her purple Uggs were proof of that.

Ms. Hatfield pushed past the others. Her weathered but delicate hands reached over to Tracy.

"Are you all right?" she asked.

The girl with big brown eyes that set the standard for just how much eye makeup a sixth grader could wear kept her steely gaze focused away from her teacher. She faced the trail, eyes cast downward.

Tracy could be a crier and Ms. Hatfield knew she had to neutralize the situation—whatever it was. And fast.

"Honey, I'm sorry if the squirrel story upset you."

The girl shook her head. "That wasn't it, Ms. Hatfield."

The teacher felt relief wash over her. *Good*. It wasn't something she *said*.

"What is it?"

Tracy looked up with wide, frightened, almost Manga eyes.

"Are you sick?" the teacher asked.

Tracy didn't say a word. She looked back down and with the tip of her purple boot lifted the feathery stalk of a sword fern.

At first, Ms. Hatfield wasn't sure what she was seeing. The combination of a stench—far worse than anything emitted by skunk cabbage—and the sight of a wriggling mass of maggots assaulted her senses.

Instinctively, she swept her arm toward Tracy to hold her back, as if the girl was lunging toward the disgusting sight, which she most certainly was not. It was like a mother reaching across a child's chest when she hit the brakes too hard and doubted the ability of the safety belt to protect her precious cargo.

All hell broke loose. Carrie started to scream and her voice was joined by a cacophony. It was a domino that included every kid in the group. Even bully Cooper screamed out in disgust and horror. Angie Bowden yanked out her ear buds as if she was pulling the ripcord on a parachute.

No one had ever seen anything as awful as that.

Later, the kids in Ms. Hatfield's class would tell their friends that it was the best field trip ever.

CHAPTER 3

Birdy Waterman parked her red Prius on Olalla Valley Road behind a row of marked and unmarked Kitsap County sheriff's vehicles. She pulled on her badly wrinkled raincoat, also red, from the passenger seat and called over to Deputy Gary Wilkins, who stood next to the main trailhead. At twenty-six, he was a young deputy and this kind of thing, a *dead* thing, was still new to him. He was a block of a man, with square shoulders and muscular thighs. He nodded in her direction and his gray eyes flashed recognition and anxiety at the same time.

"Your turn?" he asked, already knowing the answer.

Birdy shut the car door. It was *her* turn. The county had a PR nightmare on its hands the previous year when a coroner's assistant screwed up a homicide case. In an embarrassing and ultimately futile attempt to save himself, he put the blame on the sheriff's detectives and their evidence-gathering process. It was a colossal error that hadn't yet healed over when the coroner and the sheriff decided a "working together" rotation was the solution to all of their problems.

People in both offices could still recall the subject line of the email:

There's no "I" in "Team."

It was an eye-roller of the greatest magnitude.

Because of that memo, and the weeks of touchy-feely training that ensued, Birdy was standing in the muddy parking strip while the nephew she barely knew was probably burning down her house, making that sad frozen pizza she'd offered as his best bet for a hot meal. She almost never visited crime scenes, but she was in the rotation when Ms. Hatfield called 911.

"How's the family?" Birdy asked Gary, slipping on her coat as a seam in the sky tore just enough to send down another trickle of Pacific Northwest springtime weather. She picked her way across the little ridge that separated the forest entrance from Banner Road, a nine-mile thrill ride of a two-lane blacktop that hopped up and over the hills of the southernmost edge of the county. She wore street shoes instead of boots, because distracted by her nephew's sudden appearance on her doorstep, she hadn't considered she'd be traipsing through the woods until she was halfway there.

Banner Forest. Stupid me, she thought.

"Good. I mean, not really," Gary said. "Abby got a stubborn cold, which means I'm next," he went on, referring to his two-year-old. Birdy liked Gary and right then she especially liked that he didn't ask for advice on how to help his daughter get over her cold. She was a doctor, of course. She'd had the same training as any MD, but her patients had little need for a calm bedside manner.

They were always dead.

"What happened here?" she asked.

"No one has really said anything to me. Other than, you know, the kids apparently found part of a dead body down the trail. They were pretty freaked out."

"I imagine they would be," Birdy said. She indicated the row of sheriff department cars.

"Kendall here?"

Gary tipped his head toward the dark, tree-shrouded funnel-like opening of the trail that led deep into Banner Forest.

"Yup," he said. "They're all down there by—and you'll love this—Croaking Frog."

Birdy arched a brow and looked down the pathway.

"What's that?" she asked.

"The name of the trail," he said. Gary had found something amusing in the worst of circumstances. He'd make a very good deputy.

"Croaking Frog?" she repeated, though she was pretty sure she heard him correctly.

"Welcome to South Kitsap County," he said. "You'll find Kendall and the others about a hundred yards down that way."

Birdy followed his fingertip toward the rutted trail into the woods.

Kendall Stark was a homicide detective Birdy liked working with more than the investigators in her unit in the sheriff's office. That wasn't to say that Birdy thought others in the Kitsap County Sheriff's Department were any less competent at what they did. They were skilled investigators, no doubt about that. It wasn't because Kendall was the only woman either. If that had been the reason, Birdy would never say so anyway. Saying so would surely invite more sensitivity training.

And yet, if she'd been completely honest with herself, the forensic pathologist did believe that Detective Stark had an ability to empathize with a victim's family to a greater degree than some of her male counterparts. It wasn't solely her gender—there were plenty of women in law enforcement who were so cerebral, so clinical, that emotions were sealed behind a fortress of their own making. Birdy had trained with several at the University of Washington who were all about CSI and crisp white lab coats and heels that thundered when they walked down corridors—an obnoxious drumbeat announcing their impending arrival.

Kendall was different from those women, Birdy thought, because she was a mother. And a good one. In Birdy's world, a good mother—and God knew she learned that little fact the hard way—had the ability to understand the loss and suffering of others and the hurt that becomes a festering wound. Those were the cases in which a child was murdered, the darkest, saddest, of any that came across either woman's desk. The obvious truth about any homicide was that no matter the victim's age, he or she had a mother.

Kendall was where she needed to be—at the scene or with witnesses. Birdy needed to be in the lab.

Or at home with her nephew.

Cross training, she thought, *was so irritating.*

She glanced at a trail map on a sheltered kiosk behind Gary, but it looked like a crudely executed rendering of a sack full of snakes. The forest was crisscrossed by a series of hiking and horseback-riding trails that had lately been taken over by dirt bikers. Several trails—including

Tunnel Vision—featured earthen ramps that sent bikers soaring into the air. When the forest was saved from development, the vision of the committee that had fought for it had been to see it used as a nature preserve, a hiking and horseback-riding trail.

Not a speedway for dirt bikes.

Birdy wondered how a dismembered foot had turned up in Banner Forest. Birdy knew that cougars had been spotted there, as well as the notorious case in which a black bear mauled a man when his dogs frightened the mother bear's cubs.

There were two lessons there. Never let a dog off its leash. And never, ever anger a mother bear.

Birdy followed the muddy trail to the intersection of Tunnel Vision and Croaking Frog. The ground was damp from the rain, but so compacted by the dirt bikes that it wasn't as gooey as it might have been. Tire treads laced the pathway.

As Birdy passed a NO HUNTING sign nailed to an old growth cedar stump, another possibility ran through her head.

Maybe a hunter accidentally shot a child? Thought a small figure in the woods was a deer? Deer were thick in that part of the county. Even with NO HUNTING signs posted all over the place, there were plenty of rule breakers—especially midweek when fewer people frequented the woods.

As she drew closer to Croaking Frog, she recognized the voices of the techs and Detective Stark.

Kendall looked up. Her short blond hair had grown out some and softened the angular features of her face. The spikiness was gone and the look flattered her. Even her deep blue eyes benefited from the change. "I wondered if it was your turn to be a team player," she said.

Birdy glanced past the detective.

A tech was hunched among the sword ferns.

"There's no *I* in *Team*," Birdy said, recalling the obnoxious training they'd all been forced to attend to ensure that mistakes would never happen again.

"You make an Ass out of U and Me when you assume something," Kendall said with a sigh. "Thank goodness the ass that got us all into this mess got fired."

Birdy was grateful for that too. "No kidding," she said. "What have we got here?"

"Not much," Kendall said.

"No visible sign of cause?" she asked.

It wasn't Kendall's job to determine what happened to any victim, of course. But that didn't stop most detectives in most jurisdictions all over the country from announcing what they were "pretty sure" had occurred.

Kendall shook her head. "No, not that. What I mean is not much of anything." She pointed downward. "All we've got is a foot."

Birdy wedged herself into the mossy space next to a human foot painted with a writhing mass of maggots.

"I'm not eating dinner tonight," Kendall said.

Birdy had seen worse. There were far more hideous images etched onto the tissue of her brain than a mass of maggots on a dismembered foot. If she'd been asked to make a top five list of the worst things she'd ever seen, it would include the case in which a Silverdale mother held a toddler's face against the red hot coils of an electric stove, killing her. That haunted her every now and then. Also, a case in which a Bremerton woman poured battery acid over her sleeping husband and seared out his eyes. He survived for four agonizing months in a Seattle burn unit before mercifully succumbing to his devastating injuries.

But that wasn't the worst of them all.

The most revolting case of all was that of a Port Gamble man who killed his wife and literally put strips of her flesh to dry on a clothesline behind one of the historic homes in the darkly charming town at the very northern edge of the county she served as the forensic pathologist. He sold her remains as jerky at a store in nearby Kingston.

A maggot-infested foot? Piece of cake.

"I can't exactly say this is doing much for my appetite," Birdy said, though it really didn't bother her that much. Decay was a part of the cycle. It had its purpose. She saw the sense in how all things return to the earth. She knew, for example, that the trees all around them had been fed by the decomposed flesh of animals and human beings.

She moved closer. Lighting was intermittent. Saucers of illumination spotted the space from breaks in the canopy of cedars that rocketed skyward. She did a quick assessment, while the investigative team pulled back.

The foot was human.

Small.

And although it was hard to say for sure, it appeared that some of the toenails had been painted a lively shade of pink.

Birdy looked up at Sarah Dorman, one of the crime scene techs who still held anger over the blunder that not only bruised the entire department, but, more crucially, let a killer go free.

"I'm doing my job, Dr. Waterman."

"I know that, Sarah."

Sarah, with her long red hair and pale complexion, could never really hide her feelings. She looked back at the foot and scowled.

"I don't make mistakes," she said.

"Of course not. I'm not here to try to catch you making a mistake, Sarah. I'm here for the training protocol." Birdy took a short breath. She knew Sarah wasn't mad at her, but she'd been the first on the scene and no doubt had to put up with some boneheaded comment about the collection of evidence and who was responsible for what.

"Now, will you brief me on what's been done? And really, Sarah, can you at least fake a smile? Our work is hard enough."

The other deputies stepped back to give them some space—and more than likely to escape the stench. Birdy crouched closer. The wind blew and shifted the canopy. The foot under the fern glistened in the light.

"Upon my arrival deputies had already secured the scene," Sarah said. "Because of the wet trail and the likelihood that we'd lose any potential trace—probably lost any when the kids were here anyway—we've already photographed and searched the immediate area."

"How immediate?" Birdy asked.

Sarah kept her grim face. "Twenty-five yards."

"That's a big area," Birdy said with a tone that was more approving than questioning.

Sarah lightened a little. "Right, but we wanted to go wide because of the weather and the, well, you know, the possibility that there might be other body parts nearby."

"Good work. Find anything?" Birdy asked.

"Not really anything we think is connected to this. But we did pick up a Doublemint gum wrapper, a used condom, and a couple of beer cans."

"Somebody used this place for a make-out spot," Birdy said.

Sarah shrugged a little knowingly. "Yeah. I mean, I grew up here and well, yeah. Kids, probably."

Birdy scanned the trampled scene. "Any footprints collected?"

"Yes, a few," Sarah said. "But to be honest, things were pretty trashed by the time we got here. Lots of kids running around screaming and stuff. The teacher did her best to keep everyone away, but I have a feeling that a bunch of them got a good look at the foot."

Birdy understood. "I know I would have."

Sarah smiled for the first time. It was a genuine smile and not one offered up to soothe the feelings of those angry about the training session.

"Good work, Sarah," Birdy said.

Kendall, who'd been talking to another deputy, joined Birdy. When Birdy stooped down low, the detective followed her lead. Without saying a word, Birdy put on a pair of gloves. The two women held their breath and the forensic pathologist lifted a frond of the fern that had partially covered the ankle. It was too dark to see, so she crouched lower and took a small Maglite from her bag. She turned on the flashlight and sent a beam over the maggots. In response, the mass writhed like the crowd doing the "wave" at a Seahawks game.

"Can you tell how long the foot's been here?" Kendall asked.

Birdy leaned in—almost close enough to touch it—though she never would have done that.

"Hard to say if it is third or second molt," she said. "We'll have to look at them back at the lab. Since we're all hovering here, I'm presuming this is all you have for me."

"Search under way," Kendall said.

"Who found the foot?" Birdy asked.

"A girl named Tracy Montgomery. She's a sixth grader in Suzanne Hatfield's class at Olalla."

"Nature walk day," Birdy said, looking upward as the sun cracked through the sky, once more revealing the blue that reminded her of her father's faded chambray shirts, his practical uniform for the outdoor work he did in the summers. Birdy grew up on the Makah Reservation at the very tip of Western Washington. Nature was always around her family. The woods were a second home.

She turned to Kendall. "Did you talk to her?"

"Yes," Kendall said. "She says she didn't get near it. Didn't touch it. Her teacher confirmed her story."

"All right then," Birdy said. She looked over at the tech. "Sarah, when you collect the evidence I want the top six inches of soil. That sword fern too."

"What kind of square footage are we talking about?" Sarah said, knowing full well that the word *footage* was probably on the edge of inappropriate. She hadn't meant it; it just came out that way.

"Four feet all around," Birdy said, this time with a smile back at Sarah.

Sarah scrunched her brow and went to work with another tech. They finished taking photographs, carefully bagged the foot, and started on the soil samples.

Each scoop of black loamy dirt was tagged with coordinates inside a four-foot grid that had been staked around the decomposing body part.

Birdy walked along the trail, scouring it for any sign of who might have left the foot—or the body that had been severed from it.

Kendall called over to her. "You think a bear mauled someone?"

A piece of pale pink fabric caught Birdy's eye and she motioned to Sarah to collect it.

"Don't know," she said.

"We had that mauling a few years ago," Kendall said.

"Right. Read about that." Birdy set a yellow collection marker by the fabric, a shred of nylon, probably an undergarment. "I don't think so," she went on. "I think an animal would have dragged that foot to its den or, even more likely, consumed it on the spot."

"If there were any footprints—animal or human—they've been obliterated by the rain and Ms. Hatfield's class," Kendall said.

Satisfied there was no role for her right then—and she'd followed the orders to be there—Birdy started down the trail toward her car. "Let me know how the search goes," she said. "I'm heading back now. I have unexpected company and a foot to examine."

"You seem less excited by your company than by the maggot-infested foot," Kendall said. "Who is it?"

Birdy turned around and looked at her friend. It was one of those looks that said far more than words. "My sister's son."

Kendall blinked back with surprise. "Your sister's? That's interesting. You almost never mention her. In fact, I didn't really even know you had a sister for the first year you were here."

"Don't get me started." Birdy sighed. "You don't have enough time to hear my family story."

"Try me sometime," Kendall said.

Birdy unbuttoned her raincoat and walked toward the light coming from the roadway. She knew the detective meant it. Kendall was a real friend, but Birdy's family baggage was of such serious tonnage that she barely could carry it, let alone see a need to drop it on the shoulders of someone she admired.

CHAPTER 4

Elan didn't come to the door to greet his aunt when she arrived at her place on Beach Drive. He stayed planted in front of the TV wearing the lilac bathrobe and a sullen look.

"If your friends could see you now," Birdy said, taking off her muddy shoes and making her way to his spot on the sofa.

"I don't have any friends," Elan said in a tone that sounded like he meant it and wasn't reaching for pity.

Birdy picked up the remote control. She turned the sound down a little—not off, not on mute.

"Elan," she said, "we need to talk."

He looked at her and then over at the TV. It was some kind of action flick involving explosions and minimal dialogue. It seemed completely riveting to the teenager.

"I don't want to talk now," he said.

"Is it that you don't want to talk now, or talk at all?"

He shook his head a little. "I don't know."

Birdy sat down. She was soggy, hungry, and she had to get back to work. She didn't have time to try to draw things out of him. She needed him to focus on what she was saying. She needed to know why he'd shown up like some uninvited pizza delivery boy.

She clicked the remote control once more. This time she turned off the television.

Elan stared at the blank screen.

"Elan," she said. "Talk."

"Aunt Birdy," he answered, his voice growing soft. "I don't want to go home. Ever."

It was a start. Vague, but a start.

"All right," Birdy said. "You don't want to go home. I understand that, Elan. But what I need to understand is *why*. Why don't you want to go back?"

The teen stayed silent.

"I need to call your mother," Birdy said, holding her exasperation to a minimum. She hated the idea of calling Summer. Their last few encounters had been less than cordial. There was always the lingering sting in Summer's comments that Birdy was selfish and preoccupied with her own life. Her life away from the others. That dead people mattered more to her than her own living family members.

"You think you're too good for us, don't you, sister?" Summer had asked the last time they spoke, a repeat of a conversation they'd had many times before.

Birdy took a step back. "I never said that."

Summer pointed her index finger, one—like all of them—that was coiled with silver rings.

"You *inferred* it," she said.

Birdy smelled alcohol, but made no mention of it.

"*Implied* is the word, Summer. But no, I didn't."

Summer threw her hands in the air. It was a showy

move, but within the confines of her living room—
where her husband, oldest son, and the family dog
watched TV—it didn't spark the slightest bit of interest.

"There you go again," Summer said. "Making me—
making all of us—feel like we're stupid."

Birdy had heard that one before. Part of it made her
angry. The same song over and over. And yet, the other
side of the coin was that Summer didn't have to end up
the way she had. She was intelligent. She was creative.
She was all of those things when she was a teenager.

"You could have gone to college," Birdy said. "You
were the smart one."

Summer didn't say another word. She had been dis-
armed by the truth and she had nothing to do but accept what her sister had said. Summer had been at the
top of the class. She was the sister who taught Birdy
the joys of reading, of dreaming of a life beyond the
reservation with its endless gossip, heartache, and fu-
tility. All of Summer's dreams evaporated when she
dropped out of school, became a mom, got married. Waf-
fled on what she'd do. After that, Summer foundered like
a wreck off the edge of Neah Bay. She never got her foot-
ing again. She never fulfilled the promise that her intel-
lect had once assured.

Instead she drank, drifted, and watched from afar as
Birdy escaped the reservation and the life there that
was never going to be anything but hard.

"Call her," Elan said, meeting his aunt's gaze. "But
I'm not going back. If you try to make me, I'll just run
away. I'll go somewhere far away where no one can
find me. And if I do, it will be your fault."

Birdy wasn't sure what she should do. She knew that while she and her sister had their differences they did have a bond, a history that wasn't always so strained. There were things that kept them wound together like the jute twine they'd used to make bracelets when they were kids.

"Can't I stay with you?"

"You have to be in school, for one thing. For another, I don't really even know you, Elan. I don't know how to take care of you."

"I'm sixteen. I don't want to go to school anymore."

Birdy didn't like that response at all. Education was the only way to a better life. She didn't want Elan to fail. She just couldn't have that happen. Even though Summer was older, she'd always felt that there was truth to her sister's insistence that Birdy had abandoned her when she left for the university in Seattle.

"If you stay here," she said, "you have to go to school."

Elan brightened a little. "You mean you might let me stay?"

"Are you on drugs?" she asked.

"No," he said, his tone a little hurt. "I mean I smoke a little. But not much. Not like the crowd back home."

Birdy pressed him. "How much is a little?"

"Once a week, maybe? I don't have any with me if that's what you are worried about."

"If you stay, it is only until the end of the school year."

Birdy could scarcely believe her own words, but her sister's complaints resonated. They were unfair, but they still hurt. She had gone away. She had created a new life outside the reservation. Maybe she owed Summer something? Even if Summer was harsh, mean, a bitch, she was her blood.

So was Elan.

"If I call her and tell her that it's all right for you to stay here, would that be okay with you?" she asked.

Elan looked at Birdy. His eyes were so dark brown they were almost black. They looked wet, pooling with tears.

"Do you promise I can stay?" He wasn't going to cry. Elan was toughing it out. It might have been because he was a teenager, and no teenage boy wants to fall to pieces in front of a grown-up. It might also have been that he'd been cried out. Something painful had forced him from his home to hers.

"Yes," she said, "on three conditions."

The boy looked hopeful. "What?"

"You'll have to tell me why you're here."

"I can't," he said. "Not now."

Birdy landed her hand softly on Elan's shoulder. She felt a slight tremble, and then he rolled his shoulder to shake her off. "Fine, but later you will, won't you?"

"I'll try," he said.

"Promise?"

"I promise."

Birdy got up and went to get her phone from her purse on the console table by the door. Elan's muddy footprints had dried on the gleaming wooden floor of the old house. Birdy hadn't wanted to be one of those "take off your shoes" type of people, but she'd spent a lot of money refinishing those floors.

"What's the second condition, Aunt Birdy?"

She turned and faced him with a serious look.

"You have to get your own robe," she said, staying deadpan. "You look ridiculous."

Elan smiled. It was a disarming smile, one that was at once sad and happy at the same time.

"I have my stuff in the dryer," he said, indicating the rumbling machine in the other room.

"Good. I like that you know how to do your laundry. Might be good having you here for a visit."

"I'm good at lots of stuff," he said. "What's the last condition?"

"School, Elan. You miss one day and you're on a bus back home. Understood?"

He tugged at the belt of the robe and offered what his aunt considered reluctant agreement.

"Yeah," he said. "Understood."

Birdy went into the kitchen and left a message on her sister's cell when Summer didn't answer.

"Summer," she said. "Elan is with me. He's fine. Don't know why he's here. Do you? Call me."

Elan appeared in the kitchen doorway, now dressed in his original clothes and radiating the warmth of the dryer.

"She never answers her phone," he said.

"She will call me the minute she gets the message."

"You think so?" he asked.

"She's your mother."

"You don't know her, Aunt Birdy."

She stared at him for a second, assessing, wondering, processing.

"What do you mean by that?" she asked him.

"Nothing."

"Elan, talk to me." Her words were direct but tempered with concern.

Elan crossed his arms. It was a gesture that was right out of a seminar she took on body language, which she thought was a complete waste of time because her patients were all dead and the only language they spoke was silent.

Elan wasn't going to talk.

"Don't you have a dead body to go look at?" he asked.

His tone was a little smart-alecky just then, but he was correct.

Or at least partially.

It was only a foot.

That night at dinner in the family's comfortable log home in South Kitsap, Tracy Montgomery picked at her chicken fingers when she discussed finding the human foot in the woods. Her older sister Monica and her brother Waid were clearly up to their necks with their sister's need for center stage.

"You don't even seem traumatized," Monica said, texting her friend Carli while the three siblings were eating in front of the TV. "Finding a dead person—or even part of one—would make me hurl."

"I *did* hurl," Tracy said, dipping her chicken into a pool of catsup. "It was totally gross. But I got to talk to the newspaper and Ms. Hatfield said that I can have a counseling session tomorrow. If I need it."

Waid rolled his eyes. "Some people have all the

luck. I never get to miss any school. Both of you have crappy teeth," he said, looking at his sisters. "So you get ortho. You have stupid dance, so you get that time off. Not me. I get nothing. I wish I could have found a dead body."

"Well, you didn't," Tracy said. "And you're probably never going to. I'm the lucky one."

CHAPTER 5

The Kitsap County coroner's autopsy suite—Birdy Waterman's undisputed domain—was in the basement of an old white house on Sydney Avenue adjacent to the courthouse, the sheriff's office, and the other government buildings that hugged the side of the hill like barnacles. A new building across the inlet on a hill above Bremerton was being built to house the coroner's offices. All had been designed to be state of the art. That was good. It was not a surprise to any civic-booster that progress had occurred across the water, and not in Port Orchard proper.

Port Orchard, the Kitsap County seat, was tattered, bruised, and a little rusty around the edges. In truth, the town of about ten thousand had always been a lovely location in search of a better town. It had its bright spots—no one who lived there couldn't name at least a half dozen places that out-of-towners simply had to visit when they came—especially in the summertime. There were good restaurants and antique shops along the waterfront, and it was in close proximity to Seattle. But what made Port Orchard almost cool was its slightly ratty seaside vibe that was just waiting for hipsters to discover it. It was a town along the shore without a salt water taffy stand or a bevy of shops selling dried starfish, brass portholes, and seafaring bric-a-brac that had more to do with Nantucket than Washington's inland sea, Puget Sound.

That was good too.

Birdy could see all of that when she took the job, her first after medical school. She rented that little house on Beach Drive on a lease option before she fully knew that Port Orchard was destined to be the comeback kid of Kitsap County. It had to be. It was quirky and diverse. Traits Birdy loved. The town had, she liked to tell others, potential. When she told colleagues that she conducted autopsies in the basement of an old house, many were more charmed than horrified. Or at least that's how they acted.

After enrolling Elan in South Kitsap High School, driving to the coroner's office and conferring with the staff upstairs, Birdy went down to the basement and changed into pale green scrubs and gloves. She retrieved the foot from the walk-in refrigerator, a space that was large enough to hold several bodies at a time. That morning, it was empty, except for that sad little maggot-infested foot. Birdy noted that Sarah had taken great care to ensure the evidence was protected during transport in an Igloo brand Styrofoam ice chest purchased from the Walmart on Bethel Avenue. She peered inside a second foam container. It held some soil and the sword fern that had been shading the dismembered foot where it had been discovered in Banner Forest.

The foot was small and its very size saddened Birdy. She wouldn't cry about it, but it pained her. She knew that someone was missing someone. There was a dinner table with an empty space. Maybe a classroom with a desk that sat vacant. Someone out there was missing the person who belonged to the foot.

At the other end of the spectrum, someone out there somewhere had done this to another human being. Why? The *why* was not Birdy Waterman's job, but she couldn't stop thinking about the situation. Why do people do things like this to each other? What drives the depraved? She knew her psychologist friends in Seattle always had a quick answer for that particular query, but Birdy saw evil and destruction as something that was often more random than those who espouse to know the reasons for things insist with their edicts and theories.

The little foot belonged to someone. It was *part* of someone. And now it had been removed from a body by someone or something. Someone who might be skilled in dismemberment? A butcher? A surgeon? Or maybe, it was just someone who had a knife and the twisted notion to use it on another.

There was something strange about the examination of a body part. There was no face for her to talk to, to soothe—even when it was a conversation, or a prayer that she said only in her head. It was part of someone.

It was also evidence.

Birdy wheeled the foot to her autopsy table. She

made a mental note to plant the fern if it turned up nothing of evidentiary value. The plant didn't have to die too.

Chilled by the icy air of the refrigerator, the maggots had ceased their incessant bobble-dance. Once the light over the autopsy table warmed them, Birdy knew they'd wriggle in that way that makes most—but not her—vomit.

It was just a foot, but it could tell the forensic pathologist a million things about the person to whom it had once been attached. Unless there were indicators of toxins in the tissue, it likely wouldn't, however, be able to tell the story of how the person had died.

Or if the person had really died at all.

Birdy considered the possibility that there was a victim out there who had survived the unimaginable—the severing of a limb while still alive. It had happened before. She remembered a case in California many years ago in which a young woman had been abducted, raped, butchered, and left for dead in a remote area. But the young woman hadn't died. Despite the fact that the monster that'd held her captive had chopped off her arms, she climbed from a dumping spot on the side of a road and was rescued by a passing motorist from all but certain death.

Birdy put the foot on a stainless steel tray on the table and swung the beam of a light over it. It sparkled with the glistening bodies of the massing larvae. They beckoned for her to look closer. No problem. Forensic etymology had always been a captivating subject. Birdy had never been the girly-girl who cowered at the sight of a spider or beetle or slug among the deadfall of the forest. She knew the role of bugs—as she called them when she was a kid—was crucial in the way nature worked.

She slowly passed a magnifier over the foot, confirming what she'd already seen back in the woods.

Insect larvae, like those of the blowfly, were fierce flesh eaters. They latched onto dead bodies—or body parts—with little hooks that keep them attached like Velcro. Once they start feeding, they secrete enzymes, which further hasten the natural process of decay. They grow, molt, change, and eat more.

Birdy remembered one textbook fact that never left her:

Larvae can consume an entire human body in a week.

As she examined the fly larvae, Birdy collected and cataloged specimens for the state crime lab in Olympia. She was fairly certain that a second molting had occurred, which put the foot at about three days of decomp. Of course, that didn't mean that the victim had been *dead* three days. If it had been dumped there by a human predator it was possible that it might have been chilled somewhere, the way some serial killers prolonged the enjoyment by keeping body parts as souvenirs.

And if a cougar or bear had killed the owner of the foot, then presumably the rotting appendage would have been out in the elements also since Monday.

Birdy scraped off bits of soil for a better look at the wound where the foot had been severed at the ankle. It was hard to determine if the stump had been excised cleanly or if it had been torn away. She threw more light on it and took photos, the flash bouncing off the gray, water-stained ceiling.

A disgusting story lurked behind that stain. An assistant before Birdy's time punctured a body cavity during a postmortem with a little too much gusto. The poor guy hit a gassy pocket in the lungs that sent a geyser of putrid fluids into the air and onto the ceiling. The staff cleaned the mess with bleach and elbow grease, of course, but the county refused to paint over the blemish.

"You're getting a brand-new facility and we don't need to spend the money," one of the county commissioners said.

That was four years ago.

Since that time JOE'S SPLAT, as she dubbed it, had been hovering above the table.

As Birdy continued to examine the evidence, Kendall Stark arrived and stood in the doorway, watching and gathering her nerve to come get a closer, probably disgusting look.

"Anything?" she asked.

Birdy pulled the overhead light away from the foot.

"I'd say a young woman, maybe as young as fourteen or as old as twenty-five."

"Not a boy?" Kendall asked.

Birdy turned her attention back to the foot. "Well these days, anything is possible. But I see traces of bubble gum pink nail polish on two of the toenails."

Kendall moved closer. "How long has she been dead?"

"Hard to say. I'd start looking for someone who

went missing Monday, maybe Tuesday. But that only presumes the victim was killed right away. Anyway, that's a start."

"All right," Kendall said. "Cause? Any ideas?"

Birdy scanned the small foot and shook her head.

"At first I thought it might have been a mauling, but when I cleaned the stump I could see that the foot had been severed neatly. The tissue around the bone is a mess between the bugs and the dirt, but there is a single cut between the joints with damned near butcher quality."

"Homicide?"

"I think so. You'll know for sure when you find the rest of her." Birdy motioned for the detective to come closer, and Kendall somewhat reluctantly did so.

"Look here," she said. "This is kind of interesting."

Kendall strained to see. She looked back up at Birdy. "I'm missing something," she said.

"Here," Birdy said, pointing her gloved fingertip on the side of the foot. "See those?" She indicated three indentations in an arc. They were slight and a maggot had settled into one of them, making it difficult to see. She flicked it off with a scalpel.

"Yes. What is it?"

Birdy twisted the light on its stand to redirect its beam. The maggots who'd been chilled to stillness were now happily awake and they moved like a wave.

"Bite marks," she said.

Kendall's eyes widened a little. "Bear?"

"Not sure. Maybe. Maybe human. I'll try to do an impression here. I think we'll lose it if we transport to Olympia and have it done at the state lab."

Human?

Kendall took in the idea of a human predator. It was her job to catch men and women who do evil to each other, but a human bite mark? She'd investigated gunshot, stabbing, and strangulation cases. She'd never had a case in which someone had actually bitten another person. And while Birdy hadn't suggested cannibalism, the idea of it lingered.

"All right," Kendall said, pulling back from the autopsy table. Birdy shut off the water. The stench from the decomposing foot and the writhing of the maggots had intensified under her lamp. Birdy clicked off the light and turned to the detective. Her expressive dark brown eyes looked upward as she pondered something.

"Kendall," she said. "I've been thinking about those feet washing up on the beaches up north."

The detective nodded. "That crossed my mind too."

"Do you know anything about those cases?" Birdy asked.

"Not much," Kendall said. "Just what I've read in the reports. Some have been found with shoes on. A few haven't. And, all have been found on the shores— mostly in the Strait. I think the first one was found up north on the shores of Jedediah Island. Was it ten years ago?"

"No. Not quite," Birdy said. Kendall was right, however, about the location. It had been on the shores of Jedediah Island, a six-hundred-acre island off the coast of British Columbia.

"A beachcomber from Washington found what she thought was just a running shoe—until she looked inside and noticed that it wasn't empty," Birdy said, mixing the plaster for the impression of the bite marks before transport to the crime lab.

Over the few years that followed, more feet washed ashore on both Canadian and American coasts.

"There were some differences, of course. Our foot wasn't wearing a shoe," Kendall said, recalling one of the more intriguing aspects of the unsolved cases.

"Right," Birdy said. "Most of the dozen or so found were wearing running shoes. The first foot was wearing a shoe popular in India, sold in the aughts."

"I hate that I'm about to use the word 'floated' in this context," Kendall said with an annoyed grimace. "But was the idea floated that some of the victims might have been killed in the tsunami?"

The horrific Japanese tsunami had been a source of all sorts of mini mysteries as pieces of debris related to the catastrophe had found their way to Washington and Oregon. Some things were expected—pieces of boats, docks, and even car parts. Other items were either strange or heartbreaking. Part of a McDonald's golden arch, a mannequin fully dressed for an evening out, and a child's playhouse complete with toys had drifted thousands of miles to land on the craggy beaches of the Pacific Northwest.

"They could have been," Birdy said. "Bodies sometimes break apart at the joints when they've decomposed. But as I recall, it was determined that one or two were locals—not tsunami victims. I'm pretty sure one was a suicide."

As Birdy checked the foot against notes she made, the two talked and pieced together the bits of the "foot" stories they'd heard or read about. None of the feet found involved Kitsap County residents or were discovered there, so neither Birdy nor Kendall had worked directly on any of the cases. And yet, there was such mystery, such macabre lore, attached to the severed feet that everyone had an idea or theory.

Gang violence?

Pirates?

Slaves murdered at sea?

Every ugly scenario one could conjure was a possibility.

"There hasn't been much to go on," Birdy said. "But there were lots of feet. A dozen in total. Only two were a pair belonging to the same person. Others came from different people. Mostly men, but some women too."

She logged more information on the paperwork that would accompany the foot to Olympia.

Kendall, having grown up along the Washington coast, knew that finding a dead body along the shoreline was not an uncommon occurrence though it didn't happen every day. Or every week. The mysterious feet, however, still made beachcombing in the Pacific Northwest a little uncomfortable for the squeamish.

"Okay, but why was it so hard to ID who these feet belonged to?" Kendall asked. "Is that going to be a problem with our foot?"

"No. I mean, not for the same reason," Birdy said. "The ones found in the Pacific or on the Strait were compromised." She set down her pen and met Kendall's gaze. "More like transformed.

"It was difficult for the examiners to identify feet because they had been transformed into a waxy residue, somewhat like soap," she said. "The buildup was caused by a lack of oxygen in the sea water and the growth of anaerobic bacteria that converted the fat into adipocere."

As Kendall took it all in, a story came to mind.

"Like that famous case from your old stomping grounds," she said. "The one everyone calls the Lady of the Lake."

That Kendall had recalled a fascinating case made Birdy smile. It was one of the most baffling and interesting in the annals of Northwest crime. She stopped what she was doing.

"The Lady of the Lake," Birdy repeated. "Yes, that's the one."

The Lady of the Lake was so named for a crime that had occurred in Lake Crescent, a deep chasm of water not far from where she grew up on the Makah Reservation, though decades before Birdy was born.

It started when a pair of men found a body while out fishing in the summer of 1940.

It was a woman, face down, floating on the surface.

"The woman had been hog-tied and weighted down in the icy waters where anaerobic bacteria did a number on her, turning her into a creamy, putty-colored substance that resembled soap," Birdy said.

"That's disgusting," Kendall said.

"Disgusting is also fascinating, Kendall."

"I guess you've got that right."

"The discovery was a sensation," Birdy said. "I remember studying about it in school. Picnickers and curiosity seekers swarmed the banks of Lake Crescent to see just where the Lady of the Lake had been found."

"Right, but more to the point, however, was just how did she get there . . . and, of course, who in the world was she? That's the stuff of a classic murder mystery, don't you think?"

"Of course," Kendall said. "I'm grabbing at a memory now, but I can't recall how they figured it out."

Birdy smiled. "I remember it. In fact, I wrote a paper on it in college."

"Why doesn't that surprise me in the least?" Kendall asked.

Birdy ignored the tease. She never forgot anything. Every case she ever studied, especially the big ones, was burned onto her brain.

"A medical student in Port Angeles examined the corpse for the police and reported that it would be difficult, if not impossible, to identify the vic. Even though she'd been preserved by the cold, deep water, she was missing her face and fingertips. A dental plate removed from her mouth was the sole clue—and eventually led to her killer."

"Her husband, right?" Kendall asked.

Birdy recalled more details. "Yes, the victim was identified as Hallie Illingworth, a waitress from Port Angeles, married to a truck driver named Monty. No one had seen her since just before the Christmas holidays a few years before."

Kendall watched as Birdy moved around the autopsy table.

"People were suspicious of her husband, a brute who'd beaten her black and blue, but the idea that she might have run off with another man seemed plausible," she said.

"He was convicted, right?"

"Yes, he eventually served nine years in prison for the crime," Birdy said.

Kendall let out a sigh. "And we think they get off too easy today. Illingworth was the worst kind of killer. He basically beat her, strangled her, hog-tied her, and tossed her into the lake to conceal his crime."

"And he almost got away with it," Birdy said.

"Sometimes they do," Kendall said, thinking of the case that had been the source of so much contention in the department, the case that brought Birdy to the crime scene the previous day. Kendall lingered a bit more, before saying good-bye.

The list of what Birdy knew for sure about the foot was devastatingly brief. The victim from Banner Forest was likely female because there were traces of pink polish on two of the toenails. But really, Birdy knew, that was kind of an assumption that didn't necessarily mean much. The foot might have belonged to a boy playing around with polish or one who simply wore nail polish for his own fashion sense. That was fine. Jumping to conclusions was not a course of action she wanted to follow anyway. The size of the foot indicated a younger person or a female. The stump was so damaged that Birdy feared no matter what equipment they had in the lab in Olympia, there was no real hope they'd be able to determine exactly how the foot had been severed from the rest of the body.

Next, she looked at the leafy humus that the crime scene tech Sarah Dorman had collected to see what if anything had been left behind. She ran the forest soil under a field of UV lights to see what, if any, biologicals were present, though she knew that test would yield very little that was helpful.

Soil might look dead, but it was full of living things.

As she expected, it glowed like a photograph of the Milky Way.

Under a scope, she searched for any overt particles that might be out of place given the context of the foot's discovery in the middle of Banner Forest.

Nothing.

The sword fern that Sarah had dug up and brought to the lab had just begun to sprout new fronds with its fuzzy crown unfurling slightly. The budding fronds were like a perfect bird's nest with a clutch of soft brown eggs.

Birdy looked for hair, for fibers, for anything that might not belong in the dirt and on the fern.

Again nothing.

The foot was put back into the cooler and her assistant would see that it was properly transported to Olympia. She'd wondered about those feet on the shore years ago. She had to admit that she considered only for a split second that the foot found by the school kids might be related to something like that.

And yet, a foot in the forest was far, far different. It had been exposed to air and all the handiwork of the larvae. The feet on the coast were distorted, but preserved.

Birdy looked at the fern. She did not consider it of any evidentiary value, and she didn't want it to die. She went over to her sink and filled a bright orange Home Depot bucket with water and stuffed the plant into it.

She went to the locker room to shower and dress. Her scrubs were deposited neatly into a basket next to the door. The water doused her body and she let it run over her face, closing her eyes and wondering about the foot from Banner Forest. She sensed it had belonged to a girl, a young woman. It had danced. It had run. It had tapped to the music. And someone for some sick reason had sought to take it from the body and carry it to the woods for a cruel and unceremonious disposal.

Who do you belong to? Where is the rest of you?

Those questions and more came to her as the water, nearly scalding, splashed down over her shoulder-length black hair. The questions above all others were the ones she would always ask whenever a patient showed up on her autopsy table.

Who did this to you? I need you to tell me. What is your story?

Over and over she'd ask as she thought about the violence that men reserve for female victims: *What mistake did he make? What evidence did he leave behind?*

She turned the faucet to the off position and reached blindly from the shower around the corner for a towel. She was going to miss many things when she went to the new building in Bremerton, but the grime of that old shower was not among them.

CHAPTER 6

The place on Olalla Valley Road was notorious among those who lived in the area or passed by it on a regular basis. It wasn't the site of a colossal accident, though it always brought that kind of rubbernecking. So much so, in fact, that a driver had once been so distracted she ran off the road and sunk her SUV deep into a cattail-ringed ditch.

It was the house and the yard. Or rather what its owner had done to them that caused all the distraction and disdain.

If a home could be a train wreck, this was a Burlington Northern catastrophe.

The place had started its days as a charming little farmhouse when it was built in 1914. Old postcards from the time prove that in glorious, rich sepia tones. The original couple who built it—James and Delia Christensen—had farmed strawberries and then later chickens on twenty-five acres that stretched from the road to a small spring-fed lake in the back of the property. It had once been idyllic, a place of pastoral beauty.

That was a long time ago. Owners had come and

gone. With each one, an addition, a change, a pockmark was deposited unceremoniously on what had been so lovely and serene.

In the early 1990s, Tess Moreau, the great grand-daughter of the original owners, had settled into the old farmhouse. The acreage around the place shrunk as parcels were sold off. The accumulation of things collected over the years began to constrict and overtake the yard. In time, it appeared that the only parts of the earth near the house that felt the rays of the sun were a pathway from the mailbox on Olalla Valley Road to the front door. Everywhere *and* anywhere were piles of trash, garbage, and debris.

Outsiders who passed by mocked Tess and wondered how anyone could live in such a state of filthy confusion, but those who knew her held a more sympathetic view. Tess had lost her husband and a daughter in a car accident when she was only twenty. She raised another daughter, Darby, by herself on her income as a records keeper at the women's prison in Purdy, about seven miles away. At work, no one knew what her situation was like, because she never invited anyone over. She always looked tidy. She followed the rules of her job with the kind of precision that indicated an understanding of doing things the proper way. Her desk was devoid of personal effects outside of two photographs, both of her daughter. Those portraits were put away each night.

And yet, all of that was a kind of mask for what was going on at home.

Tess started collecting things in the early years of her broken heart and it simply couldn't be stopped. People tried to help her, of course. A social worker from the county offices in Bremerton made a note of Tess and her state of mind in a court-ordered home visit:

Ms. Moreau is a kind woman. While her propensity to hoarding is most certainly debilitating, it is not creating an entirely unsafe environment in her home. Her daughter is a student at South Kitsap High School this year. Tess hoards because she has a compulsion to hang on to everything—no matter its value. She has suffered the greatest loss imaginable. Hoarding is a coping mechanism.

After work earlier in the week on Monday, Tess Moreau looked around her house and knew that something wasn't quite right. Everything seemed to be in its chaotic place. And yet something was missing. Darby's book bag wasn't hanging by the door.

She called out to her daughter.

"Honey, you home?"

Tess knew every inch of that debris-blown home. She knew what had been moved, added, subtracted. She knew if someone had attempted to organize things for her. She didn't understand why people did that, when she had no problem finding what she needed *when* she needed it.

She followed the path she'd left between the stacks of papers, toys, kitchenware, and assorted collectibles to Darby's bedroom and twisted the doorknob.

It didn't take Tess more than an instant to confirm that Darby wasn't at home. The sixteen-year-old kept her room spotless. Operating room clean. There wasn't a paper not in its place. Clothes were put away. The bed was made.

"Darby!" she called out once more.

All mothers have a sixth sense about their children. Despite her problems, Tess Moreau was no different. She might have lived in squalor of her own doing, but she'd been imprinted with her daughter and the love she felt for her from the moment Darby was born. Tess was certain something had to be wrong.

Very, very wrong.

As Monday evening turned into night, as night turned into early Tuesday, Tess sat amid the disarray of her life with her phone clenched in her hand. She knew the right thing to do. She expected that she needed to phone the sheriff. Tears rolled down her cheeks. By calling the authorities, she knew she was opening the door for them to assess her one more time. She knew that when Darby was found, she would lose her forever. The social worker had said as much.

"Look, I know you're a good mother. I know you have issues. Look around. You have to see what others see. But between you and me, I'd at least make an attempt to clean up the outside appearance of this place. You are just asking for someone to come here and take away your daughter."

Tess got ready for work and made the early morning drive to the prison, but once she arrived, she could barely keep it together. She started to cry. She pretended to focus on one of the dozen sad African violets she'd been trying to revive on her desk by the window facing the sunny south side of the prison yard. She'd never considered herself a plant person, but she'd found the violets in the "free" section at Home Depot in Gig Harbor and was determined to give them a second chance with some TLC and the right amount of sunshine.

Amanda Watkins, a co-worker, noticed something was wrong and approached her.

"I don't think all the fussing in the world will make that thing bloom again," she said.

Tess looked up. Her eyes were leaking tears, but she said nothing.

"This isn't about the plant, is it?" Amanda asked, inching closer.

"Darby's missing," she said, looking around to make sure they were alone in the prison's records office. They were. "I don't know where she went."

"You've got to call the police," Amanda said.

Tess turned her eyes downward. "I'm afraid," she said, though that was only partly true.

Amanda pulled at her shoulders. Amanda was a tall woman, a little uncomfortable with her height. Her nest of unruly silver hair, almost like fine wire, didn't help her cause to be smaller. It had a mind of its own, and that was always upward. In her fifties, she was still in search of the right look. None of her clothes fit right, and the sweater she was wearing was a case in point.

"Something could have happened to Darby," Amanda said, giving up on the sweater.

"I know," Tess answered. "But in case she's run off, I don't want to lose her."

"Some freak might have her."

"You don't think I've already considered that?" Tess asked.

Amanda shook her head. "Considering where we work, I'd hope so. Call. Call now."

"There's something you don't know about me," Tess said.

Amanda put her hands on Tess's shoulders once more and stared into her eyes. "I know. We all know."

Tess let the tears fall. It was a silent cry, the kind that only allows tears to roll over cheeks and onto the floor. Quiet. No trembling lips. In many ways, the silent kind is the most heart wrenching of all the countless ways people show their hurt and grief.

"It's all right," Amanda said. "Call. Go home. I'll cover you here."

Tess went for her jacket, one of a hundred she had collected from garage sales, department store clearance centers, even one from an open box left at the Goodwill drop-off in Port Orchard.

"Everyone knows?" Tess asked. She looked so hurt, so ashamed. Her eyes filled with more tears. "I didn't know that. No one has said a thing to me about it. This whole time?"

Amanda hugged her friend.

"It doesn't matter," she said. "Darby matters."

"I know. Going home now."

Amanda watched Tess as she turned around to leave. People had laughed and talked about her behind her back for years, but they respected her too. She was so capable, so amazingly confident about how to handle things in the records office. It seemed impossible that she could be the kind of woman who lived in a pigsty. One time, Amanda and another co-worker looked up

Tess's address in the computer at work and drove by her house in Olalla just to see it for themselves.

Amanda hated that she had done that. It was a small betrayal of someone she admired. She never told her and she wondered now if she had if Tess would have confided in her about her daughter's disappearance.

On her way home from the office, Birdy stopped at Walmart to pick up some clothes for Elan who'd arrived with nothing more than what he was wearing and a smartphone. Guessing the teenager's size, she selected a couple pairs of jeans and some graphic T-shirts. She nervously picked up some boxer briefs after asking a young clerk what a teenage boy would probably prefer to wear. She selected a plain black backpack and added some toiletries into the cart. She didn't care if he was trying to grow out a wispy chin beard. She hoped that razors would give him the hint that the look wasn't appealing now. Maybe in a year or two.

She'd talked with Summer. While the conversation was brief, it wasn't as strained as it might have been. Summer said that Elan had been acting out and missing school and was having a hard time. When Birdy pressed her for more about the underlying cause of whatever it was that was making him difficult, Summer balked.

"No one can do anything right. You'll see. You might think you can. Good luck with that. I bet you throw him out by the end of the week."

It was a challenge. Birdy could feel it.

"How's Mom?"

"As mean as ever."

"How's Cal?" she asked about Summer's husband.

"Look, Birdy, you see how you can deal with Elan and I'll do what I can here."

"I'm worried about you."

"That's nice." Her voice was tinged with sarcasm.

Birdy resisted the urge to shoot back, and it was a good thing.

Summer amended what she'd said. "I mean, I appreciate it. I have to go. Working nights at the casino."

Birdy had texted Elan a few times during the day, but only got a few cryptic responses.

Her: How was school?
Him: Sux.
Her: Going to get you some clothes on the way home. We can shop for more this weekend. You can't wear the same thing two days in a row.
Him: I do at home.

When she arrived home, she was surprised to smell something cooking that wasn't pizza.

"I know how to cook, but you wouldn't know that," Elan said. "You don't really know anything about me."

Birdy didn't take the bait. "I brought you these," she said.

He took the bag and peered inside. "Thanks. You know it's true, don't you?" he asked.

"That I don't know you?"

"You don't know who my father is, do you?"

Birdy changed the subject. "Let's eat. Smells good. What is it?"

"Lasagna," he said.

"That's impressive."

Elan shrugged a little. "I don't know how good it

will be. All you had was ground turkey, which I don't like that much."

The lasagna was good and Elan was right. She really didn't know him. But he knew *her*. He'd Googled every case she'd worked on. He asked thoughtful questions. He was very, very good at that.

Answering any she had for him however was not his strong suit.

She let her first condition pass. She'd find out what was troubling him and what brought him to her later.

"Where'd you learn to cook?" she asked.

"I could say that Mom's drunk all the time and I had no choice, but that's not really the truth. I worked last summer on a boat cooking for the crew. I can make pretty decent lasagna."

"You can. What else?" she asked.

Elan laughed. "That's pretty much it, Aunt Birdy. I lasted two weeks."

Getting to know him was going to be a very good thing.

The rain had turned to ice pellets the week after the previous Christmas season. A small dark car parked outside of the house and its driver watched the figure through the window. At first, just a girl. Then her mother. The images were fleeting, but unmistakable. They were taking down the Christmas tree. Adrenaline pulsed and fear rose up. The driver held an envelope and deep inside seethed with rage for what had to be done. Too much was at stake, too much had been lost already. Over and over the voice on her cell phone spoke in a biting and harsh manner.

"You do this or I'll ruin you. Don't you even think about defying me! You, remember, are my bitch."

"I don't want to do it," the driver said.

"I don't want to kill you. But that's the way life goes."

CHAPTER 7

Birdy Waterman stood at the front of the line at the latte stand in the Kitsap County administration building, a mammoth structure that faced west to the shipyard and beyond to the Olympics. Birdy normally didn't go there for coffee—the coroner's office had a kitchen with a refrigerator, stove, and coffeepot. That sometimes the refrigerator held errant body parts while waiting for exam was of no matter. It was an old house. That the coffeepot had broken, however, was a big concern. She needed that third cup.

She looked down at the paper on the counter and read while she waited.

The *Kitsap Sun* had a screamer of a headline across the top of the daily's front page:

HUMAN FOOT FOUND
IN BANNER FOREST

A girl on a field trip with her class from Olalla Elementary School made a grisly discovery Wednesday when she found a human foot just off one of the main paths in Banner

Forest, a county park between Port Orchard and Olalla.

The foot did not belong to any of the students on the trip, according to district spokesperson Julianne Starr.

"All of our students are fine and accounted for," Starr said. "A few were traumatized by the discovery, but no one has been injured. We have made arrangements for a counselor to be at the school to help any students who might have needs related to what happened on the field trip."

The foot was collected and transported to the county morgue.

Four years ago a man walking his dogs in the park was viciously attacked by a black bear. County officials indicate that there have been no recent bear sightings. The location has also been the habitat of cougars.

Banner Forest remains closed pending a thorough search.

"Hi, Kendall," Birdy said, looking up and noticing the detective joining the queue.

Kendall smiled in her direction. "Birdy, what are you doing over here?"

"No coffee, no autopsy," the forensic pathologist said, more for effect than the reality of what she was saying. Actually, there was no pile of bodies waiting for her back at the office. A pile of paperwork, yes. Birdy knew the importance of paperwork, but she'd almost rather dive face first into the rancid depths of a body cavity than deal with the most tedious part of her job.

"Got a call from a woman in South Kitsap," Kendall said. "Says her daughter has been missing."

"How long?"

Kendall pulled out her frequent coffee drinker card and the barista stamped it.

"A few days," she said.

"How old?"

"Sophomore at South."

Birdy lingered as the barista handed Kendall her tuxedo mocha.

"You still drink those?" Birdy said.

Kendall took a sip. "You still drink drip?"

"I'm a traditionalist, Kendall," she said. "You know that. Comes from my culture." Birdy held a sly smile on her face. It was a reference to other training they had to do—diversity training. Birdy, being a Makah Indian, was the only non-white person in the room. Every time anyone posed a question about how people from other cultures might interpret something, the others looked at her.

They walked over by the floor-to-ceiling windows and looked over at the mountains and down at the shimmering water of Sinclair Inlet.

"Want to ride along? She's the daughter of a local celebrity of sorts."

Birdy took a drink. The coffee in the county admin building was superior to the stuff she'd been drinking in the coroner's office. It might have been a good thing that the coffeepot died, after all.

"I didn't know we had any celebrities around here," Birdy said.

"Very local," Kendall said. This time *she* smiled.

"All right, Kendall. I'm game. You drive."

On the drive down Sidney to Bay Street and then onto Highway 16, they spoke about what was going on at home. Birdy talked about her nephew and the complications that came with his arrival. Kendall talked about how her autistic son, Cody, was progressing. They were friends, but with extremely busy lives and careers that knew no time clock. There was never enough time for catching up.

"You think the missing girl is the source of the foot?" Birdy asked.

Kendall glanced at the forensic pathologist.

"Possible," she said.

"Right age," Birdy said. "Close to the dump site."

"That's what I'm thinking."

Birdy's focus was always about *how* a person died, not so much of the *why*. The *why* was the domain of detectives and prosecutors. They needed the *why* to prove a case. Not always, of course. But it helped.

"Except, most killers are not so careless," Birdy said. "Killers who torture and mutilate—if that's what this guy did—are pretty careful about where they deposit their victim's remains."

"I guess so," Kendall said. She pulled off the highway and drove west on Mullinex.

"Gacy kept his victims' bodies in the crawlspace of his house—so he didn't run the risk of detection," Birdy said.

Kendall turned the car toward Olalla Valley Road.

"Yes, and the Green River Killer dumped many of his victims within a few miles of his home," Kendall said.

Birdy finished her coffee. "Lazy, that one," she said.

"Yeah," Kendall said. "The laziest."

* * *

Gregg Olsen

The two women meandered their way along the trail between the berms of garbage and things that would soon be garbage that led to Tess Moreau's front door.

"Local celebrity, huh?" Birdy said softly, shooting a teasing glance at her friend.

"Well, yes," Kendall said without a trace of irony. "Everyone knows her."

The detective knocked. After what seemed like a very long time, a woman opened the door. What greeted them was surprising considering the surroundings. Tess Moreau was a pretty woman. Her hair was long, but not too long. She had smooth, even-toned skin, and bright blue eyes. She wore blue jeans with a slight crease as though they'd been ironed. Her top was a crisp, white blouse. If Birdy had been presented a photo array lineup of people and was asked to pick out the hoarder, she'd never have picked Tess. Her own mother, yes. Her neighbor, yes. Kendall, maybe. Tess Moreau was the epitome of neatness.

Not a hair out of place.

"We're here about your daughter," Kendall said, identifying herself.

"I'm with the department too," Birdy said. There was no need to say she was with the coroner's office. No need to sound the alarms. It was bad enough to have a detective show up, but a forensic pathologist— that was beyond what most moms could endure.

"Have you found my daughter?" Tess asked.

Kendall shook her head. "No, we haven't, but we do need to talk to you. We need to make a report."

Tess stood in the doorway.

"I suppose you need to come inside," she said.

"It would be easier," Birdy answered.

Tess looked over her shoulder, back into the cluttered space of her home.

"I already know what you are thinking," she said.

"No one is thinking anything," Kendall said. "We're here about your daughter, Darby. Not your house."

Tess opened the door wider. "Then you were thinking about it."

"Only because you are," Kendall said.

She motioned them inside.

Birdy wanted to say something about the Precious Moments that filled the foyer. Her mother collected them too. But not to that extent. She doubted anyone did. There were scores of them.

"I'm not the best housekeeper," Tess said. "But I'm a good mother. No one could say otherwise."

She bent down and moved a stack of newspapers off the sofa and indicated with a nod that her visitors could sit there. She took a spot on a piano bench across from them. The place was musty and cluttered, but it didn't stink. She was a hoarder of stuff; that was true. But Tess Moreau wasn't a hoarder of animals and that was good news for her visitors' olfactory senses.

"When did you see Darby last?" Kendall asked.

"Sunday night when I went to bed. I get up and leave for work early. Darby gets herself off to school."

"Darby's sixteen? A sophomore at South?"

"Yes, just sixteen."

"Did you have any communication with her? Texts? Phone calls?"

Tess tried to calm herself. She took a deep breath. "We don't bring our phones into the prison. Policy.

Darby knows not to call me because of that stupid rule. No point in it. I did check my phone when I got out Monday, but nothing."

"But you did get a call," Birdy said.

"No, I didn't."

"Not from your daughter, from the school."

Tess nodded. "Yes, I did."

"Did you call them back?"

"Yes, I did."

"What did you tell the school?" Kendall asked.

Tess's eyes flooded. "Why are you being hostile?"

"Look, I'm not being hostile. I'm being direct. That's my job. Now, Ms. Moreau, when you talked to the school what did you tell them?"

"I told them she was sick. I told them Darby was out sick."

"Why did you do that?" Birdy asked, jumping in.

Tess didn't say a word.

"All right," Kendall said, pushing on. "You lied to the school and waited a whole day before calling to report she was missing. Is that because she's left before? Are there problems between you and your daughter? Is there something we should know about?"

Tess's lips tightened before she spoke. "No. No. No. That's not why. She's a very good girl. Mostly As and Bs. She's never been any trouble whatsoever."

"But you waited and you lied," Birdy said.

Tess started to shake. "I waited because of this." She got up from the piano bench and pointed all around them. "I know what people think of me. I know you know."

Birdy looked directly at Tess. "No, I don't know."

"Crazy lady. Tess the Mess. Pig Woman. I am not deaf."

Birdy looked over at Kendall. She had heard of Tess the Mess, but she didn't realize it was *her*. It didn't seem it could be. Yes, the place looked like a terrorist had let off a bomb in a department store, but the woman standing in front of them was so put together.

"I don't know what you're talking about," Birdy said, a lie that she was happy to make.

"I didn't want people to say what I felt they would say," Tess said.

This time Kendall spoke. "Which is?"

Tears puddled her eyes. "That I lost her here in the house."

"We're not saying that," Kendall said. "We know you didn't. But we do need to figure out where she's gone."

"How about her father?" Birdy asked. "Where's he?"

Tess tried to mop her eyes with the back of her hand. "Buried up at the cemetery in Port Orchard with her sister. That's where."

Birdy blinked. "I'm sorry," she said. "I didn't know."

Kendall turned to Birdy. "A terrible accident on Highway 16."

"I'm so sorry," Birdy repeated.

"It has been a long time," Tess said. "Long enough for some people to forget, but not so long that I don't think about them every day."

For the next half hour they talked about the missing girl. She played tennis on the JV team. She wanted a horse. She kept a journal. She had lots of school friends, but none who came to her house—for reasons that neither Kendall nor Birdy needed amplified. Darby was the quintessential good girl.

"Here's a recent picture," Tess said, handing over a photograph that showed a pretty blond teenager next to a chestnut mare. Her fingers gripped the reins.

"She's beautiful," Kendall said.

Birdy took the photo. "Yes, very pretty. Did she always do her nails?"

Tess nodded. "Yes, fingers and toes."

"Can we see her room?" Kendall asked.

"Of course, but be prepared for a big shock."

"What's that?" Birdy asked.

"She doesn't take after her mother," Tess said. "It's at the end of the hall on the left."

It was a jarring experience, both women would later say, when the mother of the missing teen opened the bedroom door.

The walls were painted white. Cream-colored linen curtains pressed with accordion pleats hung over the sole window in the room. A bed with a plain white comforter was pulled up tautly and a pair of pillows in pink cases sat in squared off uniformity.

"I told you she didn't take after me," Tess said.

Birdy turned around. "That's all right. I don't take after my mother either and I turned out all right."

Tess smiled weakly. "Thanks."

Kendall moved deeper into the space. "There are worse things than being a collector, Ms. Moreau."

"I see your daughter loved pink," Birdy said, looking at the pillows.

Tess's gaze tracked the forensic pathologist's. "The singer and the color, yes."

Kendall indicated a small white and gray purse. "Is this her purse?"

Tess shook her head. "No. She really didn't carry a purse. I found that at the Goodwill on Friday and gave it to her. I don't think she liked it. She didn't like most of the things I gave her."

Kendall looked inside the empty purse.

"Were you two getting along?" she asked.

"Oh yes," she said. "She didn't run away, if that's what you're getting at, detective."

"Just asking," Kendall said. "Tell me about her behavior in the last week or so."

Tess looked confused. "What do you mean?"

"Was she happy?" Kendall asked.

"She is a teenager," Tess said. "She was happy once an hour and miserable the rest of the time."

Kendall pushed for more information. "Did she have boyfriend issues?"

"The only issue was that she didn't have a boyfriend."

"Well she is only sixteen," Kendall said.

"At sixteen, these days, you might as well consider yourself a loser or a spinster if you don't have a boyfriend."

"Right," Birdy said, cutting in. "Things have changed."

"Is this her backpack?" Kendall asked.

Tess reached for it, but Kendall held on to it. "Yes, her old one. She had several. I couldn't stop finding new ones for her."

"I'd like to look inside, if that's all right with you."

"I got that one from a yard sale in Burley," Tess said, indicating that it was fine for the detective to open it. "One of the things she actually liked. It was brand new with the tags."

Kendall dumped the contents of the REI backpack on the white laminate top of the teenager's spotless desk. A navy blue moleskin notebook, a copy of *Pride and Prejudice*, a pen, two packs of chewing gum, a tin of breath mints, some makeup, a couple of tampons, and something else that caught the girl's mother by surprise.

A small box of Roughrider brand condoms.

Awkward silence filled the room.

"What does she have that for?" Tess asked, her eyes fluttering.

Neither Birdy nor Kendall gave the obvious answer.

"Is it possible she had a boyfriend? Maybe one you didn't know about?" Birdy asked.

Tess was flustered and embarrassed. Not because her daughter might be having sex, but because she thought they were so close that she surely would have confided in her.

"No," she said, gathering herself. "Absolutely not."

Kendall opened the moleskin and noted that it was only partially filled. Some of it appeared to be poetry. Some pages were filled with lists of things Darby needed to do on various days.

Missing were a couple of items no teenager ever went without.

"Do you know where her phone is? I don't see it here."

Tess, still upset over the condoms, looked around.

"No," she said. "No. She never left without it. That phone was superglued to her hand."

"Keys too?" Birdy asked.

"She doesn't drive yet, and we never lock the front door."

When those words tumbled out of her mouth, all three women had the same thought. They wondered if Darby hadn't left willingly or if she'd been abducted from home. If there had been a struggle anywhere in the house—other than her room—there would be no way of knowing.

"We'll need to talk to her friends," Kendall said. "Teachers as well."

"Her best friend is Katie Lawrence," Tess said.

Birdy looked down at the bed and picked through the makeup that had come from the backpack. A bottle of pink nail polish called Car Nation held her attention.

"We should take that along with the notebook," the forensic pathologist said. "If that's all right."

Tess didn't answer with words, just a slight gesture that it was all right to do so. By then she was in another world, considering what she might have missed, wondering if something terrible had occurred under her own roof and if the mess that had been her life since her husband and child died had somehow helped to obscure the truth.

"We'll need her hairbrush too," Birdy said.

"I watch TV," Tess said, snapping back into the moment. "I know why you want that. Have you found Darby?"

Kendall faced the worried mother as she stood on the outskirts of the cyclone of her household debris and looked her straight in her eyes. "No. No we haven't found anyone."

It was at once a lie and the truth. A body hadn't been found. Only a foot.

When they got into the car and backed away, Birdy turned to Kendall.

"Why didn't you tell her?" Birdy said.

"Because we don't know who that foot belonged to."

Birdy kept her eyes on Kendall's. "I think we do. We just have to confirm it."

"Then confirm it, Birdy. Until then, we aren't going to tell a mother that her daughter has been butchered by some maniac."

"No. I don't expect we would," she said.

Birdy watched as the house faded from view and the pastoral beauty of Olalla Valley took over the scene. Daffodils jumped from the black earth along the road-side. A goat nibbled at some foliage by someone's front door. A school bus pulled out in front of them.

"What happened to Darby, Kendall?" she asked.

Kendall slowed down as the yellow bus with its flashing lights, now dimmed, pulled over to let cars pass.

"I don't know."

CHAPTER 8

South Kitsap High School sits on the edge of a ridge overlooking the Olympics to the west. For decades, SKHS had been one of the largest high schools in the state. At any time, the home of the Wolves had at least two thousand students—where most high schools in the nearby region were about half that size. It drew kids from the wealthy subdivisions such as McCormick Woods to the trailer parks south of Burley. Because of its massive student body, it was difficult for kids to find their place, their former status from junior high. A girl who'd been among the best distance runners at Marcus Whitman might not even make the varsity track team. A boy who'd been the first chair trumpet player at one junior high might find himself battling it out for second or third. Cliques were rampant.

While being the new girl—almost *any* new girl— carried huge importance among teenagers, it simply wasn't the case for the new boy. Elan Elliot was none of the things that would make him stand out from the crowd. He was Native American, but in the Pacific

Northwest that wasn't a big deal. The Northwest Indian culture had been an indelible part of the region long before casinos and smoke shops proliferated on tribal land. Seattle was named for a revered chief. Tacoma was the original name of the mountain that dominated the state like a snowball of immense proportions.

Elan's story traveled through the school's gossip channels. He was a runaway. He lived with his aunt who worked in the county coroner's office. Coming in so late in the year, there wasn't much of an effort to size him up or get to know him. All the sports teams were winding down. He kept his head down and went from class to class. He didn't even try to get noticed.

The first day, the kid with the locker next to his was the only one who spoke to him.

"Showing a little wolf pride, huh?"

The tone was dismissive and Elan didn't get it.

"What?"

"Your wolf shirt."

Elan looked down at the black and gray T-shirt with a stylized wolf howling at a blackened moon. "My aunt got it for me," he said. "I didn't even know the Wolves were the school mascot. If I did, I'd have used it to polish my car."

Now the kid seemed interested. "You have a car?"

Elan threw his backpack over his shoulder. "Yeah."

"I'm Chase. Can I get a ride?"

Elan shook his head. "Sorry, it's at home."

Chase shut his locker. And outside of art class, that was the extent of Elan's interaction with anyone other than a quick nod.

* * *

The principal notified Katie Lawrence's father that Kitsap County Detective Stark was on campus asking to talk with Katie about her friend, Darby. Katie's dad, a fireman, didn't hesitate. He told the principal it was fine and that he knew Kendall Stark by reputation as a good investigator.

"I doubt Katie knows anything," he said. "She is pretty much a loner."

Kendall waited in the hallway by the trophy case. She'd gone to South Kitsap herself and while not a stellar athlete, she had left her mark there. Her name was on a plaque shoved in the back of the case. She found it and it brought a smile to her face.

WOMEN'S VOLLEYBALL CHAMPIONS
Peninsula Division

"You in there?" a girl's voice said.

"A hundred years ago, yeah. Katie?"

The girl was taller than her friend and she walked with a slight limp, the result of a birth defect that had been corrected over multiple surgeries since she was a toddler. She had dark brown hair and light-colored eyes. Kendall led the sixteen-year-old to a small room adjacent to the attendance office. On the other side of the glass that faced out to the hallway, other kids who'd managed to get out of class meandered around, staring at them like they were a zoo exhibit.

"This is kind of embarrassing," Katie said, catching the eye of a girl who had lasered her attention in their direction.

"Want me to draw the blinds?" Kendall asked.

Katie looked warily at the scene through the window. "Yeah, I'm a background person. I don't like to be front and center. Neither do my friends."

The detective pulled the cord and the dustiest mini blinds on the planet slowly unfurled. She turned the plastic wand that adjusted the space between the slats slightly, not enough to block out the world, but it offered a little privacy.

"I'm here to talk about Darby," she said.

"Yeah, my dad texted me," she said, putting her ten-pound backpack on the table in front of her. "I'm cool with whatever you want to know."

They both sat down on hard-molded chairs that had become ubiquitous in schools and prisons all across the country. They were uncomfortable, but easy to clean. "Thank you. Before we talk about the last time you saw her, because that could be very important, I want you to tell me about her."

"She was cool," Katie said, fishing for a Tic Tac. "She was into art."

"All right. That's good," Kendall said. "How long have you been best friends?"

"Just this year. I mean, I wouldn't exactly say we're best friends. I've never been to her house or anything."

"Was there a reason for that?" Kendall asked.

Katie popped a mint into her mouth. "You know the reason. I mean, we never really talked about her mom or, like you know, her situation." The teenager offered Kendall a mint, and the detective declined.

"But you know who her mother is, right?" she asked.

"Duh. Everyone does. I didn't care. I mean, why should I? Sometimes I hate my mom too."

The comment interested Kendall. It didn't surprise her, however. There had been times when she had hated her own mother. It came with being a teenage girl.

"Did Darby hate her mother?" she asked.

Katie chomped on her mint. "Hate, I guess, is the wrong word. She felt sorry for her. Like her mom had a disease or something. Lots of kids think Darby's mom is lazy or crazy, but Darby told me that hoarding is a disease. She hated that her mother had that disease."

"I see," Kendall said. "What did other kids think of Darby? Having a mother like Tess couldn't have been easy. Did they bully her? Did she have anyone who might want to harm her?"

Katie thought a beat. "She was tough. She didn't let anyone knock her down. I've had some problems in the past and I'm tough like that too."

"Did she have a boyfriend?"

"No. She didn't. She told me that she probably was doomed here at South to never have a boyfriend. Guys liked her okay, but she didn't let anyone close."

"Let's talk about the last time you saw her," Kendall said.

The girl made a face. She was good at that one—irritated. "What about it? I mean," she said, "there wasn't anything special. I barely saw her. She had art class last period and I think she was going to stay around with Ms. Mitchell. She was doing a lot of that."

"Ms. Mitchell? That's her art teacher?"

"Yeah. I don't like her. But Darby did. She even went over to her house one time. Maybe more times. She didn't tell me much about that."

Kendall didn't react to the disclosure. She knew that no kid had any business going to a teacher's house. If that was true, Ms. Mitchell was going to be in trouble.

"Katie, I need you to think about the past few weeks. Was there anything different about Darby? Anything out of the ordinary?"

The bell rang and Katie got up. "Not really. Like she did spend a lot of time with Ms. Mitchell. We were supposed to meet up one weekend at Starbucks, but she didn't show. She was over at Ms. Mitchell's."

"I might need to talk to you some more," Kendall said as the teen hoisted her backpack up onto her shoulder and started for the door.

"That's okay. I hope Darby's okay. She's really a cool girl. Never mattered to me who her mom was."

Kendall watched the girl with the limping gait merge into the sea of other teens in the hall as they made their way to their next period classes. Katie Lawrence had found a kindred spirit with Darby. The like-minded had found each other. They did what all teens wanted to do—blended in. As the teenagers moved down the hallway, Katie disappeared.

But not like Darby. Darby was really gone.

CHAPTER 9

Birdy Waterman was good with color. She always had been. Before she decided on a career as a forensic pathologist she had dabbled in the art world. She loved painting. Watercolors mostly. One year she and her sister, Summer, painted Salish-inspired designs on scraps of driftwood to sell to the tourists who came to Neah Bay for fishing or whale watching. They sold quite a few pieces, but it felt compromising and dishonest. The hottest sellers had nothing to do with their own culture, but owed more to what was expected by those who wanted something to match a sofa or comforter cover. When she started painting with authenticity that fit how she felt, Birdy found she really didn't like the subjective nature of the art world. Everyone had an opinion. Nothing, quite ironically, was black and white.

Science *was*. Science was conclusive and incontrovertible.

The office was quiet. Her assistant had gone for the day and the coroner was away at a conference in Maui. Who knew there were so many trade shows and conferences for those who deal with the dead? Always in such lively and lovely places, of course.

While she worried what might be going on with her nephew, there was no place on earth she'd rather be than right there in her office trying to figure out what happened to the girl from the hoarder's house on Olalla Valley Road. Grateful that the office coffeepot was working again, she poured herself a big steaming cup.

In front of her, fanned over her ancient Boeing-surplus-store desk, were photographs she'd taken of the foot found in the forest. With the maggots removed, the foot appeared smaller than when the kids found it.

It was a pale gray and white. Not hideous, just so very sad.

As she tilted a close-up taken on her autopsy table, the pink lacquer on the nails came at her like falling cherry blossoms. She was all but certain that the color matched the bottle that sat on her desk next to a hairbrush that had been bagged and tagged.

A visual examination wasn't enough, however.

She took off one of her good luck gold hoops, picked up the phone, and tapped the buttons for the state crime lab where the foot had been transported.

Percy Smith answered.

"Percy, Birdy here," she said.

"Yup, I know," he said in his chirpy upbeat voice. "We have caller ID now."

"Of course," she said.

"Hey, are you going to invite us up to your new digs?"

Birdy looked over at the calendar. She didn't like to

be reminded that the move was coming up. She liked where she was just fine.

"Yes," she said. "But we're not ready yet. We'll have some kind of an open house after we get settled in and have all the kinks worked out."

"You don't sound all that excited, Dr. Waterman."

"I don't know," she said, looking around. "This sort of feels like home."

"Think of all that new equipment," he said.

"Right," she said. "But we do all right with what we have here. Anyway, of course, you'll all be invited to come and take a look. In the meantime, I'm calling about that foot."

"Figured. We put her in the footlocker," he said, waiting a beat.

Birdy didn't laugh at his pun. She'd heard enough of those already.

"Sorry. Couldn't resist."

"Were you able to turn up anything?" she asked, ignoring the apology for his lapse.

"Female, but you already indicated that in your report. About twelve to nineteen years old."

"Sixteen," she said.

"Could be." He went on. "The toenail polish—or is it fingernail polish that's been applied to a toe? Anyhow, the polish is made by Mayfair. Color is called—"

"Car Nation," she said, cutting him off.

"You know who she is," he said.

"I think so."

"Who?"

"Missing girl from South Kitsap. I went with one of the detectives to her house."

"Wow, that cross training is really something up there," he said.

"It wasn't because of that," she said, not happy that everyone in the world seemed to know they'd endured mandatory team-building sessions. "Anyway, the girl is Darby Moreau. I saw the fingernail polish in her back-pack. I have her hairbrush; I'll pack up some samples for you to confirm it's her DNA."

"Okeydokey," he said.

Birdy moved on. "Can you tell me anything about the cut?"

She could hear Percy flip through some papers.

"Okay, so like you know, the tissue is in bad shape," he said. "But I did see some striations on the bone that indicated whoever did it wasn't some professional butcher, if that helps."

"Tell me more," she said.

"Not much more to tell," he said. "Whoever cut her was somewhat tentative. That can mean it was a first time or that they were grossed out by what they were doing—I know I would be."

"Post or anti mortem?"

Percy hesitated. "Pretty sure, post."

"That doesn't sound conclusive," she said, drumming her fingertips on the edges of the evidence photos on her desk.

"Sure enough that if I testified in court, I'd say so," Percy said.

"Can you rule out animal activity?"

"Nope. Not at all. I think you'll need to find the rest of the body to determine that. Anything new with the search for the rest of her?"

Of course she would have told him that. It was the

kind of question that irritated. A teenage girl doesn't just vanish, leaving only a foot behind.

That was about to change.

The last time Darby Moreau's mother saw her daughter, the sixteen-year-old was doing her homework as she always did. Tess Moreau held that final image in her brain as though it were a photograph. *No, an etching.* It wasn't exactly real, or rather she wouldn't allow her memory to capture the last visage in bold strokes of light and color. Just the black and white of what she'd seen when Darby looked up from her geometry assignment and smiled at her.

"You about ready to call it a night?" Tess asked as she poked her head into Darby's room. She was tired from a long day of organizing what couldn't be organized and was distracted by a box of Beanie Babies ("with the tag protectors!") that she'd found at a barn sale at the other end of Olalla.

"Just about, Mom," Darby said. "I'm all caught up, but I'm doing a little looking ahead on the next geometry Mr. Barringer will want us to do. I don't want to get behind before the week even starts. You know me."

Tess walked in the room and put her hand on her daughter's shoulder, feeling her silky hair. A gentle and sweet caress.

"You don't have to be perfect," she said.

"No one's perfect, Mom," Darby said. "Besides, those people who actually think they are perfect are really full of crap."

Tess made a face, but kept her hand right where it was.

"Don't talk ugly, Darby."

Darby shrugged a little. "That's not ugly, Mom. Hang out at South in the commons between classes if you want to hear ugly."

"I don't think so," Tess said as she started to retreat from the only neat space in the house.

Darby grinned. Her braces had come off the month before and her bright perfect smile still looked like magic to her mother. "No. No, you wouldn't," the teenager said.

Tess turned away and started down the hall, but Darby called out to her.

She stood in the door frame. "Mom, I was thinking we could organize the stuff in the living room tomorrow night." She paused and waited for her mother's inevitably delayed response.

Tess moved toward her. "I like the idea, but, honey, I wouldn't know where to begin."

The girl gripped her mom's hands and stared up into the eyes that looked like her own, just sadder.

"Mom, you just have to start," Darby said. "We can do it together. I can teach you."

"I know you can," Tess said. "You can do anything."

Deep down, Tess knew she couldn't. No one could. No amount of wishing, yelling, begging, threatening, or cajoling could get Tess to rid her house of the clutter that consumed most of the airspace.

After Birdy Waterman and Kendall Stark left with Darby's hairbrush, some makeup, and a few other odds and ends, the recollection of that last evening together brought a stream of tears down Tess's cheeks. She scanned the room for a box of tissues, but she couldn't find any despite the fact that somewhere in that house she had a case of Kleenex. She picked up a lace curtain from the couch and dabbed at the corner of her eyes.

This was all her fault. A social worker from the county, a young woman with straight black hair that she pinned back over her shoulders, and gorgeous almond eyes that never once ridiculed, told Tess in the kindest way possible that her daughter would eventually abandon her if she couldn't change.

"It won't be because she won't love you anymore. Clearly she does. She will leave because," the social worker said in a low, kind voice, "leaving is the only way for her to relieve her stress. It is the only coping mechanism she has. When she goes—and she will—you'll have to take responsibility for it. I know you don't want that. No mother would. You can change, Tess. You have to."

Tess folded herself into a sliver of a bare spot on the denim blue sofa in the living room. She clutched the tear-soaked lace curtain and let out a cry loud enough to rattle her Precious Moments collection in the overloaded whatnot shelf that had been her mother's. She needed to let it all out. Every last bit of her regret. It was deep inside of her, coiled like a snake she'd swallowed when her husband and baby died. She needed to focus on Darby and wherever she might have gone.

This is my entire fault. I know it. I made this happen. I'm responsible. God, please find Darby. Please forgive me.

CHAPTER 10

Connie Mitchell was in the middle of her planning session. It was an hour-long period that the teachers' union had somehow managed to hang on to, despite the cutbacks that left its members hoping against hope that they'd not only be able to teach young people, but would be able to pay their mortgages. Connie was a lovely woman with short, dark hair that she spiked a little—she was the fine arts teacher, after all. With the exception of large, flashy jewelry, she favored a simple, monochromatic look.

In a very real way, she embodied what she taught the budding artists in her class.

"Simplicity with a sparkle, that's how you command a viewer's attention. Throw too much dazzle at them and well, they are turned off and overwhelmed."

When one kid, a resolute attention-seeker with destructive tendencies, created a multimedia project that used everything in the classroom and bits of the rubberized track around the football field, she praised him for his ingenuity.

And reported him for defacing school property.

Connie liked sparkle and creativity, but she also liked order.

When Kendall Stark poked her head inside the classroom, she saw Connie standing like a statue in front of the room looking at a row of student work that she'd laid out on the floor. Kendall watched as the art teacher reordered the pieces like the judge on a dog show.

"Are you ranking them?" Kendall asked.

Connie didn't look up. "There's no ranking in art," she said.

"But you've shuffled them," Kendall said. "I saw you."

"Just looking for a more pleasant way of presenting this as an experience," Connie said. "Parent and Guardian Night is next week."

Kendall introduced herself as a member of the Kitsap County Sheriff's Department. She didn't use the words "homicide investigator"—that pairing usually brought a measure of panic. And rightly so.

Connie looked up and studied her visitor. "You're here about Darby?"

Kendall was surprised. "Yes, how did you know that?"

"We have a lot of students here and word travels fast," Connie said, looking once more at the artwork on the grungy and dinged linoleum tiled floor. "I thought she was sick."

"Why did you think that?" Kendall asked.

"Attendance office called her mother. I checked." The teacher switched the first two paintings and then surveyed the entire row one more time. "But she isn't sick, is she? Has she run away?"

Kendall had liked the sequence before the teacher

moved the first two, but she didn't remark on it. She wasn't an art critic, but she knew what she liked. Nothing on the floor appealed to her. They were dark, moribund. Two had images of violence; at least it appeared as if they did. Nevertheless, they were not gallery bound. The mothers would store them until their children moved away and then unceremoniously toss them.

Like her mother had done to her stuff.

"Why would you think that?" she asked.

Connie led Kendall over to her desk and sat down. "Beanbag there." She pointed to a black pleather orb, but the detective preferred to stand.

"We got close," Connie said, her clear brown eyes riveted on her classroom visitor. "I don't want to talk about it."

Kendall let that comment slide. She'd circle back to it later. It was the kind of comment that usually led to a shutdown of information, and she wasn't going to let that happen right then. She eyed the beanbag, but doubted it would be easy or graceful to extricate herself from it.

"We're concerned about her. Her mother is concerned. She's vanished."

Connie looked worried. "Where is she?" she asked.

"That's what I'm here to find out. Tell me about her. Tell me about Darby."

Connie stood up and paced. "I love that girl. She is special."

Love. Special. Those were pedophile code words.

"How so?" Kendall asked.

"We have a mix of students here," Connie said. "This is a big school. We've got a lot of kids who think they are entitled. They want to be the next American Idol or think they are the second coming of Macklemore. They want to be famous, make a lot of money."

"Everyone has dreams, Ms. Mitchell, right?"

"True. So true. Darby is wiser, older than her years. She has a wry, sardonic kind of sense of humor. She understood the balance and order of the universe. You could talk to her about things that were important. She isn't like a lot of the kids I have now in class."

"What do you mean? Special? Different?" Kendall was leading Connie to where she needed to go.

"Vulnerable, but strong. Resilient. I saw a lot of myself in her—you know when I was younger and trying to find my identity."

Again, Kendall let that slide.

"She spent a lot of time with you," she said, adding a quick, "here."

"Yes, she did," Connie said. "She is my best student. Certainly this year. There's always one. Sometimes two that stand out."

"Does she have any friends, other than Katie Lawrence? Others who might know what, if anything, out of the ordinary was going on in her life?"

"Other than Katie? No. I think she had a crush on someone, though."

You? Did she have a crush on you?

"You're being vague here, Ms. Mitchell. I need you to be direct. I need you to tell me what a sixteen-year-old girl was doing at your house?"

Connie sprang to her feet. "What are you getting at? She was never, ever at my house! That's improper. Are you saying that because I'm a lesbian?"

Kendall didn't care if the art teacher was gay, but there were instances—very few—when female predators plucked the vulnerable from the classroom.

The special ones.

"Look, I don't care if you are gay or not," Kendall said. "It makes no difference to me. But if you were involved in any improper way with Darby, you have some explaining to do. And depending on what the investigation turns up, you will probably be out of this classroom before your art show."

"You have it all wrong," Connie said, her eyes now wet with tears. "I was never involved. I'm in a committed relationship. My girlfriend and I are getting married this summer. Darby wasn't gay. Darby never, ever came to my house."

"She told Katie that she did," Kendall said.

Connie was pacing back and forth, scrambling, trying to extricate herself from what she surely knew was a career-ruining accusation.

"Look, I think she had a boyfriend. I think, well, she didn't tell me who. She said she thought she might be in love. She didn't tell Katie. She couldn't. She and Katie were sort of the outcasts and she didn't want Katie to be hurt that this boy liked her. And that she liked this boy."

"You seem to have gotten awfully close to Darby."

"I told you," Connie said defensively. "I saw a lot of myself in her."

As the teacher wrapped her arms around her now heaving chest, Kendall noticed her fingernails. The color. It was so familiar.

"Did you give Darby gifts? You did, didn't you?"

"No. No. I'm telling you."

"When she disappeared she wore the same polish that you're wearing now."

Connie looked down at her hands.

"Oh. I did. I gave her a bottle."

"That's a little personal, isn't it?"

Connie put her fingers to her lips. She motioned for Kendall to follow her to a small room in the back of the classroom, where she flung open a storage locker.

Inside were row upon row of nail polish. All colors. All in order of light to dark. It was like a cosmetic display on steroids.

"I don't understand," Kendall said.

Connie's words were caught in her throat and she struggled a little to get them out.

"I don't like to talk about it," she started to say, before stopping herself.

"Take a moment," Kendall said.

"It's okay. Darby and I had so much in common. My being a lesbian had nothing to do with it. My mom is a hoarder too. She sends me this shit all the time. I used to throw it away, you know . . . just clean sweep it away from my life." She stopped and caught her breath. "I don't do that anymore. I know my mom can't help it. I bring it here. I give it away."

Kendall felt a rush of sympathy. If they had been friends, she would have hugged that woman right then. She didn't, of course.

"Please don't say anything about my friendship with her," Connie said. "I can assure you Darby never, ever came to my house. I never saw her not even once outside of this classroom. And yes, we spent a lot of time together. I'm worried about her, detective. You have to find her."

Kendall believed the art teacher.

"We're doing the best we can," she said. She didn't tell her about the foot, the polish, what had happened to Darby Moreau. It wasn't something she could tell, not in the middle of the investigation. She knew that when the news broke, Connie Mitchell would be heartsick.

"Which boy?" she asked. "Do you know?"

"What?"

"Which boy was she crushing on?"

Connie shook her head and closed the cabinet.

"I don't know. She never said."

CHAPTER 11

It was a perfect spring Saturday—the kind that residents of the Pacific Northwest don't want the rest of the country to know about. Having people believe it rains all the time isn't good for the travel industry, but it does keep people from moving to a place that's considered gray with gloom most of the year. While snow fell like sanding sugar on Denver, and temperatures dipped on the East Coast to near freezing at night, the Seattle area was enjoying the kind of weather that invites men to go shirtless—even when a long winter of football and snacking offered more reasons to cover up.

A dirt biker named Martin Best had been riding the humps and bumps of the Limerick Trail in Banner Forest when he got off his bike to smoke a cigarette. Martin, a small but muscular guy in his mid-thirties, settled himself on a log riddled by the beak of a woodpecker to such a degree that it looked like it had been sprayed with buckshot. As he puffed away, he took in the silence of the forest.

Life was good. He'd made up with his girlfriend. His employment prospects were looking up. A second interview at a coffee roaster in Bremerton had gone well. It was a start-up company, but that was all right with him. He had turned the page on some dark times in his life. Nothing was going to stop him now. Looking up was a very good feeling.

He finished his smoke and snuffed it out with his fingertips and stuck the butt in his pants pocket. When he got up to get back on his bike, he noticed a large black plastic trash bag.

What's with people, anyway? he thought.

The bikers had a bad enough reputation as it was. *Why,* he wondered, *would someone give the county commissioners any more reasons to boot them out of the best trails for riding in the entire county?*

Martin bent down to pick up the bag, but when he lifted it, it split in half.

Jesus! What's that? He pulled back from the worst smell he'd ever whiffed in his entire life. It was like railroad spikes driven into each nostril with a sledgehammer. He winced hard and his eyes watered. It was sharp, acrid, and gassy. All of a sudden, the young man vomited. It was a reflex, something far beyond his control.

His eyes had mapped out what it was that was in that plastic bag.

Curled inside was the body of a girl. Long blond hair, matted with twigs, lay on the forest floor. What Martin Best saw was blood-soaked and rotten and foul as foul could be. It was gooey, disgusting, but heartbreaking at the same time. He'd read the papers. He knew the park had been searched after the school kids from Olalla Elementary discovered a severed foot on one of the trails.

Martin squatted and braced himself with his arms on his knees. He coughed out all he had left in his stomach—a grilled cheese sandwich and a diet soda from the deli at Safeway on Bethel. His hand trembled as he reached for his phone, but he confirmed what he already knew. No service in that part of Banner Forest.

Goddamn! 911 I need you!

Unaware that he had screamed out when he saw the body in the bag, he got on his bike and made his way down Limerick. The forest whizzed by and he nearly crashed into a stump, but despite his accelerated pace, the smell stayed lodged in his nostrils. So did the image of what he'd seen. Martin Best had served in Afghanistan. Proudly so. He'd seen things that were beyond words.

None of it compared to what was in the bag.

A woman walking her dog in the forest made the first call to 911.

"Hey, I'm in Banner Forest and I heard a man scream bloody murder. You need to get out here."

"Are you sure it wasn't some kids just messing around?" the Comm Center operator asked.

The caller took a gulp of air. "Look, the man that screamed out 'Oh God it's a body!' wasn't some kid playing a game. You better get here now. Hurry. He might be having a heart attack or something."

The operator took the woman's name and told her to wait at the trailhead for the responders.

A minute later, the second call came in.

This time it was Martin Best. He was out of breath and desperate.

"I'm in Banner Forest," he said. "You need to get someone here right now."

"Sir, please calm down," the operator said in a voice that indicated she was more about procedure than actually calming him down. It was the same tone a call center in India used on Martin one time when his laptop crashed.

"I am goddamn calmed down," he said, this time yelling. Martin was nearly hyperventilating. His back was striped in sweat. "I think you got to get here."

He stopped talking and started dry-heaving.

"Help is on the way," the operator said. "Go to the main entrance on Banner Road. Someone will be there in a few minutes. Hang on."

Soon a swarm of deputies and crime scene techs were on the site. Birdy had taken Elan up to Silverdale to buy some more new clothes at Macy's. Her phone had the worst possible service, so she missed the call.

No matter. The remains would be waiting for her in the chiller in the morgue. Quietly. And yet, Birdy knew of this case as she did of all the murder victims who'd found their way to her office: "They bide their time until someone finds them and brings them to me. Then they'll tell me what I need to know."

At least that's what she always hoped.

A badly decomposed body is a stew of information. Sometimes, as Birdy Waterman knew as she prepared to autopsy Darby Moreau, the clues most needed are lost among the rotting flesh. If an individual dies from an overdose, for example, the residues of lethal drugs are often recovered in the lab. If a person has been shot, the remnants of a bullet are easy enough to discern. Sometimes an X-ray will even turn up the bullet or a fragment of one. Birdy Waterman was no lightweight, but she put on a mask that she'd swabbed with mentholated ointment to diminish the stench that had knocked Martin Best to his knees.

Items collected from the scene included the plastic bag, which Martin Best said he'd touched. His fingerprints were expected to be found somewhere on its slippery black surface, as were, Kendall and Birdy hoped, the killer's. The bag, the girl's clothes—jeans, a running shoe, a bra, a T-shirt—were all sent off to the county's crime lab at the sheriff's department. There, they'd run a battery of tests on all of that. They'd dry the clothes, superglue-fume the plastic bag in a fish tank they'd set up for that purpose, and with the use of scopes and a small vacuum scour for trace evidence.

If there was anything to find, the county techs there were up for it.

The body, however, was Birdy's. With its obvious missing foot, it would take only science to confirm what she knew.

Darby Moreau had been found.

Beyond the damage to the tissue there was a slight glimpse of what the victim's face might have looked like before she died. Birdy had seen the dimple in her chin in the photographs collected from her mother. Her hair was thick and long. It was blond and in life, it must have been lovely.

Darby Moreau's spirit, however, had gone elsewhere. What remained in the woods for the young girl to discover and later the dirt biker, was only the vessel that held the spirit. The body was but a shell. Once the life had been drained from it, it was ready to be given back to the earth. Birdy knew others made their livelihoods from dealing with the dead, but she saw her role as something different. A mortician did his or her job for the benefit of the living, to aid the grieving process.

Birdy was doing her job for the dead. She was there to give them the voice to tell what had brought them to her table.

"Victim is a decomposed teenage female, well nourished, no indications of drug use . . ." she dictated.

As she'd done before with the foot, she took measurements—both weight and length—and recorded every bit of it on a digital recorder that would be transcribed later for the final report on the one-hundred-pound victim. After a thorough exam for biologicals—and other evidence, she made the Y incision, turned on the saw, and removed and cataloged each of the dead girl's vital organs.

". . . all unremarkable, all intact . . ."

That finished, she rinsed the body to get a better look at the condition of the derma. *Had the girl been shot? Strangled? Just how did Darby die?*

There was no sign of sexual assault.

The condoms. She had a boyfriend. Who was he? Why hasn't he come forward?

Birdy looked at the stump, the only indicator of any trauma to the body. She had hoped that there'd be something there. Percy at the state crime lab indicated the appendage had been severed crudely by someone without much experience in butchering.

Birdy magnified the stump.

A small bone fragment, no, a tooth.

She almost sighed with relief. It was not human. It was far too small. She cleaned it and bagged it.

The foot hadn't been severed by a person, but by an animal. It had been dragged across the forest floor and summarily deposited under the cover of the sword fern where sixth grader Tracy Montgomery first pointed the tip of her purple Ugg boot at it.

Birdy's mind wandered back to the roadkill in front of her house on Beach Drive. If she had a visitor in the autopsy suite she'd have bet them dinner that the animal that had dragged the foot from the garbage bag was an opossum.

Another reason to despise the creepy-looking interlopers that had come up from southern climates and were reviled by Northwestern environmentalists as an invasive non-native species.

A zoologist at the state crime lab in Olympia would confirm the source of the tooth. That would be necessary for the case, but Birdy already knew it. She'd collected animal skulls, bones, and teeth as a child back on the reservation. Her prized possession until Summer wrecked it in a fury was a reconstructed skeleton of a harbor seal pup.

What happened to Darby was not a mauling, obviously. No bear, no cougar, bags their kill in what appeared to be a Hefty brand garden trash bag. That was good news for nature lovers who liked the solitude and beauty of Banner Forest. Since the discovery of Darby's foot, those types had stopped coming to the park. Instead teens looking for more of the body or those dirt bikers were the only ones who'd ventured back.

Birdy's eyes lingered on the five toenails and ten

fingernails, all pretty in Car Nation pink. For Dr. Waterman that hue would always hold a sad memory. It would remind her of the sixteen-year-old girl who'd been dumped in the woods.

But how did she die? And who dumped her there?

CHAPTER 12

Tess Moreau stood out amid the debris that surrounded her house and overtook her yard and screamed at the sky. She'd seen Birdy Waterman and Kendall Stark as they pulled into her rutted dirt driveway and ran toward them.

"Say it!" she said. "Say it!"

The forensic pathologist and the detective wound their way through the fringe of spring grass and a row of doghouses that stood like a mini housing development for troll families. There was no hiding the sadness on either visitor's face. The long walk to a murder victim's front door is the most unpleasant task of law enforcement. The first visit, the one in which there is still hope, is far different. Both women knew that from the experience that came with the job.

Birdy had only done two home notifications as an employee of the coroner's office. Kendall, however, had done many over her years as a detective in the Kitsap County Sheriff's Department. The second visit to a family's home always cuts deeply. That's the one that brings out the tears. Kendall had seen grown men fall to the floor. She'd seen mothers hurl themselves into her arms.

Tess Moreau knew why Birdy and Kendall were there. While she knew from TV shows that DNA profiles take a little time, they don't take days.

"You better tell me," Tess said, running toward them. "Tell me right now!"

Kendall spoke first. "I'm so very sorry. So, so sorry. Yes, your daughter is gone."

Gone was such a peculiar word. It was as though the girl with the long blond hair and love of art had been vaporized by some kind of bizarre death ray.

"You mean dead. My baby is dead!"

Birdy could not sugarcoat it. *Gone* was such a stupid word. She'd never use it again when telling someone what they really needed to know.

"Yes, Ms. Moreau. I'm so sorry, but yes. Your daughter is dead."

Tess clutched her stomach and then buried her face in her hands. She didn't fight to control her grief. It had been welling up inside since Birdy bagged that hairbrush with those silken strands of her precious Darby's hair. She knew the reason for it. She hadn't eaten all day. She hadn't gone to work. She'd waited by the window. When she saw the sheriff's car, she knew.

She screamed out. Tess Moreau let nothing stay inside. She didn't care if she was a spectacle. When a gawker slowed by her place, Tess didn't wave them away.

Like she normally did.

She had nothing left. No one. No husband. No children. For some reason God had sought to hurt her above anyone else. She could think of reasons for it, but she'd never say them out loud. Too ugly. Too painful.

"Take a breath, Tess," Birdy said.

"I don't want to breathe. I want to die too."

Birdy held the crying mother in her arms. Her eyes met Kendall's and neither could imagine being in that woman's shoes right then. Kendall had a little boy. Birdy didn't have a child of her own, but she knew that nothing could ever hurt more than that loss.

Kendall asked if they could go inside.

Tess pulled away and the three women made their way past Tess Moreau's collection of junk into the overstuffed living room.

"Do you know who did it?" Tess asked.

"No, we don't," Kendall answered. "We're in the middle of the investigation. We'll keep you up to date as we can."

"Do you know how?" Tess asked, before holding up her shaking hand. "No, don't tell me."

"We don't know yet," Birdy said.

Tess shifted on the sofa and picked up a pillow. She wrapped her arms around it and rocked slightly.

"When will you know who did it?" Tess said, her voice now soft and cracking.

"There is no timeline, Tess," Kendall said, now using the mother's first name.

"Can you think of anyone who might have done this?"

Tess sobbed some more; it was guttural and startlingly loud. Birdy put her hand on her knee, but Tess flicked it away.

She tossed the pillow to the floor. "I don't need your

pity," she said. "I need you to find out who did this to Darby!"

"We're working on it," Kendall said. "That's why I asked you to tell me if you can think of anyone who might have harmed her. Have you thought any more about the condoms? She obviously had a boyfriend."

Tess's eyes were puffy and red. The forty-five-year-old took short gulps of air. Every muscle in her neck tightened.

Birdy looked at Kendall. She was worried that Tess was going into shock.

"We might need an ambulance," she said quietly.

Tess fought hard to control her breathing. She didn't want more people in her house. She didn't want more people talking about what they'd seen once inside.

"No, she didn't," she said. "Darby didn't have a boyfriend. She was too young. Those condoms probably belong to Katie. Darby loved her, but I think she was a bit of a tramp." Tess stopped herself. "I'm sorry. I don't know why I said that. I like Katie."

"It's all right," Birdy said. "You're upset. Is there someone you can call? Someone who can be with you tonight?"

Tess, tears still streaming, shook her head. "I never have anyone over here. I guess you probably figured that out already."

"I think," the detective said, "it would be best if you had someone with you. Can you go to a friend's house?"

Tess looked for her phone. "I can call Amanda from work. She's a good friend."

"Fine," Kendall said. "I want you to do that now.

While we wait. I want to talk to her when you are on the phone. All right?"

Tess punched the buttons with a shaky fingertip. She started crying before she could say much of anything.

Kendall reached for the phone and Tess let it go.

"Amanda? This is Detective Kendall Stark with the Kitsap County Sheriff's Department. I'm afraid Tess has had some very upsetting—that isn't even the right word—*devastating* news. We've confirmed that her daughter has died."

Birdy watched Tess as her red eyes followed the floorboards down the hall to Darby's room. She wondered if Tess was replaying memories of her daughter. As a little girl? As the only one who understood her? That last evening she said good night?

All before Darby vanished.

Tess slammed her fist hard against the seat cushion of the sofa. The hurt was deep. Whatever she was thinking about brought more frustration than tears.

"Tess is having a very hard time," Kendall said. "Are you in the position to come and get her?"

Tess got up and started down the hallway.

"You know where it is?" Kendall asked. "Okay, fine. I'll stay here until you arrive."

Kendall, still carrying Tess's phone, found the grieving mother on her daughter's bed. Birdy followed. Tess was rocking back and forth with a pristine white pillow in her arms.

"I knew this day would come," she said.

While Birdy looked on, Kendall sat on the edge of the bed.

"Tess, what do you mean?" she asked.

Tess met the detective's gaze and then looked over at her daughter's perfectly ordered desk. Pictures were tucked under crisscrossed grosgrain ribbon on a bulletin board that she'd picked up at Target. The images were of a life now gone.

"Nothing," Tess said.

Birdy pressed her gently. "You meant to say something."

Tess wrapped her arms around herself, tightly, with an almost constrictive force, as if binding herself would keep the hurt from spilling out.

"Nothing. I meant that all I have now is nothing," she said. "I knew that what little I had after the car accident was a tenuous gift. I knew, somehow, I don't know how, that it could all be taken away in a flash."

"We're going to stay with you until your friend arrives."

"She doesn't have my address," Tess said. "It will be dark soon. She won't know how to find me."

"Tess, Amanda knows where you live. She's coming from Gig Harbor. Let's pack an overnight bag. Can I help you find one?"

Tess looked at the women, one by one. "I know what you think about me. Both of you. But I know where everything is. The overnight bags are in the barn."

"I'll go with you," Birdy said. "Let's go get one. Your friend will be here soon."

The detective stayed in the house as Birdy and Tess walked toward the barn. With each step, Tess Moreau felt the weight of the world crashing down on her.

"How much more can I take?" she asked.

Birdy didn't answer. She didn't know what was to come. No one did.

CHAPTER 13

While Elan valiantly resuscitated her old laptop on the sofa in the front room, Birdy Waterman ruminated over all that had happened that day. The notification she and Kendall had made to Tess Moreau was an anvil of immense weight on her shoulders. When she'd talked to other victims' families, it was without exception at her office. The location was removed from who the person belonged to and where he or she had come from. Even in the clutter of Tess Moreau's home there was evidence everywhere of Darby's life. School photos. Books about vampires. Blue jeans that were not the style of a mother. No victim was anything less than a human being when he or she arrived on the autopsy table, but few were as known to Birdy as Darby.

Cross training was annoying, but she didn't doubt that it held a benefit.

"Everyone's talking about that dead girl on Facebook," Elan said.

"I'm sure they are," Birdy said. She changed the subject. "How's that laptop coming along?"

"No offense, but it is a piece of crap," he said. "But

what about that girl? Heard that she was sliced and diced."

Birdy sipped her beer. She needed one. Maybe two.

"We don't talk about people like that, Elan."

He glanced up from the screen, a satisfied look on his face. "I was hoping that this POS wouldn't work. But it does."

Birdy studied the now lit up screen. "Good. That means you can do your homework."

"I don't have any," he said.

"Find some," she said. "You're not on vacation, Elan."

"Whatever, Aunt Birdy." The teenager powered down and closed the lid on the laptop. "What happened to the kid?"

"She has a name. Darby Moreau."

"I know all about her," he said.

The comment interested Birdy. "What do you mean, you know all about her?"

Elan brightened. "Well, for one thing, I know her mom is a total freak. Do you know what they call her?"

Kendall had told her that Tess was a local celebrity. It wasn't an exaggeration.

"Yes, her mother has a problem."

"She should be on that hoarder's show on TV. One time I watched it and the lady had two dead cats buried under a pile of newspapers. She thought they ran away. Those people are so messed up."

Birdy knew he was right. They *were* messed up.

"It is an obsessive-compulsive disorder, Elan. With-out extensive therapy, they can't change their behavior."

"Do you feel sorry for everyone, Aunt Birdy?"

"Not everyone," she said. "I never feel sorry for those who kill someone, even when I can see their reasons for it."

Elan went to the refrigerator and took out a beer.

"Put that back!" Birdy said.

Elan flashed a sheepish grin. "Just testing you."

"I don't need to be tested," she said. "I've had a top-ten worst day."

He took a can of soda, popped the top, and returned to the sofa. "So was she?"

"Was she what?"

"Sliced and diced?"

Birdy admired his persistence. Persistence was a positive attribute—when applied to something like homework.

"We're not going to talk about the case, all right? That's a ground rule that I should have added to the conditions of your staying here. I'm dealing with some sensitive things at my job. I can't talk to you about any of them."

Elan shrugged and sat up. "Be that way. I don't have any friends and I just thought if I could get some insider info it would help. But I guess I don't care. Bunch of losers at this school anyway."

"When are you going to talk to me about what's troubling you so much at home?"

"We didn't set a deadline," he said. "I have homework to do, remember?"

As Elan disappeared into what was once the guest bedroom, Birdy's thoughts about Tess and her loss shifted to her own strained relationship with her mother.

The last time she'd seen her had been just after the New Year.

That visit, like the others before it, felt like a failed reconciliation. Birdy needed to escape. One beer became two. Two became three. While Elan did whatever he was doing in his room, she sat in the office in her craftsman-style bungalow and replayed the visit with her mom and re-experienced the worsening frustration that came with the encounter.

"You are a selfish girl," Natalie Waterman had said while she stared at the TV. "You don't give a shit about anyone but you."

"That's not true, Mom. I'm not like that."

Birdy put her hand on her mother's shoulder, but she brushed it off like the long ashy tip of her cigarette.

"Keep telling yourself that, Birdy," Natalie had said in that ever-deepening voice of hers. "Always trying to be better than anyone from around here."

"Why does it always come to this, Mom? Why does it come to me leaving? Dad wanted me to leave."

"Keep him out of it, Birdy. You are too good for all of us. Why don't you just go?"

Birdy looked at her mother's reflection on the old TV. Her jaw was clenched, her eyes unblinking. "Why do you hate me?"

"Just go," Natalie said.

"Why, Mom?"

"Because you are who you are. That's why."

Birdy didn't cry. She never let her mother see her cry. Not since she was a little girl. *Maybe there was some truth to it? Maybe she had thought she was better than everyone who stayed on the reservation?*

"What am I?"

There was a slight flutter of her mother's eyes, almost a hint that she'd say something.

Reveal something.

"Just go," Natalie finally said. "All right? I want to watch TV and I don't need you pissing me off. Just leave."

Birdy drove from Neah Bay to Port Orchard, vowing she'd never go back—though she knew her resolve would fade. If she really was that girl—the one who thought she was better than her family—then she'd hate herself. And the fact that she didn't want to hate herself made her wonder if, indeed, her mother was right after all.

Maybe she did think she was better than everyone back home.

She thought of calling her mother, but dialed her sister instead.

It went straight to voice mail.

Doesn't she ever pick up? Or doesn't she pick up because it's me calling?

"Summer, just wanted to chat. Give you a little update. Elan is doing fine. I'm happy to have him here. Still not sure why he's here. He's not talking. And since you never seem to answer your phone, I guess I'll just hang in there until he talks," she said, realizing that she was rambling. The beer had gotten the best of her. "Love you, bye now."

She hung up.

CHAPTER 14

Amanda Watkins lived in a small house on Sound-view Drive in Gig Harbor. Except for its contents—neat, new, fresh, and not too much of any one item—it was comparable to Tess Moreau's farmhouse in Olalla. Amanda had done most of the talking on the drive along Crescent Valley and to her house in the harbor. Tess cried and uttered one-word answers to whatever Amanda said.

She offered to call family, anyone, to let them know.

"No," Tess said.

"What can I get for you?"

"Darby."

"Honey, I'm so sorry."

"Hurts."

"I know. I know."

When they got inside, Amanda led Tess to a spare bedroom. Amanda lived alone. She and her husband divorced two years prior, when their youngest of three graduated from high school. She had known it was coming. He had a girlfriend. Just as they got to her daughter's old room, Amanda changed her mind.

The room was a teen's dream with a beautiful maple bed and deep purple cushions. The boys' room would be better.

Fewer reminders of what her friend had just lost.

"You need to eat," Amanda said.

Tess slumped into a chair. Amanda planted herself on the edge of one of her sons' beds. Both boys had graduated from college and her daughter was away at school in Oregon. A Seahawks poster dominated one wall, a Mariners the other.

"I'm not hungry," Tess said.

"Of course not," Amanda said. "But you have to eat."

"Why?"

Amanda, who was ten years older than Tess, didn't have all the answers. No one in a time like that really did. A minister maybe? Someone who had undergone the same kind of tragedy? The worst thing that happened to Amanda was that her husband had left her. And that hadn't been so bad after all. She wanted to help her friend, but something else was on her mind.

"Do they know what happened?" she asked, finding the nerve.

Tess put her fingertips to her mouth. Silence filled the room. This wasn't easy. It was the hardest thing Amanda had done in a long, long time.

"Do you know?" she asked, her eyes riveted to Tess's.

Tess, who'd stopped crying, looked away.

"Why would I know?"

Again, awkward silence passed between the two women.

"You know, because of Brenda."

"Brenda," Tess repeated. "I don't see how."

Brenda Nevins was a lifer at the prison. She'd been incarcerated for only five years, but her anger at the world and anyone who crossed her was legendary. She was a classic narcissist who saw no value in anything that didn't benefit her directly. She'd drugged her husband and daughter and set fire to her house in Yakima, a farming community on the eastern side of the Cascades, the mountains that divide the state in two. To cover the evidence of murder, she set fire to the house.

She did it all for insurance money—which she promptly spent on a new car, cosmetic surgery, a trip to Hawaii, and a condo overlooking the Columbia River. She nearly got away with it, until, in a ballsy and exceedingly stupid move, she did it a second time. This time she killed her boyfriend, a swimming coach at the local high school. She drugged and drowned him at the pool.

Her trial for that murder had been a media sensation. Washington State had seen its share of famous criminals—Ted Bundy, Gary Ridgway, to name a couple at the top of any killers hit parade. The likes of a woman like Brenda Nevins, however, had never been seen.

Brenda's mass media appeal had as much to do with her cunning approach to her kills as to her stunning looks. She had emerald green eyes and a mane of blond tresses that dropped to the small of her back. She had a porn star's figure—courtesy of the implants she'd received from her State Farm payout. A psychologist testified that her IQ was in the genius range, but that her narcissism prevented her from understanding the most basic of all human emotions.

Love.

It was true that Brenda could intellectualize about feelings and their place in the world. She could use emotion in the way that an impressionist mimics the voices of others as part of a Las Vegas review—close, but not quite right.

Brenda didn't let her incarceration stop her from doing what she did best.

Seduction.

It was late fall and Tess Moreau had to run some files from one end of the prison to the other. That meant going through security gates outside and then back in. It was cold outside and Tess hated the cold, but she'd never said no to any request her boss or co-workers made. While some office women preferred to sit on their butts all day eating donuts and bitching about something that didn't matter one bit, Tess was a doer. That's how she'd been named "Support Person of the Quarter." On the other side of the steel ringlets of barbed wire that crowned the walls around the women's prison, however, she was seen as a pathetic creature.

On the inside, she was the employee the superintendent wished she could clone. None were better. None more indispensable in a place that needed order.

As Tess made her way down the corridor where the prison had its inmate dog-grooming and pet-boarding program, she heard strange moaning. At first, she thought it was a dog fussing about being away from its owner. That happened occasionally, though not often. The prison's program was surprisingly popular. It allowed pet owners to leave their animals with inmates, for smaller fees than other kennels in nearby Gig Harbor or Olalla. Price wasn't the sole benefit. The inmates were carefully screened. They were animal lovers. They might have been meth addicts on the outside, but inside they cuddled up with dogs, walked them, and combed them.

The moaning got a little louder.

"You like my tits," a voice said.

Another voice murmured something, but it was unintelligible.

Tess had serious doubts that a dog was involved. It was possible. She'd heard of all sorts of things over the years going on between inmates. Some women were gay while in the prison; others tried to seduce male guards. One even managed to get pregnant and sue the state for abuse.

"Ooh that feels good," the first voice said.

Tess thought about turning around and reporting it right then and there. She didn't need the visual of what was going on, but those files needed to get where they were going. She turned the corner and caught a glimpse in the open doorway

Brenda Nevins was on top of a grooming table on all fours. She was completely naked and moving her head to and fro in faked ecstasy. Those bought-with-blood-money breasts looked like a pair of 777s nose-diving to oblivion.

Licking her vagina from behind was Missy Carlyle, last year's Corrections Officer of the Year.

Tess, stunned by what she'd seen, dropped her files. Brenda and Missy looked over.

"You say anything, you'll regret it," Brenda said, pushing Missy away with a foot and twisting herself upright on the table.

Missy, her eyes popping from her head like some

cartoon depiction of someone seeing the shock of her life, gasped.

"It isn't what you think, Tess!" she said, picking a hair from her mouth. "Please don't say anything."

Tess scrambled and picked up her files. Her heart was pounding. She hurried back toward Control.

"We've got a serious problem in pet grooming," she said when the officer answered the buzzer.

"Dog get out again?" he asked.

"I wish," she said. "I need an officer here now."

A protracted, but very quiet, investigation ensued. Missy was put on paid administrative leave and Brenda was sent to the hole, a section of the prison that sounds worse than it really is. Some prisoners actually prefer isolation, only one hour of exercise, and the opportunity for endless "me-time." Brenda, not surprisingly, was not happy about it at all. After the investigation of the incident concluded, which the inmates and officers had nicknamed "Doggy Style," Missy was fired. Shortly afterward, a series of threatening letters were delivered to the prison addressed to Tess and marked *personal* and *confidential*.

The first one:

You bitch. You're going to pay.

She tore that one up.

The next one came to her home in Olalla.

Pay for what you did.

Tess tore that one up too.

When the third one arrived, two weeks later, Tess

confided in Amanda in the employee break room—a cluttered space of floor-mounted tables, beat-up romance novels, and a cobalt blue couch with tufts of white poly protruding like a row of bunny tails from one side.

"I've been getting some weird, threatening mail," she said when the room had cleared of the other employees. .

"Me too," Amanda said. "I call mine bills my ex didn't pay."

Tess didn't smile.

"Something's wrong," Amanda said. "What kind of mail are you talking about?"

Tess pulled a folded slip from her pants pocket and slid it over the battered surface of the tabletop. Her eyes stayed on Amanda's as she unfolded it and read.

Amanda looked up. "Holy cow," she said. "This came to your house?"

Tess's eyes were awash with worry and Amanda picked up on it.

She pushed the paper back across the table.

It read:

You took from me. I'll take from you.

"You think it's related to the investigation?" Amanda said. "You need to report this right now. Brenda or Missy could be behind it."

Tess grabbed her friend's hands from across the table. "No. I don't want to cause any more trouble."

"Come on." Amanda said, still letting Tess hold her hands. "You are being threatened. This is serious stuff. It could be any one of the creepy women inside here."

"Or someone on the outside," Tess said, releasing her grip.

There was truth to that. A lot of truth. It was easier to smuggle something out of prison than inside. It didn't matter what prison or what gender. There was always someone out there who would do something for money or payback. One woman used her canteen money to hire another prisoner to get her boyfriend to burn down the trailer of the man who'd turned her in for making methamphetamines. The price for arson? Seven Twix candy bars.

The state somehow managed to keep the Doggy-Style investigation out of the press—it was beyond embarrassing for the institution and its new superintendent. That meant that Missy Carlyle was only fired. She easily could have been charged with inmate abuse. Brenda could have pushed for it, but she didn't.

"She has something on Missy and that could come in handy one day," Amanda had said at the time.

As the women faced each other in Amanda's sons' room, they could only wonder if that time had come.

"You've got to tell the detectives," Amanda said. "You have to tell them about the letters now. Do you still have that one you showed me?"

Tess nodded. "And the one after that."

Tess's eyes widened. "There was another? Why didn't you tell me?"

"Because I was afraid you'd make me report it. I didn't want to be the subject of any kind of scrutiny," Tess said, hesitating as if the words were stuck in her throat. "You know, Amanda, I didn't want people to know who I was."

"You mean how you live?" Amanda asked.

Tess still couldn't stop her face from going red with the shame that had consumed her for so many years. Even in the presence of a close, trusted friend.

"Right," she said, looking away. "I didn't want to call attention to myself. The social worker from the county said that if I didn't get my act together, I could lose my daughter. She's all I have."

Amanda put her arms around Tess. The irony in her friend's words was heartbreaking. It *had* happened. She had lost her daughter.

CHAPTER 15

The call came in at 7:02 a.m.

The operator at the Comm Center in Bremerton dispatched an ambulance after confirming the address and assessing the need. The woman making the call said that her husband had been ill for quite some time and had become unresponsive. She identified herself as Jennifer Roberts and her husband as Ted Roberts.

"Please no lights and sirens," she said, her voice oddly flat. "There's no point in it. He's dead."

"I need you to check and see if he's breathing," the operator said. "Can you do that? Can you check for a pulse?"

"I did. Nothing."

"Jennifer, please stay calm. I need you to do what I'm asking until help arrives. All right?"

"I *am* calm. And it's no use. Ted's deader . . ." her voice trailed off to a distracted mumble.

The operator couldn't quite make it out, but she had an idea of what the woman had just said.

Ted's deader than a doornail? Who says that about her husband?

The operator finished the call and picked up the next line, this time a fire called in by a neighbor in a housing development in Silverdale. The caller was unsure, but thought the family was on vacation and no one was inside. The fire department was on its way.

And yet with all the drama that comes with her job, the call with Jennifer Roberts hung in the young woman's memory, the way one or two a week did.

Deader than a doornail? Who says that at that particular time?

A paramedic team led by Danny Ferry filed a report that accompanied the body to the Kitsap County morgue:

Upon arrival, at 09:07, the respondent, Jennifer Roberts, 43, indicated that her husband, Ted Roberts, 42, had expired shortly after she served him breakfast. She was angry that we'd used sirens. She said that she'd requested no sirens. She led us upstairs to his bedroom and told us he had been ill for the past six months and attributed his declining health to alcoholism and emphysema. She could not provide any additional information. She asked when she could have the body returned to her. Transported deceased to the morgue. Arrived at 09:35.

Paramedic Ferry, with his small, compact stature and bright red beard, looked more like a cereal box leprechaun than the lifesaver he often was. Birdy was in her office to receive the body.

"Something definitely hinky about this one," he said, handing over his notes.

Birdy set down her coffee. "How so?"

"Most of it's there. But the one weird part on this one was that his wife couldn't name his doctor. She said she'd have to look it up."

"She was probably too distraught," Birdy said.

Danny scratched his beard. "*Distraught* isn't the word. This lady was all over the map, I'm telling you. All over it. She cried. She laughed. She didn't know which end was up, and then she offered me a cup of coffee like I'd come over for a visit. Weird."

In her line of work, as in Danny's, Birdy had seen all sorts of reactions when it came to traumatic situations. "Danny, people handle shock and grief differently. You know that."

Danny fidgeted for something in his pockets. A cigarette, maybe.

"Yeah, I do. And I can tell you this lady was off the Richter scale of strangeness. Her kids too. They stood there and watched their mother like they were watching some play. Not once did either comfort her."

"She sounds hysterical." Birdy turned her gaze from Danny to the paperwork. "You've seen people out of their minds with grief. Impacts the way others behave too. The report doesn't mention the kids."

Danny didn't like to make mistakes, even an omission. His face flashed red. "Sorry," he said. "My bad, Dr. Waterman. A boy and a girl. High school age."

"All right," she said.

After Danny and his team departed, Birdy took care of all the intake prep work that accompanies the dead when they arrive under her jurisdiction. Getting everything ready and ensuring that things were properly documented. This was crucial not only in the possibility that a criminal case was involved—which was rare because most autopsies were not about a crime, but about a determination as to cause.

She put on her scrubs and wheeled Ted Roberts's remains toward the autopsy table.

The circumstances surrounding this latest visitor to the morgue would have raised the eyebrows of even the most inexperienced forensic pathologist. Ted Roberts was relatively young. He'd been ill for an unspecified period of time, but there was no certainty that he was under any doctor's supervision. He died at home. Home deaths were always treated with the utmost caution. Beyond all of that there were a couple of things that troubled Birdy more than others. Red flags. The widow had asked for the ambulance to arrive silently.

She didn't want to wake anyone. Or was it that she didn't want anyone to see?

And she wanted to know when she could get the body back.

That was more than a red flag. That was a big crimson banner.

Birdy put on her scrubs and mask and went to work. She started by taking photographs of the body as it appeared on arrival. He was thin, but had decent muscle tone. A tattoo on his right bicep was of an eagle clutching a heart in its talons. It was crude, she suspected probably gotten when he was young.

He was navy. Even his haircut suggested it. Not buzzed, but close cropped and all one length.

She checked his eyes. Yellowish, but no petechial hemorrhaging.

Next she cut off the pale blue pajama bottoms that he'd had been wearing when the paramedics found him.

Over the next couple of hours she "sliced and diced" him, as her nephew would surely consider it. Elan had such an inappropriately direct way of putting things.

As Birdy went about her protocol, she collected specimens for the lab. A tox screen was a given in cases in which there were no outward indications of trauma. Ted Roberts hadn't been strangled. Stabbed. Shot. No wounds indicated he was an intravenous drug user. She examined his lungs for damage and was surprised to find that none existed. They were pink. It was doubtful that Ted Roberts had been a smoker at all.

The widow had suggested emphysema.

She had also suggested alcoholism.

Despite the yellow hue of his eyes, his liver fell in the normal range for a man of his age. If he'd been a heavy drinker there would have been plenty of markers for that.

The kidneys, however, were in dire shape.

For such a relatively young man, the kidneys' condition was shockingly bad. Although more tests were needed to determine if she had been correct with a visual assessment, Birdy considered cause of death was probably renal failure. The manner? She wouldn't put money down on it until tox analysis was completed.

Throughout all of it, Birdy recorded her observations on tape, both video and audio.

With the clean palm of her gloved hand she pushed the button on the CD player and listened as Stan Getz played softly in the background.

Music made the last part easier, because it was so very sad. Birdy returned all of Ted Roberts's organs to the body cavity. Unlike some in her profession, she put them back where they belonged. Some medical examiners—especially those in large cities who were pressured by time constraints that come with assembly line processes—stuff the organs back inside with no rhyme or reason. Birdy considered that disrespectful. No matter what had been planned for the remains—burial or cremation—the body was once a person, a creation that only a higher power could have conjured.

A little time. A little care. Dignity restored.

She stitched him up and notified Kendall Stark.

"I don't have all the answers," she said, "but the case that came in this morning looks like a probable homicide."

"Nice way to start the day, Birdy. Are we talking Ted Roberts?"

Birdy was surprised.

"Did you know him?" she asked.

"Oh no," Kendall said. "But someone who did called 911 five minutes ago and you'll never believe what she said."

Birdy liked the sound of that.

"Try me," she said.

"She said Ted Roberts was murdered."

That was good.

"Who was it who called?" Birdy asked.

"Don't know. Didn't give a name. It was a female. Young. Want to come to meet the widow?"

Birdy put Kendall on speaker so she could set down her phone and finish what she was doing when she called.

"I thought we were done with cross training, Kendall," she said.

"You know you love it," the detective said. "Pick you up in five minutes. Unless you're too busy to come

along. I understand your compulsion to make your reports a thing of incontrovertible beauty."

Birdy looked at Ted Roberts, naked as the day he
was born.

"Let me put a sheet on Mr. Roberts and roll him into
the chiller. I also need to change. I'll be ready in four."

"How can you be ready that fast?"

"I'm younger than you," she said.

"Two years."

"Detective years are like dog years, Kendall."

Kendall laughed. She wasn't about to argue that
one.

Four minutes later, Birdy slid into the passenger seat
of Kendall's white Ford SUV, one that was in bad need
of a good washing.

"Incontrovertible beauty?" she asked. "Where did
that crack come from?"

Kendall smiled. "You liked that, didn't you?"

"Not at all. It seemed a little like a dig."

"Not meant that way, Birdy. In fact, quite the opposite.
A friend of mine in Seattle complained about a pathologist's report on a rape-murder over there. Thought it was
part of a serial and the pathologist blew it by not detailing
the defensive wounds. Didn't write them up. And sure as
hell didn't photograph them for court. Said she wished
the pathologist's report were as good as the ones we get
over here. Called your work a thing of 'incontrovertible
beauty.' "

Birdy liked what she heard, but she made a face anyway.

"Oh, Birdy, that's a compliment," Kendall said.

"I guess so," she said. "Makes me sound like a per-
fectionist control freak."

Kendall smiled as they drove down Sidney toward the Roberts's residence. "And, in case you're wondering, that's why I like working with you so much."

On the way their conversation turned to the Darby Moreau case.

"Tess called me this morning," Kendall said.

Birdy could barely sleep the night before because she felt so sick about what Tess was going through. "Oh God, that poor woman," she said. "I already know the answer, but how is she?"

Kendall's face held a grim expression. The lightness of their banter evaporated. The air in the car felt heavy and sad.

"Tess is a mess—sorry, I didn't mean it that way." Using the words *Tess* and *mess* in the same sentence was a cruel reminder of the insults hurled at the woman for the way she lived. "She is upset. She thanked us for helping her last night. Getting her friend to take care of her was a good thing. She said that Amanda stayed up with her all night. They talked about Darby and what might have happened to her. She wants Darby's body back so she can have a memorial service. And, more than anything, she cried and cried."

Getting the body back was not going to be anytime soon, which Birdy knew would only compound the agony.

"We get sad cases all the time," she said, "but this one just seems worse than so many of the others. Not that we can measure someone else's hurt. But if we could . . ."

"Tess had been through so, so much. But that's not what I wanted to tell you. She's remembered something that she thinks might be helpful."

Birdy hadn't expected that. "What's that?"

"She didn't say. Wants to tell you. She knows that you don't judge her and that you care."

"We both do," Birdy said.

"I know, but that's what she wants, and given all she's going through right now, I think it's a reasonable request. We can go see her after we pay a visit to Mrs. Roberts."

Kendall parked her SUV in front of the white and blue house at 511 Camellia Street.

"Let's see what the grieving widow has to say," Kendall said with a smile. "She probably won't like or trust either one of us."

CHAPTER 16

Jennifer Roberts wore a crisp white top and dark-dyed blue jeans, expensive ones, not the dreaded mom jeans that other women of her age still wriggled into when they felt the need for a competitive advantage. Jennifer didn't need to do any wriggling whatsoever. She was magazine thin. Jennifer's eyes were so blue that when Birdy first saw her standing in the doorway, she'd have sworn those eyes had been enhanced by tinted contact lenses. A sideways glance, however, indicated they were real, the color of aquamarines. Her hair was a shade too light of blond to look natural, but there was no denying that the widow was lovely.

She also seemed frazzled and sad.

"Why are the police involved?" she said after Kendall made their introductions.

"Sheriff," Kendall said, correcting Jennifer. People always thought the police and the sheriff's department were interchangeable. "We investigate cases like this. Routine procedure."

Jennifer wrapped her arms around her chest and

started to tear up. "There's nothing routine about losing the man you love," she said.

Birdy waited for a tear to roll and Jennifer blinked hard.

Down one went.

"I've examined your husband," Birdy said, her eyes full of sympathy. "In order to complete my report I need to follow up on some things you told the paramedics."

Jennifer indicated she understood and motioned for the women to come inside. They followed her to the living room with its massive flat screen and a brown leather recliner positioned front and center. Next to the recliner was a small end table with an empty water bottle. Next to the water bottle, a coffee cup. Over the fireplace was a sunset scene from the American Southwest, all pink and orange with the silhouette of Pinnacle Peak. The view of the water and the Olympics from the window couldn't have been more different.

"Ms. Roberts," Kendall said, "we need to go over what happened this morning. We'll also need some background about your husband."

Birdy wanted background about Ms. Roberts as well, but this was Kendall's investigation.

"Coffee?" Jennifer Roberts asked. "I have some cookies too."

"None for me, thank you," Kendall said.

Birdy shook her head, declining the offer.

While Jennifer went to get herself coffee, the two women looked at each other, telegraphing in that way they could—since cross training—that something was very extraordinary about this woman and her behavior.

Danny, the paramedic, was spot on.

"Her husband died a few hours ago and she's offering cookies? Why not hold a party?" Kendall said, her voice a low whisper.

Birdy didn't say anything, but she was thinking the same thing.

When Jennifer returned she sat in the recliner and rested her hands on the armrest. Her blue eyes snapped shut.

"I can still feel his presence here," she said, her eyes still shuttered. "Teddy, how I love you."

Awkward silence filled the room. Birdy and Kendall exchanged glances.

Jennifer's amazing blue eyes opened.

"We're sorry for your loss," Birdy said.

Kendall asked Jennifer for some background information. Ted Roberts's widow got teary again. She talked about how she and her husband had met online. She lived in Arizona and couldn't imagine leaving the sunshine, pool, and margarita scene for soggy, rough and tumble, Port Orchard.

"But when you are in love you go where your heart leads you," she said. "I can't say that I regret it. Teddy was an amazing husband, lover, father."

"How long ago was that?" Birdy asked. "When you moved up here?"

"Longer than a year ago," she said. "I'm terrible with dates. If you asked me what day of the week this is, I probably would get it wrong. I live in the now. Always have."

"The paramedics said you have a couple of children," Kendall said.

Jennifer nodded. "Ruby and Micah, from my first marriage."

"We might need to talk to them," Kendall said.

"Oh, I don't know about that. So upsetting to them."

"You understand," Kendall persisted, "as part of wrapping up our investigation."

Jennifer indicated a pair of school pictures on the wall. Ruby looked like her mother with long blond hair and sapphire blue eyes. Micah was a handsome boy with dark, medium-length hair that he wore parted in the middle. Like his sister, he could be a teen model.

"They went to a friend's house," Jennifer went on. "With all that happened here, they needed some space."

"Their stepfather just died," Kendall said.

"They weren't that close," Jennifer said. "I wanted them to be, but you know, you just can't make a blended family because you want one."

"How old are they?" Kendall asked. "What school do they attend?"

Jennifer sipped her coffee and closed her eyes again. "Ruby is seventeen. Micah is sixteen. Irish twins. They both go to South Kitsap."

"Last names?" Kendall asked.

"Roberts."

Kendall was surprised. "Mr. Roberts adopted them?" she asked. "That's a little unusual. At their age? I thought you said they weren't close."

Jennifer pushed the other cup and water bottle aside and made a place for her own cup. She looked toward the window, its frame filled with the blossoms of a pink dogwood tree.

"Teddy loved that tree," she said. "He couldn't wait for it to bloom. I'm so happy that he saw it."

"Yes, it is beautiful," Kendall agreed, "but tell me

about the adoption. Just so I can make sure I get every-thing correct in my report."

Jennifer swallowed. "Oh yes. Your report. Their daddy died years ago. They were little. And, well, when I found Teddy he wanted to be a father so much. He's been alone forever. That's the military for you. Anyway, when we enrolled them in school, I told Ruby and Micah to use Roberts for their last name."

Kendall opened a little black book and started writ-ing. The homicide investigator was an obsessive note taker and Jennifer was giving her plenty to remember. Birdy made a mental note to say something about the "incontrovertible beauty" of Kendall's detailed scrib-bling when they left the Roberts's place.

"So they weren't officially adopted by Mr. Roberts?" Birdy asked.

Jennifer sighed. "Oh no. I lied, I guess. I just wanted them—for us—to be a family. I won't be in trouble for having them do that, will I?"

Jennifer's phone rang and she looked at it.

"My daughter," she said. "I know she's very upset. Can I take this?"

"Of course," Kendall said.

Jennifer reached for her phone and started talking on her way to the kitchen.

"The police are here, honey . . ."

Birdy and Kendall looked at one another.

"I want to know what happened to the first hus-band," Birdy said.

Kendall nodded.

"Me too."

They both waited in silence, listening to bits and

pieces of the conversation Jennifer was having with her daughter.

"... I took a Xanax ..."

"... they say this is routine ..."

"... pizza sounds fine ..."

"... I don't know."

"... don't worry."

When she returned, Jennifer looked more upset than she had when the detective and forensic pathologist first arrived.

"My daughter Ruby," Jennifer said, taking her place in the recliner. "I don't know how we're going to get along without Ted. I don't work. I don't have any source of income. With him being sick we were barely hanging on. What are we going to do?"

"I'm sorry," Kendall said. "The Red Cross might help with some emergency assistance."

Jennifer looked around as though she was lost. Maybe she was?

"Your church?" Birdy offered. "Mr. Roberts's other family members?"

Jennifer shook her head. "No, we don't go to church. Ted didn't get along with his family. They didn't want him to marry me. I don't know why. All I did was love him to death. He was my everything."

The irony in what she just said was lost on her. She drank her coffee and watched the breeze blow the dogwood blossoms, making them flutter like a thousand pink butterflies.

"I don't have enough money in the checking account to pay for a funeral," she went on. "What am I going to do?"

It was all about her right then.

Birdy already knew the answer, but she couldn't resist the question.

"Does he have life insurance?" she asked.

Jennifer's demeanor shifted. "Oh yes," she said, her mood brightening a little. "I completely forgot about that. Yes, through the military. I think he has some supplemental too. I should start looking for that paperwork." She got up and started for a cabinet across the room.

"That should help," Birdy said, locking eyes with Kendall.

Jennifer, her back to the women, sifted through some papers. "I'll have to file a claim, won't I? I don't know how to do that."

"It isn't difficult," Birdy said. "Once we clear the case, you'll have the documents you need. Despite what you might have read or heard on the news, the one thing the government can be counted on is paying out when those who served have died."

"That's a huge relief," Jennifer said, turning around. "I'll find the paperwork later. Now I have to just take all this in."

That random discussion on insurance over, Kendall refocused the interview back to the time of Ted Roberts's last breath.

"You told the paramedics that he'd eaten breakfast," she said. "And he didn't feel well."

"Yes. French toast with orange marmalade."

"He was upstairs?"

Jennifer fluffed her hair, apparently still damp from a shower.

"Yes, he'd been too weak lately—too drunk if you want the ugly truth—to come down to eat," she said.

"He was a heavy drinker?" Birdy asked.

Jennifer's eyes fluttered. "There's no use lying. I wouldn't have married him if I had known. I've had bad experiences with other men who drank too much."

Birdy was looking for medical facts to weigh against her own findings. "Was he treated for alcoholism?" she asked.

Jennifer ran her French-manicured fingertips through her long hair. "You have to admit you have a problem in order to get help."

They talked a while longer, but Jennifer was oddly vague on her timelines. It was possible it was due to stress. That happened all the time. One time when Kendall asked a distraught mother the birthdate of her child, the woman couldn't even come up with the right month.

Molly O'Rourke lingered between her house and the Roberts place. She had come off her shift at the convalescent center and gone two doors down to the neighbors who watched her dog Candy during the day. Lena loved animals, but her husband Sam was a grouch and wouldn't let her have a pet of her own. To appease his wife, he reluctantly agreed that Lena could watch Molly's dog a couple of days a week. The two women joked they had the first dog-share program in Port Orchard, maybe even in America.

When Lena answered the door it was evident that something was wrong. Her face was awash with concern and anxiety. She was not one for dramatics. She was a straightforward type who'd worked in the county clerk's office for decades before retiring. Serving the public makes one straightforward. She called it survival mode.

"Is Candy all right?" Molly asked.

"She's fine," Lena said. "She's with Sam. But you missed quite the hubbub this morning," the neighbor said.

Molly loved that dog and was instantly relieved. The feeling was a flash.

"What happened?" she asked. "Did those tweakers at the end of the block get busted again?"

Lena dismissed that notion. "No. I think Ted Roberts died. That bitch finally did him in."

Those words were a sucker punch to the gut. Molly gasped. She nearly doubled over.

"What happened?"

Lena's eyes misted up. "The ambulance came a little after Kathie Lee and Hoda came on the *Today* show. I was walking Candy and saw the whole thing. They came with the sirens blaring and, well, they left quietly. That's not a good sign when they leave without lights and sirens. Means they don't have to hurry to where they're going."

Molly was shaking. She felt a chill, but the air was warm.

"Are you sure it was Ted? Maybe one of the kids OD'd or something?"

"No," Lena said. "I'm sorry. I know you were close to him. I liked him too. He offered to take me kayaking one time, but I thought I was too old for a new hobby. Sam thought so, anyway."

Molly remembered the same offer once. She regretted declining it at that moment more than ever.

The neighbor went on. "After the ambulance left, the three of them—bitch and brats—got in his car. She was back a half hour later. Alone. Probably dropped off the kids somewhere."

Lena's husband came up behind his wife with Candy.

"Sorry about your friend," Sam said.

Molly took her dog and convulsed into tears.

"I knew this was going to happen," she said, sputtering around to look over at the Roberts house a few doors down. "I'm going to call the sheriff. I'm not going to let her get away with this. She was doing something to him. I know it."

"You going to be all right?" Lena called out.

"No. I'm never going to be all right," Molly said, though not to anyone in particular. She was on her way home, crying and holding her dog. "I *let* this happen. I let her do whatever she was doing to him. Something was so wrong over there. He was practically catatonic last time I saw him."

Molly went home and waited with Candy clutched in her trembling arms. She stood outside and looked over at the window behind the dogwood tree between her house and the Roberts place. She knew the car parked in front was a county vehicle by its plates. She was hoping that someone was there to do the right thing because she had seriously screwed up. She'd had her chance. She knew something was wrong.

Birdy and Kendall left a now sobbing Jennifer Roberts and went toward the car. Molly scurried over.

"Are you the police?"

Kendall didn't correct her. "You look upset," she said, "Ms.?"

"Molly O'Rourke. I live next door. I knew this would happen. I just knew it."

Birdy looked up and saw Jennifer in the window.

"Why don't you meet us at the sheriff's office?" she said, giving Kendall a sideways glance.

Jennifer was watching.

"I have to feed Candy, my dog, and then I'll come down."

"Ask for me, Detective Stark."

Molly went back inside.

"She looked scared," Birdy said as they drove back up the hill.

"I don't blame her," Kendall said. "There is something very off about Jennifer Roberts."

CHAPTER 17

"I don't know why I can't stop crying," Molly O'Rourke said, as she took a chair in an interview room at the Kitsap County sheriff's office.

"It is completely understandable," Birdy said, gently touching the younger woman's shoulder. "You've had a bad shock."

Kendall gave the young redhead with the suddenly blotchy complexion some water and a box of tissues. Both were needed.

"It isn't that," Molly said. "I'm sick about this because I knew this was going to happen. I let it happen. This really is my entire fault. Ted did not have to die."

"What is it, Molly?" Kendall asked. "What are you thinking that you've done?"

Molly dried her eyes. "I've had the feeling for a long time. But the other morning when I left for work, I just knew. I just knew something was going on. I should have called the police, but I didn't. I don't even know why."

Birdy and Kendall exchanged glances. It was crucial that Molly told them what she knew from her perspective, not with the benefit of anything they had learned so far from talking to Jennifer or the paramedics.

"That's an early start," Kendall said.

The young woman said she had to be at the convalescent center by 5:30 a.m. and that it took her at least twenty minutes to get there.

"So what did you see? What troubled you?"

"I was standing out there with my dog so she could do her business and I noticed the lights go on in the bedroom upstairs. Candy was taking her sweet time— like the little brat always does."

"It was dark?" Kendall asked.

"Right," Molly said. "Not yet five a.m."

"All right, then what happened?"

"The lights were on for a while, I don't know . . . a few minutes, and then they went off."

Kendall narrowed the focus. "What was so unusual about that?"

Molly shifted in her chair. "Well, I knew that Ted didn't get up to go to the bathroom. He was practically bedridden. I figured he'd had some kind of episode and woke up Jennifer and she went to check on him. She's a pretty lazy person so it had to be some kind of major commotion for her to get out of bed."

"Maybe it was as simple as that," Birdy offered. "That he needed some help with a bedpan."

Molly didn't think so. "This is kind of embarrassing," she said. "I really don't know why. At the center, a lot of residents wear Depends at night. But I don't know, I still think of Ted as being so vital," she said, choking up, then pulling herself together. "I saw Jennifer unloading groceries last week and I couldn't help noticing that she had a package of Depends."

"You notice a lot of things," Kendall said.

The young woman looked up, a little defensively. "Our houses are very close together."

"I didn't mean it like that," Kendall said. "I mean that you've been observant. I appreciate that. You were really fond of Ted, but you obviously don't care much for Jennifer."

"You wouldn't like her either," Molly said. "I don't see how anyone could. She was such a conceited liar. She once told me she was a runner-up to Miss Arizona. I Googled the pageant's website and there was no Jennifer listed in the past thirty years. She didn't know how to tell the truth about anything. When she came up here, she told me she was pregnant. She said she'd gotten pregnant on her wedding night."

"But she only has a teenage son and a daughter," Birdy said. "We saw their photos."

Molly nodded. "Right. They are nice enough kids. But about the baby. I kept wondering about it. At first, I thought that she was going to be one of those pregnant movie star types that barely shows and then has the baby and they are suddenly back in a bathing suit. She kind of took care of herself like that."

"But what about the baby?" Birdy asked.

"I don't think there ever was one. I think Ted thought there was one, for sure. He told me one time that he had some very bad news. He said that Jennifer had a miscarriage. He was devastated."

"I'm sure he was," Kendall said.

"Yeah, but guess who wasn't? I went over there with some mums that I thought were pretty and a card and told Jennifer that I was sorry for her loss. She thanked me and was nice about it, but the next day was garbage day. I took my trash to the street, you know, next to the Robertses' and do you know what I saw?"

"No," Birdy said. "Tell me."

"Well, their can's lid wasn't down tight and I noticed some stuff sticking out. I thought that I should shut it because if the raccoons got into it, then I'd be the one that had to clean it up. The wind always blows stuff into my yard. You know what was sticking up, holding the lid up?" she asked, not waiting for Birdy or Kendall to answer. "That potted mum. Jennifer had just thrown it out. I only gave it to her the day before. I opened the lid and the card was there too. She didn't even open it."

It was cold, but neither Kendall nor Birdy said so.

"What about Ted's health?" Birdy asked. "What do you know about it?"

"Nothing. I mean, honestly, I don't know what was wrong with him. He was fine until she showed up. Seriously. At first he complained of stomach cramps and she put him on some special raw foods diet, but it didn't seem to work. She told me about that. Said it was all the rage down in Scottsdale. I didn't know anything about it, but I did watch him get better, then sicker, then, well never better again."

"What did he or she say was wrong with him?" Birdy asked.

She pondered the question before answering. "God, there were so many stories. One time she told me he had stomach cancer. I asked who his oncologist was— I'm not exactly really in the medical field, but I wanted to be a nurse—and she said it was someone in Seattle. I Googled that too, but couldn't find anything."

"I seems like you were very suspicious," Kendall said.

A look of recognition came over her. Molly had heard that before. "That's what my mom says. She thinks I'm overly dramatic. But I was suspicious. One time I kind of confronted her about it. I said that Ted looked really bad and I worried that he might die."

"How did she react?" Birdy asked.

The memory brought Molly to tears again. "I'm sorry," she said, taking another tissue. Her eyes were red; her face was suddenly very white. "I think I'm going to throw up," she said.

"Can you make it to the restroom?" Birdy asked.

Molly gripped the armrests of her chair. "It'll pass. I'm just upset. Give me a second."

Kendall slid the wastebasket a little closer to Molly. Just in case it was needed.

Molly acknowledged the gesture by holding up her finger, indicating just a second. She could get through the interview with a little more perseverance.

"When I confronted her, she just looked at me with those weird blue eyes of hers and said, 'there are worse things that could happen.' It was like Ted's dying was expected and meant nothing to her. It was after that . . . it was after that . . ."

"Go on, please," Kendall said, pushing her a little. "I know this is unbelievably hard."

"I should have called nine-one-one," Molly said. "I really should have."

"None of this is your fault. We don't even know what happened," Kendall said.

Molly bucked up. She was tough. She could get through this.

"You might not," she said. "But I sure do."

Color returned to her face and along with it, a bit of resolve.

"She killed him," she said. "Jennifer killed Ted. It is as simple as that. There was nothing wrong with him until she showed up here in Washington. I really liked Ted. He was a good man. She was trouble and he just didn't have a chance."

CHAPTER 18

It was almost 5 p.m. when Tess Moreau arrived at the coroner's office. It looked as though the life had drained from her. If her eyes were shut, she would look no better than Ted Roberts did when he was wheeled under the lights of the autopsy table. Her hair was flat and stuck to the nape of her neck as though she hadn't showered. She also smelled, rather reeked, of wine.

A merlot, Birdy thought. *And not a good one.*

The forensic pathologist knew better than to ask if Tess was all right. That question had never been uttered a single time in her office. Never would be. No one who came there had ever been all right.

"I went to see Detective Stark, but she's away. I don't want to talk to anyone but her. Or you."

"Kendall's at a school meeting," she said. "She has a little boy."

Awkwardness took over. Tess had something on her mind, but she didn't seem able to get it out right then. She held her hands together. Her knuckles were white.

"You need some coffee, Ms. Moreau. May I call you Tess?" Birdy didn't wait for an answer. She went to the house's old kitchen and found a couple of old, but clean Fathoms O' Fun mugs. The coffee had been on the heat for hours and smelled like it, but Tess didn't balk. She needed caffeine.

More than that, she needed Darby.

"Black coffee okay? We're out of creamer. And unless I buy it or swipe a packet from the coffee stand, no sweetener either."

Tess was happy for anything with caffeine. She was tired and every bone in her body ached from the kind of hard sobs that come in the middle of the night.

"Black is fine," she said.

Birdy filled the mugs.

"When can I have my daughter back?"

"I expect tomorrow," Birdy said.

Tess took a sip. "I want to see her," she said.

"That's not a good idea," Birdy answered. No mother should ever see her child in that condition. In cases in which the body can be presented intact, unblemished by decay, Birdy understood the importance of having a mother or father look at the departed.

"But I need to," she said. "To make all this real."

"Darby was a beautiful girl, Tess." Birdy motioned toward her office for Tess to take a seat, and Tess obliged. "Hold on to that. You don't want to see her. I don't want you to imagine the worst either. The girl you loved is gone, but she will always live inside of you."

Tess set her cup down on the edge of Birdy's desk and produced an envelope. It had been folded and unfolded so often that it almost appeared as if it would break apart.

"Did you bring something of Darby's?" Birdy asked.

Sometimes parents did that. They wanted people in law enforcement to know who had been taken from them. That the victim of the car accident, drug overdose, or homicide had been a real person. One dad brought his son's last report card to prove that he was not some loser. That the drug overdose had been an anomaly. Another father brought in his little girl's favorite Barbie. Tess didn't speak. Birdy didn't force her to either. She drank her terrible coffee and waited.

"I should have done something about this," Tess said.

"You couldn't have prevented it. We don't think Darby was targeted by anyone. Her murder was random and as senseless as senseless can be."

Tess didn't say a word for the longest time. She looked deep into her black coffee, her own sad reflection looking back at her. "No. No. It wasn't."

"What do you have there, Tess?"

"Where?"

"In your hand," Birdy said. "The envelope."

Tess looked down. It was almost as if the frayed paper had landed there of its own accord. Fluttered down from the sky into her lap. She nearly seemed surprised to see it.

"I brought this for Detective Stark."

"What is it?"

"See for yourself. You will see what kind of a mother I really am. What kind of a mother I *was*."

Tess had been drinking. A lot.

Birdy held her hand out to receive the paper, but Tess didn't hand it over.

"Do you have a family? Husband? Kids?" Tess asked.

Birdy shook her head. "No. I haven't been so lucky. I do have a nephew staying with me, but I know it's not the same thing."

"No, it isn't," Tess said.

"Let me see what you've brought. Maybe I can help?"

"Can you bring my daughter, my husband, my baby back from the dead?"

"You know the answer."

She handed Birdy the paper.

"Can you forgive me? Can anyone?"

Birdy kept her eyes on Tess, who was now wobbling a little. Birdy was not going to let the woman drive home. She didn't want her back in the office on the autopsy table. The envelope had been addressed to Tess's house on Olalla Valley Road, but the stamp hadn't been canceled. She opened it and pulled out the brief note held inside.

You took from me. I'll take from you.

"What's this?" Birdy asked.

"A warning I didn't heed. A mistake that cost me Darby."

"Who sent it?"

"I have an idea."

"Who?"

Tess stayed mute.

Birdy wanted to tell her to spit it out, but she chose a kinder set of words.

"Please tell me so I can help."

Tess swallowed more coffee. "Brenda," she said. "Brenda Nevins."

The name was so well known that Birdy couldn't quite believe her ears. It was like hearing the name Michelle Obama and thinking that there must be some other woman with that identical name.

"The killer?" the forensic pathologist asked anyway.

Tess wobbled and started to crumble.

"But why? What did you take from her?"

"Her time. That's what."

"But she's never getting out," Birdy said.

Tess shifted in the chair. "Her time in the spotlight," she said. "A TV crew was going to film her for some big interview. She thought she could charm them. You know, tell them she was framed."

"She wasn't framed," Birdy said.

"Of course she wasn't," Tess said. "But she lives in her own world. She's the star of the show and the rest of us are the bit players who do whatever she wants. We're there to make sure she's the prettiest, smartest in the room. She pushed things so far that she spent half her time in the hole."

"Why was she in the hole?" Birdy asked.

Tess gave her a knowing look. "Oh. It was a good one, I'll tell you. I caught her having oral sex with a guard on a dog-grooming table."

"Nice," Birdy said, though it was so outlandish it was hard to process the scenario Tess had described.

Tess drank some more coffee, replaying that image in her head one more time. It was one of those once-in-a-lifetime images that never fades from memory, like seeing a baby's first steps. Except that particular prison porn scene fell completely on the other end of the spectrum of unforgettable images.

"She threatened me," Tess said. "The guard too. Said I'd be sorry if I ever told."

"What was his name?"

"The guard?"

"Oh, it gets even better," Tess said, watching Birdy's expression. "You mean, *her* name."

"I just assumed," Birdy said.

"A lot goes on inside, Dr. Waterman, but I figured you would know that. Her name is Missy Carlyle."

"What happened to her?"

"She got fired, of course. Took a while. The union fought for her. Honestly, I liked Missy. Some of the gals working in corrections are a little scary, but she was very nice. Very good at her job. She won an award the same year I did."

Birdy was speechless.

"She turned on me though," Tess said. "Said I was a liar and everything. Then they produced a tape of the encounter and she was gone."

"Why do you think that Brenda's behind the threats?" Birdy asked. "Why would she bother?"

"Dr. Waterman, you might be an expert at what you do, but you don't know much about the people who do the really nasty things in life. I mean, I get that you see their handiwork in your job, but you don't understand the motivations behind it."

Birdy bristled, but didn't fire back. She didn't lose sight of the fact that the woman sitting in her office had lost a daughter, had too much to drink, and had been the victim of some kind of terrible harassment from a homicidal maniac.

"No, I guess not. Enlighten me." Her request was

said in the kindest way possible. It wasn't a pushback, but a genuine call for some kind of an answer from someone with a unique perspective.

Tess looked at her. "I've worked in the prison for a decade," she said. "Every now and then someone like Brenda comes in and you get to see evil close up. Like they really are there in a zoo, a place of observation. They think they are there to do their time. Most of them do. Brenda's there because it is the only place where she can continue to be what she was born to be."

Birdy was fascinated. "Tess, tell me, what is that?"

"A game player. Brenda was playing a game when she killed her husband, her child, and then later that poor sap of a fiancé. Just because she's been put away doesn't mean the game is over."

"May I keep this?" Birdy asked, indicating the letter and the envelope.

"I guess so," Tess said. "I was going to give it to the detective."

Birdy slid it into another envelope. "I'll take care of that." It was doubtful that there would be any latent prints on the paper. There would be no DNA lurking under the stamp. It, like the seal to the envelope, was self-adhesive.

No one's tongue had licked either.

The image of Missy and Brenda on the dog-grooming table came to Birdy's mind and she wished it hadn't.

"I'll take you back to your friend's place in Gig Harbor," she said.

"Dr. Waterman," Tess said. "Are you sure about me not seeing Darby?"

"Yes," she said. "If you do, you will wish for the rest of your life that you didn't. Trust me."

Tess let a single tear roll from the corner of her eye to the floor.

"I do trust you," she said. "I have no choice and really, nothing left to lose."

CHAPTER 19

Elan was waiting by the door when Birdy pulled her red Prius into the driveway. Actually, she almost *lurched* the eco-friendly car into the driveway. She'd been in a hurry. She carried a pizza from Round Table in Gig Harbor.

"I'm starving," the sixteen-year-old said, pouncing on his aunt before the door shut. "Don't you ever buy groceries?"

"I told you I was going to be late. Here's a pizza," she said, pushing the box at him like a lion tamer with a chair. "Cold, probably. I'm a very bad aunt. I hurried."

Elan took the greasy cardboard box and flipped it open. A piece was missing.

"I was starving," she said. "Hadn't eaten all day."

Elan shrugged. "Not that bad of an aunt," he said, separating a congealed slice from the others. "I like pepperoni. How did you know that?"

Birdy shed her coat and it fell in a heap on the sofa. "You've told me that five times since you got here. And yes, I buy groceries. You, on the other hand, eat them at a rate to which I'm not accustomed." She stopped and regarded Elan. "Looks like you like the pizza."

He stuffed another bite in his mouth. "You want some? Some more?"

Birdy made an exaggerated expression of disapproval.

"Don't talk with your mouth full," she said, thinking that was the most motherly thing she'd ever said to a kid. *Maybe ever*. But certainly in a long, long while. "And yes, I want some more and I want *you* to sit at the table."

That was a little motherly too.

Elan started to speak, but his mouth was still full. He led Birdy into the kitchen while she rummaged around for some napkins, ultimately giving up. She put a roll of paper towels on the table and took another slice of pizza for herself.

"Never said it would be fancy here," she said. "If you wanted full service you'd have stayed with another favorite aunt."

There was no favorite aunt. No other aunt period.

Elan smiled and continued to eat. "Hey, the police came to school today," he said. "People were talking about that case you're working on. You know, the one you won't tell me anything about?"

Birdy swallowed. "Yes, *that* one," she said. "What are they saying?"

Elan glowered a little, but it was a good-natured glower. "How come you get to ask me about it, but I can't ask you anything? People know you're my aunt. They think I could give them all the gory details about how that kid got butchered out in the woods. Like was it an ax or a machete?"

Birdy set down her pizza, her appetite quelled by his insensitivity. He was young. He had a lot to learn. He was of that generation that didn't see the horror behind the spatter.

"Her name was Darby Moreau," she said, keeping her voice even. "She wasn't some kid who got butchered."

He looked a little embarrassed. She'd made her point.

"I know that," he said. "I also know her mom is a freak. And I know some stuff about her and our art teacher who's been doing her."

"Elan," Birdy said, resuming her pizza, "please don't talk like that."

His eyes met hers. "Like what?"

Birdy selected another slice, her third. And yes, she was counting. Normally at this point, she'd have blotted the pepperoni with a napkin to save some calories, but this pie was too cold. She'd eat every fatty bit of it. "Like what happened is some video game and you don't understand that we're talking about real people," she said.

He pulled an errant piece of pepperoni from the box and stuck it on his slice.

"I didn't mean to be disrespectful or anything," he said. "I was just repeating what I heard. The cop came and kids in art class starting talking about the girl." He took another bite but waited until he'd swallowed before speaking again. Birdy doubted that he chewed it. She imagined the contents of his stomach just then, like she'd seen in other cases. It was random, but things like that happened. Determining the last meal of a kid like him would be easy.

"About Darby, and I thought maybe if you told me

something," he continued, "I'd be cooler. It isn't easy to start over."

"You aren't starting over," she said. "And you don't need any cred. You are cool enough."

"Why can't you just talk to me about your work?"

Hadn't they had this conversation?

She appreciated his interest, but he didn't seem to understand the reasons for the very need for confidentiality in a criminal case. It wasn't a reality TV show. It was real life.

"Because I'm part of the criminal justice system and we have rules, protocol, procedure. The whole process depends on it."

"Whatever," he said. "I guess you don't want to know what I heard?"

Birdy was interested, but she played it cool—his word, not hers.

"You can tell me or not."

"I choose not to," he said.

In a way, that made Birdy feel a little better. Gossip was often hurtful and destructive. That Elan was enough of his own person to keep things to himself said something positive about his character. She liked that.

"Let's change the subject," she said. "Tell me about your mom and dad. Did you phone them today like you said you would? You don't have to gulp. *Chew*. And *then* swallow."

Birdy got up and retrieved a small bottle of water from the refrigerator for Elan and a beer for herself and returned to the table.

The teen looked at the beer, accusingly. Their family

had a history of alcoholism. Birdy could see a flicker of judgment in his piercing brown eyes.

"I had a very hard, very sad day," she said, offering up an explanation for something that didn't need explaining. Being with Tess and hearing the dog-grooming table story was enough to drive anyone to drink. More than a beer was in order, but that's all she had in the house.

"I don't care," he said. "And no, I didn't talk to my mom or my dad. But I did leave them both texts. I talked to grandma though."

Her mother. Natalie Waterman managed to infiltrate Birdy's world in some way every day. Just when Birdy thought her mother wouldn't be on her mind for a single day, something pushed her there like a bird flu alert on Drudge. Like a tornado that rips apart a small town. Like a flash flood in the desert.

"Really?" she asked, playing it calm. "How did that go?"

He smiled. "She mostly complained about you."

Birdy grinned back. That was very familiar.

"Did she say I was ungrateful?" she asked.

The kid was enjoying himself. "You really want to know?" he asked.

She cocked a brow.

Elan liked this little conversation. "Ungrateful bitch was what she said."

Birdy rolled her eyes upward. "I miss my mother," she said.

"I miss mine too."

The two of them sat there at the table, both realizing for the first time, they had some genuine common ground. It wasn't that they shared the same cultural history. That was a given. It wasn't that they were related by blood. It was more than that. They were bonded by destructive and bitter relationships with their mothers.

"Have another slice, Elan. There isn't going to be enough for lunch tomorrow."

After Elan went to study or sulk in his bedroom, Birdy took a second beer and settled in her office. It was after 9 p.m. Too late to call. She texted Kendall on her personal cell phone.

Meet me tomorrow for coffee. First thing. Hope all is well w Cody.

As she shuffled a few things around, her mother coming in and out of her thoughts, she discovered Darby's moleskin. That was a lapse, but it had only been collected for the possibility of DNA. Kendall had reviewed it and thought that it could be returned to Tess. Birdy thought about what she'd told her nephew—that Darby Moreau was a girl, not a victim of a butcher. That what she was in life was still all around, living in those who knew her.

She caressed the outside of the navy blue notebook and sipped her beer.

Inside was a mix of poetry, songs that Darby liked, lists of things she was going to do. Some of the pages contained sketches. Birdy wondered if they were preliminary to pieces she was doing in her art class.

Darby's handwriting wasn't like a teenage girl's—or what Birdy recalled hers was like when she was sixteen. Birdy had been fascinated with calligraphy and for a time, never knew a curlicue that she didn't think had its rightful place on every letterform. Darby's was spare. It had a kind of heft and maturity. There were no real flourishes. It was all about order. Like her bedroom, it was an oasis in a stormy sea.

One seven-line free verse touched Birdy's heart. She wondered if Darby was daydreaming or if she had someone in mind.

> *I wish I lived in a house on the Sound*
> *And was free*
> *To fly like a bird*
> *I wish he knew that*
> *I have been waiting so long*
> *I am ready*
> *That's what makes me beautiful*

The book was only partly filled. It had been a work in progress, one that had been stopped by her killer. Her eyes dampened as she went through it page by page. It was a holy book—a girl's heart in pencil, pen, and the occasional splash of watercolor.

Birdy wondered about the kind of person who could just come and steal someone's life. Someone like Brenda Nevins, maybe? Someone bent on revenge? How was it that the earth could even host a parasite, an organism of evil like that at all? Tess was right. Those people who did evil to one another were always there—planning, hoping, and enjoying.

How was it that there were people walking among the innocent who had no idea they were at risk? Not even the slightest clue.

That the nice guy next door was a pedophile?

*That the woman who doted on one child was tortur-
ing another?*

*That the middle-schooler planned to kill everyone in
his classroom?*

Birdy finished her beer and rejected the idea of another. She knew that in all of those cases—cases she
consulted or studied in medical school, the innocent
never had a warning. The innocent never had a second
chance.

Tess Moreau had been warned. Darby didn't have to
die.

If Brenda had instigated the murder, she did so by
remote control. She managed to keep her hands clean,
her distance safely behind the razor wire of the prison.

The neighbor's cat walked atop the fence that separated the two yards. She paused every few feet looking
for a shrew or field mouse. Jinx was a hunter. A good
mouser. She could spring from the fence top and pick
off the unsuspecting rodent with precision and skill.
She didn't eat the mice, the shrews. Instead she left
them at Birdy's back door.

A trophy. A gift.

Had Darby been bundled in that plastic bag and deposited in Banner Forest in the same manner? Had
someone killed her to fulfill a promise? Or to prove a
point?

As she turned out the desk light, Birdy couldn't help
thinking that it wouldn't be long until Tess Moreau returned to her office. Not as a visitor, but as the subject
of an autopsy. She knew of no way that the woman who
had lost everything could go on.

She padded down the hall past Elan's room. A sliver of light slipped from under his door. It crossed her mind how quickly it had become *his* room, and no longer the guest room. Just having him there made it his. She could hear the teenager talking on the phone. It was late, but it was okay. He had friends. Maybe back in Neah Bay or maybe in Port Orchard. It didn't matter. She worried about him. She wanted him to be happy.

She'd go grocery shopping *before* work. She was not going to be the aunt who never had food in the house.

CHAPTER 20

Birdy arrived a few minutes later than she'd hoped, but the line at the coffee stand at the Kitsap County Administration Building had been long and Kendall was just getting her drink.

"You look like crap," the detective said.

"Thanks," Birdy answered, knowing Kendall's assessment was the undisputed truth. Her eyes were hollows and her normally luxurious black hair looked like it hadn't been brushed. Or washed. "Didn't sleep well. Got up early and, believe or not, went to Walmart to do some early-morning grocery shopping because, apparently, I'm starving Elan half to death."

Kendall put her change in the tip jar. "Kids are great, aren't they?"

Birdy nodded. "How did it go at the school? Is Cody making the kind of progress you were hoping for?"

Kendall's eyes sparkled and she smiled. "Better, Birdy. He's doing so much better. We're so happy. When Steven and I count our blessings this year, we'll add this to the top of the list."

"That's wonderful news," Birdy said, her mood

shifting back to the reason they were meeting so early. If it had been any other time, they'd have talked more about the specifics, but not now. Not with what had been weighing on her in the Darby Moreau case.

"We can't talk here," Kendall said. "And I have something for you too."

The women walked across the broad plaza between the administration building and the venerable courthouse toward the ivy-clad entrance to the sheriff's department. They passed by the security desk and wound their way to Kendall's office via a circuitous route that was a result of too many add-ons to grow the size of the building to fit a growing county.

"Maybe we'll get a new building someday, Birdy," she said as they went into her small windowless office. A green banker's lamp provided most of the light.

"Don't be jealous. I'd rather stay here. I like being with the courthouse guys."

Kendall checked her email while Birdy took off her coat and settled in one of the two visitors' chairs— chairs like her own that were usually occupied by people who'd rather be anywhere but there.

"You sure you didn't need any coffee?" the detective asked, looking up from the computer screen.

Birdy declined. "I've had three cups already," she said. "My first cup was gas station coffee at five a.m."

"Ouch," Kendall said with some exaggerated irony in her voice. "That's rough."

"Right. That might be one of the reasons I look so good today."

"Sorry about that. I was just saying."

"No worries," Birdy said. "This case has just gotten to me. Worse than many."

Kendall understood. "You're closer to the victim because you've been more involved. I get it. Not that you don't feel the pain of others, I know you do. But it is different when you see where they lived, walked through their lives."

Birdy had to admit that Kendall was right. A dead body could tell her a lot. A visit from a family member for more information, even more. But there was nothing quite like going into Darby's bedroom, reading her journal. And nothing like taking Tess home after her visit the day before.

"Tess thinks Brenda Nevins could be involved."

Kendall processed the name. It was so far out of left field.

"*The* Brenda Nevins?"

Birdy let Brenda's name swing like a pendulum in the air.

"Thank God there's only one," she said.

Kendall's eyes nearly popped. "That came out of nowhere, Birdy."

The forensic pathologist couldn't argue that point. Never in a million years. She told Kendall what Tess had confided to her at her office and on the ride to Amanda's place in Gig Harbor. She covered it all—the altercation at the prison, the threats, the letters that Darby's mom had received.

Kendall just sat there, taking it all in. Eyes still wide.

"A dog-grooming table?" she finally repeated.

Birdy looked upward and made a face that telegraphed everything she thought about that incident. "Yeah, I know. No comment on that." Next, she handed over the envelope with the threatening message tucked inside.

"The lab might be able to get something off this, but

I'm doubtful. Tess has handled it quite a bit. My guess is her friend Amanda did. I did too."

Kendall slid it from the evidence envelope and pulled it from the one the note had been mailed in. She held it by its edges and read.

"We'll try. Maybe there's something there. Maybe we can determine the paper." She held it to the light. "Nothing remarkable. No watermark. Might be able to find out what brand of toner it was printed on and, well, you know that'll narrow it down to about a million possibilities."

Birdy apologized again for touching it. "I wasn't thinking."

Kendall waved her hand, dismissing the concern. "Don't worry about it. This paper's been around a long time. We'll process it regardless. You never know."

"There's something else," Birdy said. "I think that Darby was seeing someone."

"The teacher?"

"You know about her?" she asked.

"Yes, I talked to her."

"How did you know?"

"Elan told me," Birdy said. "Rumors going around South."

"I don't suppose the rumors indicate just why two women would need condoms," Kendall said.

"I don't suppose," Kendall continued, looking over at a copy of the photograph of Darby that her mother had given them when they first saw her. By then the smile was haunting, the eyes familiar. It was as if the dead girl was there. "But it's possible no one knows about the condoms."

"Rumors are ugly," Birdy said. "And they aren't always true."

"I know," Kendall said. "Besides, I talked to the teacher. There's nothing there. They had a personal bond. Nothing else. But you said you knew that the rumor was false. How did you know that?"

"Back to the condoms," Birdy said.

"Her mom said they probably belonged to her friend. Katie denied it," Kendall said. "Darby didn't have a boyfriend. She said that neither of the girls did."

Birdy opened the moleskin journal and tapped her fingertip on the verse that the dead girl had written.

"Darby had a boyfriend, Kendall. It's right here. Right in her poetry. She talks about being ready."

Kendall's eyes ran over the verse, and then she looked up.

"Then who was he?"

Birdy's phone buzzed and she looked down at a text message.

"Tox is back on Ted Roberts," she said.

"What's it say?"

"Encrypted. Just a notification. Have to go to my office to read. I'll let you know."

CHAPTER 21

"**A**nd you say she's a widow once before?"
It was the incredulous voice of Percy Smith of the state crime lab.

"That's what I said, Percy. Two times a widow."

Birdy took off a silver hoop earring that was starting to irritate her phone ear. "A young widow at that."

She swiveled in her chair and looked over at the computer screen as Percy discussed his findings. Pages from his fax were falling onto the ratty green carpet that covered the floor of the old house, the soon-to-be abandoned Kitsap County coroner's office.

"The first death was in Arizona," she said.

"You're going to have to tell the authorities down there," he said. "Hey, I might be able to do that for you. Kind of like a mini vacation. Love the sun."

"We've had three beautiful days in a row," Birdy said. The printer stopped dropping pages, signaling that the job was done.

"Which means that we're about to have rain for a month. Hang on. Getting a hard copy of the report."

It might not have been Jennifer Roberts's lucky day,

but it was shaping up to be a better one for Birdy. She managed to scoop up the pages of the report in the correct order—that was a good thing. Sometimes it took five minutes to figure out what went where. For some unknown reason Percy's reports never had page numbers.

"Ethylene glycol poisoning," she repeated from the report. "How often do you see that?"

"Once before, but other places have more than their share of antifreeze poisonings," Percy said. "Georgia had a good case a few years back."

"Any chance that it was accidental?" she asked. "Suicide? He'd been ill."

"If you think Prestone is a good mixer, I guess so," Percy said in that oddly upbeat voice he had for everything. "Suicide is possible. I looked it up. It has happened. But from what you told me, I'd say highly unlikely. Jessica Roberts is probably the killer."

"Jennifer," Birdy said, correcting him.

Percy let out a little laugh. "Whatever. I always screw up on those J names. Anyway, I'm one hundred percent certain that there was enough of the stuff in his body to keep cars running in a Dakota blizzard."

"If she'd been poisoning him, how was it that he just let her?" she asked.

Percy let out a short, clipped laugh. "I wasn't kidding when I said it could be a mixer. Seriously. The stuff is actually kind of sweet and hard to detect when served up to someone. You know, as a mix in. Heck, pets manage to find a pool of it under the family car every now and then. That's without it even hidden in food or drink. Straight. They lick it because it tastes good and pretty soon, bam, kitty's dead."

As Birdy listened to Percy on the phone, she reached for her own report.

"His lungs, heart, looked good," she said, scanning its pages. "His kidneys were shot."

"Yup, that's what killed him," he said.

Kendall was on the phone in her dark little office when Birdy found her. Kendall caught Birdy's intense gaze and abruptly ended her call.

"Ted Roberts died of renal failure," Birdy said.

"Right," she said. "You said that in your report."

"Kendall, the Roberts samples were analyzed by the crime lab. Percy said that the poor guy's tissues were practically 'marinated' in ethylene glycol."

"Antifreeze?"

Birdy handed her the papers that Percy had faxed. "Right. Barring suicide and accidental poisoning, manner of death is homicide."

"You're missing an earring."

Birdy touched her right lobe. "Thanks. Just in a hurry."

"Me too. Let's see what Jennifer Roberts has to say."

Kendall picked up her phone. "Tell her you have some important news about her husband's death."

"Well, I do," Birdy said. "Are you going to arrest her?"

"Let's see how it plays out," Kendall said.

She handed Birdy the phone and looked at her notes with the phone number Jennifer had given for her cell and started dialing.

"You tell her to meet at your office at her earliest convenience."

Birdy listened and then passed the phone back. "No answer."

"Keep trying. Don't leave a message. In the meantime, I'll do a little more digging into Jennifer's background in Arizona."

Jennifer Roberts arrived at the coroner's office in a force field of perfume and wearing a skirt that was so short it had to have been borrowed from her daughter's closet. She teetered on five-inch heels. Her eyes were obscured by sunglasses. She apologized for not picking up her phone the first three times Birdy had tried, but she said she'd had her nails done and they were still wet when the calls came through.

"You said you had some important news about Teddy?"

Kendall appeared, right on time.

"Oh, detective, I didn't know you'd be here," Jennifer said.

"No worries," she said. "Just doing my job."

Birdy spoke up, answering Jennifer's original question. "I do. I'm glad you're both here. Let's go in my office. I have some very upsetting news, Ms. Roberts."

The three women took their places. Birdy behind her desk with the copy of the report that Percy had faxed her, fanned out. Kendall and Jennifer facing her. Kendall adjusted her chair so that it angled a little in Jennifer's direction.

"I'm afraid that your husband died of poisoning," Birdy said, holding the last word an extra beat.

Jennifer looked over at Kendall, then back at the

forensic pathologist. She took off her glasses. Her eyes appeared puffy and red.

"That can't be. Poisoning? That's horrendous!"

"Yes it is," Birdy said. "I'm afraid it is."

Kendall just watched, observing every tic and movement. Jennifer stood up and reached for the report.

"I don't believe you," she said. "Teddy never would have taken any poison. Except for his drinking he was a complete health nut. For God's sake he even ate quinoa. Who eats that? There's no way he could have been poisoned."

Birdy persisted. "But, Jennifer, he was."

"Let me see," Jennifer said, stretching her hand outward. "I don't believe you."

Birdy handed her the report. She tapped her finger on the words *ethylene glycol*.

Jennifer looked up. "What's that?" she asked. "I don't know what that is."

This time Kendall answered. "Antifreeze. But you already know that."

"That's crazy! Why would he take antifreeze? That's for cars, isn't it?"

"So you're familiar with it?" Kendall asked.

Jennifer stared at Kendall. "Are you accusing me of something?"

"No. Just asking a question, that's all."

"I resent your tone," Jennifer said. "I had a very loving relationship with my husband. I adored him. He was my everything and you're . . . you're accusing me of doing something terrible. I would never, ever. Ever." She stopped to catch her breath. Tears had filled her eyes and her hands were trembling.

Jennifer looked over at Birdy.

"And you, are you the grim reaper? You invite me over here to tell me about my husband and you treat me like this? What kind of people are you? I have lost something very, very precious to me. My children are orphans again. This is one of the worst—maybe *the* worst—thing that has ever happened to me and I've had my share of hardships. Life has not been a bed of roses."

"I'm sorry about your loss," Birdy said, finding her voice in the spectacle that was swarming in front of her. Jennifer Roberts was on a very defensive rant.

"You should be," Jennifer said. "If you had a heart you would be. But I think that people like you and the detective here get all warm and fuzzy by delivering such hateful news."

"The fact of the matter, Ms. Roberts, is that your husband was murdered. We want to find out who did it," Kendall said.

"Blame me," Jennifer said. "Blame me for not taking better care of him. Maybe it is my fault, but I did not poison him. I loved him. I don't know how I'm going to survive. I don't even have any insurance money."

"How much insurance did Mr. Roberts have?" Kendall asked. As long as Jennifer was going to talk, the detective was going to ask her. She hadn't been charged and she wasn't officially a suspect. No Miranda applied. *Yet*.

"I don't know. A couple hundred thousand. Through the military."

"That's a lot for a government policy," Kendall said.

"We had some supplemental. He wanted to make

sure that Ruby and Micah could go to college, you know, if anything ever happened to him."

"And now something has," Kendall said.

"You are so out of line, detective. I'm going now. I'm going home and am trying to put all of this harassment behind me."

With that Jennifer Roberts spun around on her five-inch heels, like a pair of compasses stuck into the floor. She scurried toward the door and slammed it shut.

"What in the world was that all about?" Birdy said. "I've never seen anything like that in my life. Grim reaper, indeed."

Kendall got up. "It'll tell you what that is. That's a guilty woman trying to make a run for it."

"Why don't you get an arrest warrant?" Birdy asked.

"There isn't enough evidence, Birdy."

Birdy looked at her friend. It didn't completely compute. "She practically confessed, Kendall. She said this might have been all her fault."

"We're not there yet. She's not going anywhere anytime soon."

"What makes you say that?"

"Because of the motive. She killed the supposed love of her life for money. She needs to make the claim. In order to do that she'll need a death certificate. How long does it take you to have one of those recorded?"

"Five days, sometimes longer with the county workers' furlough."

"When will you put it in?"

Birdy understood where the detective was going and it made her feel a little uncomfortable.

"How long do you want me to delay it?" she asked.

"A week?"

Birdy nodded. "Doable. Any longer and I'd feel funny about it."

"Good. In the meantime, I'll contact the sheriff down in Maricopa County. We need to file some paperwork on an exhumation. You'll be going to Arizona."

CHAPTER 22

Port Orchard, a town of under ten thousand, didn't have many strip malls, but among the few, it did manage to have four tanning salons. After her meltdown with the Kitsap County detective and forensic pathologist, Jennifer Roberts parked in front of the Desert Enchantment location on Mile Hill Road. She held her phone to her ear for a minute or two, listening. After hanging up, she went inside. She lingered in the waiting area while her daughter, Ruby, finished upselling a customer a one-year "Guaranteed Gorgeous" tanning package (a package that workers there called "Guaranteed Cancerous").

"You can come in any time, five times a day if you want," Ruby said. "We don't really recommend that, but I just want you to know."

The woman, white as a porcelain platter, burbled something about an upcoming Mexican vacation and thanked Ruby.

"Room six," Ruby said, as the woman started down the hallway, past the airbrushed posters of the most beautiful human bodies ever committed to paper.

Ruby acknowledged her mom with a sympathetic look.

"New bulbs in there," Ruby called out to the new customer. "I'm only giving you six minutes."

"Mom," Ruby said, reaching for her mother, "you look terrible."

"I know," Jennifer said.

"Let's go in the dryer room so we can talk." She turned toward a semi-orange girl named Lucerne who'd appeared with a sanitizing spray bottle from one of the rooms. "Lu, watch the counter. Mom and I need some privacy."

The girl took the spray bottle and went to the front desk. "Sorry about your loss, Ms. Roberts," she said.

Jennifer started to cry behind her dark glasses, mouthed a thank-you, and followed her daughter down the corridor past the pretty posters to a small room outfitted with four large LG red-enameled dryers. It looked like an appliance dealership. All but one was on the tumble cycle.

Ruby had her long blond hair in a messy bun. Silver and turquoise earrings that she had made herself from looking at a magazine photograph dangled. She was tanned, but not overly so. The seventeen-year-old wore a pretty pink, almost nude shade of lip color. She probably looked exactly like her mother did when she was a teenager. She didn't have her mother's figure, of course. She'd been saving up for that.

Ruby shut the door and put her arms around her mom.

"Mom, you're not doing okay. What happened?"

Jennifer looked away and then started to sob. It started slowly, like a kettle just beginning to simmer. A moment later, it was a roiling boil. The sound of the spinning dryers muffled her outburst.

"It'll be okay, Mom," Ruby said. "Everything will work out."

Jennifer pulled back and took off her glasses.

"Can I?" she said, looking at one of the white towels.

"Here," Ruby said, getting her one. "It's still warm." She dabbed at her mother's eyes.

Jennifer acknowledged the gesture with a slight smile. "Thank you. I've just come from the authorities. They think that this is my fault. They think that I poisoned Ted."

Ruby put the towel down. It was tear- and mascara-stained and would need to go back in the wash.

"They don't," she said.

Jennifer held her daughter. "Yes, honey. They do."

"Why?"

Their embrace was short-lived. Jennifer stepped back and started to pace. "I don't know. Because of what happened to your dad, I guess. Maybe they are jealous. It could be anything. The people are so suspicious up here. I loved Teddy. He was my dream come true. Now that he's gone they are trying to turn it into something very ugly."

"You don't deserve this, Mom. What are you going to do? What are we going to do?"

"I don't know. I mean, I didn't do anything to Teddy. I loved him."

"I know, Mom. I know. What do you want me to do?"

"Nothing," Jennifer said. "There's nothing you can do."

"They aren't going to arrest you. Are they?"

Jennifer stopped moving about the small room and looked at her daughter, dead-eyed.

"No," she said. "I don't see how. I didn't do anything."

"Do you want me to talk to them? Tell them they are all wrong? That Molly next door could have poisoned him? She gave him that stupid cake. I got sick eating some of that. So did Micah."

Jennifer pondered that. "I don't think so. Molly is a stupid girl, but she's not a murderer. I can't think of any reason why she would want to hurt him."

"She was in love with him," Ruby said.

"Let me think. I don't know if I should get a lawyer or what."

"Why would you need a lawyer?"

"Honey, they are looking for someone to blame. I just talked to your aunt Stacy. She said that the detective called down there asking all kinds of inappropriate and cruel questions. Her friend who works at the sheriff's office told her. I just talked to Stacy right now."

Ruby's eyes widened. "About Daddy? Why are they asking about him, Mom?"

"I think they think I killed him," Jennifer said.

Lucerne poked her head into the dryer room. She looked concerned.

"What is it, Lu?" Ruby said. Her voice carried a snap.

"Sorry to bug you, Ruby and Ms. Roberts. I know you have a lot going on. But a sheriff's detective is here. She wants to talk to you."

"I'm not talking to her," Jennifer said. "I've said everything I'm going to say."

Lu shook her head. "Not you, Ms. Roberts. She's here for Ruby."

Kendall Stark had only been in a tanning salon once in her life. Three years prior she reluctantly agreed to be in her cousin's December wedding in Spokane. Someone suggested the hideous pale purple dress she'd been forced into wearing would look better if she had a little color added to her winter-white body. She ended up getting a spray tan that made her look like an orange and grape Popsicle.

Never again.

"Why are you harassing my family?" Jennifer said as she and Ruby faced Kendall in the lobby of Desert Enchantment.

"Lu, go fold some towels," Ruby said.

Lu, miffed about missing out on some family drama, left.

"I'm not harassing anyone, Ms. Roberts. I'm investigating the case."

"I want you to leave my family alone."

"Your daughter can talk to me," Kendall said. "She's free to do so."

"I don't—I *won't*—and neither will my brother," Ruby said. "We love our mother and you've got her all wrong. We loved our father. He was a good man and you are making this worse."

"Stepfather, Ruby," Kendall said. "He was your stepfather."

"He adopted us," Ruby said. "He loved us. We were a happy family."

The detective turned to Jennifer. "It would really

help the investigation if your daughter and son came in for a statement. It'll be all over the news tomorrow."

"What will?" she asked.

"That Ted Roberts was the victim of a homicide."

"Why are you putting that on the news?"

"I don't put anything on the news," Kendall said. "The *Kitsap Sun* has already talked to the coroner's office."

Ruby looked at her mother. "Mom, shouldn't Micah and I make some kind of statement?"

"Absolutely not. We have nothing to hide, but it's obvious that I'm being blamed for all of this. I know what you think. I still have friends in Arizona."

"Mom?" Ruby asked. "What's going on?"

Jennifer kept her eyes on Kendall. "She thinks I killed your father too."

Ruby's face went a shade darker on the spray-on tan scale. "He died of a heart attack, you bitch!" she said to Kendall.

Kendall took a step back. "Look, I know you're upset. I understand. But real life is messy. Things aren't always what they seem." She glanced at one of the posters. It showed a woman in a retro bikini standing at the edge of a pool, a forest of saguaro cactus marching into the background of a flawless blue sky. There was nary a wrinkle on her face, a bulge or ripple on her lithe figure. She noticed the sloppy edge of the Photoshopper's handiwork.

"No thing and no one is perfect," she said. "Mistakes can always be found."

CHAPTER 23

irdy Waterman was old school enough to get the daily paper delivered to her home. A copy was also delivered to the office. The top story had to do with the homecoming of a Trident submarine that had been out at sea for more than three months on some hush-hush mission. In a navy town like Bremerton, the editors at the paper knew the importance of those kinds of stories. In a way, Bremerton, Washington, *was* a company town. Its business had been either war or peacekeeping, depending on one's political perspective.

It was the second article that held her interest.

NAVAL OFFICER ROBERTS VICTIM OF POISONING

The *Kitsap Sun* reporter did a fair job with the piece, as he always did. He wrote how autopsy results indicated that the victim had died of acute kidney failure caused by ethylene glycol.

> Ethylene glycol is a key ingredient in antifreeze and unlike other poisons is readily

available in grocery and automotive stores throughout the county.

There were no quotes from Birdy, just some vague attribution—"according to the county's forensic pathologist."

That was just as well.

Kendall, however, did get a shout-out.

> "We have no suspects at this time," said Kitsap County homicide investigator Kendall Stark. "However, we are looking into a person of interest closely associated with the victim."

That designation was a favorite line of law enforcement. A person of interest was just a mere notch below "suspect" and was frequently used to apply a little pressure on the case. Not in a public relations way, but pressure on the perpetrator and those surrounding him or her. Sometimes the specter of being a *person of interest* accelerated the momentum of a case.

Sometimes people lived the rest of their lives as a person of interest.

With the information coming out of Arizona, it was possible that Jennifer Roberts had experienced both— or was about to.

Birdy flipped through the pages to the obituaries and funeral notices. Some people skipped right to the sports page, or the classifieds. Her go-to spot was always the section in which people were remembered. It was work-related, but not completely. Most who died were not autopsied. Even most of those who were, were examined in the hospitals in which they'd died. Birdy was fascinated by the continuum of the living process.

She always had been. She'd collected those bones. She'd attended more funerals than weddings. She sent sympathy cards to strangers when it looked like there were not many left to mourn their passing.

Tess Moreau had told her that her daughter's memorial would be that afternoon. And while she almost never went to anyone's funeral that had been a part of an ongoing case, she felt like Darby's would be a bit thin on the mourners' side because of the way she'd lived—isolated in that catastrophe of a household in Olalla. She looked at her phone.

11:45.

The service was at noon. Birdy grabbed purse and jacket. There was still time to get there.

No funeral is a happy occurrence. Really. Even when it is wrapped up with the words "celebration of life," there is seldom any genuine celebrating. Birdy Waterman parked her car in the lot at Sunset Lane Memorial Park at the bottom of Mile Hill Road. She wore her office attire that consisted of dark slacks and a plain blue jacket over a powder blue blouse. Her long dark hair was pulled back in her usual clip. She hadn't planned on going to a funeral that day, but it crossed her mind on the way there that she often dressed like she was ready for one.

From across the grassy expanse of markers and flags, she saw the small gathering that had assembled to memorialize the girl found in the woods off Banner

Road. A girl who'd been murdered by someone who was still at large was being laid to rest next to her father and her sister.

There had been no viewing for obvious reasons. This was Darby Moreau's good-bye.

Birdy spotted Tess and her friend Amanda, along with some adults she assumed were co-workers from the prison. Also there, a small group of teenagers—friends of the deceased—she assumed. A few adults stood with the kids and Birdy wondered if they were also from the school.

Just behind her, Birdy noticed Kendall approaching. She slowed her pace so they could walk together. They both had the same idea. Tess acknowledged them with a slight, but appreciative, nod.

The minister, a large round man with photosensitive glasses that obscured his eyes, spoke about Darby and her dreams, but he really could have been talking about any sixteen-year-old girl in the world.

"An unfinished life never seems like it is part of God's plan, but it is. Praise the Lord! Darby has gone home and she will always live there in the celestial kingdom, but also within all of us who knew and loved her."

He pressed a button on a small CD player and P!nk's song, *Glitter in the Air*, played at a respectful volume.

Darby's favorite color. Her favorite musician.

Tess let out a cry during the chorus and one of the teenagers went over to her.

"She was my best friend," Katie Lawrence said.

"Katie?" Tess asked. "I hoped you'd come. I didn't know how to call you."

"I'm here," she said. "A bunch of us are here from art class. She had a lot more friends at school than just us, and we had to get special permission to be here."

Tess gripped the girl's hand. She looked over at the kids and the teacher.

Like a switch, her face went from sad to anger. "Is she Ms. Mitchell?"

Kendall looked at Birdy. This was going to be trouble. Kendall wished the song were shorter.

Tess let go of Katie's hand and lurched toward the art teacher.

"I know who you are," the grieving mother said, her voice beginning to crack into tiny, bitter pieces. "I know *what* you are!"

Connie Mitchell took a step back, away from the casket.

"I was her friend, Ms. Moreau," she said over P!nk's soaring and heartfelt vocals. "I'm here because I loved her too."

Tess wasn't having any of that. "Your kind of love is sick. She was just a girl. You had no business getting involved with her!"

Kendall moved in and stood between the two women. "This is not the time or place," she said.

The song was over.

"I didn't do anything wrong," Connie said, now shattered into tears of her own. "I was only her friend." She looked at Kendall. "Tell her that!"

"Tess," Kendall said, "she's telling the truth."

Connie looked at the detective. "You said you wouldn't say anything. I trusted you."

Birdy wished she hadn't come.

"I didn't," Kendall said.

Katie looked around for some support, but there wasn't any. "*I* did. I'm sorry. I did. I just thought that—"

Connie spun around. "Katie, how could you? I've been in a domestic partnership for more than a year. Millicent and I are going to be married this summer. I'm not ashamed of that, but I'm ashamed of you." She turned to face Kendall. "I'm not a predator. You've ruined my life. How do you sleep at night?"

"Wait a minute," Kendall said. Everything about what was happening at Memorial Lane was wrong. Could not be more wrong. "Please not here."

Connie stood up straight. "I won't be silenced. I'm going to sue you and Kitsap County. If I lose my job over this, I'll sue the school district."

"Look, you're getting ahead of yourself. I didn't ruin your life. I believed you when you told me there was nothing to the rumor."

The rumor.

Katie let the floodgates open. Not tears for her friend. Not tears for Ms. Mitchell, but tears of regret.

"It's all my fault," she said, tears now streaming down her cheeks. "I'm sorry. I started the rumors. I did. I thought that Darby had a boyfriend and it made me so mad. I wanted to get even with her. She told me that she was spending time with you, but not in a bad way."

One of the art boys went over to Katie and put his arm around her.

"You didn't mean it," he said. "I know it."

The minister pushed a button and the casket slowly dipped into the hole, disappearing from view. Tess had brought a basket of Beanie Babies to let each person lay one on top, but no one did.

Tess just stood there, next to the hole. She looked over at the gravestones for her husband, her other daughter. She had nothing. No one to blame. No one to stab in the heart for doing what they did to her daughter.

No one. Not really. Only herself.

Amanda said something about having a small gathering at her house in Gig Harbor, but she understood that the drive was too far for most people to come.

"Tess appreciates everyone for being here," she said. "Darby is with the angels now." She stopped and looked to the minister for some kind of closing remarks, but the man just stood there like a memorial park statue. He might have been blinking in shock about all that had been going on around him, but with those dark glasses no one could tell.

As far as funerals go, the one for Darby Moreau was unforgettable for all of the wrong reasons. It was, most definitely, not a celebration of anything.

CHAPTER 24

Kendall Stark and other officers from the Kitsap County sheriff's office conducted a thorough search of the Roberts home on Camellia Street early the next morning. Ruby and Micah stood out in the front yard with their mother. None of Jennifer's haters on the block were there to watch the show. Lena and her husband had gone to Seaside, Oregon, to visit her sister. Molly O'Rourke was working at the convalescent center in Silverdale.

Molly more than anyone would regret that she hadn't called in sick.

"They aren't going to find anything," Jennifer said to her son and daughter. "Because there isn't anything."

The warrant Kendall had presented was specific. She was looking for the source of the poison that killed Ted Roberts. The judge who'd signed the warrant allowed the search in only a few specific areas—the kitchen, the garage, a shop—if any—and the bathrooms. The bedroom, living room, and the kids' bedrooms were considered out of scope.

"Can I at least get a coat?" Jennifer said when Deputy Gary Wilkins's blocky frame passed by.

"I'll ask," he said. "Hang on."

"Can my kids go to school?"

"I'll find out about that too," he said.

Minutes later, the deputy returned.

"Yes to both. Detective Stark says you can get a coat. I'll take the kids to South."

"I don't have my backpack," Micah said.

"I don't have my purse," his sister chimed in. "I have to have my keys. I have to close up the shop tonight. It's my job."

"All right. No harm in that."

Jennifer donned a stylish leather trench coat, then returned to the yard to watch the crime scene investigators—techs and deputies—emerge with boxes of household cleaning supplies, bottled water, food that had been stored in the refrigerator.

She hugged her daughter and son and admonished them not to worry.

"Truth is on my side," she said. "I've faced this before and they didn't beat me down."

Later, after depositing the Roberts teenagers at school, Deputy Wilkins approached Kendall. She was supervising the collection of items from the kitchen. He told her what he'd overheard earlier.

"She actually said, 'I've faced this before and they didn't beat me.' I think she was referring to the dead husband in Arizona."

"Don't worry about that, Gary," Kendall said. "She's not going to get away with this."

"What makes you so sure?" he asked.

"That." She pointed to one of the large plastic totes

that the team had brought in. Each had been filled with paper bags of evidence.

The young deputy looked confused and went over to peek inside. A flash of yellow caught his eye—a plastic bottle of antifreeze.

"That was in the house?" he asked.

Kendall nodded. "In the kitchen under the sink."

"She's going down," he said.

Kendall agreed. "Oh yeah, she is."

Kendall made a quick call to the sheriff and then went outside where Jennifer had been standing by her car. Kendall told the deputy to follow her, which he gladly did.

"Am I free to go?" Jennifer asked, looking completely put out in her nightgown, slippers, and winter coat. "I'm hungry."

Kendall kept her expression flat. Deep down, she loved this part of her job more than any, but she wasn't a gloater. She didn't see any need for that.

"They'll feed you where I'm taking you," she said with the tiniest trace of snark in her delivery. She just couldn't help it. Jennifer Roberts was the type of woman who just did that to other people. She was the type of woman who rubbed other women the wrong way. It wasn't her gorgeous looks, not really. It was that air of entitlement that seemed to come from every utterance from her perfect mouth.

Jennifer brightened a little. "Where?"

Kendall reached in her pocket and pulled out a card. "Jennifer Marie Roberts, you're under arrest for the murder of your husband, Ted Roberts."

"I didn't do it," Jennifer said.

Kendall started reading. It was standard procedure to make sure that no defendant could ever say that their rights were violated because the arresting deputy had made a mistake on Miranda. Kendall read it word by word, instead of a more conversational fluid fashion.

"You have the right to remain silent . . ."

As the deputy cuffed Jennifer, she wriggled a little. "Steady," he said, leading her to the open door of a cruiser.

"I don't need a lawyer," Jennifer said. "I'm innocent. You are so wrong about me, detective."

Kendall didn't answer. Instead, she turned to another deputy.

"Pick up her kids, Ruby and Micah, from South Kitsap High. I'll be back at my office. I want them to be together in the car, but separated when you arrive. Let's see what they know about their mother's activities."

"You think the kids know something?" he asked.

"The girl does. She hates her mom. She sees her as competition. I got a whiff of that at Desert Enchantment where she works. She'll crack."

While the cars and the bins and bags of evidence filed past Kendall as she stood in the Robertses' front yard, she phoned Birdy at the coroner's office.

"How'd it go?" Birdy asked right away.

"Better than hoped," Kendall said. "She's halfway to booking now."

"What'd you find?"

"A jug of Prestone in the kitchen. Under the sink like some big yellow warning sign on a highway somewhere. Couldn't miss it."

"That's pretty careless, Kendall."

"No one said she was a criminal mastermind. She's no Brenda Nevins."

"Most of them aren't."

"When are you leaving for Arizona?"

"Tomorrow."

"Lucky you. You'll get some sun. I wish I could go. The county's too cheap to send us both."

"Right. And in case you haven't noticed I'm already tan, Kendall."

"Sorry. I wish I tanned."

"You could always go to Desert Enchantment, Kendall."

"Hey, speaking of which, Ruby and Micah are coming in for some questioning. Want to observe?"

"You bet I do," Birdy said before switching the subject. "I have a favor to ask. A personal one."

"What do you need?" Kendall asked.

"Can you look in on Elan?"

"You're only going to be gone two days."

"I know," she said.

Kendall smiled at the thought of her friend doing a little mothering. It was good for her to have someone to worry about—someone she loved and, more than anything, was alive.

Even so she teased her a little.

"He's sixteen, Birdy. He can handle it. Honestly, how old were you when your parents left you and your sister alone?"

Birdy knew that Kendall was right, even so she felt compelled to give her friend a glimpse into her life— something she seldom did.

"Not a fair comparison," she said. "My dad was on a fishing boat in Alaska and my mom was, or rather *is*, an alcoholic. I don't remember a time when we weren't left alone."

Gary motioned to Kendall that the evidence had been collected and the house was sealed.

"Gotta go," Kendall said, hanging up.

Birdy put down the phone and went to the kitchen for some more terrible coffee. Not that she needed a jolt of caffeine. Talking about growing up on the reservation—something she tried to avoid—had got her to thinking. And thinking meant pacing.

Even years later, the memories still hurt.

Birdy looked down at the stack of magazines that had been there forever like dental office rejects.

On the cover of *People* magazine was an inset photograph of Brenda Nevins with the headline:

FATAL BEAUTY CLAIMS
ABUSE IN PRISON

Boy, Brenda, that must have made you mad when Kelly Clarkson got the cover? Birdy thought.

She smiled at the thought and poured some coffee.

CHAPTER 25

With their mother in booking at the Kitsap County jail, Ruby and Micah were led into separate interview rooms in a kind of divide-and-conquer technique that investigators employed when talking to witnesses who might lie in order to protect each other or another family member. Jennifer's children were in a bind. They had no other family in the area. Their stepfather was dead. And, of course, their mother was in custody. Teenagers, in general, hate any kind of inconvenience. This was very, very inconvenient.

Family ties were frequently like steel at first, but in time, Kendall Stark and other cops knew that steel could rust, then crumble.

"What do you want me to do?" Birdy asked as she looked in through the two-way mirror that separated Micah's room from the hall. His sister's room had no such window. Micah laid his head on his folded arms on top of the table. The teenager was either very tired, or completely distraught. He might have just been bored.

"You'll tell the kids what the autopsy results were.

You're free to answer their questions, of course. Be yourself," Kendall said, opening the door and leading Birdy inside.

Micah lifted his head right away. "I'm thirsty," he said.

Kendall introduced herself and Birdy.

"I'll get you something in a moment. Let's go over a few details first." She and Kendall sat facing the boy, who leaned back as he verified his age, address, and who his mother was.

"You keep calling me Micah Roberts. That's really not my name. My last name is Lake. Just wanted you to know that. Ted never adopted me or my sister. It was my mom's idea to use his name."

"Why didn't he adopt you?" Kendall asked. "Was there a reason for that?"

The boy seemed uncertain, picking at his words. "Not really. I mean, my mom always rushed things. I think he would have adopted me and Ruby. He was a cool guy."

"You got along with him?" Kendall asked.

Micah jangled his house keys, picking at each one with his fingertips while Kendall spoke. "Yeah."

"Your mom too? She got along with him?"

He folded his arms across his chest and sat there silently.

"Was something going on with your mom and step-father?"

He put the keys in his pocket. "Ruby said you'd try to blame Mom. My mom loved Ted. I know you don't think she did. But you're wrong about her." His eyes puddled a little and he looked away. There was no way that kid was going to cry in front of two women.

Not in a zillion years.

"Look," Kendall said. "I know this is hard. You've been through a lot. I understand."

"You couldn't understand," he said. "This was our mom's big 'let's start over' move away from Arizona and all the crap down there. I didn't want to come. Ruby didn't want to come. Mom told us that if we didn't like it we could go back. But we liked it. At least I did. Ruby hated the cold weather here."

The boy was struggling and Birdy's heart went out to him. In some ways, he reminded her of Elan and how he'd just transplanted himself in a new environment, a new school. No kid likes to start over.

"I'm sure it was quite a change," she said. "It takes some getting used to."

Micah rubbed his eyes with his sleeve.

"Let's talk about the morning Ted died."

Micah pulled himself together. "Wow," he said. "That's hard. I was asleep. I didn't even know what had happened until my sister came and woke me."

"When was that, do you know what time?" Kendall asked.

"I didn't look at the clock. I didn't get out of bed. Ted was always puking and I just didn't care."

"Was it nighttime or morning?"

"I don't know. Still dark. But it seems like it is always dark here."

"You didn't get up, though. Is that because you didn't like him?"

He shook his head. "I told you *I* did."

"Right, but you didn't get up when he was in trouble."

"I didn't get up because I thought it was more of the same. I didn't think he was dead or dying."

"All right," Kendall said.

"I'm thirsty," he said. "My mouth feels like it's full of cotton balls."

Kendall stood. "Let me get you a drink. We have a pop machine down the hall."

"Mountain Dew?" he asked, suddenly happy at the prospect of getting something to drink.

"Sorry. Coke all right?"

He shrugged. "Yeah, I guess. Thanks."

Kendall went out and disappeared down the hall.

"I know you're going through a lot, Micah," Birdy said. "I'm sorry. So is the detective."

"She doesn't seem sorry. She's blaming my mom for everything. You know, my mom isn't as bad as you guys make her out to be," he said.

Birdy shifted in her chair. "Poisoning someone is a pretty serious crime."

"She didn't do it. She's not like that."

"If she didn't, then someone else did."

"He was depressed. He was sick. He wasn't getting any better. He told me one time that he knew that every one of us would be better off without him."

Kendall returned with a can of Diet Coke.

"Sorry," she said. "No *real* Coke."

Micah took the can and flipped the top. "It's okay. Better than nothing."

"Why didn't you get up?" Kendall asked. "The night your stepfather died. I don't understand."

He swallowed his drink in a big gulp. "Look, it isn't nice to say so, but the truth was he was always puking. Ted was a drunk. I didn't see any need. I just wanted to get some sleep."

There was callousness to his words, beyond what

was said. How he said it. The kid didn't really care at all.

"So he died at night," Kendall said. "Your stepfather. It wasn't in the morning, was it?"

Micah just sat there. "I don't know when he died. Can I go back to school now?"

A few minutes later, both the forensic pathologist and the detective took seats in the small interview room where Ruby Lake had spilled the contents of her purse to pass the time. She'd sorted her cosmetics and was in the middle of texting and scrolling through her Facebook account—looking every bit the teenage dream that she most undeniably was. She was pretty like her mother. Maybe prettier. Her teeth were blindingly white—a service the tanning salon offered on its upsell chart. Her lightly tanned skin amplified the brightness of her smile, the blue of her eyes. Her hair was long, blond and streaked, as though the sun had done its job.

"I know why I'm here," she said, looking up after hitting the SEND button.

"Right," Kendall said after introducing Birdy. "Because your stepfather died of poisoning and we're investigating the case as a homicide."

"Whatever," she said.

"And you know that your mother has been arrested," Kendall said.

She didn't answer. She looked down at her phone.

"I need you to put that away," Kendall said.

Ruby sighed. "I thought this was a free country."

"It is," Kendall said, "but I need you to focus on what we're doing here. Not on your phone."

Ruby rolled her eyes upward. "I didn't mean *that*. I meant charging my mom for murder. That's what. Like you have just railroaded her like she's guilty because he's dead and she's married to him."

"You're half right. He is dead and she was married to him. But he died of poisoning."

Birdy spoke up. "That's right, Ruby. Your stepfather had been poisoned by doses of ethylene glycol over a period of time."

"My mom wouldn't even know how to pronounce that, let alone poison him with it."

"It's in antifreeze," Birdy said. "It's used to keep cars running in the winter."

"We're from Arizona. I doubt my mom's ever heard of it. And besides, if anyone killed my dad it was that bitch Molly next door. That's who."

"You mean Molly O'Rourke?" Kendall asked. "What has she got to do with this?"

Ruby looked back at her phone, but then slipped it into her purse. She scooped up the rest of the stuff that had occupied her time while she was waiting for the interview.

"She hated that Mom married Ted," she finally said. "I don't like throwing shade on anyone. So you should ask her. She wanted him for herself. She acts all nice, but I've seen that kind of girl down at the salon. They think the world owes them something and when they don't get it, they do the crazy."

"Your stepfather died because he was poisoned," Birdy said. "How would Molly poison him?"

Ruby fiddled with the back of an earring. "Look, you don't get it. Do you? She was always bringing stuff over. Cake. Cookies. She made a big show of it. Always acting like she cared so much for Ted, but my mom knew what she was all about."

"Seems like both you and your mother are acute judges of character," Kendall said.

Ruby held her ground. "We're not stupid if that's what you mean."

"No one is saying that. It's just that I find it hard to believe that your neighbor had the kind of access to your house to poison your stepfather."

"She had a key."

"She did?"

"Yeah. Ted gave her one long before we moved up here. He had some fern that needed watering whenever he was away doing whatever he did for the navy. Secret shit. Molly came over all the time."

"You don't like Molly very much, do you?" Birdy cut in.

In a change in emotion that surprised both the women, Ruby started to cry. She'd been tough. She wasn't going to let anyone push her around. The mask that she wore to be cool, detached, had shattered.

"I don't like that you're blaming my mom for something she didn't do. My mom has made some mistakes in her life—like we never should have moved up here—but she's not a bad person. She's had some really hard times and now you're blaming her for something she didn't do. I think it sucks. I think both of you suck."

Kendall ignored the last comment.

"Do you have any relatives here?" she asked. "You and your brother are underage. We need to make arrangements for either a family member or CPS to take you in."

Ruby shook her head. "I'm eighteen. At least I will be next week."

Kendall looked down at the report. Ruby was turning eighteen the following week. Maybe she wouldn't have to involve Child Protective Services. In a way, that brought a little relief. Kendall hated splitting up family members who had already suffered the trauma of a homicide, an arrest, and the media coverage that made life harder than those who'd never been in the center of a murder investigation could possibly understand.

"I'll see what I can do, pending your mother's release. If she makes bond."

Ruby met the detective's gaze straight on. "We don't have any money."

"The Red Cross can help," Birdy said.

The girl ignored Birdy. "We'll manage somehow," she said. "We've been through crap before."

"We're going to need to get your fingerprints, Ruby."

Ruby pushed back from the table. "Why? I didn't have anything to do with this."

"We need them for exclusionary purposes. We know you lived there and it is likely that your prints are all over everything. We have to match your prints so that we can identify which ones belong there, and which ones don't."

Ruby sighed. "My mom lived there too. Her prints. Micah's prints. We're all over the place. So what if they are on your evidence?"

"I understand it's confusing and difficult."

"You should be getting Molly's prints," Ruby said.

"That's who. If there's some poison in the house at all you should look for hers on the bottle."

"We'll do just that," Kendall said.

Ruby got up. She'd had enough. "Where's my brother?"

"He's done," Birdy said. "He's waiting for you."

Kendall opened the door and Ruby went out first.

"When can we see our mom?" she asked, as they walked down the hall toward the reception area where Micah was waiting.

"She's still being processed," Kendall said. "She'll be arraigned this afternoon."

"She doesn't have a lawyer."

"We'll get her one."

"She's innocent. She really is."

"I know you believe that," Kendall said. "But we've already found her fingerprints on the poison."

Micah stood and went toward his sister, but the two didn't embrace.

"Ruby, are you okay?"

"Yeah," she said. "I told them about Molly. They'll see. They've made a big mistake."

The next morning, Birdy texted Elan's phone number to Kendall and got on an airplane for Phoenix's Sky Harbor airport. She smiled at the idea of the name, that a landlocked region could have a harbor. She'd grown up all around water. It was everywhere. As she sipped coffee and nibbled on a bagel she bought from the airplane's food cart, she thought of all the stories of regret that had come her way. Molly felt regret for not saving Ted. Tess was full of remorse and regret for not doing more to confront her tormenter, Brenda Nevins. Even Jennifer expressed regret for letting Ted's sickness progress to his demise.

All were sorry for something.

And yet, she knew that one of them was twice as sorry—the one who brought her to Arizona and an exhumation.

Sorry she killed twice.

CHAPTER 26

Birdy Waterman perched herself on a barstool at the Pinnacle Peak Hotel's restaurant, Proof Canteen. There was room outside on the terrace, but the heat of day kept her close to the AC. On the drive from the airport and to her destination off East Crescent Moon Drive, she marveled at the landscape that she'd only seen once before—at the Big Thunder Mountain Railway attraction in Disneyland when her family went there the year before her father, Mackie, died. Back then the images of the Southwest were as fake to her as that Disneyland ride. She'd grown up in the Pacific Northwest, all green, drippy, and mossy. The very concept of a landscape of wind-worn red rock boulders and the sentinels of saguaro seemed almost too foreign, too fantastic to be factual.

It was real. The splendor of the desert was all around her.

She sipped a glass of Oak Creek Amber Ale and ordered the chicken and waffles—because in all her life she'd never had the opportunity to have the dish that sounded like half breakfast and half dinner, but not brunchy at all. It came with a bourbon syrup and bacon brittle that tasted sublime with the crispy-skinned chicken.

"Not exactly diet food," she said to a server, who hovered nearby. It was late and she was the only patron. A couple—newlyweds probably—nuzzled next to a mesquite-fueled chimera outside as the sunset poured pink and orange over Pinnacle Peak.

"Nope. But you're on vacation. Live a little."

"Not hardly," Birdy said. "Here for work."

The server, a handsome man in his fifties, nodded and smiled. "Me too. What's your line?"

Birdy didn't often tell strangers what she did for a living. Some people reacted with affected horror and it was embarrassing. But the bar was quiet and she didn't see the harm.

"The case I'm working on," she said, picking at the smoky and sweet brittle, "involved one of the people who used to work here."

"I've been here a long time," he said. "What's his name?"

"Oh not the victim. The person we have locked up in Washington is a woman."

He sat down. "That's something. Who is she?"

"Jennifer Roberts."

He scanned his memory.

"Doesn't ring a bell."

"Jennifer Lake. That was her name when she lived down here."

The man stood up. "No shit? Jenny Lake?"

Birdy's eyes widened a little. "You know her?"

"*Know* her? Hell, I dated her. Half the guys who worked here did. And the other half were gay. If you get my meaning."

"I guess I do," she said.

"It wasn't that she was a slut, though she was pretty good at what she did. She was kind of a sad girl, really."

"Oh? I don't understand."

"She was always looking for Mr. Right. She kept getting Mr. Right Now. Girls who try too hard sometimes aren't able to get the job done."

"She wasn't a prostitute or anything?" Birdy asked, the thought just popping into her head as the beer left her a little looser than she liked.

He looked around. "Hell no. This isn't that kind of place. She wasn't that kind of a girl. I mean she was easy on the eyes always wearing her favorite color pink. She called it 'Sugar Bowl Pink' after that ice cream in Old Town. She was easy in every way possible, but she just couldn't close the deal. Not until she married Don Lake."

"Did you know him too?" She looked at his nametag and added a quick, "Eddie?"

He noticed how she'd seen his nametag and he hated how people were so familiar with others because of a piece of plastic affixed to a uniform.

"Yeah," he said. "Don ran our catering for a while. Got fired though."

"Why was that?"

"He was doing jobs on the side. He was doing really well too. Probably a good thing he got fired because then he got his ass in gear and opened a place of his own. Big success too. The Brass Cactus was a moneymaker. Jenny worked up front. Had a couple of kids. And then, poof, like snow in the Sonoran it was gone."

"What happened?"

"He died. Simple as that. He had a heart attack on

the links at Troon. She sold the restaurant. After that, I don't know what she did. I thought I heard she got married, but don't think that lasted too long. Anyway she had a big place over by the mountain. Never saw her again."

He pointed to her beer glass but she shook her head.

"You can't fly on one wing," he said.

"Got to drive to my hotel," she said.

"You're not staying here?"

Birdy smiled. "You kidding? I'm a county employee. I'm staying at a little place down the road called the Comfort Inn."

He grinned back knowingly. "Luxury at an affordable rate."

"That's right."

"So what's Jenny in jail for up in your neck of the woods?"

"Murder," Birdy said. "Her husband was killed."

Eddie smirked a little. "Playing golf?"

Birdy opened her purse and retrieved her wallet. "Nope. He'd been ill. He was poisoned. Google it when I leave. There have been a few stories in the paper up there. Roberts is her last name. Husband was Ted."

She gave him her county Visa card.

"You know Don Lake's twin brother lives here in Scottsdale," Eddie said. "He hated her. You ought to give him a call. Might help with what you're doing."

"Thanks," she said. "I'm not really that kind of investigator. Remember, I deal mostly with dead people."

She looked down to sign the bill that he'd coiled neatly in a jelly jar, a charming nod to the western theme of the restaurant and bar.

Across the top of the slip, the server had written a phone number and a name—Dan Lake.

Birdy surveyed her room at the Comfort Inn. It was clean, but hardly luxurious. A tired painting of a Navajo woman holding a water jar hung over the bedspread with a faded chevron design. She turned up the AC and phoned Elan.

"You all right?" she asked.

"Yeah," he said. "I'm having pizza tonight because someone assumes that's all I'll eat."

"Someone is sorry about that," she said, vowing not to mention that she had chicken and waffles and bacon brittle. That would rub it in too, too much.

"Hey, Aunt Birdy, the 'S' has really hit the fan at school. My friend Micah told me about how you arrested his mom and then questioned him and his sister about the murder of his dad."

Birdy sat on the edge of the bed. "Stepdad," she said. "I didn't arrest her. Kendall did. I didn't know you knew those two."

"He's new," Elan said. "I'm new. We've hung out a few times. I don't know him, but when he found out you're my aunt he really laid into me about what a bitch you and Kendall were."

She kicked off her shoes. "Actually, I thought we were pretty nice."

"I kind of told him that. I mean, I know that you are a really good person."

"Wow," she said. "Are you trying to make me cry?"

"Nope. But I just wanted you to know I have your back."

Birdy was touched by the sweetness in her nephew's voice. It wasn't out of her head that he was still dealing with something back in Neah Bay and she needed to get to the bottom of it. But that would have to be later.

"Me too, Elan," she said. "I'm on your team too."

"All right," he said. "Have fun down there digging up the dead guy."

Birdy smiled. "You know I will."

The TV in the women's section of the Kitsap County jail almost never knew a time of day when it wasn't playing some talk show. Such shows provided comfort and solidarity. Most were about how rotten men had been to the women in their lives. Many of the inmates sat there bobbing their heads in unison as some cad tried to sweet-talk his girlfriend or wife.

"Heard that before," one gal from Sunnyslope said. "My old man cheated on me, big time. And I fell for it. Hook, line, and sinker, that's me."

"Yeah, we should be out on a fishing boat, you and me," said the other, a woman arrested in Bremerton for soliciting a police officer.

Jennifer Roberts wasn't like the other two women in the TV room. She could have been. She probably started in the same place—born in a family with little means. A childhood of ups and downs, mostly downs. Yet, she got out of there. She climbed out of the gutter and made something of herself.

She owed it all to a movie she'd seen when she was ten years old. She'd seen a mention of the film on the TV guide section of the *Kitsap Sun* and made a note not to miss it.

"You gals mind if we turn the channel?" she asked, breezing into the room. "There's a movie on that I really want to watch."

"Can't it wait? We're about to find out if this slut has picked the right guy as the father of her baby or if she's going to have another paternity test done."

"Yeah, like number four," Sunnyslope said.

"Please," Jennifer said. "I just have to see this movie."

The first woman looked at the other. Jennifer Roberts was completely irritating, but she was interesting and they relented.

"Thanks," she said. She picked up the remote and flipped it to the movie channel showing *An Officer and a Gentleman*.

It was her second favorite scene. Her favorite, of course, was when Zack Mayo played by Richard Gere carried Paula Pokrifki played by Debra Winger in his arms in his dress whites. This was the scene where Paula stood her ground. She still wanted her man, but not at any price. She wasn't some dumb whore. She was trying to be a comfort to him. To show him love. That he was worth it—and by extension both of them were.

Sunnyslope looked over at Jennifer.

"Did you find your officer?"

Jennifer nodded. "Yes, that's why I moved up here to Washington."

"Then why'd you off him?" Sunnyslope asked.

"I didn't," Jennifer said. "I didn't do it."

"Yeah," the other woman said, "and I didn't offer a cop a blow job."

CHAPTER 27

In her small office, Kendall Stark looked at the lab report and did a double take. From the black plastic garbage bag that had held Darby Moreau's body, the techs had been able to retrieve multiple latent prints, though none of them were of the quality to offer any evidentiary value. They were what the lab tech called "smeary" and "blurred out."

Only one, a palm print, seemed to hold enough of its imagery to match anything—that presuming there were any in CODIS that matched it. Palm prints were not as common. Some jurisdictions only started pulling palms in the past five years. Government entities were among the first to take the full palm print as a standard practice.

It was a good thing they did.

Kendall looked down at the name. It sent her pulse racing. *Could it be?*

The detective typed in the name *Millicent Carlyle* and scanned the database. She had to call Birdy. She had to tell the sheriff. Two things came at her like a kettle of boiling water splashed in her face. Millicent had worked as a corrections officer at Purdy, but no longer.

Her current place of employment? Kendall scrolled down the page.

There it was.

Carlyle was listed as an employee of the South Kitsap School District assigned to South Kitsap High School.

Tess was right. Darby's mom was right!

It was after hours, so Kendall dialed the assistant vice principal at home.

"Stacy, this is Kendall Stark of the sheriff's office. Sorry to bother you at home. Just doing some routine checking."

"At this hour? Jeesh, detective, I thought my job was bad. What's up?"

"Sorry. I lost track of the time. Millicent Carlyle. Is she employed there?"

"She's looking for a new job?"

"Can't say," Kendall said. "What does she teach?"

Stacy laughed a little. "She's not a teacher at South. She's our lead custodian. And if the sheriff is looking for a new one for your office, he's going to have to arm-wrestle the principal to get her away from us. Millicent is the best we've ever had. She's more reliable than the crew of misfits we've had around here. She's a real peach. She keeps everything shipshape. She was in the navy."

As they talked, Kendall pulled up the DMV photo of Millicent. She was an attractive woman with soft brown eyes and a flattering short, asymmetrical haircut. She wasn't a model, but she wasn't scary either.

"Yes, I know," Kendall said.

"She worked at the prison too," Stacy went on. "I think it sort of helps her do her job around the school in a kind of not so ironic way. The kids here think they're in prison. Bitch and moan they do. Can't have cell phones on campus. Can't smoke. Have to go to every class to get at least a C. They don't know that this is the easiest part of their lives, not the most difficult."

"I get what you're saying, Stacy," Kendall said, adding a quick "keep this on the QT, will you?"

Stacy sighed. "Everything's confidential these days."

"Have a good evening, Stacy. Thanks."

Birdy Waterman looked down at the picture of the deceased and waited for Don Lake's twin brother to come into the Starbucks at Ashler Hills in Scottsdale. Daniel Lake had told her to meet him there at 7 a.m.. It was early and the temperature was already closing in on eighty degrees. The weatherman had said there might be a thundershower later in the afternoon, but Birdy couldn't see how that prediction could be any-where near possible. There wasn't a speck of a cloud in the sky.

The drive to the Starbucks had been as lovely as any she'd ever made. The saguaros were in bloom. Those with a crown of blooms looked like they were figures wearing headdresses of flowers, like the girls had worn on May Day or at a wedding she once attended on the beach. One specimen looked like it was flipping off the speeding drivers in their showroom-worthy BMWs, Mercedes, and some foreign cars that the forensic pathologist couldn't identify as anything other than out of her budget forever. From its landscape to the interests of its well-heeled residents, Scottsdale was like a for-eign land. Birdy had picked up a travel magazine at the airport and read it before bed. It was a salute to mothers of the regions. They looked like no mothers she'd ever seen before. They posed provocatively in designer clothes and burbled about the rigors of shopping and eating out. One complained that it was difficult being the prettiest one at her club, but she faced the jealousy with the help of a therapist.

Near the end of each profile, one of the women mentioned she adored her children too.

Birdy wasn't dressed like a tourist. She wore a light blue suit and heels and carried her best handbag, a Marc Jacobs that she purchased online for half price. It was large enough to carry a few of the tools of the trade that she'd need for the exhumation that morning. She sipped her latte and looked at her phone. She thought of calling Elan to see how he was doing, but she thought better of it. He was, after all, sixteen as Kendall had rightly pointed out. He'd be just fine.

Right on time, Daniel Lake, wearing khaki shorts, a Tommy Bahama shirt, and flip-flops, came into the coffee shop.

Their eyes met and it must have been painfully obvious she was the out-of-towner, despite her fancy bag. All the other early birds—a term she despised for obvious reasons—were tan, bleached, whitened, and lipo-ed to perfection. He waved and indicated that he needed something to drink. She looked down at the photo. Yes, like he'd said on the phone, they were indeed identical twins. Daniel was more than a decade older now, but in the old Arizona DMV photo of Jennifer's first husband that she brought with her along with the original autopsy report, it looked as though Donald had come out of the grave.

Which was exactly what he was going to do later that morning.

"I know you're going to dig my brother up and frankly, I'm not unhappy about it," he said, sitting at her wobbly table. "Not in the least."

Birdy introduced herself and put out her hand, which he accepted.

"I'm sorry about putting your family through this," she said.

He waved her concerns away. When he moved, she noticed a slender gold chain nestled in his silver cholla chest hair.

"Hey, like I said I'm really glad. My mom, not so much. But she's old and sick and it doesn't matter what she thinks anymore. She actually liked Jenny. I forgive her for that because, well, she's my mom."

Daniel Lake was instantly likable.

"I take it that you feel a little differently?" she asked.

He toyed with the plastic lid on his cup, before removing it and sipping his coffee.

"There's no point in lying. I'm a straight shooter, Doctor. Always have been. I told my brother she was trailer trash from Gila County and she might have been a fine piece of ass, but she'd ruin him."

"That's a little harsh, don't you think?"

He shrugged his broad shoulders. He, like all the others in the magazine she'd read, worked out.

"Which part? Piece of ass? Trailer trash?"

"Either. Both, I guess."

"Actually, funny thing, Don and I grew up trailer trash too. Dad worked for the forest service and did a little mining. We never did have much except a dream

to get out of Star Valley and make something of our-
selves. Don made it in a big way with his catering business and his restaurant. It makes me sick that that bitch
pissed it all away after he died. Couldn't hang on to a
dollar if you duct taped it to her fake boobs."

Birdy really liked Dan. He wasn't careful. He just
said what was on his mind.

"You don't hold back, do you?"

The man raised a shoulder and let out a laugh. "I
read the articles up there in Washington. Everyone
from Gila County who knew my brother has read them
too. I know what Jenny did up there and I'm pretty sure
she did it down here too. I thought so at the time. Not
poisoning, but something."

Birdy picked at the cinnamon scone she'd purchased
with her latte. She wasn't hungry, but nervous about
the day ahead. She thought having something in her
stomach would calm her a little.

"Talk to me about your brother's marriage," she
said. "What was going on with him and Jennifer at the
time he died?"

"A lot," he said. "That's what. I need another cup of
joe. Hang on."

Dan got up and placed an order, chatting with the
barista like he knew her. He might have. Or it might
have been his personality. The guy liked to talk and
that was a very good thing.

When he came back he gave Birdy what he called
"the unvarnished" truth about what he'd observed during the course of his late brother's courtship and marriage. He talked about how Jennifer had set her trap at
the hotel and that Dan was the only one dumb enough
to fall for it.

"Look, the irony is that she was a gold-digger, but she hitched her wagon to a catering guy. That's a dumb gamble. Catering? Anyway, I'll give her a little credit for pushing him in the right direction, but hell, he would have gotten there eventually on his own. He wasn't dumb. And he was pretty handsome too."

He waited for a response to his attempt at a punch line, but she said nothing

"Twin joke," he said. "You're supposed to laugh."

"I'm sorry," she said. "I get it."

"Your job or your personality?"

"Huh?" she asked.

"You're wound up a little tight."

Birdy knew he was right. "Probably a little of both. Doing an exhumation is about my least favorite thing in a job that has more than its share of negatives."

"Yeah, then why'd you pick it?"

The forensic pathologist was taken aback a little. No one had asked that question in a long time. Her standard answer up till then had always been because she wanted to help people who couldn't help themselves. Those who didn't have a voice. Yet after doing it for so many years, she doubted that motive or at least how it sounded to others.

"It's the kind of job that picks you," she said. "You don't pick it."

"Like a minister or something?" he asked.

"Something like that."

They talked some more about how Don had been so happy when Ruby was born, and then Micah.

"She let my brother name the kids. We're rock hounds. Coming from Gila County, there isn't a whole lot to do but look for rocks."

"He was happy then," she said.

"Yeah then."

She looked down at the photo. "And then what?"

The wistful smile faded from Dan's face. He was handsome, like his brother had been. The sun had weathered his face over the years, but the deep creases looked good on him. His eyes were faded denim blue and his hair had silvered a little.

"Jenny starting running around again, that's what. He told me that she was stepping out on him and that he was going to divorce her and get custody of the kids. Told me that she was probably entitled to half the business and that getting rid of her would be worth it."

"Except for the custody issue, what would be so awful about that? For Jenny?"

He finished his second cup. "You should have figured that out by now, considering what she's done up there."

She wondered if he was going to get another cup, but he didn't. "I guess so," she said. "But tell me what made you so sure?"

"One time I was over there and she was drunk and you know what she told me? She thought that I was my brother. You know what she said?" he asked, shaking his head. "You won't believe it. I told the sheriff. But he didn't do a damned thing about it."

Birdy leaned in. This had to be good.

"She said, 'I'm going to kill you one day. No one will know how, but I'm going to do it just when you least expect it.' "

"That's a pretty scary threat," Birdy said, steadying the wobbly table.

"It was a goddamn promise. Dr. Waterman, get this.

It gets even better. It happened two weeks later. Donny hadn't been feeling well for a while and finally when he got better he went out with his buddies golfing at Troon. And bam, he has a heart attack! He died right there on the golf course."

"I saw the autopsy report, Dan. He *did* have a heart attack."

Dan stood up. "Maybe. Maybe not. But I know something you don't know, I bet."

"What's that?"

"She was doing the doctor who did Donny's autopsy."

Birdy was surprised. She didn't even try to hide it. "No," she said.

"Sure as shit she was," he said, stepping away. "Hold on to that thought. I got to use the bathroom. I had two cups before I got here. My eyes are going to turn brown."

He disappeared into the restroom.

While he was away, Birdy pulled the autopsy report from her purse and scanned it for the umpteenth time. When he died, Donald Lake was forty-two. He'd had no history of heart trouble. The notes indicated that it had been an extremely hot day, more than one hundred degrees. Birdy wondered who in their right mind would golf in that kind of weather. But she put that out of her mind. This was a strange land, with strange people.

Dan returned to the table, this time with a bottle of water. A smart move, she thought. She noticed that the table was no longer wobbling. The restroom break had helped. He started talking right where he left off. Dan Lake didn't need a prompt. It was like he'd held a fingertip to a passage he'd been reading and was ready to keep going.

"I confronted the doc a few months later when I found out they'd gotten together, but he denied and denied. Some chump. You know what he did?"

Birdy shook her head. "I have a feeling you're going to tell me."

"Get this. He *married* her. He married her in Las Vegas."

She could scarcely believe her ears. "You have no reason to kid me, but really?"

He gave her a knowing look. "It lasted about as long as most of those marriages over there. That doctor divorced her in six months. Never heard why. Haven't seen him since. He lives around here though."

"Someone should talk to him," Birdy said.

"Yes you should," he said. "And I'll make it easy on you."

"How's that, Mr. Lake?"

He got out his wallet and handed her one of his business cards. Like his brother, he was in the restaurant business too. Birdy looked confused.

"Look on the other side," he said.

She turned it over. It held the name and address for Bobby Drysdale.

"I don't have his number, but it's not far from the cemetery. After you dig up my brother maybe you can dig up something with the old doctor."

She smiled. "Another joke, right?"

Dan grinned back at her. "You really do need to lighten up."

She got up. "It's kind of hard, considering what I

have to do now. But I'll try. Thank you for helping me. You'll be sure to know if I find anything."

"Doctor, do me a favor."

"Of course. If I can."

"Tell Ruby and Micah that their grandma misses them. Hasn't seen them in way too long. Would mean an awful lot to the old bird. Might keep her around a while longer. Losing your son is hard, but you've probably seen a lot of that in your line of work."

Birdy couldn't deny that she had.

"I'll deliver the message personally," she said.

"Oh, and one more thing," he said. "Call me Danny. Everyone does."

Birdy watched Danny Lake leave and get into his Mercedes convertible. He revved the engine and pulled away.

She noticed his license plate. It matched the name of the restaurant that had been on his card: DONDANS.

Birdy sat there for a few more minutes, looking at the autopsy report and the printout of the directions she'd made in the Comfort Inn's tiny business center that morning. She was expected at the cemetery at ten. She dialed Kendall, but it went to voice mail.

"Nothing really earth-shattering, but Donald Lake's twin brother thinks that Jennifer killed Donald. That's not really news. What is interesting is that Jennifer—who everyone down here calls Jenny—actually married the doctor who conducted Donald's autopsy. You heard right. That marriage, however, was very short-lived too. With one big difference. That one is still alive. I have his address and if I have time I'm curious enough to pay him a visit. Let me know if you think that's out of line, helpful, whatever. I'm not a cop, but I think I can handle the interview. If I get to meet him, that is. Anyway if you're still listening to this rambling message its eighty-five degrees down here and I'm about to dig up a dead body. Jealous? Thought so."

CHAPTER 28

The cemetery on Pinnacle Peak Road was the veritable oasis in the desert. Its verdant acreage swathed the top of a lumpy landscape like a green velvet coverlet on a grandmother's old feather bed. A family of bobwhite quail cut in front of Birdy as she walked toward the front door of the Welcome Center. It was proudly named, but looked like one of the dozens of taupe, tan, and cream-colored adobe-style mansions that hugged the base of the peak dominating the terrain. The funeral director, a deputy from the Maricopa County sheriff's department, and the cemetery administrator waited inside.

"I hope I'm not late," she said, introducing herself and providing a duplicate copy of a court order for the exhumation.

The funeral director was Stephan Santos, a flinty-eyed fellow with damp hands and an awkward smile. The deputy was a young woman with ramrod posture and eyes shielded by sunglasses, though she was indoors. Her name was Lucy Anderson.

"I'm here just to observe," she said. "I have a sister in Portland," she added.

"That's nice," Birdy said. "Not too far from home."

The last man was the cemetery administrator. Richard Mundy was in his sixties, had caterpillar brows, and was none too pleased about what they were assembled to do.

"We don't take kindly to what you're doing here, disturbing hallowed ground," he said. Louis Vuitton bags hung under his eyes.

"I'm sorry," Birdy said. She meant it too. "I'm just doing my job."

"Who's going to pay for this?" he asked.

"Kitsap County will reimburse you. You'll need to provide an invoice for the dig and re-interment."

"What about *my* time?" Mundy said, clearly no stranger to pushing the limits. His funeral director looked to the floor, embarrassed. "This is taking *my* time."

Birdy knew this man was trouble on the phone and he'd just confirmed it.

"You can include it in your invoice," she said, trying to keep the conversation pleasant and on an even keel. She declined to remind him that what they were doing was part of a criminal investigation to show a pattern of homicide spun by Jennifer Roberts. That Kitsap even paid for his work crew was above and beyond what most jurisdictions would do. People who had homes turned upside down by a police search don't get the benefit of a paid-for cleaning crew when the rummagers for evidence leave.

Though some ask for it.

"Well," he said, looking down at the document she'd provided first by email, then under the court's seal, "since the paperwork is in order, go ahead. Do what you have to do."

"All right then," Birdy said. "Depending on the condition of the vault, the casket, the victim, this might be a very short exhumation and exam."

"The court order indicates that you are collecting tissue samples in conjunction with your case in Washington," Deputy Anderson said. "Will we need to transport to our county morgue?" She glanced at the funeral administrator. "We won't charge you for the ride."

Birdy smiled.

"Or will you be able to do it here?" the deputy asked.

"We do have an embalming room where we prepare our clients," Stephan Santos said.

His boss shot him an angry glare.

"We don't have any clients there now."

Birdy scanned the large, green expanse that ran to the edge of the cemetery. "I think that will do," she said. "Let's get started."

The group, minus the annoying penny-pinching administrator, walked across the lawn past the rows upon rows of markers. Most were flat, set into the lawn for easy mowing. A few, Birdy thought maybe belonging to the more wealthy "clients" or maybe from a time when memorial parks were less a business than a place for remembrance, jutted to the cloudless blue sky. One, a big white dolphin of all things, almost scared her.

"Founder of Sea World," Santos said.

"Pretty," Birdy said, as they walked toward a tent that had been erected over the gravesite. A backhoe and two employees in jeans and dirty T-shirts stood there with shovels.

"I'm sorry about Mr. Mundy," Santos said.

"That's all right," Birdy said. "I understand."

Santos squinted toward the sun. "I know you have a job to do. I think you're barking up the wrong tree, if I'm allowed to say."

She looked at him. "Of course. Why?"

He turned to the older of the two men.

"Carlos, cut a window in the lawn. Peel it back. Then use the backhoe. I'll tell you when to stop. Be very careful."

The man motioned to his partner to start.

"You were saying?" Birdy said, trying to keep him on track.

"I know there's been a lot of talk about Jenny being a bad person. She wasn't easy to take."

"You knew her?"

He dried his upper lip, now sweaty, with a tissue from his pocket. "Oh no. I mean, not in that way."

"But you were friendly with her?"

"This isn't coming out right," he said, looking embarrassed again.

Birdy persisted. "What are you trying to tell me?"

"Just that I worked here when we buried Donald. I helped Jenny with the arrangements. She was an emotional basket case. This wasn't some Merry Widow kicking up her heels at the thought of her husband's death."

He stopped and watched a javelina run across the southern edge of the memorial park. The wild pig's tusks were visible even at a distance. He noticed Birdy looked wilted in the heat. "Deputy Anderson, I know you're not here to run errands, but do you mind going back to the office and getting Dr. Waterman some water?"

"No problem," she said, turning to leave. "It took me years to get used to our weather."

"I thought I was holding up pretty well," Birdy said as sweat ran down her back.

"As I was saying," he went on. "In my business, I actually have seen those kind of women. Husbands too. The kind that actually bring travel brochures to the chapel to plan what they couldn't wait to do once the loved one was buried. One woman even brought her iPad last year to surf the Internet during the service."

"Right in front of the client?" Birdy asked, testing him.

"That's Mr. Mundy's stupid word, by the way," he said. "It makes me cringe whenever I say it."

The two workers finished the removal of the sod. Next, the younger one stretched out a dark brown tarp and the older one got into the cab of the backhoe and turned it on.

"Take it slow and easy," Santos said. "Be gentle. This isn't a race."

"Jennifer Lake wasn't like that," Birdy said, once more refocusing the conversation.

"Absolutely not," Santos said, his tone surprisingly indignant. "She had those two little kids and, God, she was just beside herself with worry and grief. She actually threw herself onto the casket and wouldn't let go. I had to get her brother-in-law to help me pull her off. She was absolutely out of control. She kept saying over and over that she couldn't live without him. She couldn't raise those kids alone."

The dirt piled up on the tarp.

"All right, guys," Santos said. "Let's use shovels now. Don't want to mess anything up."

"I saw her brother-in-law today," Birdy said. "He sure didn't paint a picture of a lost love like you just did. He couldn't stand her."

Deputy Anderson returned with the water.

"Thank you," Birdy said, unscrewing the top. "You're right. I'm not used to this heat. What is it about ninety now?"

Lucy Anderson looked at the temperature on her phone. "About ninety-four to be exact. Did I miss anything?"

Santos shook his head. "No, the guys are about to get to the vault. We'll need to lift the lid and see what the doctor has to work with."

"I've never been to an exhumation before," Lucy said.

Birdy wore a grim smile. "It's a little like opening up a present that you know you'll hate."

"Back to the brother, Dr. Waterman. There was some family discord. That's for sure. I wouldn't trust anything he had to say."

"What kind of discord?" she asked, taking another much-needed drink.

"He wanted Donald buried in the cemetery up in Star Valley, Gila County. I understood his reasons. Family plot. His dad was there. His mom, she'd probably be there by now too."

"She isn't," Birdy said. "So why was he buried here?"

"Jenny wanted him *here*. She wanted him to be close to her. She told me she fought with everything she had to get out of Gila County and she sure wasn't going back there to visit her husband's grave."

The workers signaled that the vault was open.

"Looks intact," Santos said, peering into the hole.

"Another happy client," Birdy said.

Santos managed a smile.

"We aim to please," he said.

The last stop before anyone is wheeled out for a viewing was behind the chapel. It wasn't like Birdy's makeshift lab in the house on Sidney Avenue. It was probably closer to what she was going to have when she moved offices to Bremerton, something she still dreaded. It was bright, with banks of fluorescent tubes overhead. Two embalming tables set up to drain fluids into a medical disposal system commanded most of the space on one end of the room. Next to that was a walk-in closet with row upon row of makeup, wigs, and the rubber and silicone plugs that are used to keep bodies from draining where they shouldn't.

Donald Lake's casket was high end, no doubt about that.

"It's number eight-nine eight-nine, but we call it by its marketing name, the Castle Keep," Santos said.

It was dark brown with a pattern relief of doves repeated in a wide band down the center. Some of its surface was streaked with verdigris.

It was impressive as it surely had been meant to be.

"Solid copper?" she asked.

"Sheeted, but thank you," Santos said. "I'll tell the manufacturer that you inquired."

"I'm going to be cremated," the young deputy said. "No offense."

"None taken," he said. "We do that too. You can even pay in advance, you know, as a hedge against inflation."

Anderson made a face. There was no hiding that she didn't like the idea of a layaway plan for the dead.

"Thanks, but no thanks," she said.

"Where's your boss?" Birdy asked Santos.

"Gone," he said. "He only came in because you two were going to be here. He almost never bothers unless a celebrity croaks and then he's Johnny-on-the-spot."

Birdy pulled a clean pair of scrubs, gloves, digital recorder, and camera from her purse.

"I came prepared," she said. "Any place where I can change?"

Santos gestured across the room. "The makeup room all right?"

"That'll be fine."

Birdy didn't expect a real need for the scrubs. There wasn't any concern that there would be any fiber transfer or that any biologicals would splatter her. It was by-the-book protocol. The makeup room was cool, the air conditioner piping in enough breeze to move the hairs on a blond wig closest to the vent. She put on the mint-colored scrubs over her street clothes.

The casket was opened and there he was. Or rather a mummified version of Donald Lake. A musty, but surprisingly not too horrible, smell wafted into the room. The deceased was in surprisingly good condition for a man who'd been dead so long. He wore a blue suit, white shirt, and a tie with a small ruby tie tack holding it in place.

As if the tie would go anywhere.

Birdy wondered if the gem on his tie tack was a nod to his daughter.

The dead man's features were desiccated, of course. His skin was the color and texture of the salmon jerky she and Summer had sold to tourists during one of their spurts of entrepreneurship on the reservation. But even in all of that, there was still a resemblance to the man he'd been. Certainly a resemblance to his brother, so many years older now.

Birdy took some pictures.

"These aren't going to end up on the Internet, are they?"

Birdy ignored him as she concentrated on what she was doing.

"Well, are they?" he asked again.

She looked in his direction with an irritated, hard stare. "No, I can assure you they won't."

"Good, because we have a policy about that."

"Can I look?" It was Deputy Anderson.

Birdy stepped back and the younger woman approached. She didn't lean over to get a close view. Just enough to gasp and then return to the other side of the room.

"Can I use that tray?" Birdy asked Santos, indicating a cart on wheels she'd noticed next to the door to the makeup room. Without a word this time, he complied.

The forensic pathologist removed some gloves, glassine envelopes, and a pair of scissors from her purse and arranged the items on the table.

Next, she took four photographs of the casket, the deceased, the room, and the table with her supplies.

While the others looked on, Birdy spoke into her recorder.

"The subject is Donald Albert Lake, aged forty-one at the time of his death, here in Maricopa County. I'm in the presence of Stephan Santos, the funeral director of this location, Pinnacle Peak Memorial Park. Also observing is a representative of the Maricopa County sheriff's department, Deputy Lucy Anderson. My name is Birdy Waterman and I'm the forensic pathologist for Kitsap County, Washington. I'm here under a court-ordered exhumation related to a case under our juris-diction. I witnessed the removal of the casket from the cemetery plot and am about to conduct my exami-nation."

She put on a pair of gloves, picked up the scissors, and started cutting the deceased's suit up the right pant leg.

"Do you have to do that?" Santos asked.

"Yes," she said, cutting the other. He was not wear-ing a belt and that was a relief. She opened his jacket, undid the ruby tie tack, and set it on the table. She care-fully snipped the fabric along the button line of his dress shirt.

Next, she opened his clothes. It was as if she'd peeled an orange. Some of the tissue had stuck like a dried membrane onto the back of the fine cotton fabric of his shirt.

When Birdy made her way to his chest, she let out a gasp.

"Something's wrong here," she said.

"What do you mean?" Santos moved closer.

So did Anderson. She was disgusted by what she'd seen, but it was like a car accident. If someone was going to gasp at something, then she had to see too.

"Look at his chest," she said.

The deputy and the funeral director hovered over the Castle Keep containing the body of Jennifer Roberts's first husband.

"I don't see anything. I mean, I don't know what I'm supposed to be seeing," Stephan said.

Birdy looked up at both observers.

"Exactly," she said. "There isn't anything to see."

"I still don't follow you, Dr. Waterman," Lucy Anderson said.

"There's no incision here," Birdy said, locking eyes with the deputy, then the funeral director. "This man was not autopsied."

"But he *was*," Santos said. "I looked it up before you came. Dr. Drysdale did the autopsy. It was a heart attack."

"Really?" Birdy asked.

"Well, that's what I was told."

"Do you have a saw?" she asked.

Stephan Santos didn't like the sound of that one bit. He went pale.

"No," he said. "Why in the world would we?"

Birdy persisted. "A good knife with a serrated blade?"

Deputy Anderson spoke up. "In the kitchen maybe. I saw some kitchen tools in there when I got the bottled water."

"What are you going to do?" Santos asked.

"Deputy, go get the best knife you can find."

Her mouth agape, Anderson hurried off.

"I have to cut him open," Birdy said. "I have the authority to do that, though I was not thinking in terms of having to do so. I need to get samples of his organs for toxicology reports we'll conduct back in Washington. You know that."

Santos looked agitated. "Yes, but I expected you'd take . . ." His words trailed off. "I don't know, maybe a finger or something."

Even though she was going to have to use a cake knife to open up Donald Lake, she thought it sounded barbaric to suggest that she would remove a finger.

"I would never extricate a finger," she said. "I had hoped to collect samples more discreetly from the body, but that's not going to happen. I'm going to have to go inside."

Birdy finished her work in less than an hour. She took her time, but there was little to be done other than collect the tissue samples to see if there were any traces of toxins—something that had never been done. If he had heart disease, that wouldn't advance Kendall's case. She thanked the deputy and the funeral director for all they had done. They had been helpful in a difficult situation.

If she'd ever taken a finger, however, she'd like to have given it to the cheap administrator, Richard Mundy.

He deserved it.

CHAPTER 29

Birdy ate alone after the tissue collection. Even though it was a barbecue place, she ordered a salad because the idea of any kind of meat turned her stomach. It had been that kind of a day. She'd wrestled with the desiccated insides of a man in the hopes of proving that he'd been murdered.

Kendall had told her what was going on back home, and she was sorry that she wasn't there. The thought that Darby's killer might be caught brought little comfort. Not when she still couldn't testify in court as to the cause of the girl's death. She hadn't been shot or stabbed. Her eyes showed no signs of petechial hemorrhaging—the tiny spider web broken blood vessels—so it was doubtful she'd been strangled. In addition, there were no indicators that she'd been strangled by way of a broken hyoid or marks on her neck. She hadn't been drugged. Tox screens were all clean. She just died.

The waitress returned with a dessert menu.

"No thanks," Birdy said. "I've got to run." She passed the young woman her Visa card.

While the waitress went off to run the card, Birdy

turned her attention to Dr. Drysdale. She looked at the address. The doctor's house was in a gated community not far from the barbecue place.

"You know how to get to Mesquite Heights?" she asked the waitress when she returned with the check. "My rental doesn't have GPS."

"Easy as pie," the woman said. "You've got friends up there?"

Birdy signed the check. "No. Not really. Just someone that I need to see."

"Take a right on Arroyo and go about five miles. The entrance is on your left. You can't miss it. Big dumb fountain there."

Birdy thanked her and went to her car and called Elan.

"Aunt Birdy, when you coming back? There's nothing to eat here."

"Is that all you care about?" she asked, turning the AC to a full, chilly blast.

"How did your day go?" he asked. "I already heard on the news you were down there poking into Ruby and Micah's dad's case. They are so pissed off at you."

"It was on the news?" she asked.

"Yeah, the paper too. Hang on."

She put the car in drive and turned right on Arroyo.

"Okay, I have it right here," Elan said. "The headline is a classic."

Silence.

"Well what does it say?"

"Right, sorry. You're breaking up a little."

"As you would say, the cell service sucks here."

"The headline says 'Is Kitsap Woman a Black Widow?' "

"I guess that's not so bad."

She braked as a coyote ran across the road. The connection was poor and she was having a hard time hearing him. He, it seemed, was having the same problem.

"What?" he asked.

"It could be worse I guess. I'll be home tomorrow."

"Good," he said, cutting out a little more. "Stuff happening with that Darby girl case too. You there?"

"I'm here."

"Aunt Birdy?"

"Elan?"

Despite the fake saguaro cactus replica cell towers that dotted the area and fooled no one into thinking they were anything but cell towers, the cell service was abysmal.

An American Beauty red 7 series BMW darted in front of her, zipped up to the gate, and waited as the enormous steel partition slowly slid open. Birdy knew just what to do. As soon as the BMW passed through and made its turn, Birdy tucked in right behind. She agreed that the fountain had been dumb, but inside was impressive. Mesquite Heights was a neighborhood of mini and not-so-mini mansions that blended in to the desert landscape.

She looked down at the back of the DONDANS business card: 824 Candlewood Lane.

She was already there.

Just as Birdy got out of her rental car, a woman in a Lexus pulled in across the street. One of four garage doors went up, and the woman stepped out and went toward a garbage receptacle that stood near the curb like several others in the neighborhood.

It had been trash day. And as lovely as the homes were, not everyone had domestic help or were retired.

"Excuse me, is this Bobby Drysdale's house?" Birdy said, indicating the house.

The woman, in a chic black and white skirt and expensive heels, looked at her and then went about her business.

"Excuse me," Birdy said, raising her voice.

Maybe the woman didn't hear her?

Again, no response.

Maybe she had earbuds in or something and was listening to music.

Birdy walked toward her. "I'm looking for Bobby Drysdale," she said. "Where I come from, you answer a question when one is politely asked."

The woman slowed, then turned around and glared.

"Then maybe you should go back to Nogales and ask your questions there," she said, cruel sarcasm dripping from her lips.

Birdy bristled. She'd been dismissed. That had never happened to her in her entire life. Yes, her complexion was dark and her hair black as a starless night.

"I'm not from Mexico," she said.

The woman shrugged it off. "Sorry. Just thought you were looking for housekeeping work. No offense."

"None taken," Birdy said, lying. The woman's attitude couldn't have been more purposefully rude.

The waitress at the barbecue place had called the city Snobbsdale. Birdy understood that nickname completely.

"Look, I don't know who you are and I don't care," the woman went on, moving the receptacle to the open garage and dragging it between her BMW and some other fancy car that Birdy couldn't identify. "But equally, I don't know who lives across the street nor do I give it a second thought. We're all very private people here in Mesquite Heights. That's why we live here."

The garage door went down like a guillotine, hard and decisive.

Birdy stood there.

"Nice meeting you," she said loud enough for any-one to hear.

If only there was someone there to hear, that is.

While all of the houses in the neighborhood were massive, low slung to blend in with the landscape, they resembled something else. She couldn't quite place it as she walked up to a courtyard planted with prickly pear, agave, and ocotillo. Then it finally dawned on her. She turned around and scanned the neighborhood. All the homes were built like fortresses with thick rounded-edged walls. Only tiny gunner windows were poked into the front of the massive front exteriors. Walls shrouded the front doors from the street. Cactus pro-truded over walkways in a way that instant-messaged visitors to back off.

She rang the bell and waited. Her hair stuck to the nape of her neck. A suit, even a lightweight one like the one she was wearing, was not the right attire for Ari-zona. She'd have given anything to be in shorts and a tank just then.

The door opened and a man with close-cropped white hair and designer glasses stood there in a silky T-shirt, shorts, and flip-flops.

Doesn't anyone wear shoes down here?

"No soliciting," he said right away. "Can't you read?"

Birdy almost said, "si" but held her tongue.

"Dr. Drysdale, I'm Dr. Waterman, a forensic pathologist from Washington looking into one of your cases."

He looked at her warily. "I'm no longer practicing medicine."

"Yes, I know," she said. "May I come in?"

"I'd rather you didn't," he said.

"I'm not used to this heat," the forensic pathologist said, adding a quick, "please."

Reluctantly, Bobby Drysdale led her inside. The room was enormous, cavernous really. Though the homeowner's furnishings were massive, they still seemed dwarfed by the size of the space. There were dark leather couches, planked tables, and a kind of sterile look that indicated he lived alone.

"I was having a drink," he said, still not smiling. "Want one?"

She shook her head. "Some water, please."

Bobby flip-flopped over to the bar.

"I know why you're here," he said, handing her a glass of ice water with a lemon slice tucked between the cubes. "It's about Jenny."

Birdy took the water and sipped. It tasted so good. The lemon was a nice touch.

"I guess word travels fast," she said.

"I have friends," he said, as he led her to the Mexican tiled patio that surrounded an oblong, irregularly shaped pool. Unlike the house, the pool was small. More for dipping in on a hot day like the one they were experiencing than doing laps.

He indicated a couple of chairs and they both sat down.

"Marrying Jenny Lake was the biggest mistake of my life," he said.

Birdy sipped her water as Bobby fidgeted a little.

"Maybe not the biggest," she said, not spelling it all out, but knowing without a doubt that he understood the meaning of her comment.

Yet he let it pass.

"You know she's been arrested for the murder of her third husband," Birdy said.

Bobby swirled the ice cubes in his glass. "Doesn't surprise me," he answered.

Birdy was the one who was surprised. "Why not?"

Bobby took off his glasses and put on a pair of sunglasses. "Jenny was nothing but trouble. That's why I divorced her. I actually caught her forging some documents. Look, I went to the police and filed a report. Go check. I didn't press charges because, well, I felt sorry for those kids of hers. They didn't deserve to be orphans while their mother went to jail."

"What kind of documents?" Birdy asked. "What was she forging?"

"Checks," he said. "Life insurance. You name it. If there was a place for her to sign my name and get something out of it, she was right there with a cheap-ass Bic pen. Jenny was a scammer. I was stupid. I was in my late forties, going nowhere, and I was ripe for the pickings for a girl like her."

"A girl like *her*?"

He looked over at Birdy and took off his shades for a second.

"She was a total looker," he said. "Hotter than a scotch bonnet chili. From what I can tell, she still is. I saw her picture on the Internet. Not bad for her age."

"You know that I took tissue samples from Donald Lake's body today."

Sunglasses back on, Bobby Drysdale got up and went back to the bar inside the house. "I'm getting another drink," he said. "And yes, I know."

A coyote lumbered by on the other side of the jail-bars of the fence that separated the pool area from the arid magnificence of the desert. The coyote limped and kept his head down, sniffing for something along the path that he'd worn along the other side of the fence.

"You listed cause of death as a heart attack, Doctor," she said when he returned to the chair next to hers.

"Yes, I did," he said. "I was actually there when he died. Golfing with him when it happened on the thirteenth hole. It wasn't that I just made it up. I tried to save the man. I think I know cardiac arrest when I see one."

"Of course you do," she said. "What was his medical history?"

"He had high blood pressure, but nothing completely off the charts. I expect it was living with Jenny that gave him HBP."

Birdy was still on the hunt for answers, and she wasn't getting many from the man who'd married Jennifer in Las Vegas.

"Had he been ill?" she asked. "Before he went golfing. Do you know?"

"Look, I wasn't his doctor," Drysdale said. "But, yeah, he'd been under the weather. Stress related. Jenny told me that he wasn't taking care of himself and she was pretty sure that something like this would happen."

Birdy took that last line in.

"Like she predicted it? Ahead of time?" she asked.

He scratched his paint-bristle white hair. "I don't re-member. I was drinking heavy back then. It might have been after, might have been before. She was a really emotional girl. Needy like. Confident too. Kind of all over the map."

Birdy recalled the same description from the para-medic when they answered the call for help at the Roberts place.

"Your report indicated an autopsy was conducted," she said. "I saw no evidence of one today. You probably know that already."

Drysdale looked down at his glass. "That's a mistake."

He returned his gaze to her. Despite the ruddy com-plexion of a drinker and the sun of the desert, it was clear that he looked embarrassed. His face went a shade darker.

"Look, I was busy," he said. "I had a lot of patients and I had what I thought was a grieving woman fight-ing over her husband's body. She wanted everything expedited."

"She was in a hurry?"

"Yeah. She didn't want him buried in Star Valley. She said that he never, ever would want that. He hated where he'd come from. Just like Jenny. She did too."

Birdy kept at him. "But what about the autopsy?"

"I had a friend do me a favor."

Birdy was incredulous. "A falsified document? Do you realize that will cost you your medical license?"

"Dr. Waterman, you didn't do all your homework before coming down here and digging up Don Lake."

"I have your paperwork," she said. "Right here."

"That's fine," Drysdale said. "I expect you would. But you don't have the rest of my story."

Birdy looked at him. "No, I guess not."

Over the next hour, Dr. Bobby Drysdale told the Kitsap County forensic pathologist that he'd willingly surrendered his medical license two years after Jenny Lake Drysdale left town. He was quietly let go for being drunk in the operating room.

"I thank God every single day that I didn't kill anyone on the table or on the road, for that matter," he said, dumping his ice cubes into a potted agave next to his chair.

"But you're drinking now," she said.

"Tonic," he said, a little defensively. "*Diet* tonic. I haven't had a drink in ten years."

She looked around. "Somehow you've recovered. You must have had a major pension plan."

Drysdale blinked. "I'll ignore your tone, Doctor, but I had some investments, yes. But like most of the people in this neighborhood, I'm up to my eyeballs in debt over this house. If the market ever returns, I'm out of here."

"Did you ever think Jennifer was capable of murder?"

He looked down at his empty glass. The misters came on and sent a vapor moisture over the patio. It was like a steam curtain, but cooling.

"I honestly don't know," he said. "I do know that we were seeing each other before Don died. I know she wanted to marry me—you know marry the doctor, it's a big thing around here. Probably up there too."

"Not *my* kind of doctor," she said.

He smiled. "Yeah, I guess that's probably true."

She pulled the report from her purse and shook her head. "I still don't understand why you signed off on Donald's death cert and indicated that an autopsy had confirmed the heart attack."

He sat mute as the cool mist fell on him. He closed his eyes.

"Doctor, can you answer, please? It's important."

Bobby Drysdale opened his eyes and looked off into the distance before turning back to face her.

"In case you haven't figured it out," he said, his eyes locked on Birdy's, "Jennifer had a way with guys. She could get what she wanted. She was good at it. She was, and I hope this doesn't embarrass you, the best sex I ever had. I did it for her."

Birdy's phone was dead. She looked around Sky Harbor for a charging station, but all the jacks were being used. She wanted to text Elan that she'd be home and to see if he needed anything. She felt warm and wondered if she had a fever. But it wasn't that. She'd been sunburned. That almost never happened to her.

She had a beer in the bar and waited for her flight, wondering about everyone back in Kitsap County. So many people were waiting for her to deliver the truth, to put them at rest—something that she wasn't always able to do.

The flat screen TV in the bar played the local news. The volume was down so low she couldn't hear, but the imagery was plain enough.

Local girl Jenny Lake Drysdale Roberts had made the news.

The man next to Birdy leaned toward Birdy.

"Pretty little thing like that couldn't hurt a fly," he said.

Birdy kept her eyes on the screen. "She'd gobble the fly down in one messy gulp, sir."

CHAPTER 30

"**M**e? Why me?"

Birdy stood in Kendall's office and shook her head in disbelief. She'd already had a bad day. Elan was mad that she came home so late, but the weather delay hadn't been her fault. She barely had time to get a cup of coffee when Kendall told her to get over to her office.

"Jennifer wants to see you because you've been poking around in the past with a sharp stick. She wants to find out what you know," the detective said.

"I don't know," Birdy said, feeling a little over-whelmed by the prospect. "She's just going to stonewall with her attorney sitting there telling her what to answer and what to avoid."

Kendall dismissed that with a wag of a finger. "That's the best part. If there could be a best part in the saga that has become the *Jennifer Roberts Show*. She said she doesn't want her lawyer there. Just *you*."

"And you, right?" Birdy asked.

Kendall shook her head slowly. "Nope. Just you."

"What if she says something incriminating?"

"No worries. Everything is recorded."

Birdy allowed a smile to cross her lips. "Thank goodness for that. I thought you were going to make me wear a wire. What do you want me to say to her?"

"Whatever you like. The point is, let's see what she wants to say to you."

The Kitsap County jail was a knot of cells and offices that connected the sheriff's department and the courthouse, which made it easy for officials to move prisoners from pickup to court to incarceration, a kind of assembly-line approach that suited the process well. Birdy had only been in the jail one time, when the coroner who hired her gave her the grand tour of the county facilities. It was a nice jail, as far as jails go.

A guard named Tobey led her to an interview room that looked a little like the shell of a gas station lavatory, plain, stark. It was tiled with white linoleum squares. A table that was better than anything she had in her office commanded the center of the space. Two bistro-style chairs were placed at either end.

"I'll be outside," Tobey said. "Just holler if you need me."

"Where's Jennifer Roberts?"

"Be down in a minute."

He looked at her with a funny expression on his face. "Have fun with that one," he said.

"How do you mean?" Birdy asked.

"Piece of work. No kidding. We don't get many like her around here."

"What do you mean?"

Tobey rolled his eyes and opened the door.

"One example," he said. "It's a good one too. She asked if we had any South Beach options for dinner. Like she was in some spa and not jail."

"I can see her doing that," Birdy said. "From what I've heard."

"No offense because you're a woman, Dr. Waterman, but she pitched a royal hissy fit when she didn't get her way."

Birdy went inside and sat down. She didn't like the way the chairs were positioned—at the opposite ends of the farthest points of the table. She shuffled them around so that she and Jennifer would be facing each other in a more intimate way. Jennifer would want it that way. She liked to be the focus of attention.

The door opened and Jennifer Roberts was led inside.

"Do I have to wear these?" she asked, holding up the handcuffs and belly chain. "They hurt."

"Sorry," Tobey said. "Procedure."

"That's ridiculous," Jennifer said with disgust as she sat down. For a woman who just lost her husband and was the subject of a criminal investigation, Jennifer Roberts held up pretty good. Her hair was in a loose ponytail, revealing not even the slightest darkened roots at her temples. Her skin was bronze and luminous. Whatever face lotion she'd used up to that moment was a winner—and probably wasn't available at any cosmetics counter in Port Orchard.

"Jennifer, I don't know why I'm here," Birdy said.

"You're here because no one is listening to me."

"That's your lawyer's job."

"Yes I know. And if I had a good lawyer, the kind that I should have, I'd do some talking to him. But I don't. The guy they gave me has been out of law school about fifteen minutes and doesn't know his ass from a torte."

"I know him," Birdy said. "He's young, but very capable. You could have done a lot worse."

Jennifer bristled. "Worse than being accused of doing something so horrible like Detective Stark and you think I've done?"

"You'll have your day in court."

"Right. In court. If I make it that far."

"Are you frightened of something?"

Jennifer fidgeted with her chains. "No. Maybe. Yes," she said. "I don't know."

"Why am I here?"

"Because I know you talked to some people down in Scottsdale about me. I know that you're trying to blame me for Donny's death too."

"Who told you?" Birdy asked.

"Ruby, my daughter. She came to see me. She told me about the exhumation. I think you're a pretty sick woman, digging up Donny like that so you could try to come up with some dirt on me for Ted's death."

"Who told her?" Birdy asked.

Jennifer lowered her head so she could brush a strand of hair from her eyes. "She reads. She's in high school. This is a big story. This tragedy shouldn't be on the news, but you've gone stirring up a hornet's nest."

"Had Donald been ill?"

"Hey, you're not here to ask me questions. You're here so I can ask you some."

The woman was nothing if not assertive.

"I don't have to answer, you know," Birdy said.

"You will. If you give a little, maybe I will too."

"Did you poison your husband?"

"Which one?"

Such a strange answer, Birdy thought.

"Either," she said. "Both?"

"You must think I'm stupid. That I would admit to anything. First of all, just so you know, I didn't kill either one of them. Donny died of a heart attack and I know you think Ted was poisoned—I don't know if that's a lie or a fact."

"It's a fact. He was poisoned."

"Says you. But if he was poisoned, like you say, why would I have done that?"

Birdy thought a second. Maybe just letting out a little of the cat would be fine. The bag was plenty big enough.

"Bobby told me that you wanted money. That you were a thief. Maybe Donald caught you? Maybe he was going to dump you and you did what you had to do to protect what you thought was yours."

Jennifer glared at Birdy. "You're a real *Law and Order* fan, aren't you, Dr. Waterman?"

"I am, but that's not the point. The point is that you have a history of getting what you want by any means possible."

"You have black hair," Jennifer said, stating the obvious. "I bet you've always hated your hair. It's thick enough. But it doesn't catch anyone's eyes. I see that you don't have a ring. Too bad. Can't find a man? I have had no problem in that regard. I could get the officer standing outside this door if I wanted to."

"Where are you going with this?" Birdy asked.

Jennifer seemed annoyed, not really angry. "Women like you are haters," she said. "You hate me because of how I look. You despise me because I have more than you'll ever have."

Birdy rolled her shoulders. "I have no feelings about you whatsoever."

"Then why are you here?" she asked.

"Because you asked me to come."

"Fine, I did. I wanted you to know that I loved my husbands. All of them. Well, except maybe Bobby."

Birdy kept her expression flat. "That's interesting," she said. "He's the only one that's still alive."

"I know you saw him down there in Scottsdale."

Birdy saw no reason to lie. "That's right, I did."

"Did he tell you that I was devastated when my husband had that heart attack?"

"I can't remember what he said your reaction was," she said.

Jennifer fiddled with her belly chains. "Did he tell you that Donny had high blood pressure?"

"He mentioned it."

Jennifer stared at Birdy with a strange and awkward intensity. "That he didn't take his medication?" she asked, sputtering out her words. "That he ate too much? Drank even more? That he was screwing the hostess at his restaurant—the restaurant that could have been an empire if he hadn't keeled over and died?"

"Look," Birdy said. "This isn't going anywhere."

The switch had been pulled. Jennifer in her orange jumpsuit, a color that she considered less than flattering, started to cry. It wasn't sniveling either. A gusher, accompanied by the kind of guttural moaning and crying that comes when a wild animal is caught in the rusty jaws of a snare.

Like Birdy felt right then.

"I loved Ted," Jennifer howled. "Damn! I loved him with all my heart. I moved away from the sun for rain-soaked rust bucket Bremerton to be with a man that gave me the safe harbor I'd always been looking for!"

Officer Tobey, a concerned look on his face, poked his head in.

"Dr. Waterman, everything okay in here?" the corrections officer asked.

She waved him away.

Train wrecks like Jennifer Lake Drysdale Roberts were dangerous, but in a twisted way they were captivating too.

"He was the man of my dreams. Honestly, you, having no husband, can't comprehend what I'm saying, Dr. Waterman. He was the love of my life," she said, gulping air.

"You're going to hyperventilate," Birdy said. "Please try to calm down."

"I can't," Jennifer said. "I'm trapped in here. My kids are going into foster care."

"The kids aren't. Ruby is about to turn eighteen. The judge might allow her—with monitoring of course—to eventually watch Micah, pending the outcome of your case."

Jennifer looked surprised. "She is? Oh, that's good." Jennifer calmed down a little.

"Yes, don't worry about them," Birdy said. "Worry about what you've done and why you're here."

Jennifer tried to dry her eyes, but the chains on her wrists made it a struggle.

"That Molly O'Rourke wanted Ted for herself," she said. "You'll see. I was set up. You have to do something about her. This is all her fault. I don't know what

I'll do when I get out of here. Since you think I'm already a killer, what would it matter? I'd slit her throat from ear to ear."

Birdy called Kendall after the interview.

"How was it?" the detective asked before even saying hello.

"Just your garden variety glimpse into a mind of a narcissist," Birdy said, as she walked across the back parking lot to her office, "if you really want to know."

"That doesn't surprise me. What did she want?"

Birdy laughed. "What they all want. She wanted to win me over. She wanted to find out what I had dug up—pun meant—in Arizona."

"Anything we can use?" Kendall asked.

"She blames Molly. So, no, not really. It would have made good TV."

"That'll come."

Birdy stopped while a car backed out of a spot. "I can hear *Dateline* producers circling now."

"Speaking of which, guess who I'm going to see?" Kendall asked.

The driver was an elderly man and he was taking his sweet time. Birdy, tired of waiting, went around him. "I don't have the slightest."

"*Dateline*'s pin-up, true crime star attraction," Kendall said.

It could only be one person.

"The one and only?" she asked.

"Yup," Kendall said. "The one and only Brenda Nevins."

"I'm not going."

"You don't have to."

"Do you think she'll tell you if she put Missy up to killing Darby?" Birdy asked, going up the steps to the front door of the coroner's office.

"Nope," Kendall said. "But like you and your interview today, I'm going because I can't wait to be manipulated."

"Manipulation is such fun," Birdy said.

CHAPTER 31

When Birdy arrived home after seeing Jennifer in the jail, Elan was waiting for her. He'd had a haircut and it looked good on him.

"I didn't know you were going to do that," she said, looking him over. "I like it. It's cleaner."

"It was getting a little on the scruffy side," Elan said. "How was your day?"

"You don't want to know," she said.

"That means I would want to," he answered.

She didn't say anything.

"Another of those 'Elan, I can't talk about it' kind of things?"

"Yeah, sorry. You want to take a walk? I picked up a couple of sandwiches at Whiskey Creek."

"Sure," he said. "We can talk about something other than whatever cool thing you did today and I can tell you about how much I hate school. Or at least most of it."

"Deal," she said. "We can talk about other things too."

"Ugh. I don't like the sound of that," he said.

Birdy acknowledged his remark but disappeared

into the bedroom to change into jeans and more appropriate shoes, and the two of them took off. The sun was
low as they walked along Beach Drive toward the little
waterfront village of Annapolis. They walked outside
to the fishing pier jutting out over the water, pointing
to Bremerton. Just as they reached the end, a floating
fishing platform, a ferry's wake rolled under the dock,
bobbing it up and down.

"This feels like being drunk," Elan said.

Birdy took a hard look at her nephew. "How would
you know how that feels?"

"I'm sixteen," he said a little sheepishly. "Not *six*.
Not that the age matters much in our family."

She handed him a sandwich. "You've been on your
best behavior here, haven't you?"

"Yeah. I'm doing all right," he said, happy to see that
there was actually meat in the option she bought for
him. "I'm making friends. I like it here."

"That makes me happy," she said.

"Can't I just live with you?" he asked.

She looked out thoughtfully as a man and little boy
went past on a small boat with a purring outboard
motor.

"You have a family, Elan."

He swallowed a bite. "Yeah, and that includes you."

"Family members tell each other the truth," she said.

"I'm not lying," he said.

"You know what I'm getting at, Elan. Talk to me."

Elan squinted into the setting sun.

"All right. Mom's having an affair with a guy at work.
I caught them in bed when I came home from school
early. By the way, it was *my* bed. Isn't that gross?"

Birdy stayed quiet. A seagull swooped down low to

grab a piece of lettuce that had slipped out of Elan's sandwich.

"Elan, that's a problem for your parents."

"It was *my* bed, Aunt Birdy."

"That is pretty bad. Did you talk to her about it?"

"Not really," he said. "It was just the end of what I couldn't take anymore. I know about everything."

His words hung in the salty and breezy air. Birdy didn't want to push any further just then. If it was what she thought it was, there would be no point in doing so. There was nothing that could be done about it.

"Does your dad know?"

Elan balled up the white butcher paper that had wrapped his sandwich. "You going to eat the other half of yours?"

"It's veggie," she said.

Elan pulled the zipper up on his hoodie, then shrugged a little. "I don't care."

Birdy handed him the sandwich.

"You know he's not my dad," he went on. "Why do you keep calling him that?"

Birdy took the wadded paper from his sandwich and hers and put it in the paper bag.

"He raised you," she said. "That's why."

Elan seemed to like the sandwich enough to eat Birdy's half in four bites.

"I hate him," he said. "I hate both of them. I wish they'd just fall into a big hole somewhere and never crawl out."

"That's a terrible thing to say," Birdy said.

Elan spoke with his mouth full, but she didn't admonish him this time. "Well, you asked. That's how I feel," he said, swallowing.

Birdy put her hands on his shoulders and looked into his puddled brown eyes.

"You are going to be all right, Elan," she said, meaning every word. "I promise you."

Elan didn't want to leave Port Orchard. He'd settled in. He was trying to make a new life before his old one, back home, circling the drain, sucked him down, into oblivion.

"You know everything, don't you, Aunt Birdy?"

"Your grandmother says I do have an answer for everything," she said. "But really, I'm just like everyone else. We're all doing the best that we can do. You'll get to a good place. I believe in you. So I guess, I'm sorry to say, I do have an answer for everything."

She smiled warmly at Elan. This was a good kid.

"I can forgive you," he said.

"Thank you. You know that I love you, Elan."

He turned away, not wanting her to see him cry.

"Someone has to."

They returned to Birdy's house, mostly in silence, though the subject of a dead opossum in front of their house and how it had gone from mush to bones did come up. Birdy didn't give him all the gory details about how that little feat was accomplished. He didn't ask.

On the front steps was a Target shopping bag.

"Wonder what this is?" Birdy said, struggling to open the knotted opening.

"Does Target deliver now?" Elan asked, dumping their dinner bag into the trash can on the side of the house.

Birdy stayed silent, peering inside.

"What is it?" he asked.

"I'm not sure. I think they're some letters."

"Don't we have a mailbox for that?"

"That we do." She closed the white plastic bag peppered with red bull's-eye logos.

"Do you have any homework?"

Elan made a face. Their bonding time was clearly over.

"Some," he said.

"Good," Birdy said, heading to her office. "Let's get to it. So do I."

With the exception of one, each in the bundle of letters had been addressed to Ted Roberts, 511 Camellia Street, Port Orchard. The return address was what appeared to be an apartment on E. Dynamite in Scottsdale. All but one had been sent by Jennifer Drysdale.

As a precaution that there might be something related to the case on the envelopes or on the papers held within, Birdy put on latex gloves. She arranged them in date sequence.

The first one had been written on lavender stationery. She lifted it to her nose to see if it had been scented. Jennifer Roberts had seemed like the type to send perfumed love letters. This one hadn't been. It was, however, handwritten.

Dear Teddy,
   I don't know why I haven't heard from you since our meet up in San Diego. Or as the kids like to call it, Sand Diego! I had the best time. It

*must be amazing to have a job that brings you
all over the world to places like San Diego. I
haven't traveled much at all. A lot of people
think that Arizona is so glamorous and that the
desert is intriguing, but not me. I'm so sick of it.
I've been through so much. I haven't had it easy
being widowed at such a young age. I know that
God intends for me to get through all of this.
Somehow.*

*Love,
Jennifer*

The missive was interesting for a couple of reasons;
Birdy had no idea how Ted and Jennifer had met, and
yet they'd rendezvoused in San Diego. The navy was
there, so maybe it was just happenstance that Jennifer
and Ruby and Micah had been there. The other oddity
in the note was the return address and the postmark.
Birdy knew that Jennifer and Bobby had split up by
then, but Jennifer never alluded to that marriage. She
acted like she was merely a widow and not a two-time
loser. Maybe she was embarrassed about the short-
lived marriage to Bobby, but it was also possible that
she didn't want Ted Roberts to think she was unstable
and went from man to man?

As she had been doing all her life.

Birdy called Kendall and told her about the letters.
She could hear Steven talking to their son Cody in the
background and the clatter of dishes.

"Sorry to bug you," Birdy said. "Thought dinner
would be over."

"It's *never* over around here," Kendall said with a short laugh. "What's up?"

Birdy explained that someone had dropped off letters that might have been written by Jennifer Roberts.

"I have two questions," Kendall said. "I wonder who did that? And also, don't keep me hanging, what do they say?"

"I don't know the answer to the first one, and so far, nothing much. I've only read one. But I wanted to give you a heads-up. I'll bring them to your office first thing tomorrow."

"Sounds good," Kendall said. "The boys are loading the dishwasher and they still don't know how to do it the right way. See you tomorrow."

Birdy thought the same thing about Elan and the way he attempted to help out around the house, but she never told him. Loading dishes at all was a blessing. After he went to bed for the night, she found herself putting plates and glasses in the order they needed to be.

It must be a guy thing, she thought.

She put down her phone and started on the next letter, though it was not really a letter, but a greeting card. It was sent about two weeks after the first. The outside was a picture of a prickly pear cactus, with full moon-glow yellow blooms and a glistening webbing of spikes ready to wreak havoc.

Inside the manufacturer printed: *The only thing that hurts more than bumping into one of these is not seeing you.*

The message was handwritten on the bottom of the card and continued to the other side:

Dear Teddy,

The sound of your voice kept me up all night. I'm not embarrassed to say I had a very nice dream about the two of us. ☺ When I got up this morning I felt a little sad inside. I just kept thinking of all that you are doing and wondering how a woman and her kids (teenagers, no less!) could ever fit into a life like yours. I've made my share of mistakes in life, but somehow I still am able to dream about that perfect life with the man of my dreams. Silly me. Anyway, I saw this card a few days ago and I thought of you. Not the prickly part, but the part that says I'm missing you. I'm thinking that you must be extremely busy doing all that official secret stuff that you do for the navy. Protecting our country is an important job. Being a mother has been my life's work. I am ready to start a new life in the Pacific "Northwest" if you're still serious.

Love,
Me

Birdy stopped reading and fished for her drugstore readers. Her eyes were tired, and Jennifer had a teeny tiny handwriting. Having found her glasses, Birdy went to get something to drink. She opted for a diet soda over a beer. Elan's crack about her family's problems with drugs and alcohol resonated a little. She passed by his bedroom. He was on the phone. She could only pick up bits and pieces and she didn't linger.

"She's a lot nicer to me," he said. "I like her a lot. I haven't been this happy probably ever."

He was talking to his mother. It was sweet, but if she'd had to bet on it, she figured his comments probably didn't set well with his mom. Summer thought life was a competition and she'd been saddled with the losing team.

Birdy sat down and opened the next envelope from the Target bag.

This one was postmarked two months later. It was a pretty big gap in time.

Dear Teddy,

This is not easy to write. I'm sick about what happened. I really didn't expect you to act that way at all. I've left messages. You don't call me back. I get it. Being blond doesn't make me stupid. I thought things were moving in the right direction when we made love on your visit here. My children thought you were cool. Now, I'm almost 40 and pregnant. I'm very, very religious. I don't have a say in the matter. This is all in God's hands. If you don't want to be a part of our lives, just say so. I am crying as I write this so I guess it is just as well that you're not answering me. I won't ask for anything. Don't worry. I'll just fade away and you can live your life the way you want it to be. No thoughts of me or your son or daughter.

Good-bye,
Jennifer

Birdy thought of calling Kendall just then. Jennifer had set a trap. If she'd been pregnant, then where was the baby? The gestation for an elephant was about two years, not for a human. And they'd been married for almost a year and a half.

The next envelope was also addressed to Ted Roberts; inside was the identical prickly pear cactus card.

The same card? Who does that?

At the bottom written also in Jennifer's minuscule handwriting:

How are you? I miss you. I am elated about the baby. I think we should get married before I start showing. I'm from a very small, conservative town outside of Phoenix. My family would be humiliated if I had a shotgun wedding at my age! So excited!

Love,
Jenny

The card had been addressed to Ted, but its tone didn't feel right to Birdy. It seemed like it was written to someone else. She double-checked the date. It had been sent *after* the first pregnancy note. Something was wrong, out of sequence. She looked closer. The envelope was not the same as the first one that held the other prickly pear card. She placed it on top of the first card. The new one was slightly larger. Normally, she knew, greeting cards came with matching envelopes.

The next letter was addressed to Ted, three weeks after the pregnancy note.

Dear Teddy,

I know you are at sea and doing whatever you are doing to keep our country safe. The kids and I will be up as soon as school is out down here. I have never been this happy in my entire life. After losing my husband, Donald, I never thought I'd get married again. I never thought that I could find someone to love me like you have. You are my heart, my soul, my everything. Making a new start in a new place with the man of my dreams and my children is a great blessing to me. Ruby and Micah are thrilled to say the least. Oh, they'll miss the sunshine but we've been looking on the Internet for places to explore in Washington and there are so many. It almost seems like a foreign country compared to down here. I've been feeling a little sick the past couple of days, but the doctor says not to worry. Just to be on the safe side, he's told me to have an amniocentesis (spelled right?) because of my age. Boy, did that make me feel old. Most people think I'm in my twenties! I just changed the beneficiary on my life insurance to you as secondary and the kids as primary. Don't forget to do that for me too.

> *Love and kisses,*
> *Me*

The next letter was addressed to a Rodney Roderick in Denver. It had been postmarked Scottsdale, but had been returned to sender: Jennifer Drysdale.

Dear Roddy,

I never thought I could feel the way you make me feel. I just woke up from the most beautiful dream. You and I were making love on a beach in Hawaii. A car with tourists drove by and honked at us, but we didn't care. We just kept on going. Nothing was going to stop us from showing how much love we have for each other. You are one sexy man. Men half your age should look so good and be able to go so long. You make me blush right now when I think of you holding me in those big strong arms of yours. Come on back to Scottsdale. The kids adored you. Can't wait to see you!

Love,
Me

Birdy sat there, thinking of the letters and what they meant—and almost as importantly—*why* had they been left on her doorstep and by whom? It seemed obvious that Jennifer was on a mission. She was looking to find a husband—and she was doing whatever it took to do so. She'd played the pregnancy card. The religion card. The I'm-so-beautiful-it-hurts card. She had more cards to play than a Vegas dealer.

Desperate and on a mission.

Whoever had left them there wanted to make sure that Birdy Waterman and Kendall Stark held no doubts about Jennifer Roberts.

She wondered if it was the same person who had called 911 insisting that Ted Roberts's death was a murder.

It had to be. But who?

Above her desk was a picture of Darby Moreau. When her eyes landed on it, Birdy put Jennifer and Ted Roberts out of her mind.

Darby, what happened to you? What did Missy do to you? What did that monster Brenda Nevins set in motion?

CHAPTER 32

Brenda Nevins was everything the media had portrayed her to be. She'd done her hair and makeup for the interview with Kitsap County sheriff's detective Kendall Stark like she was going to be chatting with Ryan Seacrest. Kendall couldn't take her eyes off her. Not only was Brenda stunning, she acted as though Kendall was there to court her when the women sat down in a small interview room at the Washington Corrections Center for Women near Gig Harbor.

"I hope you'll give me a good report," she said.

"What report would that be?" Kendall asked.

"People will ask about how I look. They seem obsessed with my appearance. I finished first in that online poll about the sexiest woman behind bars. And I was against Lindsay Lohan at the time."

"Well, Lindsay has had some major bumps in the road," Kendall said.

"This hasn't been a bed of roses either," Brenda said. "Sure I have my admirers inside and out of here and I do what I can to keep myself ready."

"Ready for what?"

"The day I'm free. You see, I know it will come. Sooner or later."

"What makes you so certain about that?"

"I'm innocent," Brenda said. "I haven't done anything wrong."

Kendall let that one sit there. It was like a UFO had landed. There was no way to even comprehend the audacity of Brenda Nevins.

Jennifer Roberts was looking like a Girl Scout.

"I'm here about Tess Moreau's daughter, Darby," Kendall said, keeping her gaze locked on Brenda's eyes.

Brenda's eyes didn't blink. "I read the papers and I watch TV. Mostly TV. I expected someone would try to blame me for that too."

"So you're not surprised?"

She shook her head and unbuttoned her third button. "Hot in here," she said.

"Why aren't you surprised?" Kendall repeated.

"Because bad things happen to bad people."

It was snark bait, but it was too good to pass up. "So, you must be a bad person, Brenda."

"I've noticed that your eyes are on my breasts," Brenda said.

Kendall ignored the remark. This woman probably was mentally ill. A killer, for sure. A self-delusional narcissist that thought everyone lived to wallow in the splendor of her charms.

"Let's focus on why I'm here."

"Those were idle threats," she said. "If you're talking about what happened between me and Tess Moreau and that other guard, what's-her-name."

"Missy Carlyle," Kendall said.

Brenda smiled. Her veneers needed a little rework. *Too bad*, Kendall thought. Oral repair work was one of the benefits the state didn't offer inmates. They'd pull teeth, provide dentures, but no one got one bit of cosmetic dentistry. That perfect smile wouldn't be perfect forever.

"Yes, Missy Carlyle," Brenda said. "Fun, that one."

"You didn't think it was so fun at the time. In fact, you swore you'd get even."

"I guess I did. So what? I'm here in prison and the kid's dead out there somewhere. I had nothing to do with that. Maybe you should ask Missy Carlyle."

"We intend to," Kendall said. "I want to show you something."

"That sounds vaguely dirty, detective. I'm all yours."

Kendall retrieved the note that Tess Moreau had provided Birdy. She put it on the table and turned it so that Brenda could read.

And she watched her every move.

Brenda looked down at the note.

"How original," she said, her tone annoyed and deadpan at the same time.

"Did you send this?" Kendall asked.

"No," Brenda said. "I didn't. I don't even know where Tess the Mess lives."

Kendall tried to disarm Brenda by playing up to her. "I bet you could get someone to do anything for you."

Brenda rotated her shoulders a little. "You have no idea."

Kendall didn't take the bait. She had a pretty good idea what Brenda was getting at. If she was going to have lunch later she didn't want the visual to impede the enjoyment of her meal. The idea of Brenda and Missy on the dog-grooming table had already been seared into her imagination. That was enough.

"Have you ever asked anyone to do your bidding? You know, Brenda, would you have ever thought to maybe manipulate someone into doing something for you on the outside?"

Brenda smiled. "Of course I have. I have more money in my canteen account than I had in my bank account when they arrested me."

"Right," Kendall said. "I suppose people just give it to you."

"No one just gives you anything, detective."

"Right. You have to ask for it."

Brenda fidgeted with the fourth button on her blouse.

Oh God, please stop, Kendall thought.

Brenda moistened her lips with the tip of her tongue. "You don't know much about how to get what you want, detective. You don't ask for anything. If you ask for something, that implies that the person you're asking can say yes or no. With me that's not an option. I don't like leaving things to chance."

Brenda liked to brag and Kendall sent her in that direction.

"So what do you do?" she asked.

Brenda grinned. "Easy. I tell them to do it."

"Or what? Or else?"

"If I have to," Brenda said.

"Is that what you did to Missy Carlyle? After all, if she hadn't been so loud you wouldn't have been caught and you wouldn't have been in the hole when you were going to get that big TV special. You know, the one that was going to make you an even bigger star."

A cold smile came over Brenda's face. "I know what you're doing. You're mocking me. But I'd rather be in prison than have your humdrum boring life."

Kendall got up. She wasn't mad, just disgusted. She tapped the window in the door for the guard.

"Hey, don't go," Brenda said, her tone now pleading.

Kendall turned around and looked at her. "Are you telling or asking me to stay?"

Brenda turned her shoulder, her blouse opening a bit. "You know how I do things," she said.

"Yes, Brenda, I do," Kendall said. "That's why I'm leaving now."

On her way out to the superintendent's office, the Kitsap County detective passed by the employees of WCCW Wall of Fame. Tess's photograph caught her eye right away. The records clerk—Support Person of the Month for October—was wearing a light gray blazer over a dusty pink blouse—the same style but a different color than the one she'd been wearing when Kendall and Birdy first met her. Tess probably had one in every color. All on sale, of course. Or maybe, even better, from a representative's sample sale.

Kendall found her way to the offices upstairs. She hadn't met the new superintendent. While she knew confidentiality laws would keep information gleaning to a minimum, she asked the floor secretary if she could stop in.

"She's expecting you, detective," the secretary said.

The superintendent was a surprisingly cheerful woman named Janie Thomas. In her early fifties with soft, pearl gray hair and a ready smile, Janie had been on the job for a very short time. Already, it was clear, she suffered serious Brenda Nevins fatigue.

"The shows still call for her," Janie said, getting up to greet the detective. "Not network, but cable. And not as much," she said with obvious relief.

"I can see why they love her—and she loves the attention, doesn't she? She'll probably try to go over the wall the day they stop asking her for interviews," Kendall said.

Janie offered coffee, but Kendall's stomach felt queasy from the encounter with Brenda and she declined.

"You get what you needed from the interview?" she asked.

"This was more a due diligence interview than anything concrete," Kendall answered. "People like Brenda don't know how to tell the truth. They only know how to try to get what they want. They'll do anything. And if anyone wrote a book on the world's biggest narcissist they'd put Brenda's picture on the cover."

Janie smiled. "Did she unbutton her blouse?" she asked, already knowing the answer.

Kendall rolled her eyes. "Oh yeah, she did. I honestly don't know why she bothers with buttons when Velcro would be so much easier for her."

Janie laughed. "It doesn't matter if you're a man or a woman," she said. "She's so blatant about it that it would be hilarious if it weren't so twisted. She did that to a reporter from the *Seattle Times* last week and the poor guy practically wet his pants with embarrassment. He didn't even finish the interview."

"She thinks she's all that," Kendall said.

Janie sat down behind her desk, cluttered with paperwork, and Kendall took a seat across from her.

"What can you tell me about Missy Carlyle, Ms. Thomas?"

"Not much," the superintendent answered. "Not that I don't want to. But the state keeps info around here on lockdown. I can tell you the basics, from what I know. When she worked here, when she left."

"Why did she leave?"

Janie shook her head. "Personnel matter. Confidential."

Kendall thought it might go this way. "I'll come back with a court order."

"And I'll give it to you on a silver platter. Believe me, this is a black mark on all of us here."

"Without getting into specifics, can I ask you a few things?" Kendall asked. "Just to confirm?"

"You can try," Janie answered, a wry smile on her face.

"Dog-grooming table?" Kendall asked. "Always used for grooming dogs?"

Janie saw that this was going to be a bit of a game. She was up for it.

"Mostly but not always," she said.

Kendall liked this woman.

"There was a photo missing from your Wall of Fame," she went on. "Was it Missy's?"

"Yes, I believe it was taken down."

"Is every inmate's mail read before it goes out?"

Janie sighed, but it was an exaggerated sigh, the kind that says so much more than words. "Yes, detective, every sordid and boring word."

"Right. Incoming too?"

"Yes every word of those too."

"Tess Moreau is one of your best employees?"

"Her photograph hangs on the Wall of Fame," Janie said. "Deservedly so."

"Is she truthful?" Kendall asked.

Janie met Kendall's gaze head on. "Her portrait is on the wall, detective. She is the best employee—and most trusted—we've ever had."

Kendall picked up her badge, phone, keys, and ID from the locker provided for their storage. She glanced over at a display case showing the craft items made by the inmates. All were hideous in her opinion. She wondered whose murderous hands had done the crocheted tea cozy. She got Birdy on the phone.

"Hi, Birdy, I'm just leaving the prison."

"How'd it go with Brenda Nevins?"

"You and I are going to have lunch today and a psycho-bitch-from-hell throwdown. If you thought Jennifer Roberts was something else when you chatted her up in jail, you ought to have experienced Brenda Nevins."

"That bad?" Birdy asked.

"I feel like going to the curb and scraping the bottoms of my shoes. She practically tried to flash me."

"She sounds like a charmer," Birdy said. "Did you get anything you can use?"

An elderly couple walked from their Oldsmobile to

the front entrance of the prison. Visiting hours had started. They looked so sweet, so upset that they had to go see their little girl there. Suddenly, Kendall didn't feel sorry for them. It was possible that they had a hand in whatever it was that turned their little princess into a drug addict, a murderer, a child rapist. After sitting with Brenda Nevins for an hour, she wanted to blame someone.

Kendall slid into her car and turned on the ignition.

"Not sure," she said to Birdy. "That depends on what Missy Carlyle has to say."

CHAPTER 33

Birdy Waterman would have bet money on a different outcome than what appeared on the lab report of the organ tissue samples she'd removed from Donald Lake's body.

No sign of any poisoning. *None.* No heavy metals. No arsenic. No strychnine. The chemists did pick up traces of an HBP medicine, warfarin, which had been used by killers in the past. That might have given her a little satisfaction, but the concentrations were so light that it couldn't have been fatal.

Ethylene glycol degrades rapidly. Birdy knew that going in, but she thought it was doubtful that a woman living in Scottsdale could easily get her hands on antifreeze. She figured that Jennifer must have selected a different poison for the deed down there. Arsenic and other heavy metal poisons stay in the tissues for years.

Danny Lake was sure that Jennifer was his brother's killer. Bobby Drysdale ruined his life over her, and yet, as a parting shot had told Birdy that he was all but certain that he'd been the lucky one.

"I'm the one who got away alive," he said.

But as she sat in her cozy home office, poring over the report, she knew there was nothing but a cloud of suspicion hovering over Jennifer Roberts. A photograph of Birdy's father holding a massive king crab on a boat in the Bering Sea hung above her desk. It was rendered in black and white, which only served to make his dark eyes sparkle more. His smile was wide and there was a little anxiousness on his face.

That was one giant crab.

She called Kendall.

"Nothing turned up in the tox report on Donald Lake," she said when the detective answered.

"No antifreeze? No poisons?" Kendall asked.

"None," Birdy said. "A big fat zero. There is nothing here to indicate that she killed Donald. But she *might* have."

"Don't feel bad. You did your best."

"We can only go where the evidence takes us. No matter how we feel inside."

"Right. If Jennifer hadn't hooked up with that doctor down there, maybe things would have been different."

"Yeah, maybe a proper autopsy would have been conducted. And if it had, Ted Roberts would never have met her. He'd be alive kayaking or running laps."

"We can't change any of that, Birdy."

"You don't need to tell me that. By the time a case gets to my office, I'm pretty much the end of the line. In fact, my office really is the literal end of the line."

"The papers down there in Arizona—and our own *Kitsap Sun* here—sure are loving the story," Kendall said, changing the subject.

"I guess nothing beats a 'black widow' case."

"I know. A guy can kill his wife—and they do all the time—and unless they're super rich or super handsome no one gives it much of a thought. But put a flashy woman at the defense table and you've got a winner, media-wise."

Birdy asked Kendall what her next step was.

"I've been thinking about that. We have motive. We have opportunity. We have a history of a person who doesn't stop at anything to get what she wants."

"Prejudicial, detective."

Kendall laughed. "I know. The defense will fight tooth and nail to keep all of that Arizona crap out, but the bell will have rung louder than St. Gabriel's. Everyone knows what kind of person she is. The prosecutor wants more evidence, but I don't know where we can get it."

"Her son and daughter," Birdy said. "Lean on them. Elan tells me that they're the talk of the school. They think you and I have been mean to their mom. Especially you."

"Great, Birdy. Well, they've been on my list. How's your tan holding up?"

"I'm Native American, remember? Tan *is* my skin color."

"Oh I was thinking maybe you'd like to go visit Desert Enchantment with me. I'm thinking of signing up."

Birdy looked up at her father's portrait. She always favored his coffee-with-cream skin tones. "Come to think of it, I am looking a little peaked."

"Be there in five."

* * *

Ruby Lake stood behind the counter; the Ocean Scene suntan product line's endless commercial on the big screen in the lobby was on mute. Jennifer's daughter, her blond hair artfully tangled, looked up and her nirvana of sun, fun, and piped-in music was over. A grim look came over her pretty, but surprisingly not overly, tan face.

"What do you want now?" she asked, clearly irritated. "Haven't you done enough? Because of you and what that bitch Molly accused her of doing, mom is in jail. She's going to have to fight to stay out of the gas chamber."

"We don't have the gas chamber in Washington," Birdy said. She didn't add, "but we do have death by hanging."

Ruby glared at Birdy. Her phone sounded indicating a new text, but she didn't take her eyes off the forensic pathologist.

"I know all about what you've been up to," she said. "My uncle Danny called me. He said that you think that my mom killed my dad."

It was interesting that Danny would do that, but Birdy didn't remark on it. She had thought Danny and his nephew and niece were estranged and that she'd been tapped as the messenger for a reunion with his ailing mother.

"I do, but so does he," Birdy said. It was a tit-for-tat answer, but that's the way Ruby seemed to like to deal with things. She was a know-it-all-button pusher. A mini-version of her mother, except she hadn't killed anyone. And that along with the fact that she almost eighteen, as Birdy knew, was a pretty big difference.

Ruby glanced at her text and made a face. Whatever it was it wasn't important.

"I hope you called your grandmother," Birdy said.

Ruby rolled her eyes upward. "Oh my God," she said. "Are you lecturing me? My brother knows Elan. I know a few things about you. So don't go telling me what to do or who to call. People like you are always trying to act all perfect and making sure that others do what you want them to do. What you think is right. My mom hates my grandma and I hate her too. So stay out of it. Fix up your own issues."

Though she was sort of enjoying the give and take between her colleague and the teen, Kendall circled back to the reason they were there.

"We are here for the truth about what happened the night Ted died, Ruby," the detective said.

Ruby picked up her phone and texted a short message.

"I don't know anything," she said, finished with what was so much more important.

Kendall pushed. "Ruby. You *do*."

"You wish I did, because your case is weak and you know it."

"We wouldn't have arrested your mother if we didn't think we could prove our case in court, but I admit that it would be helpful if you told us the truth."

The dryer made a pinging sound that signaled the end of the cycle.

"Excuse me, I have work to do," Ruby said, leaving the counter for the hallway of desert photos. She tapped the mute button on the TV, and the commercial with its oiled and bronzed bodies frolicking in the surf had sound again.

"Looks like Fiji," Kendall said. "I've always wanted to go there."

"It's all right," Birdy said.

"You've been there?"

"No but I've been to Scottsdale and I've seen enough of the beautiful people. At least for a while."

"What's taking her so long?"

"Search me."

Birdy smiled. "I love it when cops say that without irony."

Ruby had been gone at least four minutes and the looping commercial started to repeat.

"Let's go find her," Birdy said.

The two women went down the hall toward the room with the bank of dryers. As they approached they heard sobbing. It was soft and then hard, like popping corn against the aluminum lid of a pot on the stove. A cry. Then quiet. Then a cry, cry, cry.

Ruby was on the floor holding a handful of towels to her face.

"Honey," Kendall said, the mother in her rising to the surface, "what is it?"

"I don't want to talk about it," Ruby sputtered out, "but I don't think I can hold it inside anymore."

Kendall bent down and put her arm on the teen's shoulder, but Ruby pulled back and sobbed some more. More like wailed. Her mascara smudged the snowy white of a towel.

"You don't know what it's like to have a mother like mine," she said, looking up at Kendall, then over at Birdy who moved in closer but still stayed behind the detective. "My mom. My mom," Ruby said, struggling to string her words together. "She's not like other moms. She's not like other people."

Kendall looked deep into the girl's eyes. The hardness that had been there when she was telling them to get lost at the counter was completely gone.

"Your mom does have a big personality," Kendall said, choosing her words carefully.

Ruby sat there, crumpled in a little ball. She rocked back and forth a little and she cried some more. "I don't know what's going to happen to me or my brother. I really don't know what to do."

"We'll help you, Ruby," Kendall said.

"I'm afraid of her."

"Who? Your mother?"

"Yes, my mom. You don't know what she's capable of. I do."

"I think we have a pretty good idea. That's why she's been arrested."

"Do you know more, something you haven't told us?" Kendall asked.

Ruby started crying some more.

A tone sounded that a customer was there.

"I have to get that," she said.

"No, I'll do it," Birdy said, leaving for the front door. A young woman stood there.

"I've been like waiting a long time," she said.

"I'm sorry, but we're closed."

"Nah-ah. I have a Sundowners Pass and I can come anytime without an appointment. And you don't close until late."

"We're closed," Birdy said with complete authority. "You have to leave."

"I paid a lot of money for my unlimited."

"I know. You can come back tomorrow."

"I'm really mad. You have to give me something for my inconvenience."

Birdy handed her a bottle of lotion marked TESTER.

"Thanks!"

"No problem."

The girl left. Birdy pulled the string cord on the OPEN sign and turned the deadbolt. When she returned to the dryer room, Ruby was just pulling herself together again.

"You know what happened to Ted, don't you?" Kendall said, her eyes barely grazing Birdy's as she resumed her place in the toasty warm laundry room.

"Uh-huh. I do."

"Can you tell us?"

"You don't understand. She's my mom. I love her. I don't want to get her in trouble."

"She's already in trouble. You know that."

"I know that she killed Ted," Ruby said.

"How do you know?"

"I saw her do it."

"Do what?"

Ruby paused while one of the dryers let out its melodic chime.

"Poison him," she said. "That's what. She put the poison in his drinks. Sometimes she added it to the spaghetti sauce. That was easy because he liked meat sauce and my brother and me didn't."

"Did you know what the poison was?" Kendall asked.

"No," Ruby said. "Not at *first*. She kept the stuff under the sink in the kitchen. I looked at it. It wasn't really poison, I mean not like rat poison with a Mr. Yuck sticker on it. It was some stuff she bought in the automotive section at Fred Meyer."

"What was the product?" Kendall asked. "Do you know?"

The teenager nodded. "Yes, Prestone."

"You just let her do it? You didn't say, 'Hey, Mom, why are you doing this?' "

"Honestly, I am not going to lie. There is no reason to. I didn't say anything at first, because I thought it was medicine or something. She even told me one time that it was something that would 'make him feel better' and I guess at first I just wanted to believe her."

Birdy spoke up. "But something changed and you began to suspect something wasn't right."

Ruby looked down, struggling for the words. "Yeah, she told me that he didn't love her and was going to divorce her. And she said something like 'I've been on that merry-go-round before and I'm not going to do it again.' "

"What symptoms did he have?" Birdy asked. This was her area.

"Throwing up mostly," Ruby answered. "I mean, he was always heaving his guts out. One time when he passed out, my mom held his mouth open and poured it right down his throat. Another time—and this was only one time—she took a can of Raid and sprayed it in his eyes."

Birdy and Kendall exchanged quick looks.

"You said she didn't want to lose everything?" Kendall asked. "What did she think she'd lose?"

Ruby was clearly uncomfortable, but she wasn't going to stop now.

"Well, when they first got married, Mom got some extra life insurance and she was afraid that he'd find out before, you know, he, like, died."

"She told you this?" Kendall asked.

"Yeah, she did. I told you my mom isn't like other people. She didn't want to end up back in Gila County with her mom and the rest of the trailer trash that she grew up with. She had—we all had—a really great life in Scottsdale. I cried and cried about leaving there for here. Mom told me, she *promised*, it wouldn't be for long."

Birdy could see that Ruby knew her mother was devious, but her last remarks indicated something she wondered if the teen quite understood. How was it that Jennifer knew they wouldn't be in Washington long? The explanation was clear to her. Ted had been a mark. He'd been snared in one of Jennifer's traps. Killing him was a means to an end. When Jennifer was convicted, and Birdy was sure she would be, she would face the death penalty. Kitsap County more so than others in Washington had a prosecutor who believed that certain killers shouldn't be shown any mercy.

Jennifer Lake Drysdale Roberts was easily going to qualify for the death row club.

"Tell us about when your stepfather, Ted, died," Birdy said. "What happened?"

Ruby's tears started anew. "I don't like thinking about it."

"We need to know," Kendall said. "What happened?"

Ruby looked down at the floor as she spoke. "My mom got me up. It was around four a.m. She told me that she needed my help. I was like a zombie. It had been a late night and I wanted to stay in bed. But I got up. She made me. She took me into Ted's room. She'd moved him into the guest room like a month ago. She turned on the light and told me to check to see if he was breathing."

"And did you, Ruby, did you check?" Kendall asked.

The girl looked up "Yeah. I did. He wasn't. I felt his chest but it wasn't moving at all. It wasn't going, you know, up and down, like a living person's would."

The dryer room at Desert Enchantment was warm. Too warm. But there was no way anyone was going to leave that space. The tumbling noise of the machinery was like a drum, padding each word with emphasis.

"What happened next?" Kendall asked.

"Okay," Ruby said. "This is really hard to talk about. I mean, this is my mom I'm talking about, but it's also something I did. I don't want to go to jail."

"You didn't give him any poison, did you?" Kendall asked.

She shook her head. "Oh no. Never. But maybe you'll think I was an accessory because I helped her. But I had no choice."

"Telling the truth like you're doing, you'll be fine," Kendall said. "I promise."

Ruby, for the first time, looked a little relieved. She was still trembling a little, and obviously shook up, but Kendall's words seemed to give her the courage to carry on—to do the right thing. The teenager swallowed hard.

This was not easy. Despite the poster promoting an after-tan lotion that hung by the dryers, life was not a day at the beach. Ruby's day certainly hadn't been.

"My mom was in a tizzy," she said. "She said she didn't know how she was going to explain why, if he was so sick, she didn't check on him all the time. Or have a nurse. She gave me some washcloths that she had got wet and soapy and told me I had to help her clean him up. He'd thrown up in bed. It was totally gross but I did it. She told me that we needed to go back to bed and then get up and act like it just happened."

One person had been left out of the conversation.

"What about your brother?" Kendall asked.

Ruby acknowledged the weirdness of her brother being so absent from the action with a shake of her head. "Micah slept through the whole thing. He could sleep through anything."

"Did he know about what was happening?"

Ruby thought he did. "Yeah, but not as much."

"So did you go back to bed?" Kendall asked. "Is that what you did?"

Ruby looked away from the detective as one of the dryers pinged. She went over and twisted a knob for an additional ten minutes.

"Yeah, the next morning Mom fixed breakfast," she said. "She even made Ted a plate of food although he was dead and she ate some of it to make it look like, you know, it just happened. But really he'd been dead for at least three hours. It's all so crazy."

"You're going to need to come to the sheriff's department so we can put this all in writing."

"Look, I don't know. You mean that I would have to testify against my mom?"

Kendall looked deep into Ruby's eyes. "You have to do what's right, Ruby."

"I don't know. I don't think I can. My mom can be scary."

"You can do it. You can be stronger than her. The truth is very powerful."

"What about my brother?"

"It depends on what he knows."

"Only enough to know that there's something seriously wrong with our mother."

The trio returned to the front desk. Birdy unlocked the deadbolt and pulled the OPEN sign light back on. Ruby went to the restroom to pull herself together. She'd promised to come to the office and give a statement the next day, after school. She'd convince Micah to come with her. In other cases, Kendall would have insisted she come right at that moment. But with Birdy there witnessing the interview, there was backup for everything Ruby had said. Ruby came out of the restroom with her hair in a ponytail and an application of fresh makeup. She looked better, but not great.

"Are you going to be all right?" Birdy asked.

"I think so," Ruby said. "I have to work. I promised my boss. And, really, I don't have any money. The house is paid off, but I don't know if I can stay there or what. Ted's family hasn't come around yet. But if they do, they're probably going to want it back."

Birdy and Kendall sat in Kendall's car in the parking lot in front of Desert Enchantment to debrief.

"I didn't see that coming," Kendall said. "At least not that easily. She just spilled her guts out."

"It's a lot to hold inside," Birdy said. "She's been carrying that around like a cancer and she just wants to get away from all the ugliness that her mother foisted on her and her brother."

"Can you imagine having a mother like that?"

Birdy didn't answer. She did have a mother a little like that. Not as bad, but one who was immensely cruel.

"In some ways, I'm not completely stunned by what she said," Birdy said. "What she said makes perfect sense. The autopsy showed no food in his stomach, but Jennifer said she'd fed him French toast and orange marmalade."

The windows started to fog and Kendall turned on the defroster.

"The timeline matches what Molly said too," Kendall said.

"The liver temp was a little off too, not so much that I'd have red flagged it. Rigor hadn't occurred yet either. That takes anywhere from two to four hours. I remember that he'd stiffened up considerably during the autopsy."

"Unusual?" Kendall asked.

"Nothing's really unusual," Birdy went on. "There are always reasons for variance in nature. Outside of cicadas every seventeen years in the Northeast and the swallows in March in Capistrano, the rhythm can be erratic."

"I feel sorry for her," Kendall said.

"I do too. My mom was bad, but not like hers."

"She knows about your mother."

Birdy opened the car door and looked toward her Prius. "I guess that surprised me more than anything," she said. "Elan will have some explaining to do."

CHAPTER 34

The turnout for Theodore Allen Roberts's delayed-for-too-many-reasons-to-list memorial service at St. Gabriel's in Port Orchard was red, white, and blue. None of the forty-two-year-old's immediate family was in attendance—his wife, of course, was in jail. His stepchildren were absent at the request of their mother who was concerned about the media bashing that had started to follow her. Ted's sister, Megan Casper from Boise, was there as were Molly O'Rourke and elderly neighbors Lena and Sam. The coffin was draped in an enormous flag. After the ceremony two of Ted's friends from the navy folded it into a triangle and handed it to Megan.

A newly hired reporter for the *Kitsap Sun* waited for Megan and Molly outside the chapel. He was looking for a short comment from someone close to Ted that he could use as proof to his editor that he'd showed up to cover the service.

He asked the dumbest question that anyone covering a funeral or memorial service could ask. And he got an earful.

"How do you feel about everything that's happened?"

Megan, a silver-haired woman in her late forties, let him have it.

"How do I feel? That my brother married a 'black widow'? That he was murdered? How do I feel about *that*?"

The reporter's face turned apple red. "Yeah, sorry."

"Fine," Ted's sister said. "I'm feeling a million things right now. I'm not a liar. My brother and I were not close and I didn't have the . . . let's say *opportunity* to meet Jennifer. I came to settle a few things with his estate, but the whole trip has been a complete bust."

The young reporter was embarrassed, but he knew enough to ask a follow-up question. He'd only had this job for a month and he didn't want to lose it.

"What's going on with his estate?" he asked.

She glared at him while Molly O'Rourke stood there, not sure what to say.

"How old are you?" Megan asked.

The reporter switched on an eager-beaver attitude. "Twenty-three next month," he said.

Megan waved her finger at him. "First of all, never say what your age is next month," she said. "It makes you sound like a four-year-old saying you're 'four and a half.' "

He blinked. "Thanks, I guess."

"You can quote me on that," she said.

He wrote that down in his notebook.

"What about the estate though?" he asked.

While mourners, mostly navy men and women, filed past and acknowledged her with sympathetic looks, Megan clutched the flag.

"That's the story you should be working on," she said.

The kid thanked her. "I'll get on it," he said.

Ted's sister turned to Molly, who was standing there with her jaw wide open.

"Nice to meet you, Molly. I'm glad you got to know my brother. I never did. He had issues. We all do."

She watched the reporter get in what she was sure was a hand-me-down car from his parents.

"I'm glad I live in Idaho," she said. "We don't put up with this kind of bullshit."

The next day, Birdy Waterman unfurled her rolled-up newspaper. There had been suspicious activity at the submarine base in Bangor, up in the northern part of the county. Neither the paper, nor the base spokeswoman, indicated that it was a terrorist threat, but everything like that seemed to be.

At the bottom of the front page, her eyes were seared by a headline:

BLACK WIDOW ROBERTS SET TO CASH IN

She read and dialed Kendall at the same time.

"Did you see the paper?" Birdy asked.

"Huh? No," Kendall said. "I haven't even made it to the office. Steven has a job interview. I'm driving him to the airport."

Ordinarily Birdy would have asked all about that. But not now. She didn't even tell Kendall to wish him well.

"Listen to this," she said.

" 'An investigation by the *Sun* has revealed that Jennifer Roberts, who is being held for the murder of her husband, might indirectly reap more than one million dollars—even if convicted of the crime.' "

Kendall piped up. "That can't be true."

"Let me finish," Birdy said, now skimming. "Says that Jennifer filed insurance claims the morning her husband died. Says there are three 'known' policies each worth between two hundred and fifty and three hundred and thirty grand."

"I thought there were only two," the detective said. "A third is a bonus, but doesn't change our case."

"Right, Kendall, but here's what's so fascinating. The article says that Jennifer is the primary beneficiary and in the event that she is unable to claim the money her children will get the cash."

"But he didn't adopt them," Kendall said.

"Doesn't matter. His estate passes to her, hers passes to them. Listen to this quote from Ted Roberts's sister Megan Casper.

" 'I think it is a travesty that someone could marry someone just to kill them and have their children get the insurance money. I mean, really? Any woman or man for that matter who wants to send their kid to college just has to kill their spouse. This is all right? This is America. Makes me sick.' "

"It makes me sick too," Kendall said.

"You may need to pull over to throw up," Birdy said.

"What now?"

"Listen to this quote from Ruby Lake."

"I'm not going to like this, am I?"

"Good guess," Birdy said, deadpan.

" 'When reached at her home in Port Orchard last

night Ruby Lake said that she was not testifying against her mother despite rumors that had been circulating around members of law enforcement.

" ' "I said some things to the detectives and they took it the wrong way. My mom is not going to prison for something she didn't do." ' "

"Just wow," Kendall said.

Birdy agreed completely. "Yeah."

"I'm heading over to the school to see Ruby," Kendall said.

"Where are you now?" asked Birdy.

"Just got off the Narrows Bridge."

"You might pass her coming the other way," Birdy said. "Here's the closing line of the article.

" 'Lake, 18, says she's returning to Arizona to stay with family until her mother's trial this fall.

" ' "I don't want to be harassed anymore," she said.' "

"Birdy, you're going to have to try to catch her before she leaves. See why she's flip-flopped on us."

"Shouldn't a deputy do that?" Birdy asked. "Maybe Gary?"

The last encounter with Ruby in the dryer room had made things a little personal when Ruby invoked knowledge of Birdy's relationship with her mother. Birdy would have preferred not to see her again. Mostly because she knew the girl was right. Birdy didn't have her own house in order and she knew it. Her relationships with her mother and sister were messed up.

"We don't have time for that. You know the case better than anyone. Certainly better than Gary."

"He's a very good deputy, Kendall."

"I didn't say he wasn't. But he's not you. I'm counting on you. We're a team on this case, remember?"

Birdy couldn't argue against that. That was the whole crux of their working together—improving relations between the departments.

"I'll go," she said without much enthusiasm. "I guess I have to, but this team work is wearing me out. I have an old man in the chiller waiting for me. Tell Steven good luck. I forgot to ask. Where's the interview?"

"Portland," Kendall said.

Birdy didn't like that at all. "You won't be moving there, will you?"

"No," Kendall said. "That's the hiring office. You're stuck with me. Steven says hi back. Bye."

CHAPTER 35

Micah Lake sat on the front steps of 511 Camellia Street. He wore dark jeans and a dark blue hoody zipped to his throat. He looked like a tough guy, but Birdy knew he wasn't that at all. He was quiet, artistic, and had a disarming smile—though he didn't use it that often. The air had chilled a little since the previous day and the sky threatened a good rainstorm with a bank of clouds coming in from the south.

"She's in the house, Dr. Waterman," he said. "If you're looking for my sister. Packing. Like a rat deserting a sinking ship."

Birdy stopped at the bottom of the steps. "Aren't you supposed to be at school now?"

The teenager was annoyed by the question. His life had unraveled and school didn't seem to be part of his priorities just then.

"I know," he said, "but with Ruby leaving and all, she told me to get my butt over here to load up Ted's car. So here I am missing history class, which I guess is better than missing something I actually like."

"How's it going living here with Ruby?" Birdy asked. "You've been through a lot."

He fumbled for a pack of cigarettes, but she ignored that he was about to smoke.

"It's okay," he said.

Birdy thought he was a nice kid. He just had the misfortune of being born to the kind of mother that usually eats her young.

"Upstairs?" she asked, as the first drops of rain splatted hard and heavy on the front steps.

"Yeah, first door on the right. The one with all the crap on the bed." He reached for a finally found cigarette and she managed to give him a scolding look.

"At this point, what does it matter?" he asked.

"Not now," she said. "Later, yes, it will. Did your mom let you smoke?"

"No," he said, lighting up.

"Then you shouldn't be doing it now."

Micah blew a perfect smoke ring. "My mom's a killer. Who cares what she thinks? My sister's leaving. My life sucks now. I hope I get cancer."

"You don't," Birdy said. "Trust me. I've seen enough of it in my office. You don't."

"Whatever," he said. "Sorry. Thanks."

She smiled faintly at him, feeling every bit of the sorrow of a boy who was now without a father, a mother, a sister who was about to do exactly what he said.

Jump from a sinking ship.

Birdy went inside looking for Ruby. Before heading up the stairs, she scanned the main living area. Ruby and Micah were not good housekeepers that was for sure. The place was in dire need of a crew of Merry Maids to pick up the soda cans, Chinese takeout boxes, and other remnants of a home without one bit of parental supervision even though it had been only a few days since their mom's arrest. Jennifer's daughter might be almost eighteen but she was no adult.

Birdy found the teenager stacking her belongings on the bed. She was extremely organized in that endeavor—all clothing was stacked by color and folded with the exactness of a Gap sales clerk working the floor.

Ruby looked up with her impossibly blue eyes, the best attribute her mother could have given her. The only thing about her that seemed pure and uncorrupted. "What do you want now?"

It was no welcome, but Birdy Waterman really didn't expect that either. Kendall should be there doing this. Her job was to look into the cause of someone's death, not shore up an investigation that didn't need shoring up. She decided that sympathy could only get her so far. A little directness was in order.

"I want to know why you've decided to be a liar," she asked.

Ruby stared hard at her. "I don't owe you an explanation."

"But you do," Birdy said, lingering in the doorway. "You made a promise to me and to Detective Stark that you'd tell the truth. You told us everything that had been going on here. We don't need your testimony to secure a conviction, but you don't need to live your life feeling like you helped your mom kill your stepfather."

Ruby looked down at what she was doing. "I'm not listening to a word you say," she said, opening a suitcase and moving the pinks and whites into separate compartments.

"You *will* listen to me," Birdy said, moving closer. "I know that you are better than your mother."

Ruby stopped. "Are you trying to make me laugh or cry, Dr. Waterman? Go back to the morgue and play with a stiff one."

"Okay, that's just tacky. Is that who you are?"

Birdy pondered saying, "Is that the trailer park of your mom's past coming out in you?" but she thought better of that. Trailer park people were people of lesser means, they weren't rotten people.

"I am getting out of town," Ruby said. "That's what I'm doing. I'm going to lay low because—and you will never understand this—because I'm afraid."

"Afraid of what?" Birdy asked. "Telling the truth?"

Ruby stopped arranging the pinks. "I'm afraid of my mother. I'm terrified of her. She's capable of anything."

"We know that," Birdy said. "I'm glad you know that. That's why you need to testify against her."

"I want to live. I don't want to die."

"She can't hurt you."

Ruby moved some things aside and sat down on the edge of the bed.

"You honestly don't know what she's capable of, do you?"

"Murder. Yes, I know that."

"My mother," she said, hesitating. "She would kill me for a pair of Manolos if she thought she could get away with it."

Birdy let silence fill the air, hoping it would prompt the girl to say more. And she did.

"Dr. Waterman, I'm scared."

For such a tough, self-absorbed girl, it was remarkable to Birdy. Ruby actually *looked* scared.

"What happened?" Birdy asked.

Ruby swallowed hard. "I saw her. I went to see her yesterday. You see, I still love her."

"Of course," Birdy said, "she's your mother. I understand that. You're almost eighteen now. She's in jail. She can't get to you."

Ruby got up and paced. "She threatened me. She begged me. She told me that if she went to the gas chamber she'd haunt me for the rest of my life."

"I told you. We don't have the gas chamber here."

"Gallows, whatever. The point is if my mom goes to prison she'll find a way to reach for me with her sharp fingernails. She'll do it. I saw her hold Ted's mouth open and pour poison down his throat. You can't tell me that she wouldn't seek revenge."

Birdy couldn't. No one could. After what Brenda Nevins had set in motion, it was possible that Jennifer Roberts could do something too. The unthinkable, the unimaginable, had already happened. Revenge from a prison cell seemed all too real.

"I hope you change your mind, Ruby. I know you're strong enough to stand on your own two feet."

"You can't promise that the police will be able to protect me. Can you?"

Birdy knew there were no guarantees and she didn't want to lie to the girl.

"No," she said, "no one can."

While Ruby turned back to her packing, Birdy stood in the door watching. She looked over at the bedroom where Ted had taken his last gasp, the master bedroom where Jennifer had set her trap, and finally Micah's room. She looked inside each space. They were little tableaus to the things that had transpired there. The king-size bed in the master bedroom with its sand-colored sheets and a comforter of dark blue, like the edge of an ocean that had swept two lovers away. Ruby's room had pictures of the desert and a shelf of books and stuffed animals, that twilight time between girlhood and adulthood. The guestroom was plain, sterile, a place to wait to die. And Micah's room was a lot like Elan's makeover of her guestroom—a desk of electronics, an empty popcorn bag, and some artwork that he'd created at school.

Micah was gone when Birdy went outside. She looked around, but he was nowhere to be seen.

She dialed Kendall and filled her in on what Ruby had said. Kendall was on her way back from the airport after sending Steven off to an interview in hopes of a job offer the family needed so much.

Birdy drove up to her office. When she walked in, Kendall had returned; she was on the phone.

"Hey, just wanted you to know that Ruby saw her mother in the jail," the detective said.

"She mentioned that," Birdy said. "Her mom threatened her."

"Really?" Kendall asked. "That's interesting. We have a tape. Come and watch when you have time."

"No time like right now," Birdy said. "Just say that this is the worst mother-daughter dynamic, since . . . well, since me and my mom."

"Don't be so hard on yourself," Kendall said.

"I was thinking more of my mother. She sets the tone for everything. Always has. See you in a few."

* * *

On the computer screen in Kendall's office, mother and daughter were about to face each other through an inch-thick safety glass partition at the Kitsap County jail. Their lifeline was a landline-style telephone mouthpiece and receiver. There was only one other person with a visitor, another woman there on a DUI charge four seats down. Her visitor was her husband, a sleepy-eyed guy who looked about half-baked. Either one could have been on the wrong side of the glass.

The chairs were fixed to the floor. The ambience was decidedly impersonal for any kind of reunion. As it should be. Jennifer smiled and drummed the tabletop of the carrel that she occupied while she waited for Ruby to take a seat. At once, Ruby picked up and started talking.

"I can't hear the audio," Birdy said.

Kendall made a face, then hit the PAUSE button. "There is no audio."

"Then why record it?" Birdy asked.

"For security reasons. We can't include the audio because of right-to-privacy laws."

"Shouldn't people visiting someone in jail expect they'd be recorded?"

"It isn't *their* privacy. The inmates' right to privacy is what's of concern." Kendall stopped talking. "And don't look at me like that."

Birdy was stunned. "Really, Kendall? The inmates?"

"Yes, I know," the detective said. "They have an expectation of privacy within a visit. Spokane County got sued four years ago. They didn't know that the person on the good side of the glass was a lawyer. So now we have to assume that everyone is a lawyer."

"Sometimes I hate what this world's turning into, Kendall."

Kendall couldn't disagree. "Sometimes? I hate it at least once a day. Now watch the vid because actually it is kind of interesting."

She clicked on the arrow and it started up again.

"Look at Jennifer," Kendall said. "She's not saying a word. Her daughter is doing all the talking."

"Ruby said her mom threatened her, Kendall. Maybe that comes later in the tape."

"Nope. But something else does."

The video was hardly high definition. In fact, it was black and white and disappointingly grainy. The camera was in a fixed position, showing the back of Ruby's head, and about three-quarters of her mother's face.

"I wish I knew what she was saying," Birdy said.

"Watch this part." Kendall sped up to just a hair before the end of the recording. "Right here. Now."

Jennifer was standing up, clutching the phone next to her ear.

"I didn't think you could wear earrings in jail," Birdy said.

"Sh! Watch."

Jennifer was saying something to her daughter, but her manner, her affectation, seemed utterly at odds with what Ruby had said about the encounter. Jennifer, who despite her jailhouse garb looked pretty good, was smiling.

"Maybe she's one of those people who smiles at you while she's slitting your throat?" Birdy said.

Kendall grabbed a picture of that in her mind. "I wouldn't put it past her."

"If only there had been some audio," Birdy said.

"If only we could read lips," Kendall added.

Birdy leaned in, then pulled away from the screen. "Yeah, but her mouth isn't visible," she said.

Kendall pointed to the screen. "Right. *Here.* Watch her eyes."

Birdy looked at Kendall. "She didn't do that, did she?"

"Watch again." She clicked the arrow, sending the video back two seconds, and pushed PLAY.

The forensic pathologist and detective looked at each other. They both saw it.

Jennifer Lake Drysdale Roberts winked at her daughter.

"What do you make of that?" Kendall asked Birdy.

"I honestly don't know. She was adamant that she'd had some kind of knock-down drag-out with her mom and that she was scared to death to testify against her. She told me that she feared for her life."

"She didn't look too scared there."

Birdy shook her head. "No, she didn't. Not at all."

The inmates at the women's prison in Purdy are allowed the use of wall-mounted telephones in a central location. Despite the idea that outsiders frequently embrace as gospel, the inmates do not have their own phones or computers. Many, however, have TV sets in their cells. That's more about keeping the population occupied than rewarding them with a special privilege. Phone calls are limited to a specific time of day—and are always made collect. Monopolizing the phones is an issue—some inmates are constantly trying to work in a call. Brenda Nevins never had a problem getting the amount of time extended. She had canteen money or sex to trade.

A newbie who was incarcerated for selling meth for her boyfriend was crying into the phone to her mother. She wanted to come home. She was terrified. Brenda came up to her and tapped her shoulder.

"I'm still talking," the girl said.

"You're done," Brenda said.

Their eyes locked. "Mommy, I gotta go."

She dropped the phone and scurried down the hall.

Brenda picked up the phone and listened.

"Kimberly?"

"Kim's gone. Bye."

She smiled, hung up, and started dialing. The recorded message played before she could speak. It alerted that the call was originating from a correctional facility. It went on to say that if the recipient didn't know someone named "Brenda," they should hang up immediately.

This recipient didn't hang up.

"Why are you calling me?" a woman said.

"Because, I dunno, I guess I just wanted to let you know that we might get to be roommates, after all."

Brenda loved every second in which she could inflict pain. One time she had an orgasm while she battered another woman in the shower; the sole blind spot provided cover from the video cameras that caught almost everything that happened inside the walls of the institution.

"Don't ever call me again."

"But you accepted my call."

"I shouldn't have."

"But you miss me, don't you?"

"Like cancer I miss you."

"Too bad. I don't often do things for other people because, well, they are always so busy doing for me."

"What do you want, Brenda?"

Brenda breathed into the phone. "I'm so horny for you, babe."

"What do you want?"

"Be that way," Brenda said. "A detective from Kitsap County came for a visit. You're about to be on the news. If you are, just make sure to mention me."

CHAPTER 36

Missy Carlyle was often underestimated. She was attractive, with soft auburn hair that she wore in a stylish bob. If someone needed some heavy lifting done, they'd look right past her. She had a small, wiry frame. But she was tough. Navy tough. She'd worked in a prison, for God's sake. Even more impressive, she worked as a high school janitor. That was tougher duty than the prison and the navy combined. And despite the good-looking package over a steel interior, she was shaken to the core. She'd never faced anything with such a grim outcome as telling her girlfriend what she'd done before they met.

And that it involved notorious killer Brenda Nevins.

Connie Mitchell was packing up her things in the classroom that she'd made a second home over her years at South Kitsap High School. Everywhere she turned there was a memory associated with something. A gift from a student. A piece of art that had been a creative breakthrough. The stain of copper sulfate in the sink that was a reminder of a boy who thought art and chemistry should be combined and nearly burned down the place. Connie's world had been shattered. She'd been placed on administrative leave with pay. The rumors about her involvement with Darby Moreau had become impossible for the school board and the principal to ignore.

She wasn't told in person, but by a letter delivered by a representative of the teacher's union—a smug man who didn't like her "kind" working in the school.

"You mean an art teacher," she said, knowing that's not what he meant at all.

"Here," he said, handing the letter to her seconds after the bell ended the day.

For legal reasons and to protect all parties involved we are placing you on leave for the remainder of the school year. A full review of any alleged or non-alleged incidents involving any improper behavior between you—a teacher— and a student will be conducted in the immediate future. Your pay and benefits will continue until such time as severance or termination is applied to your specific employment with the South Kitsap School District.

She'd texted Missy the second the man left.

Connie: I need u. I can't pack this up alone.
Missy: I need to talk to u too

Connie and Missy had been in a domestic partnership, but when Washington became one of the first states to pass same-sex marriage into law they'd planned a summer wedding at Snoqualmie Falls Lodge near North Bend,

Washington. They had selected matching dresses and had pared the guest list down to a manageable twenty-two.

Now all of that was in serious doubt.

Connie was collecting things from her desk and selected a few paintings from students that she'd miss—including one made by Darby.

"I have something to tell you," Missy said when she arrived. Standing in the doorway, she wore a grim look on her face.

Connie looked up and half-smiled, trying to lighten a very dark mood. "It can't be anything worse than losing my job."

"You haven't lost your job yet," Missy said, her voice achingly soft. "But it is a lot worse than that."

Connie looked out the door. Seeing no one in the hall, she got up and embraced Missy. She held her and quietly sobbed. It was a rolling cry, one that was not meant to be heard, but rather just absorbed into the body of the one person she'd trusted and loved above all others. Until she met Missy, Connie had never wanted anything more than to be a teacher, to shape and mold the dreams of the misfits, the outcasts, the students who reminded her of herself at that age. She'd found serenity and joy in the art she created and she knew that other teens could do the same. If only someone would lead them in the right direction.

With Missy came the dream of a more fulfilling life—a life to be shared.

"Connie," Missy said, pulling her back and looking into her weeping eyes, "what I have to tell you is even worse than you can imagine."

Connie wiped her eyes with her sleeve.

"What, baby? What could be worse than being called a sexual predator?"

"But you aren't," Missy said. "I know that. Everyone in this school knows that. It was a whisper, a rumor made by some kid to get attention. It will be seen for the lie that it is. You'll see."

Missy waited a beat. It was so hard to get out the words. She wasn't sure if she should trickle out her story like a leaky faucet, one drop at a time. Or maybe just dump it all out like a fire hydrant hit by an SUV.

Trickle. That was the only way.

"There is no way that I can be saved from my past," she said. "There is something . . . something that you need to know about me."

"Missy, you're scaring me." Connie shut the door. School was over for the day, but there were lingerers— kids who didn't have anywhere to go and stayed long past regular hours. Most of those kids seemed to drift into the arts: drama, music, and Connie's specialty, fine arts.

She turned around to find Missy facing the window that looked out toward the parking lot and then beyond to a barricade of green woods behind the school.

"Now, you're really scaring me," she said.

"I can't look at you," Missy said. "Just let me talk."

Connie stood still, trying to think of what might be so troubling for Missy. She hadn't been fired from her job. It wasn't that.

"All right," she said. "Is it about our wedding?"

Missy wished in her heart that was all the worry was about, that there was nothing simpler than that.

"No," she said, her voice choking a little. "But I expect it will eventually get to that. I don't know if you will ever be able to forgive me."

"I love you, Missy, but why are you doing this now? Why are you going to bring something up that's going to hurt me at a time when I'm the lowest I've ever been? You always seem to find a way to make everything about you."

Missy was shaking then. "This *is* about me. This is before we met. And," she added, "it is very, very ugly."

Connie tried to insert herself between Missy and the window, but Missy narrowed the space and turned away. She just couldn't face her fiancée.

"Something happened to me when I worked at the prison," she said.

"I don't like the sound of that, Missy. What do you mean something happened to you?"

Missy's eyes were still riveted to the nothingness outside the window. "I got involved with someone there and was let go," she said.

"It was against employee policy?" Connie asked. "Was it because you're a lesbian? If that's it we should sue. It's so unfair."

"It wasn't an employee, Connie," Missy said, knowing that nothing would get her out of the mess she was in just then. "I got involved with an inmate."

Connie let out an audible gasp. "A prisoner?"

Missy just stood there, unable to speak.

Connie tugged at her lover's shoulder. "Missy, tell me that this is some joke, babe. Tell me that you're being dramatic because you think that it's April Fool's Day or something."

This was the bad part, the really, really bad part. It

was like a mouthful of poison that Missy Carlyle had to spit out and just get it over with.

"It was Brenda Nevins," she said. "That's who I got involved with."

Connie felt as if the wind had been knocked out of her, and she steadied herself against one of the student chairs in the classroom. The room had been swallowed in one big gulp. There was no air. No time. Everything was frozen in that one awful revelation.

"The murderer?" she asked, though there could be no other. "You got involved with a psycho?"

"It was only once," Missy said, wishing that she hadn't thought to add that piece of information. It came off as an attempt to make something so ugly seem trivial, and Connie pounced on it.

"Got involved?" she said, trying to keep her cool, but failing. "You had a sexual encounter with a psycho?"

The disgraced art teacher was reeling. Like the snap of a finger, suddenly their life together, their plans, the Borracchini's wedding cake they'd pre-ordered from their favorite Seattle bakery—all of it was gone.

Missy tried to hug Connie.

"Don't touch me. I work in a school. You work in a school. We're two women in a relationship. We have to be better, more careful. We can't have the taint of scandal associated with us, Missy."

Missy could feel her heart breaking. "That's why I'm warning you."

Lost in her thoughts, Connie missed the word that should have, that would have, alarmed her even more.

Warning.

"We're done," Connie said. "I can't make love with you. I can't be involved with someone who could sleep with a murderer. I don't even know who you are, Missy. Maybe I never did at all."

"I love you," Missy said. "I made a huge mistake."

Connie didn't cry. She was so mad, so hurt, she couldn't. The muscles in her throat had tightened to such a degree that she almost felt like she'd pass out.

"Go," she sputtered out. "Go home, get your stuff, and get out."

Missy was crying then. "Where will I go?"

Connie was past her breaking point, past the ability to empathize—a trait that had been her greatest gift.

"Missy! That's what you're thinking about now?" she asked. "I am almost forty. I thought I had found the love of my life. I thought that I'd get pregnant next year and have a goddamn family. I will never have any of those things now."

"It was only once, Connie," Missy said. "It was before I met you."

Connie took a step back. She looked hard at the woman she no longer really knew.

"Why are you telling me now?" she asked. "Is it because you wanted to kick me to the curb a little harder when I'm already down so low? Are you some kind of sadist like Brenda Nevins?"

"I never wanted to tell you. I love you."

"Then why? Why now? Why couldn't you have just kept this to yourself?"

"Because I think I'm in trouble," she said.

Connie still cared. She hated Missy just then. Loved her. Wished she'd just go away. Wished they'd be married as planned. Everything was spinning out of control.

"What kind of trouble?" she asked.

Missy swallowed hard. "I think the sheriff wants to talk to me."

"About what?" Connie took a gulp of air. "Never mind. I don't want to know."

Missy had already said more than she knew her fiancée could handle. She couldn't tell her all she and Brenda had done. How the murderer had threatened to tell the school district the reason for her dismissal from the prison. How the whole thing had snowballed and a huge mistake became a nightmare. She had done something so terrible that it never left her thoughts. There were times, however, when she was with Connie that she could feel there would be a way to forgiveness for what she had done. But that was gone now. There was no turning back the clock.

"I'll get my things," Missy said. "I just wanted to warn you. I just wanted to say I'm sorry."

Connie watched her fiancée leave. *Former fiancée.* She held the image. It was bad. It was terrible. Reprehensible. Maybe it was, in fact, forgivable.

She had no idea right then, of course, that her wishful thinking, her hope, could not survive what would happen next.

Nothing could.

On the other side of town, Birdy Waterman conferred with Kendall Stark about a request Jennifer Roberts had made to see her again at the jail. Birdy wasn't happy about it in the least. She had paperwork mounting up and she'd promised to take Elan to see some bombastic action movie at the South Sound Cinemas.

"I don't want to do this, Kendall," she said. "I don't want to say it, but honestly, it's not my job."

"Look, we're breaking new ground here and you need to go with it."

Birdy was not amused. "Are you running for sheriff or something?"

"No, but you might run for coroner someday and it will look good on your résumé that you helped break the case," Kendall said.

"I doubt that. And I'm never running for public office."

"No *I* in *Team*, remember?"

Birdy made an exaggerated face. She was irritated, but she had no choice.

"Right now, I hate you just a little," she said, not really meaning it, but not happy about talking to Jennifer Roberts again.

CHAPTER 37

Birdy Waterman sat across from Jennifer Roberts and picked up the phone.

"Detective Stark would be a better choice to listen to your side of the story. If that's what this is about," Birdy said. "Why ask for me?"

Jennifer looked beaten down. The Kitsap County jail was a far cry from the Pinnacle Peak Patio, the restaurant where she liked to lunch with friends, or the wine bar at the DC Ranch where she and Bobby first went when it had opened—and when he thought she might love him.

"I could list some reasons," she said. Her voice was devoid of the bravado that she used like a trumpet to get people to pay attention. It was almost soft, weak.

Birdy took her up on the offer. She had nothing to lose. "Go right ahead. Start listing."

Jennifer ran her fingertips through her hair, tucking one of her blond locks behind her telephone ear.

"First of all," she said, "I'm innocent."

Birdy knew it was a mistake going there. Kendall told her to go. Kendall thought that maybe Jennifer felt some kind of connection to Birdy and that association might give them some leverage in the case. Birdy figured she wanted her there for a little attention. Nothing more.

"You summoned me over here for that? You're going to have to do better. We've got you for killing Ted with antifreeze. You fed it to him like it was nectar for a hummingbird."

A slight and inappropriate smile came over Jennifer.

"Hummingbirds remind me of home," Jennifer said. "I didn't kill Donny and I didn't kill Teddy."

Birdy thought of asking her if she selected husbands based on infantile-sounding names. Bobby was in the mix too; sandwiched between the two dead ones. She held her tongue on that, though. There was no need to antagonize.

"Look, Jennifer," Birdy said, "you'll have your day in court. You'll be able to tell a jury or a judge every bit about what you didn't do. Telling me doesn't make a bit of difference. Why do you want me here?"

Jennifer drew a breath. It actually crossed Birdy's mind that as shallow, lethal, and glib as that woman most assuredly was, she was wrought with anxiety.

"Because I'm being set up," she said. "I didn't kill anyone."

"You've already told us about Molly O'Rourke."

"You have to check her out," she said.

"Detective Stark has already done that."

"My daughter told me that you went down to Scottsdale and actually dug up Donny."

Birdy didn't answer.

"And you found nothing, right?"

She was right about that, of course. But there was

still a slim chance. Never count out the men and women in the Washington State Crime Lab. They were among the best in the country.

"The samples are at the lab," Birdy said.

"There's nothing there," she said. "I had no reason to kill Donny or Teddy."

"Bobby thinks otherwise."

"I hope you know he's a drunk. He hates me. I never should have married for money. I admit that I did. So what? I'm not the first woman who has and I sure as hell won't be the last. Gold digger? That's not who I am."

Birdy could have laughed out loud at that remark. If any woman could be put in the category of gold digger it was the woman on the other side of the thick glass partition. She was never, ever anything but a gold digger.

"Really?" Birdy said. "That's what Bobby thinks too. That you married him to get your hands on his estate. He told me that he feels like he's the lucky one. He's the one who got away from you. Alive."

"Dr. Waterman, I know you are a decent person. I don't think you're stupid either."

"I'm not here for a personality assessment from you, Jennifer."

"No," she said. "I don't mean it like that. I just want to be heard. I just want someone to understand that even though I've done some admittedly stupid and selfish things in my life that . . . well, being selfish and stupid doesn't make me a killer. If those attributes were a precursor for murder, you'd have more people in the morgue than you could deal with."

Jennifer was right. It was, Birdy thought, the only time she'd been spot on about anything during their conversation. That included her personality assessment too. Birdy was intelligent and she was decent, but she'd made some mistakes of epic proportions in her personal life—things that had come back to haunt her since Elan's arrival in Port Orchard. Things that might never be solved no matter how much navel gazing she employed.

"I don't see the point in this, Jennifer," she said.

Jennifer waited a beat. Later, Birdy would wonder if it was for dramatic effect or if she was just trying to come up with something to keep Birdy captive in that visitor's carrel.

"If not Molly, then maybe Ruby could have done this," Jennifer said.

Birdy hadn't expected that, but Jennifer was always good at coming up with a surprise. She had said so once herself.

"She was a little girl when Donald died, for one thing."

Jennifer shook her head. "Not Donny. But maybe she's behind Teddy's poisoning."

This wasn't going anywhere.

"Really, Jennifer, how low can you go? Now you want to blame your daughter. Why is that? Because she's turned on you?"

"She won't testify against me. She's not going to. She loves me."

Birdy leaned in closer to the glass. "She's scared of you."

Jennifer didn't even flinch. Not a trace of reaction, emotion, escaped her frozen face.

"She's just like me," she said. "She'll do the right thing. She'll do what's best for us."

Birdy pulled back. Jennifer was a game player. Probably a good one. But she was also a murderer and she wasn't going to get away with it this time.

"You know you were taped talking to her last night," Birdy said, knowing that Kendall probably would not have volunteered that information.

"Really? It says right here that audio recordings are not made of inmate and visitor conversations." She indicated a notice that had been laminated to the glass.

"No audio. But video. And we've got a great lip reader in the sheriff's department."

Jennifer looked a little defeated. She glanced at the angle of the camera. Birdy could see the wheels rotating. Jennifer was wondering if the angle was right to capture what she said or what her daughter had said.

"I'm not worried. I didn't do anything wrong," she finally said.

"We'll see about that, Jennifer," Birdy said, hanging up the phone and turning to leave.

Jennifer pounded on the glass.

Birdy turned to look at the former hotel restaurant hostess with the big dreams and the face and figure to get what she wanted from men. The words *master manipulator* came to mind. Jennifer was saying something and Birdy Waterman was pretty good at reading lips too.

"You're a bitch! I'm not a killer."

Or something like that.

And she winked.

The wink was strange. It was the same as the one on the tape, but it didn't mean anything. *Jennifer had a nervous tic.*

* * *

Jennifer Roberts went back to the jail's TV room. She thought about growing up in Spring Valley and how her parents had saved their money to go to Scottsdale. It was years before the city would morph into the Beverly Hills of Arizona. They walked along the streets of what was later called Old Town and sucked in the sights, sounds, and smells of a place so different from Spring Valley.

Jenny, who was eight at the time, got a big chocolate ice cream cone from the Sugar Bowl, a painted all-pink fantasy of a soda shop. She sat on a bench with her family eating that cone and watched all the pretty cars roll on by. They were shiny in a way that made her think she could go up to one and use it to make sure her hair was combed out the way she liked it. The cars were not dull and dust-caked like those back in Spring Valley. Not like the old Chevy her dad had driven.

While her father and brother, Carter, went inside a western wear store to look at belt buckles, Jenny and her mother sat in silence as women sauntered by with beautiful long blond hair and cords of gold and silver around their necks and so many bangles stacked on their wrists it looked like they were wearing armor.

It was an eyeful and, in every sense, life changing.

"That's what I want to be when I grow up," Jenny said.

"That's never going to happen, sweetheart," her mother said.

"Why not? Daddy says I'm pretty."

"You're not pretty like that. You're cute as a button. Pretty like that takes a lot of money."

She didn't want to be cute like a button. Buttons were utilitarian. Boring.

"I could get some money," she said.

"Baby, just be happy with what you have," her mother said, sitting there in cheap sandals and clean, but boring, jeans and top. "It's better that way. We are who we are."

"But I want *that*," Jenny had said with great adamancy.

Her mother, a plain woman with those same unreal blue eyes as her daughter, patted Jenny on the knee.

"The only way to get that is to get out of Gila County, and if you're at all like me—and everyone thinks so—you'll end up right next door."

Jenny finished her cone. She looked at her mother. "But I want to," she said.

"Everyone has a dream. The smart ones know that dreams don't come true. They are a desire, a want. Nothing more. Not real. Do you understand me?"

The Sugar Bowl was real. The women walking around were real. Her mom was a liar.

"Yes, Momma," she said.

Inside, Jenny wondered what it would take to get out of Gila County. She'd plan her escape. There was no way she would end up in the trailer next door to her mom. She wanted that pretty-in-pink life she saw all around the Sugar Bowl.

She didn't care what her mother said. Jenny was nothing like her mom. She vowed to do whatever it took.

CHAPTER 38

"**I** need to talk to someone," Tess Moreau said, waiting outside the offices of the Kitsap County coroner. She was completely sober this time, but her eyes still looked as hurt and haunted as they had since the day her daughter went missing. She wore her work clothes, a blazer and light-colored slacks. On her lapel was a small photo button of Darby anchoring the neatly cut tails of a pale pink ribbon.

Darby's favorite color.

Birdy smiled at Tess and with a nod indicated they should take a walk.

"I wasn't always like I am now," Tess said, as they picked their way through the still-jammed parking lot between the county buildings before reaching the plaza that overlooked the shipyard and its nearly mile-long row of gray behemoths.

An empty bench beckoned and the two women sat down.

"Of course you weren't," Birdy said, not really sure where Tess was going. "Circumstances brought you to where you are. You can change things."

Tess looked out at the water. "It isn't about Darby. I mean, not really. It's about the accident that killed my husband and Ellie, Darby's sister."

"I'm a doctor, but maybe not the kind that could help you best."

Tess studied Birdy. "I trust you," she said.

"I appreciate that, Tess. I can be a good listener, despite what my nephew says. He's staying with me through the end of the school year."

"How old is he?" Tess asked.

"Sixteen."

"Did he know my Darby?"

Birdy shook her head. "No, he came here right around the time she went missing."

"About the accident," Tess said, changing the subject back to what was heavy on her mind. "I want to tell you something that I have never told anyone. Not ever."

Birdy didn't like the sound of that. It felt a little confessional. Introspection was fine, of course. She'd be a good sounding board for that. But confessional? That wasn't her strong suit—especially if there was nothing to be done with the confession.

Tess settled back and closed her eyes. She was remembering, concentrating. The truth was that the night of the accident had never completely left her mind. Not from the moment a team of paramedics extricated her from the crushed passenger side of the Honda Civic that her husband had been driving.

First there was the sound, then the quiet, then the crying . . .

"You know what happened?" a man had asked.

Her face had felt numb. She wasn't sure she was moving her lips. *Maybe she was paralyzed?*

"Is everyone all right?" she sputtered out. "My husband? My girls?"

"We're taking care of everyone right now," the man said.

Tess couldn't move. She was pinned under the dash. She heard one of her girls crying.

"Darby? Ellie?"

"We're getting to everyone. What happened? Do you know?"

She tasted blood in her mouth, but she couldn't wipe it away. "What? I want to know how my husband is doing."

The paramedic flashed a light, not in her eyes, but in a sweeping motion over the debris of the car. A couple of CDs. A juice box. Some baby wipes.

"What's his name?" the paramedic asked. "Can you tell me his name?"

She shut her eyes. "Brad. My husband is Brad. My girls are Ellie and Darby."

More crying came from behind her and she tried to move.

"Darby? Ellie?"

"We're doing all we can," the calm voice said. "Are those your children?"

Tess gulped for air.

"Ma'am, do you remember what happened before the crash?"

A shooting pain went down her legs. The jaws of life were tearing a chunk of metal and plastic from the front end.

"A deer. A deer jumped out. Brad swerved. How is Brad?"

Tess felt her body move. She was being lifted upward by another paramedic. It was possible it was the first one who helped her, it was hard to see. It was so dark. The lights from the aid cars pulsed like a heartbeat.

"I'm sorry, but your husband didn't make it," a woman's voice said. "One of your little girls is in serious condition. We're airlifting her to Harborview."

The crying faded to a whimper.

"The car seat kept the other one in pretty good shape. The little one. She's going to be okay. Bruised, but nothing serious. No lacerations."

Darby was fine.

That was the moment frozen in time forever. Right then in that flash when she knew everything had been her fault. All of it.

Tess sat there mute. She had a faraway look in her eyes. Not sad. Just faraway.

Birdy gave her some leeway. She knew that revisiting traumatic incidents often replayed in the human mind as if they were occurring all over again. She'd seen it in her office more than one time. The worst was when a man was recounting how his wife had keeled over from a heart attack and how frantic he'd become trying to resuscitate her. He'd done everything. As he spoke, he suddenly went white and excused himself to use the bathroom—he died of a heart attack two minutes later.

"There was no deer on the highway," Tess said. "Brad and I were arguing. I was so mad at him because he—and this sounds so pathetically stupid—because he wanted to go to Ocean Shores and I wanted to go to Leavenworth for vacation that year. I was just sitting there getting madder and madder. Darby was fussing and I couldn't get her quiet. I know she was only reacting to our fighting. I reached over—"

Birdy cut her off. "I don't want you to say one more word. Not a word. Do you understand?"

They locked eyes. "I have to tell someone," she said.

Birdy held her hand out as if to push back whatever Tess was going to say.

The truth of what happened.

"Tell your priest at St. Gabriel's," Birdy said.

"I have," she said.

"Good. That's enough. You've suffered enough. It was a terrible accident. I know that whatever caused Brad to swerve is something that no one needs to know now."

There was a time when Birdy would almost certainly have felt otherwise. Even a month ago or a few weeks prior to all that had happened since those kids from Olalla Elementary found Darby's foot in Banner Forest.

"What happened to Darby has zero to do with whatever happened on the highway that night," she said.

Tess plainly disagreed. "You can't know that for sure. If I hadn't . . . If it hadn't happened . . . I wouldn't live the way I live. I know that's true. And if I didn't live the way I live, my daughter would have let me inside her life more. Her friends. Her school. All of it was walled off. We were in a bubble, a messy bubble there in that house, and I just couldn't make it right."

Birdy put her arm around Tess's shoulder. "It wasn't your fault," she said. "What happened to Darby was not your fault. You could have had a spotless home, lived in a hermetically sealed Lucite box, with not a speck of dust, and it still could have happened. Murder can happen to anyone. It absolutely is not your fault."

Tess mouthed the words "thank you" and that faraway look returned for a beat.

"Tess, I know someone you need to see."

"I can't see anyone," she said. "I can't even tell Amanda."

Birdy sifted through her purse and retrieved a business card. It was for a woman named Deanna Clarke who ran a grief group out of her home in South Colby, a couple of miles from Port Orchard.

"See Deanna," she said, giving Tess the card. "She'll help you. She had terrible guilt over a tragedy of her own. Not like yours, but with a similar outcome. You need to talk to someone. You have paid dearly already and no one could torture you with more pain than you've poured all over yourself."

"I caused the accident," Tess said.

"I understand."

"Shouldn't I go to jail? I work at a prison where people have done far less damage than I have and they are serving time."

"See Deanna," Birdy repeated.

After Darby's mom left, Birdy let her imagination take her inside that Honda Civic with the Moreaus on the night of the accident. She let herself believe that Tess and Brad had only argued. Maybe Tess even gave him a shove, in the heat of the moment. She didn't allow herself to think what might have truly occurred the night Brad and Ellie Moreau died. She would always wonder if Tess had grabbed that wheel and steered the car into that shoulder, killing her husband and two-year-old. If she knew for sure, then as an officer of the court she had the sworn duty to report what she knew.

But she didn't. And she wouldn't. No one had suffered more than the woman who would forever be known as Tess the Mess.

CHAPTER 39

Missy Carlyle was loading her Jeep when Detective Kendall Stark and Deputy Gary Wilkins pulled up in a county cruiser. The house was the envy of the neighborhood—neatly painted white, a red metal roof, and a garden boasting every kind of blooming flower. A hedge of red azaleas was the showstopper, but not right then. That day, it was the mountain of belongings on the lawn, dumped in a haphazard fashion. It looked more like court-ordered eviction than a breakup, which is what it was.

It had been the worst day ever. The love of her life had thrown her out. The love of her life had lost her job. There would be no wedding at Snoqualmie Falls Lodge. There would be none of the dreams of raising a family together some day. Every bit of it had been rubbed out by an incident so strange, Missy never really understood how it had transpired in the first place.

Missy, her muscles sore from packing and her heart broken, thought back to that first moment.

She'd been making her rounds through the prison pet program when she saw Brenda Nevins cleaning dog brushes in the big stainless steel sink. Brenda had her back to Missy and was humming some tune. Missy moved in closer. In doing so, she startled the inmate.

Brenda turned around suddenly and accidentally— or maybe on purpose—sprayed soapy water all over her T-shirt. She wore no bra. That was pointedly obvious. She laughed at how ridiculous she looked.

Ridiculously sexy.

"A wet T-shirt contest," she said, looking down at her breasts. "Do you think I have what it takes to be a winner, Officer Carlyle?"

There was no denying that she was beautiful. Missy should have known better. She should have known that Brenda Nevins was beautiful like a bouquet of night-shade. It started with her helping to dry off the inmate. And then a kiss. *How did that happen?* In her mind, as she sat there remembering it, she could only come up with one phrase and it could not be more lame.

"One thing led to another . . ."

When Missy played it over and over in her head later—the wobbly dog-grooming table, the frenzied sex atop it, the inability to stop until Tess Moreau caught them in the act—she couldn't come up with the reason *why* it had gone that far.

While Gary lingered by the cruiser, Kendall walked over to Missy.

"Connie didn't call the sheriff on me, did she?" she asked.

"Millicent Carlyle?" Kendall asked in her official voice.

Missy looked at all of her things, spread out like a tornado in the Midwest.

"I know I told her I'd get out right away," she said.

"But it is a lot harder to sift through our stuff to determine what's hers and what's mine."

"We're not here about that," Kendall said as Gary joined her.

Missy looked relieved and then concerned. She planted her feet in the lawn next to her boxes and crossed her arms.

"You're not here to evict me?"

"No," Kendall said, glancing at Gary. Two kids were riding their bikes in a circle in front of the house. This would be done in as quiet a manner as possible. No need to get anyone hurt or excited. The detective moved her blazer to show her gun, but she didn't even graze it with her palm.

Missy caught the movement of the fabric and knew what was coming.

"Millicent, please put up your arms," Kendall said. "I want you to do this slowly."

"I don't understand," she said. "I'm being arrested? What happened with Brenda was a long time ago. There were no charges. It was handled as a personnel matter."

Gary drew his gun and Kendall led the high school janitor over to the Jeep.

"Put your palms on top of the vehicle and spread your legs," she said, wishing there were a better, less unseemly way to provide the same instruction.

Connie Mitchell came running out of the house across the front lawn.

"What's going on?" she asked. Her eyes were open wide and full of fear.

Missy, handcuffed behind her back, turned and shot Connie a very hurt look.

"How could you?" she asked.

Connie had no idea what she was talking about. "I didn't do anything!"

Kendall watched Missy while the two women argued about broken dreams, betrayal, and how they'd never, ever forgive each other.

"Why am I being arrested?" she asked.

"Millicent Carlyle, you're being held on investigation of the homicide of Darby Moreau."

Connie screamed. It was a scream without any words, and the two little kids riding their bikes looked over and pedaled away as fast as they could. They'd lingered because it was exciting to see a cop car in the neighborhood, but the scream let out by Connie Mitchell was bloodcurdling.

"I didn't kill anyone," Missy said, spinning away from the Jeep. She almost fell, and Kendall steadied her.

"We'll talk about it at the department," Kendall said.

"I don't have any idea what you're talking about. I sure didn't kill that girl."

Connie lunged at her lover. "How could you? She was just a kid."

"Do you know anything about this, Connie?" Kendall asked.

"She was jealous of all my students. She was. She never wanted me to spend time with them. I told her that those kids were like we'd been. They needed someone to listen to them. I never thought . . ."

Connie burst into tears, unable to complete her sentence.

"Take a few minutes," Kendall said. "We'd like to get a statement from you."

"Anything," Connie said. "I loved Darby. She was such a sweet, beautiful girl."

"I didn't do this," Missy said. "You know me, Connie."

Kendall looked back at Connie, who wouldn't even look at the woman she had planned to marry.

"Yesterday, I knew her, detective. Today, I have no idea who that woman really is."

She walked toward the perfect little white house, holding her stomach like she was going to vomit. As Gary head-checked Missy and slid her into the car, Connie turned around one last time. She held the image of her lover for a second but directed her remarks to Kendall.

"Tell her I'll call our lawyer for her." She looked at the belongings on the lawn. "I'll put her things in storage."

"All right," Kendall said.

"But nothing else," Connie said. "I don't want to see her, talk to her, no matter what happens. My life has been ruined. I don't have a job. I don't have a future. It was like I let the devil inside my life. I was such a fool. Brenda Nevins? She had a relationship with a monster? She murdered a young girl? What does that make me?"

"What she did doesn't define you," Kendall said.

"No?" She started back toward her door. "Tell that to Tess Moreau. Darby would still be alive if I hadn't been involved with Missy. They'd never have met."

Kendall knew that her next line was supposed to be something about how the actions of others have no reflection on the people around them, but she just couldn't go there. If Connie and Missy hadn't become lovers, Darby would never have been in danger. Kendall wondered if the truth was even darker than that. Could Missy have taken the job at the high school only to find an opportunity to seek revenge for Brenda? If that had been the case, Connie had been duped. She had lain down with the devil.

Kendall Stark and Birdy Waterman had grown close over the Darby Moreau case. They had started it together in the woods of Banner Forest with the discovery of the foot. They'd joked about the ridiculousness of the cross training, but in the end, neither would say that it hadn't had its benefits.

Deputy Wilkins had gone ahead to process Missy while Kendall called the forensic pathologist.

"We arrested Millicent Carlyle. I'm on my way back to the office. Gary's processing her and then we'll see if she'll talk."

Birdy, who was reviewing lab reports on another case, set the papers aside.

"That's a relief," she said. "A huge one. A sick case that is. Killing a girl for revenge. Missy is as much of a sociopath as Brenda Nevins."

"I'm not sure. I'm sure she's a sociopath, but there is an alternate theory. It came from Connie Mitchell."

"Oh God, she was there? I feel so sorry for her."

"Me too," Kendall said. "She knows about Brenda Nevins. She just found out. But she doesn't seem to know about how twisted all of that was. She was in the process of booting Millicent out. Her stuff was on the lawn."

"What's her theory?"

"She said that Millicent was extremely jealous of Darby and how much time and attention she was getting from her."

"Missy saw the girl as a rival?"

"Think so."

"But Darby wasn't gay."

"Maybe Millicent didn't know that."

"Have you notified Tess about the arrest?"

"That's really why I'm calling. I don't want to lose momentum here and I don't want to send someone who doesn't know her to go tell her."

"Say no more. I'll do it."

"You sure?" Kendall asked.

"On my way now," Birdy said.

Birdy straightened her desk, grabbed a light jacket and her purse. Tess Moreau had been in a shambles when she'd seen her last. Birdy hoped that Tess would summon the courage to call the grief counselor she'd recommended. Tess had lost everything, but she could start over. She was barely in her forties. No matter what people had done, Birdy always believed in second and third chances. Sometimes behind bars. Sometimes out in the world. People could still do good things. The human race was not a total loss, though sometimes it seemed that way.

CHAPTER 40

It was late in the day, but there would be no waiting until tomorrow to talk to the woman arrested for the murder of a sixteen-year-old girl.

The news that Millicent Carlyle was in custody for Darby Moreau's murder was known only to a small number of people inside the sheriff's and county prosecutor's offices in Port Orchard, but Kendall Stark had no doubt that this particular case would explode in the media. For some reason, lost on her, lesbian love triangles were a red-hot media commodity. Add in the Brenda Nevins connection, and it would no doubt be the biggest case in Washington State history since, well, since Brenda's case and before that, the Green River Killer's murder spree.

An assistant county attorney named Jill Goodwin arrived for the interview that would be held in a small, windowless room in the jail. Her boss had put her on notice that with all eyes soon to be on Kitsap County, there could not be one "gnat's-eyelash-size screw-up."

Jill, an unusually dour woman with motorcycle helmet hair and lips that wouldn't know a smile if it had been spray-painted on her face, kept her mouth shut except for two questions.

"Have you been Mirandized?" she asked Missy.

Missy looked tired and scared. "Yes, I know my rights. I worked in law enforcement."

Jill gave a quick nod. "You've waived the right to counsel, and you understand the consequences of that?"

"Yes, I do," Missy said. "And I didn't do this. For the record."

Dour Jill looked over at Kendall.

"Go ahead. I'm satisfied," the assistant county attorney said.

Kendall ran down a list of items that were so benign in nature that if an observer watched unaware of the circumstances behind the meeting, they'd come away with the impression that Kendall was conducting a job interview.

In answer to the basic interview questions, Missy said she'd been born in Silverdale. She was one of three children of a shipyard worker and a nurse at Harrison Hospital in Bremerton. After high school, she knew she wanted out of Kitsap County so she enlisted in the navy. After that, she worked at the prison.

"You left the prison under less than ideal circumstances," Kendall said.

Missy knew what was coming. She shifted her frame in her chair.

"That's putting it mildly," she said. "But yes."

"You were involved with an inmate."

"You know I was."

"Who was it?"

Missy looked down at the table. The admission was

a painful one, not for what she did—which was bad enough—but for the person she'd been involved with.

"Brenda Nevins," she said.

Dour Jill looked over at Kendall. Apparently, she hadn't read the arrest warrant. She started skimming it as fast as she could. She chugged down the words and each bite was more bitter than the first.

More unbelievable.

Kendall pressed on. "Tell us about your relationship with Ms. Nevins."

Missy studied the fake wood grain on the table. "Do we have to go down this road? This is very embarrassing."

"You can quit any time, Ms. Carlyle," the assistant DA said, though she was caught up on her reading and was on the edge of her seat hoping that Missy would continue.

Missy opened a water bottle set out for her. She took a big, long gulp.

"I had a sexual encounter with her and I was put on leave," she said, twisting the plastic cap back onto the top of the bottle. "After an internal review, I was released from my job."

"Back up," Kendall said. "You had a sexual relationship with an inmate. How did it come about that you were caught?"

Missy looked at Kendall. "Tess Moreau. *An encounter.* She saw us and reported it."

"That made you really angry, didn't it?" Kendall asked.

"It made me ashamed," she said. "It made Brenda angry."

Kendall was in dog-with-a-bone mode. Her element. She'd often thought that being a trial lawyer would have been a fun job, but catching the bad guys had its perks too.

"How angry?" she asked.

"I'm not going to lie," Missy said. "Brenda wanted revenge. She missed an important TV interview. At the time, she was all about being a TV star. It was everything to her. She would have killed Tess if she could have. Really, I think she could have."

Kendall pushed on. "Did she threaten Tess?"

"I don't know," Missy said. "Not to her face. I really don't know. I don't know what happened after I left as far as Brenda and Tess."

"So you suffered no consequences from dismissal from your job?" Kendall asked. "No criminal charges? No write-up to follow you to a job as a janitor at South Kitsap?"

Missy stared hard at the detective. This hadn't been fun and games and she knew that it wasn't going to be.

"I lost my job," she said. "That was a serious consequence."

"How did you get hired on at South Kitsap?"

"I saw an ad in the *Kitsap Sun* and I answered it."

Kendall rifled through a pile of papers in the folder she'd brought into the conference room.

"Is this your application?" she asked, showing it first to Dour Jill, who then passed it over to Missy.

Missy glanced at the paper. "So?"

"You don't mention your employment at the prison," Kendall said. "Do you?"

She looked away, embarrassed. "I left it off. I didn't

lie about it. If they'd have asked about the gap, I would have been truthful. I'm not a liar."

Kendall pushed again. "Come on, Missy. You got that job at South because Darby Moreau went to school there."

Missy sucked down more water. "Are you thinking that I took that janitor's job so that it would be near the kid of the woman who turned me in? You think I was stalking her?"

"Don't you think it is an amazing coincidence?" Kendall asked.

Missy was angry, but she tried to hold it inside. "That's all it is. I didn't even know who she was until after I started dating Connie."

"That would be Connie Mitchell, Darby's art teacher?" Kendall asked.

A softness came to Missy's face. "Right," she said. "Connie."

Kendall set Darby's sophomore class photo on the table. "Connie spent a lot of time with Darby."

Missy kept her eyes on the photo, then she looked over at Jill, then back to Kendall.

"She wasn't inappropriate with her, if that's what you're getting at. But, yes, she did. She said she and Darby had similar life experiences and she wanted to help her. Connie was just being Connie. She's a really good person."

Kendall didn't let up. "Were you jealous too? Jealous of all that time?"

"A little," she said. "I kidded her about it. It wasn't anything creepy if that's what you're getting at."

"Did you have any contact with Brenda after you left the institution?"

A long pause. The wheels were turning, grinding. It was almost audible.

"Some," Missy said. "Not much."

Kendall stood and paced a moment. She just let Missy stew. It was a good technique. Always give the subject time to trip themselves up.

"She wanted you to seek revenge, didn't she?" she finally asked.

Missy didn't deny it, which disappointed the detective a little.

"Something along those lines," Missy said. "Brenda was crazy. She *is* bat shit crazy. I told her not to bother me again."

"How was she able to call you?" Kendall asked.

"I gave her my phone number."

Kendall looked surprised. It was a slightly exaggerated look, meant to rattle.

"Really? Why on earth would you give a convicted killer, your former lover, your phone number?"

"I know this sounds bad," Missy said, struggling to get her words out. "It is disgusting to me too. But at the time I was enamored with her, I guess," she said, looking up at the ceiling as if there was something interesting up there. "Infatuated. Stupid. When I look back on it, I can't even imagine that I could have felt anything but disgust for her. It makes no sense. My involvement with her doesn't define me."

"A jury probably will think otherwise," Kendall said.

"I didn't do anything," Missy said.

"Yes, you've said that. When was the last time you talked to Brenda?"

Missy put her elbows on the table and put her face in her hands. "Please don't tell Connie."

"When was the last time you talked to her?"

Missy stayed quiet. "Yesterday. She called me to say this was all about to come out. She called me to warn me."

The detective opened her folder and pulled out the letter that Tess had first given Birdy. She slid it over the table to Missy.

She looked down at it.

You took from me. I'll take from you.

"What's this?" she asked.

"You tell us."

"I've never seen this before," Missy said. "I have no idea what it is."

Kendall pounced. "I'll tell you. It's the message Brenda had you relay to Tess Moreau."

Missy was reeling right then. "Honestly, I don't know anything about this. I've never seen it before in my entire life. I don't have a clue about what it is, who it was meant for, who made it. I'm not involved in any of this. That's why I'm here."

"That's part of why you're here," Kendall said. "The other part is this."

She passed over a photograph of the black plastic bag that held Darby's remains.

"Can you identify this?" she asked.

Missy's eyes studied the photograph. It was of a heavy-duty black plastic sheet with a bright yellow drawstring tie.

"It looks like a trash bag?" she said, almost as a question.

"Have you ever seen it before?" Kendall asked.

Missy looked up. "This one? Or any in general?"

"We know you've seen this one, Missy. We know it because your palm print was recovered from it."

"Okay, I've touched this bag," she said. "What's the big deal?"

Kendall went in for the kill—her favorite part of any interview.

"The big deal is that this is the bag that you stuffed Darby Moreau's body into before you dumped her in Banner Forest," she said.

Missy blinked back. Those words had come at her with such force. It was like a blow to the chest.

"I never did," she said. "I never did!"

Kendall stayed calm. "Where were you the night of March twenty-second?"

Missy thought a second. Fear filled her eyes.

Or maybe something else?

"I was with Connie, I guess," she said.

Kendall's next questions came at Missy with a snapping sharpness. Not a beat between the answer and the next question.

"Connie doesn't remember seeing you until after nine."

"That's right," Missy said. "I went out and did some target shooting."

"Out in Banner Forest?"

Missy looked up, then down.

Was she making up a story? Was she scared?

"No," she said. "At the range. At the Gig Harbor Gun Club. I've been a member there for years."

Kendall let out an annoyed sigh. "That's your alibi?"

"I told you I didn't do anything," Missy said. "I had no reason to."

Dour Jill spoke up.

"Seriously, Ms. Carlyle? I've made a list of about five reasons why you would have done this—and frankly I hope you do get a good lawyer. Our office much prefers to beat the good ones. And we'll win this. I only see one upside for you."

Missy didn't say a word.

Dour Jill cracked something similar to a smile. It was a mean one, but a smile nevertheless.

"At least you and Ms. Nevins can get reacquainted. Maybe they'll let you work in the prison pet program. From reading Detective Stark's report I see that you're experienced with dog grooming."

Kendall never liked Dour Jill until that moment. In that single utterance the assistant DA capped off a perfect interview. The case was totally in the bag.

Or so she thought.

CHAPTER 41

Birdy's heart began to race when she arrived at Tess Moreau's home in Olalla. Cars were everywhere. There were at least ten of them lined up along the road. And they weren't part of the hoarder's collection of things.

Something's wrong here.

She jumped out of her red Prius and hurried toward the house worried about Tess, but halfway there it began to occur to her that nothing bad had happened to Darby's mother. Nothing at all. Something, however, *was* happening to her *house*. Four enormous tarps had been spread out in the yard like mammoth picnic cloths, flat and smooth. On each one was an easel holding poster board signs made with big bold red markers. One read KEEP, another GOODWILL, a third read DUMP, and the last one read SELL.

Tess was standing next to the one that said DUMP.

"I think that pressure cooker could be fixed," she was saying in a slightly animated voice. "I think I should keep it."

A woman in shorts and a striped tank top stood there, holding the pressure cooker.

"Do you know where the lid is?" she asked. Her tone was firm, but there was a perceptible measure of kindness in her voice. Whoever this woman was, she was there on a mission, and she knew that the person between her and her goal was the homeowner.

"It didn't come with a lid," Tess said. "I got it from a yard sale. Gig Harbor, I think. Maybe Port Orchard. I bet I could find another lid and then make it just perfect."

"Right," said the woman in the tank top. "I have no doubt about that. But, really, Tess, are you ever in the rest of your life going to do that? I'm looking for a little honesty here because there are seven other pressure cookers that I know about and this is the worst of the lot."

As Tess was about to answer, she caught the sight of Birdy.

"No," she said. "You're right. I'm not ever going to do it. Put it in the DUMP pile."

"Good girl," the woman said, tossing the worthless kitchen appliance onto the largest of the four heaps that were growing by the second.

"I didn't expect to see this, Tess," Birdy said.

Tess smiled faintly. "To be honest, I didn't either." Her voice trailed off into the din of all that was going on around her.

"What's happening here?" Birdy asked, taking it all in. "I mean, besides the obvious?"

Tess took a breath. "I've been sleeping in Darby's

room the past few nights," she said. "You know, just to be close to her. The sheets still smell like her."

"That's a beautiful way to be close to her," Birdy said.

Tess agreed. It was. "When I woke up yesterday, I felt her talking to me. I didn't hear anything. I'm not crazy."

Birdy moved closer and held out her hand and Tess took it. She gave it a gentle squeeze. "Of course not," she said.

Tess looked around. Birdy could be trusted. She understood Tess's pain in a way that none of the others doing the work around there really could. Birdy hadn't endured the trauma that Tess had, but Darby's mom knew that the Kitsap County forensic pathologist cried with a dozen other moms who had.

"I felt her tell me, 'Mom, let go. Let go of everything. I'll still be with you.' "

Birdy squeezed Tess's hand. "She's always with you."

Tess's eyes fluttered. "Yes, Brad and Ellie too."

A man with an old rusted wheelbarrow dumped a load of magazines onto the DUMP tarp.

"We're going to need someone to haul this one pretty soon," he called out, as the familiar yellow edges of *National Geographic* magazines slid into an avalanche of beautifully rendered images of exotic places and people.

Tess looked nervously toward the growing debris pile, but she didn't say a word about it. She'd collected those *National Geographic* magazines because she thought someone would want them. No one ever did.

"My friends from work," Tess said. "They came." She started to tear up. "For the longest time, I thought, you know, that no one really could care about me. Considering who, or what, I was. A hoarder. But my friends from work, well, they think I matter. That despite how I've lived, I *am* something. They're here, Birdy. Amanda, all of them. I'm going to get my life back in order."

Birdy hugged Tess and felt a genuine joy. Tess Moreau had taken that first step. It was a mighty one too. Birdy had come there with the other piece of what could hold her back—the not knowing of what had happened to Darby.

"Can we talk privately?" Birdy asked, as prison co-workers did their best to sort out those four primary categories, holding off on things that were of value but maybe not needed in a household that was overloaded. Fourteen Crock-Pots, many still in their boxes, were too many. But only Tess could decide if the number should be one or two.

"You didn't come to help," she said. "You came for another reason, didn't you?"

"Yes, let's step away from here." They walked toward the barn, where they had first talked when Darby's disappearance had brought Birdy and Kendall to that hoarder's mess on Olalla Valley Road.

The entire time they made their way down to the barn, Tess braced herself. She knew what was coming. She felt it in her bones.

"Did you find out who killed her?" she asked.

Birdy scanned Tess's already very sad eyes. "Yes, we think we did. This is preliminary, but you don't need to read another thing in the paper or see it on TV and be the last to know."

Tess started to shake a little, but she wanted more than anything to honor Darby with the strength that her daughter had always said she possessed. She didn't drop to her knees and scream at the sky. Not this time.

"Who was it?" she asked.

Birdy held her by the shoulders. "We're pretty sure it was Missy," she said.

Tess just stood there, still, while the breeze of a spring day blew past the barn, filling the air with the smells that come with horses and goats and compost.

"Brenda put her up to it," Tess said.

Birdy gave a quick nod. "Yes, that's what we think."

"Has she been arrested?" Tess asked.

"Yes, about an hour ago," Birdy said. "She's being questioned as we speak."

The sound of kids playing ball down at the ball field wafted through the air. The daffodils were up all over the pasture, the site of a former bulb farm. Everything was the same as it had been before Darby vanished. And yet, as Tess stood there, she knew that things would never ever be the same.

"It's not really over, is it?" she asked.

Birdy watched as a duck landed clumsily on the pond. "No, it won't be for a long time," she said, "but one day you will wake up and you will know that your daughter is at peace with her sister, with her father. And one day, a long, long time from now, you'll all be together again."

Tess hugged Birdy and whispered in her ear. "Thank you. Thank you for all you've done for me and my baby."

They went back toward the house, along a pathway that was no longer constricted by the odds and ends that Tess had collected over the years.

As if she needed a bit of a release from the reality of Birdy's revelation that her daughter's killer had been caught, Tess started toward the DUMP pile. Her gait was slow at first, but with each step velocity increased. With movement of her feet, the memory of what had been taken came at her in a flood, as the debris pile grew skyward. So much and so very fast.

She was not strong. She was not worthy. She was a woman who had lost everything. Now, they were taking more from her. More than she wanted them to take.

"Not that! None of that!" she yelled.

The man standing there looked like he'd been shot at. His face was frozen. Stunned.

"Sorry! What?" he said, stepping back as Tess pushed past him.

Tess was frantic. "That's my daughter's artwork! That is part of her! You can't ever, ever get rid of that! Birdy!"

Birdy got onto the tarp and helped Tess sift through the trash to retrieve some drawings, sketchbooks, other things that were Darby's that somehow got into the wrong pile.

"It's all right, Tess," Birdy said. "We've got it. It was just a mistake."

Tess looked at the man, a small fellow who worked at the mailroom at the prison. He was still in shock.

"I'm sorry, Tess," he said. "I didn't mean anything by it. Really."

Tess pulled herself together. "Oh, Kenny, I know it was a mistake," she said, embarrassed by the spectacle of her actions. "I'm sorry I lost it. I'm fine now."

"I really am sorry," he said.

Birdy and Tess carried the artwork back into the house.

"What happened out there?" Amanda asked, as they came inside.

"It's all right," Birdy said. "Something got mixed into the wrong pile. That's all. All fixed now. We don't need to worry about anything more."

Amanda, who had been sorting enough Tupperware to fill the back of a pickup truck, smiled with a knowing look on her face.

"It's getting late," she said. "We're going to wrap it up for a while. We'll start up fresh in the morning."

"Good idea," Birdy said.

She followed Tess down to Darby's spotless bedroom. They set the artwork on the bed.

"She was very good," Birdy said, admiring the drawings.

Tess smiled. "Yes, she was."

Birdy peered down at a charcoal rendering of a forest clearing. A deer and a fawn grazed in the foreground. The fierceness of the artist's technique surprised her. There was power, energy. It was bold and striking. She thought of Darby and her diary and the sweet yearnings of a girl. This sketch held a kind of raw power that was at odds with that personality. It was beautifully rendered, though. That couldn't be denied. The girl had a very special talent.

"I love this," she said.

"She didn't draw that one," Tess said. "Another kid at school did. It is good, though. You can have it."

She handed it to Birdy.

"Oh, I couldn't," Birdy said, pushing it back. In doing so she noticed an inscription on the bottom.

You don't know you're beautiful

Under that inscription was a name.

Micah

"Did you know this boy?" Birdy asked.

Tess didn't. "None of her friends ever came by," she said. "I think I told you that. Not even Katie."

"Sorry," Birdy said. "I remember. Did she ever talk about him?"

"I guess a little. Not much. She said he was cool or something like that. Just some boy from Arizona. I think she liked him, though. You know she was sixteen. She was a girl. I think she might have liked him more if she'd had a normal mother."

"Oh, Tess, you have to stop that," Birdy said. "You have to quit piling on the guilt like it's some of the things you've collected here. More and more. Deeper and higher. You know it isn't going to get you any-where. You know that in your bones, don't you? Tess? Don't you?"

Tess looked down at the paintings, sketches, and the drawings. She sifted through them, arranging them the way she'd had them before Kenny took them out to the DUMP pile. The room was white and the artwork was full of life and vigor.

"Right," she said. "I know it is the truth just as you say it. I really do. I called Deanna Clark as you advised and am in grief group already. I'm working on the ac-cepting my life as it is, but it's rough."

"I was going to ask you how it was going with Deanna, but I already see that it has helped you."

"I owe you, Dr. Waterman," Tess said. "I'll never forget what you've done for me."

Birdy could feel tears coming and she wanted no part of that. It had been a sad, tragic, difficult case all the way around. She was grateful that Tess was doing better.

"I gave you Deanna Clark's business card," she said. "That's all."

Tess refused any tears. She simply wouldn't allow it right then. She was stronger. "Much more than that," she said, her words now even and full of resolve. "You gave me a compass."

Amanda poked her head in and interrupted the pathologist and the mother of the dead girl in the woods.

"We're heading out now, Tess. We've made a ton of progress. We'll get more done tomorrow. We've got your back, kid."

"I can't ever thank you enough or pay you back," Tess said.

"Sure you can," Amanda said. "I could use some Tupperware. Got any extra?"

Tess laughed. It wasn't a big laugh, but it was the first she had even chuckled in a long time.

"You want the one that holds a single cupcake?" she asked, her tone lighter.

Amanda winked. "You know I do."

Tess turned back to Birdy.

"Seriously," she said, "I want you to have the drawing. I'll just put it in the GOODWILL pile."

Birdy took it, not because she loved it, but because it puzzled her. She wasn't exactly sure why.

* * *

It was late when she returned to the office. The place was empty except for Sarah Dorman, the crime tech who'd been angry about Birdy's presence at the Banner Forest scene. She sat in a chair outside of Birdy's office. Her flaming red hair cascaded over the back of the chair.

"I heard they arrested Missy Carlyle," she said, getting up and following Birdy into her office. The small room had once been a child's bedroom in the old house that the county had used for a coroner's office and morgue for decades, though not for much longer.

"That's right," Birdy said. "I've just come back from telling Tess."

"I don't think she could have done it," Sarah said, planting herself in another chair. She held an envelope close to her chest. "I know her. She's not the type."

Birdy wondered what Sarah meant by knowing her.

"I didn't know you were friends," she said.

"We were more than that. I know that she's not capable of doing something like that, Dr. Waterman."

Birdy held a couple of thoughts to herself. She wondered how close the two had been—and while it was none of her business—she couldn't help considering the possibility that the evidence could have been compromised because of a personal relationship the CSI tech might have had with a killer.

"There may be things you don't know about your friend, Sarah," she said.

"I doubt that."

"There are things that she did separate from the palm print recovered on the plastic bag."

"I think I know about some of those mistakes she

made in the past," she said. Sarah was now keeping some of her thoughts to herself too. "But about that direct evidence, the print. I did some more checking. I think I have a reasonable explanation for how it might have been left on the bag."

"All right then," Birdy said. "I'm all ears."

"The bag was made by Dow Chemical."

"Right, we know that."

"Okay, but did you know it was their industrial and institutional line? Not for consumers."

"Yes," Birdy said. "Well, that's fine. That makes sense. I don't see how it happens to help your friend's case. South Kitsap High School is a user of that line. We've already tracked that."

"All right then," Sarah said. "I know that. I'm trying to explain to you how Missy's palm print got on it. The institutional line is sold in rolls of five hundred. They're huge. They are put into special mountings at the school so that they can be dispensed with ease."

"Fine," Birdy said, though she was thinking, *so what?*

"Well, aren't you wondering why her fingerprints are not on it? Just her palm?"

"It didn't matter to me. Having her prints—any of her prints on the bag that was used to dispose of Darby Moreau—is enough for me."

"I understand, Dr. Waterman," Sarah said. "I just want you to know that I checked out how the palm print could have been made. The reason her fingerprints aren't on it is because of the way the dispenser works. It is a roll. She pulled down to get one and her fingerprints were on the one she took to use. The palm was left on what she hadn't taken yet."

It was an interesting detail, Birdy thought. "There are other things at play here," she said.

Sarah made an annoyed expression. "I know about Brenda Nevins," she said flatly.

Birdy was taken aback. "I'm surprised. Missy's fiancée Connie didn't know."

Sarah fixed her gaze on Birdy. "That doesn't surprise me. Missy and I broke up over it. My job is too important to me and I couldn't have that drama in my life. Not at all."

"That was a smart move on your part," Birdy said.

"Smart or not," Sarah said, "I still loved Missy. But not enough to risk my career. I know she could never have hurt anyone. Not a schoolgirl, especially. Did you ever wonder why there were no other prints on the plastic bag? Just her palm?"

Birdy hadn't. Not really. She'd been grateful for the evidence—any evidence. It solved a murder that had horrified Kitsap County. Before she could answer, Sarah started up again.

"Whoever killed Darby used a plastic bag from the school. That's the crime scene. That's where it happened. The killer took a plastic bag from the dispenser and through dumb luck or maybe even because he wore gloves he left no prints."

"Have you told your theory to Kendall?"

"Do you mean does Kendall know I'm a lesbian?"

"No, that's not what I meant."

"Yes, I have," Sarah said. "She's too wrapped up in the thrill of getting another notch on her gun for an arrest than listening to me. That's why I'm here. I trust you. I think you trust me. I'm telling you Missy would never, ever."

"I do trust you, Sarah. I think you are an excellent tech."

Sarah started to get up to leave, but changed her mind. "That seems like faint praise, Doctor."

"I don't mean it like that," Birdy said. "This is a lot to take in. And really, beyond my area of expertise. I'm the forensic pathologist here. I'm not a detective."

Birdy liked Sarah. "But you think like one. I know you do."

"I made this," the younger woman said. From the envelope, she handed Birdy a photo of the plastic bag. On the back she'd written out a number of questions in the dark ink of a felt tip pen.

Who had access to the janitor's closet?
Why would Darby be killed?
If the crime scene was the school, how could her body have been smuggled out of there without anyone seeing it?
The perpetrator would need to be very strong to have carried Darby's body. The killer had to be a man. Or maybe two people?

Birdy looked up after she finished reading. "A hundred pounds of dead weight is a lot," she said. "Missy is wiry, but probably not that strong."

Sarah had considered that too and said so. "That's what I was thinking on the way over here."

"I'll ponder it, Sarah. I really will." Birdy looked at her watch. It was late. She'd promised Elan she'd bring home dinner. Being responsible for another human being, she realized, was very, very hard work.

"I have to go," she said.

"Take this with you," Sarah said, giving her the photo. "Think about it."

Birdy gathered her things and started to lock up her office. "Have a good night, Sarah. Thanks for trusting me."

CHAPTER 42

A doe and her yearlings skittered across Beach Drive just as Birdy arrived home from picking up some Kentucky Fried Chicken and not feeling the least bit good about doing so. It was after 7 and a layer of dark clouds rolled in. Birdy waited for the deer to cross the road before she pulled into her driveway. A car she didn't recognize was parked out front.

Elan had a friend over. That was good. With the way her mother was, Birdy couldn't recall a time when she'd ever invited anyone to come to her house.

Birdy gathered up all of her things, the chicken and biscuits ("with lots of honey packets," he'd told her the first time she stopped in there), the photograph with the notes from Sarah, and the drawing that Tess had insisted she keep. She did a balancing act worthy of a circus performer and awkwardly turned the knob. Her hands were so full she used her right hip to push the door open. It would have been nice if Elan had bothered to come help, but so far his offers to assist always came just after she needed it.

Typical teenager, she thought. But that was fine

with her. Typical was just fine. Exceptional was the potential for some point down the road.

"Hi, Aunt Birdy," Elan said.

"Hi, yourself," she answered, looking at him in a way that was meant to convey she was struggling to carry everything inside.

"Let me help you," he said after she had set everything down on the kitchen table.

"My friend from school's here," he said. "He's in the bathroom."

"Micah?" she asked. It was the only friend he really mentioned.

"Yeah," Elan said. "You know the one with the mom in jail. I told him you wouldn't mind or judge him or anything."

"You can put some plates and silverware out," she said. "Napkins too. They never give enough."

"Did you get extra honey?"

"I never make the same mistake twice," she said.

While Elan set the table, Birdy thought of the drawing and the awkwardness she felt about having it just then. He had to be the Micah who had drawn it for Tess's daughter. She nudged it to the corner of the counter near the refrigerator.

Micah entered the kitchen. He was a nice-looking boy with haunted eyes and the kind of wavy hair that she'd always dreamed of having when she was a girl facing a lifetime of straight, coarse black tresses. She sniffed and noticed that he smelled of smoke.

"Dr. Waterman," he said, extending his hand to shake it. "Nice to see you again."

A charmer too.

His hand was damp.

And he washed his hands too. At least that's what she hoped the dampness came from.

"Hi, Micah," she said. "I hope you haven't been smoking here in my house."

"Aunt Birdy!" Elan said, embarrassed.

"No. I haven't," Micah said, jamming his hands into his pockets. "If you think it's weird that I'm here because of my mom and stuff, then I can go back home."

She waved the notion away. "No. No. It's fine. Have some dinner with us. Elan normally does the cooking. Tonight, as you can see," she said, holding up a KFC bag, "it was my turn."

Micah grinned a little. "That sounds good," he said. "My mom was a lousy cook. Me and my sister always prayed for fast food."

"All right then," Birdy said. "You boys serve yourselves. I'm going to change out of my work clothes." She left them for the bedroom and put on a red T-shirt and a pair of faded blue jeans. It was strange seeing Micah. He'd been on her mind for days. The drawing of the woods was haunting and its inscription was telling.

When she returned to the kitchen, Elan was alone.

"Micah had to call his sister," Elan said. "Cell reception for his carrier is lousy here." He motioned toward the back porch where aunt and nephew could see Micah's silhouette as he talked on his phone.

"How's he doing?" Birdy said, keeping her voice low.

"He's okay. He had a totally messed-up family. I can relate to him."

"Thanks for that," she said.

"Not you, Aunt Birdy. The rest of the family."

The door opened. "My sister's a pain in the you-know-what," Micah said when he came back inside. "I was telling Elan before you came home about her moving to Scottsdale. She always hated it here. Rains too much. I like the rain. It's a nice change from triple digit temps in the summer."

"I'll bet it is," Birdy said, though after her visit down there, she could see the appeal. Rain made everything green, but constant sunshine had its definite benefits too.

The boys lunged for the biggest pieces of chicken. It was evident right away that Birdy was going to be stuck with a single wing and a biscuit.

"Did you know Darby Moreau?" Birdy asked, thinking of the drawing.

A funny look came over Micah's face. "Why are you asking that?" He amended his response. "Yeah, we had art together."

Elan spoke up. "We heard that Ms. Mitchell's girlfriend, that custodian Missy, got arrested, Aunt Birdy."

Birdy was hungry and her chicken wing was really, really small.

"I heard that too," she said, noticing that she had likely not gotten enough honey. She was stuck with a dry biscuit. "Did you notice anything going on at school?"

"I have enough problems, Dr. Waterman," Micah said. "Is that what I'm supposed to call you?"

"Yes, that's fine," she said. "You mean problems with your mom?"

The handsome teen chomped on a drumstick. "Yeah," he said. "Not everyone has a black widow for a mom."

Birdy, who was eating her dry biscuit, mulled that little comment over. Her own mother was worse than a black widow in some ways. Natalie Waterman emotionally tortured her victims for years. Jennifer Roberts got it over and done with in a few months.

"Tell her what you told me about the custodian," Elan said, looking at Micah.

"It was no big deal," Micah said. "It's secondhand anyway. My sister was the one who saw it."

"Ruby?" Birdy asked.

"Yeah."

"What did Ruby see?"

Micah took a thigh and started in on it. "She saw the custodian Missy and Darby arguing about something the week before Darby disappeared."

Birdy put down her skimpy chicken wing. "Where was this? What were they saying?"

Micah swallowed and reached for the last biscuit. "I'm starving," he said. "My sister only gives me ramen and Hot Pockets."

"Go on," she said.

"Right," he said. "Ruby came to the art room to get me, but I'd already left. She said that Missy was saying something mean about Darby's mom. I've heard other people say trash about her too."

"What exactly was she saying?" Birdy asked.

"I don't know," he went on. "Ruby just said something mean. I knew Darby pretty well. I knew that her mom was a hoarder and that kids made fun of her. I'm thinking that some of the adults at school did too. I'm not surprised that Missy was arrested. She's a total bitch and I think I've been around enough of those to know one when I see one."

* * *

A car pulled up and the front door of Birdy's house swung open. There was no bell ring. No knock. It was Ruby Lake in her tanorexic and blond halo of hair glory. In her right hand was a gun.

"What are you doing?" Birdy asked, jumping up from her chair, but Ruby didn't answer. She handed the gun to her brother and he pointed it at the side of Elan's head. It all happened so fast. Like a tornado blowing through a small town in the middle of the night—no warning, just the destructive wake of a teenage girl.

"You got here fast," Micah said.

"What are you doing?" Elan asked.

"Shut up," Micah said.

"I've been here before," Ruby said. "Dropped some letters off in a Target bag not too long ago."

Ruby had brought the letters. Ruby wanted her mother to go down for the murder of her stepfather.

"What's going on here?" Birdy asked.

"I'm going to kill your nephew," Micah said. "Then I'm going to kill you. Isn't that what you want me to do, Ruby?"

"Show me," Ruby said.

"Over on the counter," he said, nodding in the direction of the photograph and Micah's drawing.

"Micah, put the gun down," Birdy said.

Ruby picked up the photograph, looked at the back, looked at Micah's artwork.

"I'm surprised you figured it out. I thought the other bitch cop might get there eventually, but not you. Aren't you just a doctor?"

Figured out?

"I don't know what you are talking about," Birdy said.

"Elan, tie your aunt's wrists together." Ruby tossed Elan an apron that had been hanging on the handle of the oven door. "Use this."

"No," Elan said.

Ruby got within six inches of his face. "Do you want her to see your brains all over her tacky kitchen?"

Birdy held her wrists up. The kitchen was a small, confining space. If she tried anything there was no telling what Micah and Ruby could do, *would* do.

"Elan, do it," Birdy said. Micah kept the gun to Elan's head as he took the apron and started tying the lime-and-orange-colored strings around Birdy's wrists.

"Tighter," Ruby said. "I want them to hurt."

While she held her arms in place, Birdy's eyes landed on her cell phone.

Seeing that, Ruby picked it up and dropped it into the garbage disposal and turned it on.

"Where's Elan's phone?" she asked.

"I got it," Micah said, grabbing it with his free hand from the table where it sat next to Elan's dinner plate. He tossed it to his sister and she dropped it down the disposal, which had jammed.

"Now, you sit down," Ruby said to Birdy.

Micah whispered in Birdy's ear. "I'm sorry but she's crazy. Really she is."

Birdy kept her expression even and calm. Whatever dynamic was going on between brother and sister, Ruby was the one in charge. Micah was either afraid of his sister or he was so weak that he didn't have a mind of his own. In a situation like this, whatever happened would likely turn on how he behaved.

Not what *she* did.

Ruby might have been the alpha dog, but her bitch of a brother didn't like his role one damn bit.

"Ruby, are you out of your mind?" Birdy asked. "What are you hoping to accomplish here?"

"I'm doing what needs to be done," she said. "That's what I've always done in my family."

"Aunt Birdy," Elan said, "I'm sorry about this."

"About what?" Birdy asked. "I'm not even certain what's happening here."

"About coming down here and bringing this shit into your life." He looked over at Ruby. "What *is* the matter with you?"

Ruby ignored him. She took the small coffee grinder off the counter and tried to yank off the cord.

"Give me the gun," she said.

Micah handed it over. "Here."

"Rip this power cord off this grinder and tie him up," she said.

"Hands and feet?"

Ruby let out a sigh of exasperation. "No, Sherlock, hands. They have to walk, don't they?"

"Where are we going?" Elan asked.

"After you tie him up, I want you to go across the road and see if you can start up one of those boats."

Micah seemed agitated and confused, but he didn't argue. "Okay," he said, trying to pull the cord, but it wouldn't give. So he cut it with a knife from the knife block on the counter.

Birdy wished she had been positioned closer to the knife block. A knife would be handy just then. She had never been prone to violence. She'd hunted as a girl, but that was because she needed to help feed her fam-

ily when her father was away and food was scarce.
When she killed her first deer at fourteen, she cried for
two days.

"You're kind of hurting me, Micah," Elan said.

"You're such a pussy, Elan. Your aunt didn't com-
plain," Micah said, "and I tied her even tighter."

Elan felt stupid just then. Scared *and* stupid.

Ruby slid a chair into the space next to Birdy and
her brother hurried out the front door.

"Sit there," she said. Elan did what he was told.

"Let's go back to whatever it is that you think you are
doing," Birdy said. "Do you have any clue that you're
making a colossal mistake right now?"

Ruby didn't see it that way. "It isn't going to be a mistake. I'm going to get the money from my stepfather's
life insurance policy."

"Not if you killed him," she said.

"My mom's going down for that. Your trip to Scottsdale sealed the deal there. You might not have proved
anything by digging up my father, but you sure made
my mom look like the world's worst wife. That's a bell
that the jury will hear for sure. And when I get on the
stand and tell my story—what I saw her do, my mom's
going to death row. I mean, I hope that's what happens
because I would feel bad knowing she was in prison for
the rest of her life. I mean, she is my mom and I don't
want her to suffer."

Micah, breathing heavily from a sprint across the
road to the beach and back, returned.

"I got one going," he said. "What are we going to do
now, Ruby?"

Ruby let out another sigh. Apparently, she had a lot
of practice being irritated by everyone.

"Dummy, we're going on the boat," she said. "We're going to walk calmly across the road. We're not going to scream. We're not going to run. We're not going to make any sudden moves, because if anyone does they're dead."

Jinx, the cat, ran over to be petted as they went outside, but there were no takers among that group.

"Glad it's a cat," Ruby said. "If it was a yappy dog I'd kill it. I've done that before too."

Micah looked confused. "What are you talking about, Ruby?"

Ruby let a cruel smile come to her face. She loved the power that came with hurting other people. Her brother processed what she was saying.

"Cocoa," she finally said. "I had to see how long the antifreeze would take to kill someone. So I fed it to Cocoa."

Micah looked hard at his sister. "Cocoa? That was my dog."

"You can buy another," she said. "You can buy a kennel full."

"I loved that dog, Ruby."

"You'll love another," she said. The word *love* coming out of her mouth seemed to have no meaning.

The four of them waited in the dim light until a car passed.

"Okay, now we go," Ruby said. "Anyone who speaks, moves funny, gets a bullet in the head."

The four of them silently, and awkwardly, walked across Beach Drive and down four cement steps to the pebble beach that ringed that side of the road. A small boat, with an outboard motor and named the *Little Mighty*, had been beached there. Birdy knew the boat.

She'd been on it once, crabbing off Bainbridge Island with the neighbors.

"Untie the boat and push it out a little into the water. You get on last," Ruby said to Micah. She got in the boat and kept the gun directed at Elan. She took a seat at the bow.

Micah unhooked the line, shoved the craft hard, and it floated.

Next, she directed her instructions to Birdy. "You sit there," she said. Without saying a word, Birdy took the middle seat. As she sat down, the boat rocked a little. Ruby met Birdy's gaze and seemed to know that the forensic pathologist—just a doctor—was thinking about something.

Tipping the boat over?

"And by the way," Ruby went on, "don't even think about doing anything once we're out in the water. For one thing, if you force me into shooting you and Elan, then I'll be super pissed off. Then I'll shoot Micah."

"You wouldn't do that," Micah said, knowing that his sister probably would.

"Just get on," she said to Elan. "Next to your aunt."

The teen who'd come to get away from the trouble he'd been facing at home had now landed in something far worse.

With everyone on board, Ruby told her brother to restart the engine.

"Head toward Blake Island," she said.

"What are we going to do there?" Birdy asked, as the small boat wobbled through the water.

Ruby looked forward and turned to speak over her shoulder. "We're not going to watch the tribal dancers and have salmon," she said.

Blake Island was a state park in the middle of Puget Sound. The only commercial enterprise on the island was a tourist trap called Tillicum Village, a restaurant and an auditorium that promised vacationers and out-of-towners an authentic Northwest experience.

As the wind blew across the water and the little boat cut through the wake of a Seattle-to-Bremerton ferry, Birdy turned to Micah.

"Eventually she'll kill you," she said.

"Shut up," he snapped back.

"What happened with Darby?" Birdy said.

"That's on Micah," Ruby said. "I'll take the blame for Ted and you guys, but that one's on him."

Birdy faced Micah, who was operating the outboard motor. "I thought you liked her, Micah. I saw the drawing you made for her."

"I think I loved her," he said over the sound of the engine. "It isn't on me. It's on *her*."

Ruby feigned surprise. She opened her mouth to make the shape of an O.

"Really?" she asked. "You told her about Teddy, didn't you?"

It was now a Ping-Pong match between siblings. Birdy liked that. Some dissension could be good. It could give her time to figure out what to do. "I did because I had to tell someone, Ruby. It made me sick that you and Mom had cooked this up and tried to put the blame on the neighbor. Ted was a decent guy. You killed him. All for a bunch of money."

Ruby shrugged it off. "Money is the only thing that matters, dumb shit," she said. "We caught a lucky break with that lesbian janitor and you've totally and royally screwed it up."

Micah was emotional. It was real. It wasn't pretend. Birdy could see it in his eyes. There was something lurking there that his sister didn't have.

A soul.

"You didn't have to kill Darby, Ruby," he said. "You didn't have to do that!"

"I wouldn't have had to kill her if you'd kept your mouth shut and your dick in your pants. What an idiot you are! I'd kill you too, but family is important."

"What happened to Darby?" Birdy asked, trying to keep the conversation going toward some kind of a meltdown. A meltdown, an argument, anything other than a gun-wielding teenage girl.

The wind whipped through Ruby's hair. She was stunning. That was her problem. She almost looked like one of those beautifully carved bow figures facing into the wind with her blond locks blowing back. She had as much life in her blue eyes as one of those painted figures too.

"He told her about what I'd done," she said in a near sneer. "She told him that it was wrong. And that I was a psycho. She was just jealous of me. I get that. It happens to me all the time. Being sure of yourself and knowing that you're better than other people doesn't make you a psycho."

It was nearly dark and no one was dressed for the chill of Puget Sound. Birdy was freezing and she could feel Elan shaking too. It could have been fear or the cold. Maybe both.

"What happened?" Elan asked. "I don't get it. I mean, I get that you're a psycho."

Ruby ignored the psycho comment. Or it didn't bother her at all to be called that.

"He told her," she said. "Then stupid Micah told me what he'd said to her and what she thought of it. He was having sex with her and thought he could trust her. But we couldn't. So we killed her."

"We? *You* did," Micah said. "And we hadn't had sex yet. I think we were going to, but you messed that up for me, big time."

"Whatever. We killed her together. You held her down while I kept that beanbag chair on her face."

The beanbag chair was one of the things that Connie Mitchell had taken to her car the day she left school after being put on administrative leave.

Darby's cause of death had been impossible to determine. Her body was decomposed and there were no overt signs of trauma. Smothering had always been a possibility, but until they'd learned where the crime had occurred and some of the circumstances surrounding it, there had been no exact theory. It was a homicide because of the body dump, but in the back of Birdy's mind she had thought it could have been an accidental death and a body dump. That happened on a case early in her career. The perpetrator hadn't killed the victim, but was fearful people would think he had.

"I held her down because you made me," Micah said.

"You wanted the money too," Ruby shot back. "You told me you wanted a brand-new mountain bike."

"Then what did you do?" Elan asked.

Micah answered in a shaky voice. "My sister got into the janitorial supply closet and got one of those big trash bags. We put Darby in the bag and put her on an AV cart and just pushed her out the door. I was scared shitless. A couple of kids from track asked us what we were doing and I told them we were on the Green Team doing some recycling."

Ruby laughed. "You actually showed a little flair there, Micah. Totally. One of the first times ever. I was almost a little proud of you."

"We took Darby's body and dumped her in Banner Forest," Micah said. "Ruby made me! I hate her for that! It was dark and I thought we found a good spot, but I guess not. The bag tore a little."

"Again your fault," Ruby said.

"I had to carry most of the weight, Ruby."

"I wish you would have been on steroids. You have weak shoulders."

Keep fighting, Birdy thought. Fighting between each other is good.

"You really poisoned Cocoa?" he screamed across the boat.

Ruby put her hand out as if to stop him from moving forward, when he wasn't moving at all. "Forget the damn dog."

"If you shoot us and dump us out here they'll trace the gun back to you," Birdy said, as the boat moved farther and farther from shore. "I'm assuming that's Ted's gun."

Ruby rolled her eyes like Birdy's pronouncement was beyond the obvious. "It is. And who says I'm going to shoot you?"

"What are you going to do?" Birdy asked.

"Not me. *You two. You're* going to drown. It will look like an accident."

"With a coffee grinder cord around my wrists?" Elan asked. "That won't look like much of an accident."

"Good point," Micah said, now backing his sister. "I'll take that off."

"I can swim," Elan said.

Ruby laughed. "No, you can't," she said. "Not out in that water. It's really cold. I know for a fact that you can last about ninety seconds out there. I can wait. And maybe you can swim. So maybe you have a chance."

By then they were in the middle of nowhere. Shore with its twinkly lights of waterfront homes was too far to swim. It was dark and though sound travels over water like electricity through a power cord, there was no vessel nearby to hear them call for help.

"Cut the engine," Ruby said.

Micah, still mad about his dog, did what he was told. The *Little Mighty* sputtered into quietness. The boat rolled a little in the waves of the water.

"You're going to have to shoot me," Birdy said. "I'm not going to just jump in."

"That's why you're going into the water first," Ruby said. "I'll shoot Elan in the head right here and now if you don't. I've already killed two people, so I think I know how to do it, in case you're wondering."

"I'm a good swimmer," Birdy said, looking at Elan. "Elan, you are too."

He looked at his aunt. "Not that good, Aunt Birdy. Ruby, don't do this to us," he said. "We won't tell on you."

The girl was a boulder. Unshakable. She was completely undeterred. It was like whatever was happening right then was nothing to her. She might as well be checking in some pale-skinned tanners at Desert Enchantment.

"Like how am I going to get away with this if you're still alive?" she asked. "Micah told me about the drawing he made for Darby and the list of questions you had about that lesbian's involvement in the crime. What am I supposed to do? Just pretend like you haven't figured it out? Go to prison? Not move back to Arizona? I mean, really, for an educated woman, I'd say you are pretty stupid."

Birdy felt stupid. She'd never considered that Jennifer had been set up by her own daughter. That Micah had been involved with Darby and that somehow the crimes were connected. Never in a zillion years had she thought of that, but all along it had been staring right at her face.

"Aunt Birdy, I want to say something. You know, while I still can."

"Elan, I love you too," she said.

"I know that. And I do love you. But are you my mom?"

Birdy was stunned by the question.

"Oh, honey, no."

"I did the math. You could be. I heard my mom talking about some stuff."

Ruby was annoyed by then. "Oh God, are we going to settle something here on the . . ."

"The *Little Mighty*," her brother said.

"Right. On the goddamn *Little Mighty*?"

Birdy glared at Ruby. She turned to Elan. "I'm not your mother."

"Don't lie to me. Not now."

"Honey, I'm not lying."

"I heard my mom and dad arguing about me and

how they wished they'd never raised me. That Mom wasn't my mom."

"Elan, this isn't the time for this," Birdy said, her eyes misting a little.

"We don't have any time," he answered back.

Ruby looked at Elan. "He's right. You don't. Now, Doctor, get in the water before I blow his brains out into Puget Sound for crab bait."

It was hard to see. Birdy could feel tears rolling down her cheeks.

"You're my brother," she said. "Not my nephew."

Elan had tears in his eyes. "I don't understand," he said.

Birdy didn't cry, but her heart was broken. It had been ever since Elan was born.

"Our mother didn't want any more kids."

"Grandma?" he asked.

Birdy looked over the black water. "She wanted to give you up for adoption but Summer wouldn't let her. She didn't think it was right. She didn't want that for you."

Elan was overwhelmed. If her hands were free just then, Birdy would have held him and never let go.

Ruby cut in. "Okay now that the drama is figured out, get in the water, Doctor. Or watch your brother die."

"I'm sorry, Elan," Birdy said. "It was never mine to tell."

Elan was in shock.

"I hate Grandma," he said, trying to pull himself together. "Or our mother."

"Me too. But she's the only one I've got. You have

your mom. And she loves you. Always has and always will."

"Who is my father then?"

Birdy could barely face Elan. "I don't know. None of us knows."

Micah untied her.

"Get up," he said.

"I'm not going in," she said. "This is not going to happen."

"Yes, it is," Micah said.

Birdy spread her legs apart and tried to rock the boat. She thought that if she could upset the craft, flip it over, they'd all have a fighting chance. Elan was still tied, but she could save him. It was the only thing she could do.

"Push her in!" Ruby yelled.

As the *Little Mighty* nearly listed, Micah shoved Birdy into the inky black of Puget Sound. Birdy went down fast, under the water, out of sight.

"Aunt Birdy!" Elan called out.

"She can't hear you," Ruby said. "And she's not your aunt."

"Aunt Birdy!" he tried again.

"Shut him up!"

Micah swung an oar and smacked Elan in the head. He slumped onto the deck of the boat.

"Untie him. We'll push him in and get out of here."

Micah did as he was instructed.

"I'll help you," Ruby said. The two of them hoisted Elan up to the edge of the boat and pushed him over. Elan fell into the water.

"Now you get in," she said.

"Me?" he asked.

"Yes, *you*. You didn't think that I'd let you live? All you wanted was a goddamn mountain bike. You don't dream big enough, Micah. Never have. You're not like me and Mom."

"What are you going to do? How are you going to explain this?"

Ruby smiled. "I took a video of you pushing Darby's body on that cart. I'll say that you forced all of us out here and that I could only save myself. Remember, I'm pretty and I'm believable. Video never lies."

In the blackness of the water, Birdy clawed her way to the surface. On her way up, Elan was coming down. Her body already felt numb from the cold water. It was that fast. Like an icy quicksand. He was semiconscious, but somehow she managed to bring him to the surface on the opposite side of the boat. She could hear brother and sister arguing.

"Really, Ruby?" Micah said. "You'd kill me? You'd set me up?"

"Why in the world would you think I wouldn't?"

"How are you going to get yourself out of this? I've covered for you," Micah asked. "I've done everything you wanted me to do."

"I'm blessed," she said. "I have a guardian angel. I'm untouchable."

Birdy grabbed the edge of the boat and pulled with all her strength. She wasn't a large woman. But she was strong. Like the boat's name, *Little Mighty*.

In a second Ruby and the gun were in the water.

"Micah, help me!" she said. "I'll kill you if you don't get me out."

Micah hung over the side and looked at her. "Die bitch! I hate you! Darby was my girlfriend!"

Elan was conscious and coughing. Birdy helped him cling to the edge of the boat. They couldn't see what was happening on the other side of the small craft.

"I hate you, Ruby!" Micah said.

"I'm going to kill you!" Ruby called out from the water. "When I get back in the boat. You're dead. You hear me?"

Birdy heard the ore scrape the bottom of the boat and the dull slap of something. A second later, Micah pulled Elan back in, then she pulled herself up. She and Elan shivered. Micah stood there at the bow, looking off at the Seattle skyline far in the distance.

"I really did like Darby," he said.

A pleasure boater sped toward them.

"I know," Birdy said. "You're going to be all right," she added, not to Micah but to Elan as she held him close.

Elan would be all right. Micah was going to prison. Jennifer Roberts, it seemed, was innocent. Both she and Missy Carlyle had been spun up in the web of a teenage sociopath.

Scottsdale, apparently, really *was* to die for.

EPILOGUE

All on the *Little Mighty* had survived the night in the water. Ruby had a skull fracture from where her brother had struck her with the oar. After a few days in intensive care at Harborview Medical Center in Seattle, she was moved to a room with an armed guard posted at her door. She wasn't going anywhere, but jail. Micah, Elan, and Birdy were treated for hypothermia and were released after a night of observation. Micah was arrested too, but talk was that the prosecution would make a deal for a lesser sentence for his role in Darby's murder.

They needed him to nail his sister to the wall, a task he seemed to want to do.

The day after Birdy was released from the hospital, Kendall Stark stopped by the house on Beach Drive to see her. Others had sent their well wishes too. Tess Moreau had sent flowers. There was even a note from Jennifer Roberts saying that she was sure that Ruby had been framed.

"She's really a lovely girl," she wrote.

"How's Elan doing?" Kendall asked when Birdy led her inside.

"For a kid who found out his grandmother is his mother and who was almost killed by a . . . let's see, he called her a 'psycho' . . . he's doing fine. He went home to Neah Bay. He'll be back on the weekend."

"He's been through a lot," Kendall said.

"Yes, he has," the forensic pathologist said. "He's a good kid. He just comes from a messed-up family."

"We all do, Birdy."

"I guess to some extent, Kendall, you're right. Do you want a beer?"

"I'm working. And, isn't it a little early?"

"Look, I've been through hell. And yes, it is early."

Birdy went to the refrigerator for a beer. She brought Kendall a diet soda.

"We released Missy Carlyle on the murder charge," Kendall said. "She posted bail on the harassment charge for sending the Brenda Nevins letter."

"That's good. She should pay for that."

"Sarah recovered Darby's DNA from the beanbag chair."

"Sarah deserves a lot of credit here," Birdy said. "She did really good work. We probably wouldn't have solved this if not for her. And if not for Micah's reaction to Sarah's work."

"How so?" Kendall asked.

"Sarah gave me that photo with her list and I had the artwork Micah had made for Darby. He saw it in the kitchen, jumped to conclusions, and called his crazy sister to say they'd been found out."

"Guilty consciences always jump to conclusions," Kendall said.

The TV was on mute and the screen flashed a special bulletin notice.

Birdy drank some beer. "I was thinking about how all these lives intersected—Tess, Darby, Ruby, Micah, Jennifer, Elan, Connie, and Missy. It wasn't two unrelated murders. Ted's was a murder and Darby was collateral damage."

"Turn that up," Kendall said.

Birdy looked at the screen. A picture of Brenda Nevins filled the frame.

" '. . . reports indicate that Nevins and Superintendent Janie Thomas had a romantic relationship. Thomas, who is married and has two children, was last seen late last night at the institution. Surveillance cameras show her and Nevins leaving the building around two a.m . . .' "

"Holy crap!" Kendall said.

"You just saw Superintendent Thomas," Birdy said. "And Brenda."

"I would never have thought that in a million years," Kendall said.

"You need to send a deputy out to Tess's place. *Now.*"

"On it," Kendall said.

The two women looked at each other as Kendall dialed.

She spoke to dispatch and a relieved look came to her face.

"Tess is fine," she said. "She's at county now."

"Thank God for that."

"I wonder what Brenda and Superintendent Thomas are doing?"

Kendall looked at the TV as the regular programming resumed.

"Brenda will do whatever she wants. She always has. Like Ruby. Some people are just born to kill."

Birdy took another sip of beer.

"I guess so," she said. "I have to start packing tomorrow. We're moving offices. I'll miss seeing you at the latte stand."

"You don't go there that much," the detective said. "But don't worry. We're going to work together again."

"Isn't our training over?" Birdy asked.

"Nope. In fact, the sheriff said you and I are . . . let's see, what was the word . . . 'Prime examples of teamwork in action.' We're going to continue on to partner on major cases."

Birdy smiled. Teamwork wasn't so bad after all.